A HILL
OF BEANS

A HILL OF BEANS

A Chuckwagon Trail Western

WILLIAM W. JOHNSTONE

AND J. A. JOHNSTONE

PINNACLE BOOKS
Kensington Publishing Corp.
www.kensingtonbooks.com

PINNACLE BOOKS are published by

Kensington Publishing Corp.
119 West 40th Street
New York, NY 10018

PUBLISHER'S NOTE
Following the death of William W. Johnstone, the Johnstone family is working with a carefully selected writer to organize and complete Mr. Johnstone's outlines and many unfinished manuscripts to create additional novels in all of his series like The Last Gunfighter, Mountain Man, and Eagles, among others. This novel was inspired by Mr. Johnstone's superb storytelling.

All Kensington titles, imprints, and distributed lines are available at special quantity discounts for bulk purchases for sales promotions, premiums, fund-raising, educational, or institutional use. Special book excerpts or customized printings can also be created to fit specific needs. For details, write or phone the office of the Kensington sales manager: Kensington Publishing Corp., 119 West 40th Street, New York, NY 10018, attn: Sales Department; phone 1-800-221-2647.

PINNACLE BOOKS, the Pinnacle logo, and the WWJ steer head logo are Reg. U.S. Pat. & TM Off.

ISBN-13: 978-0-7860-4406-1
ISBN-10: 0-7860-4406-3

First printing: April 2020

10 9 8 7 6 5 4 3 2 1

Printed in the United States of America

Electronic edition:

ISBN-13: 978-0-7860-4407-8 (e-book)
ISBN-10: 0-7860-4407-1 (e-book)

CHAPTER 1

Dewey "Mac" Mackenzie was settled in for the night. His horse, picketed close by, grazed contentedly. The campfire burned low, crackling softly and issuing an occasional muted pop that sent a brief swirl of sparks dancing above the flames. Evening meal resting comfortably in his belly, Mac sat cross-legged on his bedroll, nursing a final cup of coffee before he'd be ready to stretch out, pull the blankets over him, and drift off to sleep.

Life wasn't too bad, Mac decided. After spending the past several months on a pair of separate trail drives followed by a brief but memorable stopover in the crowded, frantically expanding city of Denver, he savored this period of quiet solitude. The crews of the trail drives he'd joined were, for the most part, decent, hardworking hombres whose colorful ways and rough-hewn sense of humor he'd enjoyed being around. A couple of the men had made lasting impressions he would carry in his memory for a long time, even though he had to move on and go his own way. And the time he'd spent in Denver had been an enjoyable experience, too.

But at the same time, the latter had proven beyond any doubt that he was no longer cut out for big-city life beyond an occasional visit for the good times to be had.

So now, with all that behind him, Mac was on the drift, alone, and it felt pretty good. He still had a few dollars left in his pocket, even after his generous sampling of Denver nightlife, and he had a vague notion of heading west, toward California, but without any particular sense of urgency.

In fact, the only real urgency in Mac's life was trying to ride clear of certain events that had befallen him nearly two years ago down in New Orleans. They had cost him the woman he'd once believed to be the love of his life—Evangeline, who now loathed him due to falling for a pack of lies that convinced her he was responsible for the brutal murder of her father.

The perpetrator of those lies, the true murderer yet the man she had now fallen in love with and was wed to, was one Pierre Leclerc, a cunning schemer out to attain the holdings and wealth of the family he had successfully married into.

To make sure nothing got in the way of all he had so ruthlessly gained, Leclerc had hired a virtual army of bounty hunters to track down and kill Mac to prevent him from ever returning and attempting to reveal the truth. Members of Leclerc's horde had caught up with Mac on each of his recent cattle drives, but with some luck and a little help from his new trail pards, Mac had managed to keep from falling prey to them.

For the time being at least, Mac felt reasonably confident none of Leclerc's hounds were barking anywhere close on his heels. That was the way he wanted to keep it, a big part of why he meant to stay on the move and put as much distance between himself and New Orleans as possible.

After draining the last of the coffee, Mac was slapping the grounds out of the bottom of the cup when his horse, picketed over on the other side of the campfire, suddenly perked up its ears and chuffed nervously about something. Mac had been riding the deep-chested paint long enough to have developed a trust in its instincts.

He rose to his feet, right hand absently brushing across the Smith & Wesson Model 3 revolver tucked in the belt of his pants. The horse stood poised, not overly agitated yet very alert to something. Mac swept his gaze in all directions, peering into the darkness as deeply as he could. He saw nothing and neither did he hear anything.

But then he did. A low, distant rumble. Very faint but growing louder and closer. At first he thought it might be far-off thunder from a storm moving in. However, a quick scan of the sky showed nothing but an uninterrupted wash of stars from horizon to horizon.

Then full recognition hit Mac. He'd heard that sound before. Too many times. And it only took once for it to make a lasting impression.

Somewhere not too far away, a herd of cattle had been spooked and was on the run. A full-blown stampede was underway, and as the rumble grew louder, Mac judged a pretty good-sized herd was caught up in it.

His first instinct was to saddle up and ride out to see if he could try and help turn the herd. Then he hesitated, remembering that not only wasn't he part of the outfit driving the herd but—except for a general sense that the stampede was occurring somewhere off to the south—he couldn't even be sure of locating it and catching up in time to do any good.

Once more, however, the paint had a say in the matter. It chuffed again and pawed the ground with one of its front hooves. A trained cow pony, the animal also recognized the sound and knew it had a part to play when cattle were running out of control.

Mac gave a grunt of his own. Danged if the nag wasn't right. He ought to at least *try* to lend a hand, no matter what. The damage a stampede could do, both to the cattle themselves as well as the wranglers trying to stop them, could be plenty serious. And anybody who was close enough and had the right experience should feel obligated to pitch in and offer some aid.

Moving quickly, Mac grabbed his saddle and slapped it on the paint's back. Fingers flying with well-practiced movements, he had the gear cinched up in no time. A moment later, he was mounted and wheeling the paint around, then kneeing the eager animal into motion.

The rumble grew steadily louder. Given the way sound had a sometimes-tricky way of fanning out across prairie terrain and making it difficult to pinpoint the exact location of its source, Mac gave the paint its head. It seemed to have a strong sense of where they needed to go.

Sure enough, it wasn't long before they topped a grassy hill and came in sight of the boiling mass of stampeding longhorns. In fact, the onrushing critters were headed straight toward them. Luckily, they were still far enough off to allow Mac time to swing the paint out of the way and then fall in beside the panicked herd as those in the lead went thundering by.

This put Mac in a good position to go to work on halting the stampede. The way it was done—at least the way he had been taught—was to force the lead animals to turn back against the flow of those rushing behind. This created the equivalent of a dam being thrown up against a torrent of floodwater. The resulting collision of massive bodies sometimes caused some unfortunate injuries, but still less than the trampling and goring that would take place if the stampede continued unchecked.

Mac dug his heels into the paint, urging it faster, aiming to once again draw even with the frontrunners of the rushing cattle. He felt excitement building inside him, caught up by the roar of pounding hooves, the taste of dust on his tongue, the frantic bawl of the cattle, and the reflection of moonlight in their wild eyes and on the tips of their slashing horns.

As he rode, Mac became aware of other horsemen closing in to attempt the same task. At least one on the other side of the herd and one or two more coming up behind him.

The land was a series of blunt hills and shallow draws, with a few rock outcrops poking up here and there. As he drew even with the front of the herd, Mac peered ahead, wishing for more rugged features to help slow the cattle but seeing none. But with or without any help from Mother Nature, the cattle still had to be stopped. Drawing the Smith & Wesson from his belt, he reined the paint closer to the leaders and fired some shots skyward.

"Heeyah! Ease up, cattle! Ease up!"

The horseman across the way began cracking a long whip in front of the longhorns' snouts, also shouting and cursing. Two riders closed in around Mac and started firing their pistols, too.

"Turn, cattle! Turn, you muleheads!"

Some of the leaders began swinging their heads inward toward the middle of the mass, pulling away from the gunshots and the pop of the whip, balking, slowing down slightly. But the push of the cattle in the middle and at the rear drove them on.

Then, finally, the terrain dealt a bit of a helping hand by way of a sharp slope feeding down into a wide, funnel-shaped depression with some stubbly rocks rimming the far side.

"There! There!" somebody shouted. "Drive 'em into that choke point! With the sides squeezin' in on 'em and those rocks rising up in their faces, they'll have to slow down!"

And that's pretty much the way it went. With the sloping walls of the depression pressing them from the sides, the cattle plunged into the funnel-shaped opening. There, the rim of stubbled rocks and the ongoing shooting and shouting of the cowboys did the rest—turning back the leaders and at last bringing the whole strung-out mass to a weary, puffing halt.

"Let 'em mill! Let 'em mill! They're good and tired out now. As soon as they discover there's decent grass under their feet, they'll be happy to stay right here for the rest of the night."

Mac couldn't get a good look at who was giving this advice. But whoever it was, it was good advice to follow.

As the herd steadily grew calmer, showing more and more signs that all the run was worn out of them, Mac continued to ride the paint slowly back and forth alongside them, talking low and soothingly. Just to make sure.

Only when he was satisfied the cattle were sufficiently settled down did he look around for some of the other riders who'd also been in the thick of things. He spotted three of them clustered together twenty yards away and gigged his paint toward them.

"Hey, fellas," he said as he drew nearer. "Those cows sure had themselves worked into a state. What riled 'em, anyway?"

One of the three men snapped his face around and aimed a menacing look in Mac's direction. Half a second later, he was aiming something else—the hogleg he'd pulled from the holster on his hip.

"You ought to know, you rustling polecat! And something else you're about to learn real quick is what a big mistake it is to mess with what belongs to the Rafter B!"

With that, his finger tightened on the trigger and the hammer came down—striking with an empty click that really wasn't very loud but was still enough to cause Mac to jerk reflexively in his saddle.

Twice more the would-be gunman cocked and triggered the Colt, with the same results. It was suddenly clear that he'd fired off all the cartridges in his wheel while getting the herd turned and hadn't yet bothered to reload.

That realization hit Mac along with a wave of instant anger—anger quickly whipped into rage by the thought of this ungrateful varmint trying to shoot him after he'd risked his neck helping save the skunk's herd.

Driven by this rage, and with no conscious thought beyond it, Mac dug his heels into the paint's ribs and charged straight at the man still pointing his empty gun. The paint thudded heavily against the other man's horse and knocked it to one side.

In the same instant, Mac launched from the saddle and flung himself onto the man who'd tried to shoot him. The Colt went flying, the horses twisted away, and the two men toppled to the ground in a tangle of flying fists.

CHAPTER 2

Luckily, Mac landed mostly on top. The impact of hitting the ground was still jarring, but hardly enough to curb Mac's anger or to slow the barrage of punches he continued to launch.

The man absorbing those punches was taller, a lantern-jawed specimen leaner in build and not as thickly muscled as Mac. He quickly proved to be a scrapper, though, and neither the blows Mac was landing nor the crash to earth seemed to have knocked any noticeable amount of fight out of him. His own fists and elbows shot up and around and drilled frequently into Mac as the pair rolled pummeling and kicking across the ground.

With neither man gaining any advantage that way, they broke apart and scrambled to their feet. Mac immediately went on the attack again, lunging forward and throwing a whistling roundhouse right at the point of his opponent's prominent chin. The taller man jerked his head back at the last second, however, so the blow ended up being only a glancing one. It was still enough to knock the tall man off balance, sending him staggering a step and a half to his right.

Mac moved after him, stepping in close and following up with a left hook to the ribs that landed solidly. A *whoof!* of escaping breath issued from the tall man, and he bent sharply toward the side where the blow had landed.

But then Mac got too eager and let his forward momentum pull him in too close. His opponent made him pay for it with a slashing left elbow that whipped back with blinding speed and banged hard against the side of Mac's head. Bells went off and stars danced before his eyes, and this time it was Mac who did a stutter step.

Before he could catch his balance and try to shift away long enough to let some of the stars fade, the tall man finished his spinning move and brought around a clubbing right that slammed against the side of Mac's head at almost the same exact spot as where the elbow had landed.

This time Mac did more than stumble. He staggered violently, his knees feeling momentarily rubbery, almost giving out on him. But the rage still burned strongly enough in him to force him to stay on his feet. Blast it, he would *not* go down to this cowardly cowboy who'd drawn and fired on him for no good reason.

Mac planted his heels stubbornly as the tall man came rushing toward him. Instead of trying to hold up against the rush, Mac hurled himself forward also. He barely had time to build any momentum of his own, but at the last second, he leaned forward—ducking the tall man's punch as he did so—and lowered his head so that it rammed squarely into his attacker's solar plexus.

The tall man's forward movement abruptly halted. He folded forward, his chest, shoulders, and face flopping down over Mac's shoulder as he expelled another great gush of air driven from every corner of his stomach and lungs. Mac straightened up with a sudden surge and flung his opponent off. As the tall man stumbled backward—clutching his belly with both arms, mouth formed into a perfect "O" as he tried desperately to suck some breath back in—Mac stepped after him and put all his weight into a right cross that smashed devastatingly into the inviting bull's-eye made by that mouth. The tall man dropped like he'd been pole-axed.

Mac took another step and stood over him, wavering slightly, his still-balled fists hanging loosely at his sides. He wasn't the type to stomp a man when he was down, so as far as he was concerned the fight was over.

It suddenly became apparent there were others ready to make sure of that when the sound of pistols being cocked caused Mac's head to snap around and he found himself staring into the gun muzzles of the other two riders who'd been with the tall man when Mac first rode up.

"Does everybody in your outfit draw on every stranger you see?"

Before either of the gun-toters could respond, a new voice called from a short distance away, "Hold up with those guns! What's going on here?"

Mac and the other men turned their heads to

watch the approach of two figures on horseback. One was broad-shouldered and erect in the saddle, the other, trailing a few feet behind, was barely discernible in the murkiness of the night.

The front rider reined in when he got within a few feet and revealed himself to be an elderly gent with bristly white sideburns and thick, contrastingly black eyebrows currently bunched together in a fierce scowl. In the same raspy voice that had called out a moment earlier, he spoke again. "I asked a question, blast it—what's going on here?"

"It's this hombre," said one of the cowboys, jerking his chin toward Mac. The speaker looked to be in his middle twenties, with a narrow face, sleepy eyes, and an unruly tangle of fiery red curls poking out from under the front of his hat. He went on, "When he rode up out of nowhere, Roman took him for one of the rustlers who must have got separated from the rest of his bunch. Roman tried to get the drop on him, but the sneaky devil sucker-punched Roman and knocked him down."

"He didn't try to get the drop on me," Mac countered hotly. "He flat-out tried to shoot me, is what he did! He would have, too, if he hadn't forgotten to reload his gun after firing off all the rounds working to slow the stampede. When his hammer came down on nothing but spent cartridges, you bet I tore into him. I don't see how anybody can claim I threw a sucker punch, though, not when he was already waving a gun in my face. If he'd had any bullets left in it, I'd be the one laying in the dirt—pumped full of slugs!"

The older gent peered intently at the red-haired

cowboy. "That's a little different than the way you told it, Sparky. Any truth to his version?"

The puncher addressed as Sparky shifted uncomfortably in his saddle. "Well, it all happened pretty fast . . . I mean, Roman *did* draw his gun and all. Like I told you, he figured he was lookin' at one of the rustlers . . . and why else would this stranger pop up out here in the middle of nowhere?"

"I can answer that," Mac was quick to say. Jerking a thumb over his shoulder, he went on to explain, "I was camped a couple miles back. Right in the path of your herd, as it turned out. When I recognized the sound of a stampede—a sound I know all too well, from having been in my share—I saddled up and rode out to see if I could help. And I did, too, doggone it. If there's an honest man in your outfit, somebody surely must have seen me."

"I can vouch for his claim," spoke up the second of the two newly arrived riders, moving up alongside the white-haired man.

Mac's first reaction was a surge of relief, grateful that someone *had* spotted him and was willing to say so. A moment later, when he got a better look at the second rider, he found even more to appreciate. Because what he saw, moving her horse forward out of the twilight murkiness, was a very attractive young woman returning his gaze with a self-assured boldness.

She appeared barely past twenty, a mane of thick chestnut hair spilling from under a cocked Stetson to frame a face highlighted by intelligent, challenging eyes and a wide, lush mouth. Below that, womanly curves filled out the standard trail garb she wore just fine, and it was all Mac could do to keep from gawking like some calf-eyed fool.

CHAPTER 3

"Assuming that paint horse standing over yonder belongs to the stranger," the girl continued, "I spotted them right in the thick of turning the herd. And like he said, it looked to me like he was a big help."

"That hardly sounds like the actions of a rustler," the old-timer said, frowning thoughtfully. "Unless, that is, Roman was right to suspect this fella might be part of the crew that hit our herd and somehow got separated from the others."

"Come on, Father," the girl said in an impatient tone. "Even if that were the case, what sense would it make for him to stick around? Once the cattle started running, he could have easily ridden away and eventually caught back up with the others. And especially, why would any rustler put himself at risk to help stop a stampede he was involved in starting to begin with?"

By this point, the man Mac had knocked down—referred to as "Roman"—was struggling to get back up. He groaned as he pushed himself onto one elbow, gasping and wheezing as he tried to pull some air back into his lungs.

"Sparky, Nolan," the white-haired man barked. "Climb down and give him a hand."

The two cowboys promptly proceeded to do as ordered.

The white-haired man's gaze returned to Mac. "Young fella," he said, "my daughter has me ready to give you the benefit of the doubt. But before I'm willing to commit, I think it's only right to allow Roman a chance to have his say. In the meantime, my name is Norris Bradley. I own the Rafter B spread down in Bellow County, Texas. The longhorns you apparently helped stop from running themselves to ruination are mine. This is my daughter, Colleen"—a tip of his head toward the girl—"and you've already, er, made the acquaintance of my son Roman."

Mac winced inwardly at the revelation that the man he'd knocked down was this old rooster's son.

"How about you? You got a name?" Bradley wanted to know.

Mac answered, "Mackenzie. Dewey Mackenzie. Most folks just call me Mac."

"I don't give a hoot what he's called," growled Roman, now having been helped to his feet. "What matters is what he is—and that's a dirty stinkin' rustler!"

"Now hold on a minute," Bradley responded. "You've already made your opinion plenty clear. Trouble is, there's some pretty convincing evidence you're mistaken."

"The hell I am," Roman snapped back. "If this ranny ain't up to no good, then what's he doing sneakin' around the edges of our herd as soon as we got 'em stopped?"

"That's already been answered," his sister told him.

"You would have heard if you hadn't been so busy trying to pick yourself up off the ground."

Roman glared at her. "Yeah, and why was I on the ground? Because I was quick to have this varmint pegged for what he was and what he was up to—looking to pick out a few more cows he could steal to go with however many his buddies already slicked away before they started the stampede."

"So you tried to shoot him on the spot?" Colleen accused. "Without taking even a second to try and find out if there was another explanation?"

"His showing up the way he did was all the explanation I needed!"

"And if you'd succeeded in jumping to that conclusion and following through with it," Bradley said, "you very likely would have shot an innocent man."

"Innocent? How in blazes can you—"

Bradley made a slashing motion with his hand. "Shut up! You and that hair-triggered temper of yours. Isn't the trouble it's gotten you in ever going to teach you to hold it in check—at least once in a while?"

Roman looked torn between anger and puzzlement. "I don't understand, Pa. What did I do that was so wrong? What about this piece of trail trash makes you think he's so innocent?"

"Because the reason this man is here is that he risked his neck to pitch in and help turn our herd. Does that sound like something a rustler would do?"

"Who says he played any part in turning the herd?" Roman demanded. "You taking his word on that?"

"I say he played a part. A big part," Colleen spoke up. "I already told you, I saw him right in the thick of it."

"You!" Roman practically spat. "You'd say that just to spite me."

"Now don't you two start in," Bradley warned.

The cowboy referred to as Nolan, a lean, middle-aged man with a face worn beyond its actual years by long exposure to the wind and sun, cleared his throat.

"I, uh . . . I kinda saw the same as Miss Colleen," he said. "That fella and his big paint, they helped turn the herd right enough. I seen 'em right there toward the front, makin' a big difference."

Roman shot him a dirty look.

"Okay, that settles it," Bradley said. "Here's what I suggest we do. No, make that what I *say* we'll do. Nolan, you and Sparky stay here with the herd. They're tuckered out, I don't think they'll spook easily again. But hang around, keep an eye on things, and keep 'em soothed just the same. I'll send a couple other boys to relieve you in a few hours. The rest of us are going on back to our camp. We'll finish sorting this out when we get there, and get a general idea of how many cattle we lost on the way."

His eyes settled on Mac. "That includes you. I figure, at the very least, we owe you a place to bed down for the night and a hot breakfast in the morning. You got any objection?"

Mac considered. He tossed a couple of quick glances to the two Bradley siblings. One was looking at him invitingly, the other menacingly.

"No," he replied to their father. "No objection at all."

CHAPTER 4

By Mac's reckoning, they covered more than four miles before reaching the Rafter B night camp. That was how far the stampede had carried the herd. Along the way, Bradley tallied an even two dozen carcasses of unfortunate critters who'd fallen and been trampled by their own kind. In all likelihood, ten or a dozen more lay unseen somewhere out in the darkness.

Also on the way, Mac was able to show the others the remains of his campsite. There wasn't much to see except for a scorched patch of ground where his campfire had been and a few tatters of his bedroll fluttering up out of the mangled ground. The coffeepot he'd left behind was kicked and stomped to oblivion. Luckily, most of his gear was in the saddlebags that he'd thrown across the paint's back along with the saddle when he hurriedly mounted up and rode away from the spot.

This meager bit of evidence was further proof to back up Mac's story that he wasn't part of any rustling crew. He could see acceptance and added conviction of this on the faces of Bradley and Colleen, but Roman only continued to glower, not willing to give an inch on what he stubbornly had his mind made up to believe.

As they progressed toward the camp, they were joined by other Rafter B riders who'd gotten strung out chasing the herd, among them Bradley's middle and youngest sons—Henry and George, respectively. Henry was fair-haired and handsome, middle twenties, with a sun- and wind-burned face and a quiet, easygoing manner that seemed in sharp contrast to his hotheaded older brother. George was not only the youngest brother, but he was also a year or so younger than Colleen and came across as a rambunctious sort with boyish good looks, a thatch of curly hair the same chestnut color as his sister's, and an excitable air about him that kept him talking and asking questions.

A third man to fall in with them was introduced as Shadrach Hopper, the Rafter B ranch foreman and trail boss of the drive. By the bullwhip coiled around his saddle horn, Mac recognized him as the rider he'd spotted cracking that whip on the opposite side of the herd as they were riding hard to get the critters halted. Hopper was a tall, ruggedly built man, with an easy Texas drawl and seen-it-all-before eyes set between deep crow's-feet on a battered, weathered face just this side of homely. He looked pretty good in Mac's eyes, however, when he promptly spoke up and stated his recognition of Mac and his paint horse for their involvement in curbing the stampede.

This final unsolicited testimony from Hopper pretty much sealed the deal on everybody accepting Mac for what he claimed to be. Everybody but Roman, who didn't voice any further argument but remained silent and continued to wear a bitter scowl.

The camp, when they finally reached it, was found unscathed by the runaway cattle and also left unbothered by the rustlers who had set the stampede in motion. The way the whole thing had happened, Bradley explained to Mac during the ride in, was that a pack of rustlers had hit the outer edges of the herd, driven off forty or fifty head for their own purposes, then hoorahed the remainder of the restless longhorns into a stampede to distract the Rafter B crew while the rustlers made their getaway.

The pattern was recognizable because Bradley, during a trip into a nearby town for supplies a week back, had been warned by the store clerk there about reports from other drovers who'd had their herds hit in that manner. So, even though Bradley and Hopper kept everybody as vigilant as possible, the men pulling nighthawk duty tonight had been spread too thin to catch the wide-loopers before they were able to strike again.

"I got six men pushing eight hundred head of cattle," Bradley lamented. "Plus myself, our chuckwagon cook, and Colleen. She mostly takes care of the remuda but can punch cows with the best of 'em if need be. It's a whale of a job, but by Jove, we've made it this far, and it'll take a sight more than tonight's trouble to turn us back."

"Where are you headed?" Mac had asked.

"Miles City, Montana," came the answer. Then Bradley added, "I know, you're probably wondering why we didn't sell off back at Denver. Could have, would have gotten a decent price, too. I was tempted, believe me. But I've had a buyer lined up in Miles City for some time. He locked in on a fair price and is counting on us to come through. I don't aim to let him down just because the going gets a little tough."

Mac gave a quiet nod, inwardly admiring that kind of commitment to a deal. In spite of his hotheaded oldest son, Mac decided Bradley was a tough but fair sort, the kind of man who would inspire loyalty in those around him and expect nothing less in return.

The Rafter B chuckwagon cook was a potbellied, bow-legged old rascal decked out in a derby hat and a once-white apron now splashed with so many different food stains that only the strap going up around the back of his neck retained any trace of white. Bradley introduced him as Orson Brandenburger, and the only thing Mac got in response was a grunt and a once-over that didn't seem particularly welcoming.

"I got a pot of coffee and some fresh-baked biscuits waitin'," the cook announced. "I figured after all the extra cattle chasin' and such, you'd come back wantin' something to put in your bellies, even though you already et supper. I never saw a bunch so quick to have their appetites triggered by the least little amount of work."

"Must be the high quality of your outstanding cuisine," remarked George Bradley, "that keeps us clamoring for more."

"If that was another sarcastic crack about my cookin'," responded Brandenburger, "just keep it up and see what it gets you, you pup. Might be a big surprise floatin' in a bowl of stew I dish up especially for you one of these times."

"Hey now," protested Henry Bradley. "Don't take my little brother's digs out on the rest of us."

Brandenburger frowned. "I said it'd be especially

for him, didn't I? The rest of you don't have to worry—though you might want to take fair warnin' from it."

Mac couldn't help grinning to himself. This kind of banter between a ranch crew and the outfit's cook was as common as fleas on a hound. Sometimes it was good-natured, other times not so much. His own experience as chuckwagon cook on two different trail drives had taught Mac how to toss it back and forth with even the most sour-pussed cowpoke. Luckily for him, though, he'd also learned how to be pretty good at serving up tasty grub, so the ribbing he had to put up with was mostly the good-natured kind.

As for this Brandenburger fellow, Mac was willing to reserve judgment on how deserving he might be of whatever guff he got. But, based on the half-burnt biscuits and overly bitter coffee he served under these less-than-ideal circumstances, Mac's first impression was that he just might have it coming.

CHAPTER 5

"Hey, lazybones. You going to sleep the day away?"

Mac awoke with a start, surprised to find sunlight pouring into his eyes as soon as he opened them. He was usually an early riser, especially when bedded down in unfamiliar surroundings.

Adding to his surprise was the fact that the voice rousting him was decidedly female. Looking up, blinking and pushing to a sitting position, he saw Colleen Bradley standing over him, wearing a smile even more dazzling than the sun.

"I . . . I'm sorry," Mac stammered. "It ain't like me to sleep past sunup. I must have been more tuckered out than I realized."

"It's all right," Colleen said with a gentle laugh. "Pa let everybody sleep a little extra this morning on account of all the excitement last night. Besides, it's not like you're part of the crew. You're our guest, you don't have any duties. The reason I rousted you, though, was so you wouldn't miss out on the breakfast Pa promised. If you don't get over there to the trough and grab your share when it's dished up, the rest of those inhospitable varmints are apt to gobble it all and leave you nothing."

"Well, I thank you kindly for that. Since I usually wake with a tolerable hunger, I'd hate to start the day missing out on some good grub."

Mac threw back his covers and reached for his boots. That was the extent of how far he undressed before crawling into a bedroll. He was grateful for that, what with Colleen standing there now the way she was.

Even so, he felt a little funny crawling out of the sack with a gal looking on. But since it didn't seem to bother her any, he reckoned he could tolerate it, too. Once he had his boots tugged on, he stood up and stomped into them the rest of the way. After that, he leaned over to retrieve his hat and gun, clapping the one on his head and slipping the other behind the belt of his trousers.

"Don't you use a holster?" asked Colleen.

"I've worn one on occasion, but never really got in the habit. This suits me good enough," Mac told her.

"That looks like a pretty old gun."

"It is, I guess. My father gave it to me. I hung on to it, even though for a while I never really appreciated it or took proper care of it—not until I headed out on my first cattle drive with a couple of fellas who taught me better. Even an older model like this one can be plenty reliable if you take care of it right."

Colleen regarded him. "Last night, after the stampede got stopped and after you fought with Roman, you called him a fool for not thinking to reload his gun after he'd emptied it turning the herd. The way you said it, the disdain in your voice, you sort of sounded like a gunfighter."

Mac smiled. "I'm nowhere near good enough to be called that. Although I'll admit to using this Smith & Wesson to defend myself a time or two. Mostly it goes back to those two fellas I mentioned, how they drilled into me about using a gun proper-like. It rankles me when I see somebody packing one and not having the sense to treat it that way."

"But if Roman would have shown that much sense," Colleen pointed out, "you might not be standing here this morning. He would have shot you."

Mac made a sour face. "Don't remind me. You trying to ruin the breakfast you woke me up for?"

They had started walking toward the chuckwagon but Colleen stopped abruptly. When Mac stopped, too, she placed a hand on his arm and said, "Roman's my brother and I love him. But he can be terribly hotheaded, and he hates like poison to admit he's wrong about anything or anybody. You be careful around him, you hear?"

"Thanks for the advice, ma'am," Mac said. "But I plan on lighting out right after grub, so I don't figure on being around Roman for very long. But I'll be careful for as long as I am."

As it turned out, what Colleen should have warned Mac to be careful about was another round of Brandenburger's cooking. The breakfast he dished out consisted of more burnt biscuits, a big scoop of overcooked beans, and bitter coffee to go with them. The only saving grace was a generous pile of crispy, thick-sliced bacon. All things considered, Mac had a hunch it must have been a mistake on the part of the cranky old cook to allow that much of his fare to turn out decent.

But based on the way the others were all chowing down without comment nor complaint, they were either so used to such poor grub that they didn't know any better, or they had simply resigned themselves to enduring it until the drive was over.

In any case, Mac was glad this was the last of it he'd have to choke down.

Whatever the others had been talking about as Mac and Colleen approached, it tapered off on their arrival. Mac noticed that Nolan and Sparky were present while the two younger Bradley brothers were absent, causing him to conclude that Henry and George must have been sent out to watch over the distant herd sometime during the night.

Balancing his plate of food and cup of coffee, Mac sat down next to Shad Hopper, the trail boss. Colleen opted to settle onto an overturned bucket between her father and her brother Roman.

Norris Bradley said, "So, Mac, you say you're bound for California. Is that right?"

Mac nodded. "Eventually, yes. For starters, though, I'm figuring on continuing north for a ways. Poke my nose into Wyoming, probably as far as Cheyenne, mainly just to say I've been there. Then I'll aim west, leave some tracks across the top of Utah and through Nevada on the way. No particular destination, just keep chasing that setting sun until I hit salt water."

"They say there's a big lake full of salt water in

Utah," said Hopper. He grinned. "Make sure you don't run into that and mistake it for the end of your trip."

"I'll be sure to keep that in mind," replied Mac, also grinning.

"Chasing the setting sun. Footloose and fancy free, eh?" prodded Bradley. "And no place up to now that's ever dragged at your feet a little, made you think about putting down roots?"

Now Mac felt the corners of his mouth pull down. He said, "Had some notions along those lines once. When that fell apart, well, that's when I went on the drift."

"Pa," said Colleen in a scolding tone, seeing that the question had touched something in Mac. "You're being awfully nosy, aren't you?"

"Not meaning to be. Just showing some friendly interest is all," Bradley countered.

"It's okay. No problem," said Mac.

"Sounds to me," said Hopper, "like even if you didn't put down roots in one *place*, you're leastways rooted to one *thing*. That's bein' a cowboy. You said you've been on a couple different drives in the past few months, didn't you?"

"That's right," Mac replied. "But that's pretty much the extent of my experience working cattle. I wouldn't say it makes me a full-fledged cowboy."

Hopper nodded. "Based on what I saw last night, the way you helped turn that stampede, you must've had some pretty savvy hombres teaching you the ropes then."

"I learned from some of the best, that's for sure," Mac agreed. "The thing is, though, what I hired on for at the start of both of those drives was as chuckwagon cook."

"What happened?" Roman asked with a nasty smirk. "You such a lousy cook they took away your frying pan and set you to work eating dust back on the drag as a way to get even?"

"Roman!" Colleen snapped with a flash of fire in her eyes.

Before Mac could respond, Bradley said, "Something I've been thinking, especially now that you said you were going north as far as Wyoming anyway— what would you say to sticking with us for a spell, Mac? I explained to you last night how stretched we are for help and since—"

"Now hold on, Pa! You can't be serious!" Roman exclaimed. "You know I've had a bad feeling about this jasper right from the beginning. If you ask me—"

"Nobody did," his father cut him off. "And yes, you've made your feelings toward the man plenty clear. Trouble is, nobody else sees one whisker of reason to feel the same way, including me. And the last time I checked, I still run this outfit."

"Yeah, you got the right to final say . . . even when you're wrong," Roman muttered through clenched teeth.

Bradley glared at him until he averted his eyes. Then the old man swung his gaze back to Mac. "So what do you say? You at all interested? The pay is two dollars a day, a twenty-five-dollar bonus if we make it to Miles City with seven hundred head. If you stick with us all the way, you can find that setting sun to take aim at from Montana as well as from

Wyoming. And you'll have picked up some extra cash for traveling expenses."

Mac rubbed his jaw. "Something to think about. But something else to think about—and no offense meant, sir—is that you said you started out with eight hundred head and now, in just one night, you've lost about thirty in the stampede and another forty or so to the rustlers. That makes any chance to claim that bonus mighty slim, wouldn't you say?"

"Yes, I suppose it does," Bradley allowed, scowling. "But if we're careful and don't have any more bad luck, it's still possible."

"Be a lot more possible if you got those forty stolen head back," Mac pointed out.

"Much as I hate to agree with the likes of you, that's something else I've been trying to tell him," said Roman. "But it's also something else he won't listen to reason about."

"Blast it, we've already been through all that," grumbled Bradley. "We can't spare good men to go chasing after no-account rustlers. And who's to say they aren't wanting us to do exactly that? They could be out there waiting to ambush anybody who comes after them. If they managed to pick off a couple of our crew, we wouldn't have enough men to finish the drive. Not only that, it would leave us vulnerable to those skunks coming back and hitting us even harder—stealing more cattle, doing more killing. Is the chance to regain a few longhorns for the sake of a few lousy dollars in bonus money worth that kind of risk?"

"I say it is," Roman insisted stubbornly. "It's more

than just the bonus, it's the principle of the thing, Pa. They pranced in, stole a bunch of our cattle, then killed a bunch more in the stampede they caused. We can't let them just get away with it!"

Into the tense silence that followed that statement, Mac said, "How many rustlers were there? Anybody got an idea?"

"Four," Hopper answered promptly. "I rode out early this morning, checked out the trail they left. Four riders pushing forty-five cows. Headed southeast."

"Likely aiming to loop around and sell off the cattle back down in the Denver area," Mac said. "If they've worked this kind of thing before, they probably got a buyer for stolen beef all lined up down there."

Roman glared at him. "You sound like you know a lot about how cattle thieves operate."

"It ain't hard to figure out if you keep your eyes and ears open," Mac responded, working hard to hold his temper. "Like I told you, I rode with some mighty savvy hombres. Other than maybe Mr. Hopper here, those fellas forgot more about driving cattle than most will ever learn."

"Be that as it may, it doesn't change our situation," stated Bradley, growing annoyed. "And us sitting here jawing about it don't, either. Nor does it get our herd moving again. Now, Mac, are you interested in joining us or not?"

The answer that came out of Mac's mouth was a surprise to nobody more than himself. "I reckon I might be, Mr. Bradley. But on one condition."

"We already got a chuckwagon cook!" Brandenburger was quick to say.

Mac ignored him. *Like anybody was apt to forget that sorry fact.*

Bradley scowled. "What condition?"

"That the first job you give me," Mac said, "is to go get those stolen cattle back."

CHAPTER 6

Bradley's scowl turned into a puzzled frown. "What makes that stolen stock of such great concern to you?"

"Let's just say I got a healthy dislike for rustlers," Mac told him. "What's more, the stampede they set off trampled my campsite to ruination and came close to stomping me into the ground right along with it. I take that kinda personal."

"You saying you're ready to take out after those owl-hoots on your own?" Hopper asked.

"Be better if somebody went with me."

"That'd still be four-to-two odds."

"Two men riding hard ought to be able to catch up easy enough with four pushing a herd, even a small one," Mac pointed out. "Then, if they were patient and held off until nightfall, who ambushes who might be a whole different matter."

"That don't sound like a half-bad idea, Boss," said Hopper, addressing Bradley. "Can't say I'm keen on the notion, either, of lettin' those cow-snatchin' varmints get away."

"Plus," said Mac, "since I haven't been part of this

outfit before now, if somebody went with me, Mr. Bradley, you'd only be risking one member of the crew you had before. If our gamble doesn't pay off and worse came to worst, you'd still be able to manage the herd and not be as crippled, manpower-wise, as you might be otherwise."

Bradley clearly was wavering. Pinning Mac with a hard look, he said, "If I agree to this, does that mean you'll stick with our outfit all the way to Miles City?"

A corner of Mac's mouth quirked upward. "My old grandma had a saying. 'In for a penny, in for a pound.'"

Bradley nodded curtly. "You got in mind who you want to go with you?"

Mac looked at Roman. "You were pushing for this before I was. Reckon that gives you the right for a piece of it, if you want."

"With you?" Roman sneered. "No thanks. I'm not in that much of a hurry to ride a few miles away from camp and get a bullet in the back—and I don't mean from the rustlers we'd supposedly be chasing."

"Because there's too much else going on right now," Mac said through clenched teeth, "I'm going to forget you said that. For the time being. But one of these days, mister, me and you are due to have a real intense discussion about some things."

"I'll go with Mac," Hopper spoke up. "I'd welcome the chance to dish out some payback to those polecats."

"Now wait a minute," Bradley said. "I agreed to somebody going after our stolen cattle. But I have to draw the line at you being part of it, Shad. In case anything goes wrong, you're too important to this drive."

"Oh, that's rich," Roman said. "You got no objection to *me* riding out and risking my neck. With a complete stranger who might be as crooked as a sidewinder, no less. But Shad, he's *too important* to let him take that chance!"

"You did a pretty quick job of objecting for yourself. You never gave me the opportunity," Bradley responded.

"No, and I'm not going to again." Roman turned his head and glared at Mac. "I changed my mind. I *will* take you up on your offer. I'll ride with you after those rustlers. Who knows? Somewhere along the way, we might even be able to fit in that real intense discussion you're wanting to have."

The rustlers had stampeded the main body of the Rafter B herd north, the same general direction the drive was headed anyway. By then cutting back south, as Shad Hopper had determined, and pushing all night with the critters they'd stolen, the thieves had a pretty good start on Mac and Roman Bradley by the time the pair started in pursuit.

But as Mac had pointed out, two men riding hard—especially now in the daylight—could cover ground a lot faster than cattle could be driven. By midday, the pursuers believed they'd closed the gap substantially between themselves and their quarry.

As they walked for a spell in order to rest their horses, Mac said, "The varmints we're after can't be more than a half mile ahead."

"That's the feeling I got," Roman said. "But it's just a feeling. I don't pretend to be no kind of experienced tracker. You got anything more solid to go on?"

Mac gestured toward the ground. "I learned a few tricks about tracking along the way, though I don't claim to be any great shakes at it, either. Still, following forty-odd head of longhorns over prairie grass is about as simple as it gets. Besides the stomped-down grass, look at the droppings we've been riding by. Steam's still coming off some of 'em. That means they haven't been there for very long."

"You're right," Roman said, an edge of excitement in his voice. "We must be practically on top of those devils."

Mac lifted his gaze from the ground and swept it over the landscape up ahead. This terrain appeared considerably more rugged than the rolling hills and grassy flats they'd been traveling over.

"I'm thinking of your father's warning about how those skunks might set up an ambush for anybody trying to follow them."

Roman frowned. "We haven't had any trouble so far. If they were going to try something, don't you think they would have done it by now?"

"Not necessarily," said Mac, eyes still scanning. "Think about it if you were in their boots. They know they stampeded the main herd and had to figure it would take quite a while to get that stopped, scattering Rafter B riders in the process. By the time the herd was halted and everybody regrouped, a lot of time and distance would have passed. It was full dark. Be reasonable for them to think, I'd say, that if anybody was going to come after 'em, it wouldn't be until daybreak—just like you and me did. And right about now is when they'd figure any followers might be closing in."

"Just like we are," said Roman.

Mac nodded. "Uh-huh. Add that line of reasoning to the way their trail is swinging closer to the foothills, making one of those higher knobs you can see up ahead a good spot for an ambusher to shoot down from . . . well, it's kinda making the back of my neck itch."

Roman regarded him closely for a long minute, saying nothing.

Mac shifted his gaze, met Roman's eyes. "Something on your mind?"

Roman licked his lips, took several more seconds before answering. "Look, you know I don't really trust you, right?"

"You made that clear enough. Yet you still changed your mind about coming with me."

"Everybody was looking. I couldn't let 'em think I was yellow. Especially since I was the one who'd already been making noise about chasing those rustlers."

"So you proved to the camp that you're not yellow," Mac said. "Why are you balking now?"

"Like I said before, you seem to know an awful lot about how an owlhoot might think and operate. Can't help but make a fella wonder."

"And like I told you," Mac countered, "it's just a matter of thinking and doing a little reasoning. Something you're not doing a very good job of right at the moment. If I'd wanted to do you in, you blasted fool, I could have planted a bullet or slipped a knife into you a dozen different times by now."

Roman suddenly looked at a loss for words.

"You want to talk about making a fella wonder?" Mac went on. "Look at it from my side. Knowing the way you feel about me, how could I be sure you wouldn't ride us out a ways and then decide to haul off and shoot me—again—so's you could go back and claim to everybody you were right about me all along, that I'd tried to jump you and you had to cut me down in self-defense?"

Roman bristled. "I might be hotheaded and stubborn, but I'd never do anybody that way, not even somebody I didn't trust."

The two men stood glaring at each other, nostrils flared, jaws set hard. The better part of a minute ticked by.

Finally, Mac expelled some breath and said, "So where do we go from here? Decide this can't work because neither of us can trust the other? Ride back to the camp and tell 'em it fell apart, that we failed?"

"I don't want that," Roman responded in a tight voice.

"Neither do I," Mac said. "Your father and the whole Rafter B crew are counting on us. I don't like coming up short when somebody puts their faith in me."

"I don't like it, either, particularly since my temper has led me to come up short in the eyes of my old man more times than I care to admit. I don't want this to be another of those times." His eyes bored into Mac once more, but suddenly without the rancor that had burned there moments earlier. "You seem to have a knack for reasoning things out. What do you figure's our best play for getting those cattle back?"

CHAPTER 7

"Yeehaw! Yip! Yip! Get a move on, cattle!"

Screeching like a banshee as he triggered rounds from his skyward-aimed Yellowboy Winchester, Mac simultaneously dug his heels into the paint and sent the big horse plowing straight toward the knot of long-horns grazing in the shadow-edged moonlight.

Fifteen feet away, from the back of his own horse, Roman Bradley emitted similar howls and fired off a Henry repeater as he, too, charged the small herd.

As one, the nearest cattle wheeled in panic and bolted straight into the mass of other animals behind them. Equally startled and now suddenly being crowded and slammed by the rush of their own kind, those cows also turned and began to run. In a matter of seconds, the whole bunch was racing blindly, fran-tically, aimed haphazardly on a course that would take them back out of the grassy gap between two high, rounded shoulders of rock where they had been bedded down for the night.

And directly in their path, seated in a loose circle around a small campfire, leisurely swigging cups of whiskey-laced coffee, sat the four rustlers who had sneaked the cattle out of the main Rafter B herd before hoorahing the rest into a stampede. Now, suddenly, horrifyingly, the tables had been turned and the four found themselves forced to deal with another stampede—this one barreling directly toward them with no room or time to get out of the way!

With nearly four dozen head of cattle flowing ahead of them like a bawling, rumbling wave, Mac and Roman kept yipping and shooting, urging them into a frenzied, full-out run. The wave poured over the campsite, and the four rustlers caught there had practically no chance to escape. The horses picketed close by tore free from their restraints and fled out of reach ahead of the onrushing cattle.

One of the rustlers, heavyset and ponderously slow in his movements, fell under the pounding, grinding hooves and managed only a short scream of terror and pain before disappearing in the cloud of dust that boiled around the charging animals.

The other three wide-loopers were a little better at running for their lives. One carrying a big rifle made it to some rocks on the left side of the camp. He scrambled up with horn tips scraping his boot heels. Once above the tramplers, he twisted around with his rifle half-raised and looked for the cause of the stampede.

Mac quickly reined up the paint and raised his Winchester. Just as the eyes of the rustler fell on him, Mac stroked the Winchester's trigger. His bullet struck true, slamming into the man's chest even as he was attempting to bring the Sharps to his shoulder. He fell back against the rocks, dead fingers losing their grip on the big rifle, then he twisted slightly to one side and dropped forward to fall under the last of the cattle rushing through the gap.

The remaining two rustlers also made it to the rocks. One of them got severely gored in the process, however, and although he managed not to end up under the mangling hooves, the amount of blood pumping from the ragged gash in his stomach didn't signal much hope for survival.

Ascended to a ledge just above the gored man, the last of the thieves crouched with a drawn pistol. Like the rifleman, he began peering intently through the billowing dust, looking for the cause of the stampede. He found part of it—but too late. When the man's eyes locked on Roman, the latter already had his Henry snugged to his shoulder and was drawing a bead. The Henry spoke once, sharply, and the pistoleer was knocked clean off his feet, toppling into a lifeless heap.

CHAPTER 8

It took three days before Mac and Roman caught up with the Rafter B's main herd. Almost half of the first day had been lost to burying the remains of the rustlers—something they debated even bothering with, but in the end felt obligated to do—and chasing down the stampeded cattle. The hombre who'd been severely gored lived for a few hours, mostly unconscious and moaning in pain. When they woke at sunrise the next morning, he was gone.

The smaller bunch could be pushed along somewhat faster than the main herd. Still, recognizing they had a lot of ground to make up, Mac and Roman had squeezed as much as possible out of each day—and then some. They were on the move from before the sun rose until after it sank out of sight beyond the horizon.

During this time, the feelings between the two men were considerably less tense than when they'd started out. Nevertheless, there remained an undercurrent of uncertainty.

The one area where this undercurrent was laid wholly to rest, however, was when it came mealtime. Mac had made sure to include in their provisions enough fixings to stir up some decent grub. This included ingredients for the kind of fluffy, golden biscuits he was rightfully proud of. Biscuits, in fact, were the first things he'd mastered as a cook and since his initial ranch boss held the opinion that "a cowboy will ride to Hades and back for a good biscuit," Mac's ability to meet that demand was what had landed him on the seat of a chuckwagon.

Not even Roman and his lingering reservations when it came to Mac in general could hold back praise for his cooking. "I swear," he declared at one point, "if Orson Brandenburger could cook like this, my old man could probably cut the wages he pays and still get wranglers flocking to ride for our brand just to get eats this good."

"Well, I'm glad you like the vittles," Mac responded. "But I'd appreciate it if you didn't let on about it when we catch up with the Rafter B. I don't want Orson to get his feathers ruffled and take it out on either of us."

Roman grunted. "Unless he flat-out resorted to poison, it ain't like he could do much to make his slop taste any worse."

"If everybody feels that way, why does your father put up with it?" Mac asked.

"I guess he figures we're sort of stuck with Orson," Roman explained. "He was a last-minute hire, you see, when we got ready to start out on this drive. Our regular cook all of a sudden decided to get hitched and then wasn't willing to abandon his brand-new wife for all the time it would take to push our cows to Montana. So the old man scrounged up Orson from somewhere, him *claiming* he could cook, and that's what we've been putting up with ever since."

Mac frowned. "Not to ask anything out of line, but

since your sister is along on the drive . . . well, I can't help wondering why she doesn't handle the cooking duties?"

Roman threw back his head and laughed. "One very simple reason. My beloved little sister is an even worse cook than Orson!"

Mac's eyebrows lifted. "That's hard to believe."

"Why? Because she's a woman and all women are supposed to be good cooks?" Roman gave an emphatic shake of his head. "Well, that missed the mark when it came to Colleen. When it comes to what you might call traditional womanly ways, she don't much fit the mold. She can ride and shoot as good or better than most men, took to that sort of thing as soon as she could walk, just like us boys. Ma died when Colleen was still pretty little, so whether she would have influenced her any different, nobody can say. But the fact remains, Colleen didn't turn out to be no kind of homebody. And the few times she's tried her hand at cooking for Pa and us boys . . . well, we could barely get the ranch dogs to eat what she fixed."

"I guess I got my answer," Mac said.

Roman grunted. "Afraid so. Sure would be nice if Colleen *could* have handled the cooking. But she can't. So every day and every lousy meal Orson serves up brings all of us fellas in the outfit closer to rebellion."

"Maybe so," Mac allowed. "That sounds like something to take up with Orson and your father if you need to. But like I said, leave me out of it."

It was the middle of the afternoon when they came in sight of Colleen and the remuda. Roman rode ahead to report their good fortune and spread word to the rest of the outfit. Upon hearing the news, Norris Bradley slowed the pace of the main drive in order for the stolen cattle to be allowed to close the gap remaining between the two. Once that was accomplished, Mac and Roman rode up to the head of the drive, meeting with hearty congratulations from the other cowboys along the way.

None were more pleased than Bradley himself. "You did it," the old man boomed. "I had confidence you would, but I gotta admit, the more time passed with no sign of you, I couldn't help but start to worry that . . . Well, never mind. I'm awful glad you made it back. Not just with the cattle, but especially having you safe and sound!"

Mac had figured out by now that things between father and son hadn't always been smooth. But what he saw in that moment was a genuine fondness existing between the two and, on Bradley's part, considerable pride and relief. It made Mac feel good to see it and to think that he'd helped play a small part in bringing it about.

Not that his participation went unnoticed. He got his fair share of praise and congratulations. Even, somewhat to his surprise, from Roman, who, when he related how they'd used a stampede of their own *against* the rustlers, gave full credit for the idea to Mac. Only when the question of the rustlers' fate was raised did the high spirits of the reunion turn a bit dour.

"Let's just say," Roman responded in a somber tone, "nobody else will ever have to worry about having their cattle stole by those varmints."

The sun was sinking behind the western mountains when they reached the grassy expanse that Shad

Hopper had marked for that night's bed ground. Parked close by was Orson Brandenburger's chuckwagon, with columns of smoke and steam rising from the cooking fires and the pots and pans bubbling over the flames.

Riding alongside Mac, Roman gave a low groan. "My stomach's starting to churn already."

Mac shot him a look. "Remember our agreement."

"What agreement?" Roman said. Then he snorted a quick laugh to show he was just teasing. Maybe.

When it came time for Brandenburger to ladle out supper, it was the usual fare prepared in the usual substandard way. Bland, half-burnt, served with sullen indifference. But to hungry wranglers who'd put in another long, hard day, it was belly-filling, so it went down quickly and with no complaints.

Not long after Mac had found a soft hump of grass to settle down on, balancing his plate and cup of coffee, Colleen Bradley came walking over, carrying her own meal. "Mind some company?" she asked.

"Of course not," Mac answered, quickly setting aside his plate and cup and starting to get to his feet.

"Stay put!" Colleen ordered him. "No need to stand on ceremony and jump up from where you're sitting just because I come around. After all, we're in the middle of a cattle drive, not any kind of proper dining room."

"Habits are habits, ma'am. Standing up for a lady was drilled into me early and deep."

"That's sweet, and it's certainly refreshing to run into someone who still knows how to act like a gentleman," Colleen replied as she sank gracefully down next to him. "But for the duration of this trip, I absolve you of having to carry out that particular function. Once we reach Miles City and I've had a chance to bathe and put on a dress, maybe we'll dine together. *Then* you can perform all the gentlemanly routines that were drilled into you. How's that?"

"Fair enough," Mac agreed. When Colleen smiled at him like that, he told himself, he reckoned he would agree to just about anything.

They ate a few bites in silence until Colleen spoke again. "In all the excitement today, I didn't get much chance to add my own congratulations on your success. It was a bold and very brave thing you did, going after those cattle and facing those rustlers."

"It was the right thing, that's all I know," Mac said, enjoying her praise yet starting to feel a little uncomfortable from having so much of it heaped on him. "You let cattle thieves or other lowdown types get away with riding roughshod over everything and everybody, it just gets more and more out of hand and pretty soon good folks end up getting hurt. It needs to be stopped and stopped hard."

"You sound as if you've encountered your share of lowdown types before."

"Yeah, I reckon I have," Mac said.

Colleen regarded him. "And yet you seem to have remained, for the most part, a rather gentle sort yourself."

Mac shifted uncomfortably on the hump of grass. "Being polite and treating folks decent doesn't come that hard, ma'am. But there's times when the wildcat inside me does some howling, too."

"Everybody has that right once in a while. But I bet

even the wildcat in you has never been petty or mean, not without good reason."

Mac didn't know what to say to that. Thankfully, he was saved from having to come up with something by Norris Bradley striding over to join them, coffee cup in hand.

The old rancher squatted, not sitting down. "The way me and Shad have got it figured," he said, "we ought to be crossing over into Wyoming Territory about the middle of the day tomorrow. You still got in mind wanting to pay a visit to Cheyenne, Mac?"

Mac's eyebrows lifted. "You know, I really haven't thought about that lately. What with chasing after those stolen cattle and all."

"The thing is," Bradley said after a short sip of his coffee, "the herd will be swinging a fair piece west of there. I know you agreed to go ahead and stick with us, but after the way you pitched in and helped bring those rustled critters back, I feel kinda bad robbing you of your chance to make that visit."

"My notion to make a stop in Cheyenne was no more than that—just a notion. One I had when I was on my own. Now that I've signed on to ride for the Rafter B, I go where the cattle go."

Bradley's mouth curved in a faint smile. "I'm relieved to hear you say that. You've already proven a good addition to our outfit. I'd hate for you to slip away so quick."

"I don't make a habit of going back on my word."

"No, I can see you ain't the kind who would. And that's good enough for me," Bradley said. He stood up. "Now that we've got that settled, I'll let you two finish your meal and your conversation."

Colleen watched her father walk away. When he was out of earshot, she swung her eyes back to Mac and said, "Father likes you, I can tell."

"I hope so," Mac replied. "He seems like a good man."

"Something else I noticed," Colleen went on, "is that since you two got back, even Roman doesn't seem to harbor much of a grudge against you. That's not like him, to allow a chip on his shoulder to get brushed off so easily."

Mac grinned. "Maybe it wasn't as easy as you think. I wouldn't be too quick to call me and Roman pards. But we took on a tough task and got it done together. I reckon that counts for something."

The fine lines of Colleen's brows pinched together slightly. "I'm not sure what that means." Then the brows smoothed again, and from beneath them, her sparkling eyes once more gazed very intently at Mac. "But I am sure about one thing. My father isn't the only one who's glad you're back safe and sound and that you'll be sticking with our outfit."

CHAPTER 9

"Oww!" Curses followed the exclamation.

Mac kicked back the covers and scrambled hurriedly out of his bedroll. He'd awakened some time earlier, a leftover habit from his days of being a chuckwagon cook and needing to get up ahead of everyone else.

The sudden cry came from Brandenburger. There was something about the tone—pain? panic?—that immediately told Mac there was something more seriously wrong than the cranky old cook just stubbing his toe or burning his thumb on a hot pan. Taking time only to stomp into his boots, Mac made a dash across the campsite to reach the chuckwagon.

It was still dark, daybreak no more than a pale smudge above the eastern horizon, but Brandenburger's cooking fires were stoked high enough to provide some illumination.

When Mac got to the cook, the man was standing very still, shoulders hunched forward, hands clutched together in front of him. Mac edged around on one side of him, trying to determine what was wrong.

"What is it, Orson? What happened?"

Mac could see he had the front of his apron lifted and wrapped tight around both hands. He could also see that the assorted stains covering the apron were now being obscured by a rapidly spreading pattern of wet, shiny scarlet.

"I cut myself," Brandenburger said through clenched teeth. "My hands were greasy from handling a slab of bacon . . . knife slipped when I went to slice . . . I . . . I don't want to look."

"Well, somebody's gonna have to. And by the way it's bleeding, it needs to be pretty quick," Mac said. "Who does the doctoring for the outfit?"

"Miss Colleen tends to scrapes and blisters and the like. Shad Hopper does any stitching that's needed."

"Not much doubt that's gonna need stitching." Mac looked around until he spied a wadded-up towel on one corner of the table. He grabbed it and handed it to Brandenburger. "Here, wrap your injured hand in this. Tight. Then bend your arm and hold it up above chest level, to help slow the pump of blood."

While the cook was doing this, Mac turned up the wick of the lantern that was hanging from a crossbar of the canopy that extended over the food preparation area. Hanging next to the lantern was a steel triangle and a ringing bar for signaling everybody when it was time for grub.

Mac grabbed the bar and began whirling it inside the triangle with a practiced flourish, sending a clamor all through the camp as he hollered, "Everybody roust up! Right away! We got an injury here and a man in serious need of help!"

* * *

Forty-five minutes later, the sun was partly risen above the horizon and the flurry of activity within the Rafter B camp had finally settled down. Orson Brandenburger was laid out on his bedroll under one end of the chuckwagon, resting fitfully, at times snoring, other times moaning softly.

This state was the result of consuming nearly half a bottle of whiskey meant to dull the pain from his wound and then the two dozen stitches required to close it and stop the bleeding. The deep laceration left by the slipped knife ran from the web between his thumb and forefinger down over the ball of his thumb nearly to the base of his palm. By the time he was done applying the stitches, Shad Hopper was blood-spattered, dripping sweat, and reaching to take a belt of the whiskey himself.

"That's a mean cut," Hopper reported now to those gathered around him. His voice was tight, his expression grim. "I got the bleeding stopped—I think. As deep as he sliced, I can't even swear that will hold. Plus he cut through who knows how many nerves and tendons, then ended up almighty close to that big vein in his wrist. If he's to have any chance of getting back full use of his hand, we really ought to get him to a doctor."

"Can he travel? What I mean is, will he be able to sit a horse?" Bradley asked.

Hopper's mouth twisted wryly. "When he sobers up enough to sit upright at all, he ought to be able to. Long as he don't start pumping more blood."

"The next question," said Bradley, frowning, "is where are we likely to find the nearest doctor?"

"I'd say the closest place would be Cheyenne. Can't

be more than thirty miles to the northeast. A decent start and a good horse could make it there by dark."

Bradley rubbed his stubbled jaw for a moment before saying, "Well, I guess that's the right thing to do then. We owe it to the ornery cuss to give him the best chance we can." He looked at Mac. "Looks like you may get your chance to visit Cheyenne after all."

"Not so quick, Pa," spoke up Roman. He tossed a quick glance toward Mac. "It's not that I begrudge Mackenzie making the trip. But here's the thing. Without Orson, this outfit is going to be minus a cook. None of the rest of us are cut out for that. If we were, we wouldn't have put up with the slop Orson's been feeding us up to now. But the one exception—and I'm telling you this based on experience from eating his trail cooking while him and me were after those rustlers—is Mackenzie. He can cook like nobody's business. Be a shame to let him get away and then the rest of us suffer through the kind of grub we'd have to get by on with him and Orson both gone."

Bradley frowned. "What do you say to that, Mac?"

Mac shrugged. "Well, I told you at the start I've got experience as a chuckwagon cook. And I won't deny that I'm kinda proud of the grub I'm able to rustle up. As far as going to Cheyenne, after we talked last evening, I'd pretty much put that notion out of my head. So going or not going now, on account of this new development, doesn't really matter to me. If I can help the outfit more by staying and cooking for the drive, I'm fine with that."

"I'll go, Pa," young George piped up. "I'll take Orson to Cheyenne and get him doctored up proper."

Bradley didn't hesitate in the least to shake his head. "Oh no, you won't. You're too blamed eager.

You'd get to Cheyenne, have your head spun around by the big city, and who knows how long it'd be before you found your way back to us."

"Aw, come on, Pa. That ain't fair! I'd behave myself. I'm just as responsible as—"

Bradley cut him short. "I said no, and that's the end of it!" He took a breath and then turned to his middle son. "How about you, Henry? You seem to tolerate Orson's crankiness better than most, anyway. You up for riding him to Cheyenne and seeing to it his hand gets patched up proper?"

Henry's generally mild expression didn't change. "If that's what you want, Pa. But if it's what we're gonna do, then let's start pouring some strong coffee into the patient in order to get him sobered back up enough to sit a saddle. And Colleen, will you round up a couple sturdy horses for us? If we want to make Cheyenne by nightfall, we'd better get a move on."

And so it was that Mac became, at least temporarily, the new cook for the Rafter B. But in no time at all—only as long as it took for the crew to taste a few bites of the first breakfast he served, consisting of fluffy, golden biscuits smothered in creamy redeye gravy containing thick chunks of bacon, accompanied by rich, strong coffee that wasn't so bitter it curled teeth—the compliments and murmurs of satisfaction issued around mouthfuls of the food sent a pretty clear signal there might be some powerful resistance to Orson reclaiming his position whenever he got back.

Chapter 10

Face flushed a bright red, his tone ringing with indignation, Orson Brandenburger demanded an answer. "So I'm fired—is that what you're telling me?"

Standing with his feet planted wide, not withering under Brandenburger's angry glare, Norris Bradley replied tolerantly, "I said nothing of the kind. You're more than welcome to finish the drive with the rest of us. We'll find work for you to do. But with that contraption the doctor slapped on you . . ."

Bradley's words trailed off uncertainly as he scowled down at the "contraption" covering Brandenburger's left hand and part of his forearm.

"It's called a cast, Pa," Henry Bradley said. "The doc in Cheyenne explained it's made of something called plaster of Paris. It dries hard as a rock and is meant to keep the hand and wrist protected and totally still so everything has the best chance of healing in a way that will give Orson all or mostly full use again."

"That's all well and good. And I naturally hope Orson *does* regain full use of the hand," Bradley said. "But in the meantime—that being two to three months before the doc said this cast thing would come off—I don't see how a one-handed person can perform the cooking duties for our drive. Wrangling pots and pans, building the cooking fires, cutting and mixing, even handling the mule team . . . I can't picture it. It would be too much."

"Yet you say you'd find me other work," Brandenburger huffed. "What would that be, for me and my one hand?"

"A man can sit a saddle with one hand, can't he?" Bradley replied, starting to show some impatience. "You could help Colleen with the remuda, take turns as a nighthawk. Things like that."

"Wrangler work," Brandenburger said as if the words left a bad taste in his mouth. "If I'd wanted to be a cowboy, I would have signed on as one. I am a cook!"

"And when your hand is healed, you'll be one again. But for the time being, I don't see how you could manage. Are you telling me you think otherwise?"

Brandenburger scowled fiercely, refusing to give a direct answer. Attempting to dodge the question and instead focus attention elsewhere, he aimed his scowl in the direction of where Mac was working over by the chuckwagon.

"And is that my replacement?" he said acidly. "The upstart who came out of nowhere and claims to be a cook?"

It was the middle of the day. The outfit had just finished its noon meal, and Mac was buttoning up the chuckwagon in order to start rolling again. Henry and Brandenburger had shown up when lunch was nearly over, but Mac put together a couple of bacon and biscuit sandwiches and cups of coffee for them. They'd taken those and wandered off a ways to converse privately with Bradley.

In answer to the question Brandenburger had posed along those very lines, Bradley told him, "Yeah, Mac's been filling in while you were away." Then he added, "And doing a mighty fine job of it."

The corners of Brandenburger's mouth turned downward even more. "Bah! Any saddletramp knows how to throw a piece of meat between a couple slices of bread. But can this Mac cook up a satisfying meal, time after time, that'll stick to a workingman's ribs?"

"If he's the one who made the biscuits that were wrapped around those sandwiches he fixed for us," Henry spoke up, "then I'd say that's a pretty good sign my ribs would be plenty happy to have his cooking stuck to 'em."

"Is that another dig at *my* cooking?" Brandenburger demanded.

Roman Bradley, who was standing not far away, took a step closer. "You want to know what *I* think, Brandenburger?" he said. "I think what needs help is your stinkin' cooking. We've put up with it all these weeks on account of my father feeling obligated to keep you on because you were willing to join us at short notice. And now he's willing to keep you on some more, even after you've hobbled yourself into a nearly useless condition."

"You wouldn't dare talk to me like that, you barking pup, if I had the use of both of my hands!" seethed Brandenburger.

"If that's all that's stopping you," Roman said

through clenched teeth, "I'll gladly tie one of my hands behind my back."

"No, you won't. Stop this, the both of you!" his father said.

"I demand an apology," insisted Brandenburger.

"Then go to hell and wait for it," Roman told him. "The day snow starts falling there, I'll bring one by."

Bradley's voice rose to a low boom. "Enough, I said!"

Roman eased off slightly, but Brandenburger wasn't so willing. "Enough is right. That's what I've had—enough of this whole ungrateful outfit. I've seen the wrinkled noses and heard the muttered complaints from day one. But nobody ever had the guts to say anything to my face, did they? And now, now that I'm injured in the performance of my duties, you all slide around and deliver the ultimate insult . . . Expecting me to sit a blasted horse, eat dust all day, and then eat somebody else's cooking. There's no way I'm willing to do that!"

"It's the only offer on the table," Bradley said, his words as flat and direct as his stare.

"Then cash me out," Brandenburger said stubbornly. "Pay me for the time I've put in, and I'll be on my way."

Bradley nodded without hesitation. "If that's the way you want it. Collect your personal gear and pick a horse from the remuda. When you're ready to ride out, I'll have your money waiting."

That night, after supper was done and he'd finished his cleanup chores, Mac sat apart from the others. He was leaned back against a wheel of the chuckwagon, sipping from a cup of coffee, so deeply lost in thought that he wasn't aware of Colleen's approach until she spoke.

"Any particular reason you're being so antisocial tonight?"

Mac looked up with a start. "Oh. Hi, Miss Colleen." He started to rise to his feet.

Colleen halted him with, "Hold it right there. We had an agreement, remember? You're supposed to stop popping up like a jack-in-the-box every time I come around."

Mac settled back. "I recall *you* saying that's how it should be. But you'll have to forgive me having a lot of years drubbed into my head saying otherwise."

Colleen smiled. "Okay. We'll have to just keep working on it, then."

"Fair enough."

"Now that that's settled, would you mind some company?"

"Of course not." Mac reached a couple feet to his right and overturned a wooden bucket. Patting the now upturned bottom, he said, "That is, if I'm at least allowed to pull out a chair for you."

Colleen giggled and sat down on the bucket. "There. We've reached a compromise."

"Reckon it wasn't so bad," Mac allowed.

"Now," said Colleen, "I'm going to push my luck and be forward enough to repeat my original question—why are you over here all by yourself? Sparky's playing isn't so bad it's keeping you at bay, is it?"

She was referring to Sparky Whitlock seated over by the central campfire, blowing some low, lonely notes on his harmonica. Every once in a while, some of the other men sitting around would hum along for a few bars.

Mac grinned. "No, that's not it at all. Sparky blows some right pretty music on that thing. Though I can't say all the voices joining in are necessarily of equal talent."

"Imagine," said Colleen, "what the poor cattle have to endure on nights when some of those same voices are riding nighthawk and feel moved to warble songs meant to keep them soothed."

"I know what you mean," Mac agreed. "I've heard some mighty dreadful nighthawk warbling in my time—and that's not to say I got a great voice myself. I've wondered more than once, given some of that really bad singing, why the cattle don't stampede more often than they do, just to get away from the sound."

Colleen waited a minute but then, being persistent, said, "So if it's not the music keeping you away . . . ?"

"I don't know," Mac told her truthfully. "When I was done cleaning up and putting things away after supper, I just felt like sitting here for a while and pondering on some things alone. Didn't mean for it to be offensive or seem standoffish."

Colleen shook her head. "No, and I didn't mean to imply anyone took it that way. I only noticed because . . . well, I was worried about you."

"Worried? What for?"

"Because, all during supper, you seemed . . . I don't know, distant somehow. Not like your normal self. Like something was weighing on your mind. And then, afterwards, when you stayed over here by yourself . . ." Colleen let her words trail off.

Mac held her eyes for a long moment before saying, "Well, it's nice to be worried about. Thank you for caring. But there's no call for it. Really. Like I said, I just had some things to ponder."

"Were you thinking about Orson Brandenburger?" Colleen said, not quite ready to give up. "You're not feeling guilty about taking his job, are you?"

Mac considered before answering. "I never thought about it in terms of feeling guilty. Brandenburger didn't deserve to be the cook for this outfit, that much is certain. Nor any outfit, as far as that goes. He's just plain no good at it. But you're right, I do feel a little uncomfortable horning in where another man has been put out on his ear."

"Put out due to being totally unreasonable," Colleen was quick to point out. "My father gave Orson every opportunity to stay with the drive. Even offered him limited duty based on his injury—which, not to sound unkind, came about through nobody's fault but his own."

Mac nodded his head faintly. "All that's true enough. I can't help wondering, though, if I wouldn't have been here and hadn't spouted off right from the get-go about having experience as a chuckwagon cook, would Orson still have been turned out as quick as he was?"

"If he hadn't, then that would have required somebody to serve as a full-time nursemaid to him and his bum hand for the sake of driving the chuckwagon and the cooking preparation. That would have meant being even shorter-handed when it came to wrangling the herd, not to mention having to continue eating Orson's lousy cooking." She shook her head vigorously, causing her spill of chestnut hair to shimmer in the pale light. "So you see, Mac, you've got nothing to feel guilty about. Quite the contrary—you are a savior."

Mac lifted his eyebrows. "Certainly never saw myself worthy of that description, ma'am."

Colleen smiled. "Now, in addition to working on that hopping up whenever I come around business, something else we definitely need to focus on is this 'ma'am' thing. I want no more of it. You're Mac, I'm Colleen, and that's that. Understood?"

Mac nodded. "Yes, ma—er, Colleen. If that's the way you want it."

CHAPTER 11

"I can stretch out the supplies we have for a while," Mac was explaining to Norris Bradley in the wake of another evening meal. "But some staples—flour and beans, mainly—will need to be restocked pretty soon, and Shad tells me we'll be heading into some mighty open country before long, a stretch where there won't be much in the way of places to pick up anything."

Bradley nodded. "That's true. We'll be passing near a pretty good-sized town by the name of Torrence sometime tomorrow, then after that we can't count on any resupply stops until we get up near Montana."

"Then I suggest that I make a swing over to Torrence in the morning and get some things we're going to need," said Mac. "Or I could make a list and you can send somebody else if you'd rather do it that way."

"No, you're the logical one," Bradley replied. "You know best what you need and you can load it directly onto the chuckwagon."

"I'm thinking I could leave right after breakfast. Before I head out, I'll make up an extra batch of biscuits. That way, everybody will have fairly fresh biscuits and jerky for a noon meal. Barring anything unexpected, I should be able to get back to night camp in time for supper."

"That'd take some pretty hard pushing on your part. But I know you'll do it if anybody can." Then, after considering a moment, Bradley added, "Tell you what. To make it a little easier and give you your best chance to meet that schedule, how about I send Shad along with you? He knows the land hereabouts pretty good. He can get you to and from Torrence the quickest, plus he'll have a good idea where we'll be bedding down the herd at the end of the day."

"Fine by me. Shad's good company, and if he knows the lay of the land, so much the better." Mac grinned wryly. "These rolling hills all tend to look sort of alike to me. Left on my own, I might miss Torrence and end up in Idaho or somewhere before I got my bearings."

Bradley showed a brief grin of his own. "I doubt that. For one thing, as popular as your cooking is with the crew, I expect they'd hunt you down and drag you back long before you made it that far."

Mac accepted the compliment without comment. But it felt good to hear all the same.

This was the third day since the departure of Orson Brandenburger, and things were going generally well. The drive was averaging about seventeen miles a day, helped along by the grassy, gently rolling terrain. Mac's acceptance by the Rafter B crew—or the acceptance of his *cooking* might be a more accurate way to put it—was well established by now and his own discomfort at having taken over the chuckwagon full-time had been put to rest.

He got along particularly well with Shad Hopper and the two younger Bradley brothers, often being part of the banter and good-natured ribbing they tossed back and forth among themselves. Roman, on the other hand, still tended to treat him a bit coolly, but there was nothing really unfriendly in his manner. What was more, the open friendliness and hints of flirtation aimed his way by Colleen more than made up for any amount of chill emanating from her brother.

"I'm jealous, you getting to go into town in the morning," she said to him later that evening, after word of those plans had spread through the camp. "You know how long it's been since I set foot in a town, even a dusty old one-horse kind? And how much longer it'll be before I ever do?"

"We should be in Miles City in less than a month," Mac reminded her. "That's a pretty good-sized place, isn't it?"

"So what?" Colleen pouted. "In another month I'll be so sunburned and dried out and dust-coated from plodding along on this stupid drive that I'll look like an old maid. Even if I put on a dress and tied a ribbon in my hair, who'd ever take a second look at me?"

"Come on, you couldn't look that bad if you tried," Mac told her. "And if those fellas in Miles City are too lunk-headed not to look twice—or three or four times, to do it justice—at a pretty gal like you, then they'd have to be a mighty sorry bunch."

"You really mean that—or are you just saying it to tease me?"

Mac knew she was being coy, wanting him to tell her again how pretty he thought she was. But he didn't mind playing along, at least up to a point. "No, I'm not teasing, Colleen. You know darn well how attractive you are. And anybody short of a blind man would tell you the same."

"Well, you certainly haven't been in any hurry to say so before this."

"I didn't figure you needed me to tell you." Mac was suddenly feeling a little uneasy about the way this was going. "Besides, under the circumstances . . ."

"What circumstances?" Colleen prodded.

"Aw, come on. Now who's teasing who? You're the boss's daughter, and I'm a biscuit-slinger with no past to speak of and even less of a future," Mac said. "What would be the point of me telling you how pretty you are and hoping it would amount to anything? I've been down that road before and all it got me was—"

Mac stopped short, realizing he'd come dangerously close to saying too much, revealing too much.

Colleen's expression changed, became anxious and very earnest. "What did going down that road get you, Mac? Someone hurt you badly, didn't they?"

"Never mind," Mac insisted. "It's ancient history."

Before either of them could say more, Norris Bradley walked up. He stopped short, frowning. "You two look like you're involved in a mighty serious discussion. Maybe I'd better come back later."

Colleen shook her head. "That's not necessary, Father. I was just lamenting to Mac about missing out on the chance to go to town tomorrow, but I'll survive."

Bradley's expression softened, and for the first time Mac saw some of the ranch boss shell give way to the father underneath. "Shoot, honey. I'm sorry for not thinking about that. I can only imagine how tough these long, hard weeks on the trail have been for you."

Colleen made a dismissive gesture with her hand. "It's all right. I was just feeling a little sorry for myself, but like I said, I'll survive." She flashed a wry smile. "If I was worth a hoot at cooking, maybe I could make a convincing plea for why I should go. But let's face it, since we all know how pathetic I am in that department, it's perfectly reasonable not to include me."

Bradley wagged his head sadly. "If our crew wasn't stretched so doggone thin as it is, I'd be happy to let you go. But with Mac and Roman already going . . ."

"Roman?" Mac repeated. "Where does he all of a sudden fit in?"

"It just came up," Bradley explained. "That's what I came over here to tell you. Roman has a tooth that's killing him. It first gave him trouble a couple months ago, back in Texas. You remember that, Colleen. So he went to town back then to have a doctor yank it or whatever had to be done. He came back and said it was all taken care of. But the truth, come to find out, was that the tooth quit bothering him by the time he got to town so, in spite of what he claimed, he ducked out on actually seeing the doctor. I found out about this just a little while ago from his brothers, by the way, and I also learned that for the past couple days, the blasted tooth has had him in agony again."

"Given the lousy disposition he displays most of the time anyway," Colleen said tartly, "no one would ever know."

Bradley sighed. "Be that as it may, he's in genuine misery. A rotten tooth can cripple a man about as bad as any wound. I know, I've seen it. So I'm hoping this town of Torrence has a doctor or a barber who can take care of it. Otherwise, if it flares up worse out in the open country we're headed for, the rest of the crew might have to hold him down while Shad goes after the bad tooth with a knife and pliers."

Colleen's mouth curved in a devilish smile. "Now I wish more than ever I could make that trip to town. How I'd love the chance to see big brother squirming in a doc's chair."

CHAPTER 12

The town of Torrence was a quiet-looking, tidily arranged cluster of buildings nestled in a shallow valley that it shared with a small, tree-fringed lake. As Mac and Roman started down into the valley from the east, Roman on horseback and Mac handling the reins of the chuckwagon team, they could see the distant, smooth surface of the water reflecting the cloudless morning sky like a mirror.

These initial impressions of tranquility, however, turned out to be very short-lived.

As soon as they reached the outlying buildings on the edge of town, they began hearing the clamor of angry, excited voices and the tramp of many feet. The source of this noise came from deeper within the town, somewhere down a side street that ran off to the left just ahead. A tall, weathered livery barn on the corner obscured exactly what the commotion was about and who was involved. But whatever it was, it was increasing in volume and drawing nearer.

Exchanging wary glances with Roman, Mac steered the wagon out of the middle of the street and closer to the livery. He'd barely accomplished this before the noisy mob broke into view. Around the corner they came, about thirty in number—men mostly, but a handful of scowling, red-faced women also in the mix and a few stragglers hurrying to catch up with the bulk of the mob. All were on foot except for four mounted men at the front.

All the riders wore grim, determined expressions. All, that is, except for the man crowded into the middle of the other three. His expression was grim enough, but it also looked very desperate. He was hatless, about halfway between forty and fifty, with streaks of gray in a neatly trimmed beard and at his temples. He wore a fancy shirt with ruffles in front and a black silk vest. His hands were tied behind his back, and a hangman's noose dangled around his neck. The other end of the rope was coiled and tightly gripped by the meaty fist of a heavyset, red-suspendered man riding on the left of the gent in the fancy shirt.

The throng went stomping past Mac and Roman with hardly a glance in their direction. The steady growl of words being issued from between clenched teeth and out of mouths twisted into menacing grimaces could be heard to contain phrases like "Murderin' snake!" and "Fancy Dan slickster thinkin' he could get away with it!"

Once the mob had gone on by and was continuing out of town in the direction the Rafter B men had just come from, Roman let out a low whistle and said, "Whew! That rascal has somehow managed to get a whole town on the prod."

"What do you reckon he did?" Mac asked.

"I don't know. But whatever it was, I'd say it's a real

safe bet he won't be doing no more of it. Remember that big old gnarled oak tree we saw just off the trail about a quarter mile back? It gave me a funny feeling when we passed by, and now I know why. That there's a hanging tree if I ever saw one."

Mac nodded. "I think you're exactly right. A nice, peaceful-looking little town like this, you'd think they'd be past the days of lynch mobs. You'd think they'd have themselves a sheriff or marshal or some such, and court trials and the like to settle up with lawbreakers."

"No judge or sworn-in jury was part of the bunch that just went by, I'll guarantee you that much," Roman said. "And there weren't any badges in sight, either."

"That's for sure," agreed Mac. "That big fella in the red suspenders wasn't wearing an executioner's hood—but the look in his eyes made it plenty clear that's what he's bent on becoming."

More voices came from around the corner of the livery barn. First the honking tones of a young man in his late teens, his voice having not yet fully matured and this condition made worse by what was obviously a tense situation.

"Stop it! Quit trying to jerk away like that. Please! Don't make me have to hurt you!"

In response came a female voice, equally anxious and a bit strident, yet somehow still containing a velvety quality. "Why not go ahead and hurt me? Why not go ahead and kill me the way those other ruffians are going to kill my father? What difference will the blood of one more person on your filthy hands make?"

"Please, ma'am, please! I'm just trying to do the job I was given. I don't want no blood on my hands."

Mac and Roman had heard enough. Roman went tearing around the corner at a gallop as Mac got the chuckwagon team moving again.

Halfway up the block, in the middle of the street, the two people they'd overheard were locked in a struggle. The male was young, tall, and lanky in build, with a scrawny neck, an oversized Adam's apple, and a shock of straw-colored hair he was having trouble keeping out of his eyes.

What he was having even more trouble with was the woman he was trying to keep from jerking away from the grip he had on her wrists. His captive was maybe a half dozen years older, very shapely in a skirt that flared out only after tightly hugging her hips and an off-the-shoulder blouse the struggle had tugged down to quite a daring level. Her face, even contorted by anger, was finely featured and framed by a loosely spilling mass of pale gold hair.

A dozen or so onlookers lined the street, milling on the boardwalks and watching with anxious expressions but not protesting. The young man didn't seem concerned about them, but Mac and Roman were a different story.

"Whoever you fellas are, this ain't none of your concern," he told them. "Best keep goin' on about whatever business brung you here."

"No! Please!" the woman said. "He's part of a bunch of thugs. You must have seen them on the way in. They're going to lynch my father!"

The young man gave her a shake. "Shut up, you! He's only getting what he deserves."

"You don't ease up on that gal," Roman drawled, "I'll be givin' you what *you* deserve. Better yet, take your hands off her altogether."

The young man swallowed hard, his Adam's apple bulging as it rose and fell. "You don't want to mess in this, mister. You really don't. Not if you know what's good for you. There's fellas asked me to hang on to this spitfire, and if you get in the way of me doing what they want—"

"Ain't no *if* about it, you young fool. You already been got in the way of." Almost casually, Roman drew his gun. "Now, you're the one who'd better figure out what's good for you and real quick do like you been told."

The woman suddenly pulled free and took a half-staggering step away. The young man didn't reach for her. He simply hung his head and let his hands drop loosely at his sides, defeated.

Mac swung his gaze across some of the onlookers standing on the boardwalk. "What in blazes is going on around here?" he demanded of them. "Don't you have a marshal or some kind of proper law in this town? Is this how you let a woman get treated right out in public?"

Nobody answered and when he tried to make direct eye contact with some of them, they looked away.

"They locked the marshal in his own jail cell," the blonde said. "He tried to stop them but they over-powered him. Even his own deputy turned on him. They were like . . . like a pack of rabid dogs. They wouldn't listen to reason from anybody!"

"What the devil did your pa do to rile them so bad?" Mac wanted to know.

The woman's eyes darted down the street to where a gaudily painted wagon was parked. Bringing her gaze back, she said, "We run a medicine show, my father and I. He makes and sells a health elixir. But something went wrong with the batch he brought here to Torrence. Bad ingredients or . . . or I don't know. But instead of helping people, it started making them sick. Terribly sick. It nearly killed some. But it was a mistake. A tragic one, true, but my father never set out to hurt anyone. We've sold gallons and gallons of his concoction in towns all over Colorado and Wyoming without ever having a problem remotely close to this!"

A sudden buzz of voices from the folks on the boardwalks caused Mac and the others to look around. Down the street, past the gaudily painted medicine wagon, a horse-drawn buggy was approaching at a good clip, its thin wheels whipping up a cloud of dust. As it drew nearer, the words "Doc Middleton" became discernible out of the muttering.

When the buggy reached them, its driver—a rather portly, weary-looking gent wearing a bowler hat and a frock coat straining to contain his girth—reined up. A pair of round spectacles perched near the end of a bulbous nose and sharp, inquisitive eyes peered over the top of them, darting first to the folks lining the street and then coming to rest on the blonde and those gathered around her.

"What's going on here? What's happened?" he demanded.

"A lynch mob has broken my father out of jail," the

blonde said. "They locked up the marshal and they're dragging my father to someplace out of town to carry out their murderous intentions."

The young man with the bulging Adam's apple lifted his face and said dully, "It's Hiram Chamberlain leading 'em, Doc. He whipped up the Hayes brothers and a bunch of others after they spent most of the night drinking. They're set on stringing up that professor fella out at the old Vigilante Oak east of town. You know, the place where they used to—"

"Yes, I know the place," spat the doctor. "The blasted fools! Hiram's mother pulled through. I just came from their farm. In the middle of the night I thought sure we were going to lose her, but she rallied. She's going to be fine. Hiram, in his grief, took off when she was at her worst, when it looked like there was no way she was going to make it."

"You've got to stop him! You've got to save my father," the blonde wailed. "He doesn't deserve to die!"

"I agree," Middleton said. "But how much time do we have? When did they leave town?"

"Just a few minutes ago," Mac said. "But most of 'em are on foot. We can catch up if we hurry."

Middleton's eyes swept over Mac and Roman. "Who are you fellows? What's your part in this?"

"Let's just say we're passersby who know a raw deal when we see it and don't much like it," answered Roman. "Since you got townsfolk who appear shamefully short of gumption, we're willin' to pitch in and help crash the necktie party bein' planned for this gal's pa."

The doctor frowned. "No doubt we could use some extra persuasive power. But we really need to try and get the marshal involved again, too."

"If we wait around too long," said Roman, "ain't nobody gonna be in time to do any good. Somebody point me to the jail, I'll go free the marshal and fetch him along. The rest of you get a move on and find a way to throw some cold water on the proceedings until I can get him there!"

CHAPTER 13

When Mac and Doc Middleton arrived out at the hanging tree, the mob already gathered there was worked up into even more of a frenzy than when they'd stormed out of town. They had fueled one another into a kind of blood lust that by now could only be appeased by the taking of a life. And by the appearance of things, getting that accomplished wasn't very far off.

Their intended victim sat his horse under a fat horizontal arm of the towering oak. The rope extending from the noose around his neck had been flung up over the branch—the latter exhibiting numerous scrapes and scars from past ropes having been there—and its coiled remains were once again clutched in the fist of the big man in the red suspenders. He sat his horse a couple yards back from the man in the noose. Crowded up closer on either side of the captive were two bleary-eyed hombres in dirty, hard-worn trail garb. They had skeleton-lean faces that shared a resemblance so strong it marked them as certainly being brothers. The one who appeared to be the older of the two had a shiny black pistol drawn and was holding it aimed at the man hemmed in between them.

Slowing his rig only slightly, the portly doctor plowed straight into the mass of people forming a semicircle around the horsemen, eagerly craning their necks to get a good look at what was about to take place. Those in his path scattered frantically, cursing and stumbling, knocking others out of the way. Two or three ended up getting knocked to the ground. Mac came behind, following close in the wake of the juggernaut.

Middleton reined up only after he had swung his buggy directly in front of the horse carrying the man about to be hanged.

"Hold up there, Doc! What do you think you're doing?" bellowed the man in the red suspenders.

"That's my question to you, Hiram, you infernal idiot—what do you think *you* are doing?"

"We're dishin' out just deserts to a murderin' piece of trash," sneered the man holding the pistol on the elixir peddler.

"My father's not a piece of trash, and he's not a murderer!" said the young woman, who had climbed into the buggy with Middleton back in town. She attempted to clamber down now, but the doctor restrained her with a backward sweep of his arm.

"You ought not be messin' in this, Doc," snarled the red-suspendered man now identified as Hiram Chamberlain. "You need to stick to tryin' to heal the sick and hopefully savin' the rest of those this lowdown skunk poisoned. I'll forgive you for not bein' able to save my ma, but that forgiveness don't stretch to lettin' you think you're gonna stick your nose in—"

"I *did* save your ma, Hiram!" Middleton cut him off.

"She's alive and coming around just fine. You need to go and be with her, not stay here and be part of this."

Hiram looked bewildered. "But last night, you said . . ."

Middleton wagged his head. "I know what I said. And I regret it deeply. I should have never given up hope that way, and even worse, I never should have let you think there was no hope. But what matters now is that I was wrong and she's pulled through."

"How do you know he's tellin' the truth?" prodded the younger of the skeleton-faced brothers. "Maybe he's lyin' just to try and bust up what we're fixin' to do here."

"Could be Billy Bob is right, Hiram," said the brother with the gun. "But even if the doc is tellin' it straight and your ma did pull through, this poisoner still put her through hell. Just like he did a whole bunch of others. And some of them are still hangin' on by a thread and might not be lucky enough to come out of it. We ain't gonna let this lowlife scum get away with that, are we?"

This got a loud rumble of assent out of the rest of the mob.

Doc Middleton passed his gaze over the surrounding faces, his expression suddenly more crestfallen than angry.

"What's wrong with you people? Who *are* you?" he said in a mournful tone. "I thought I knew most of you. I've cared for the ills and injuries in our town for going on two decades. But this . . . this disease I see here before me now . . . it's something I thought I'd never have to deal with again. Not since the old days when this tree—this ugly growth that we should have long ago burned to the ground out of shame—got put to use far too often. I thought our community had grown past that and had welcomed civility and proper law and order in the form of a town marshal and court hearings and justice meted out only after due deliberation and—"

"We did all the deliberatin' we needed," the gunman snarled. "All that other monkeyin' around takes too long. Marshal Sweet couldn't even make up his mind what to charge this phony varmint with. But he admitted nothing he could think of amounted to hangin' charges and so he locked up the weasel more for his own protection than anything else. Ain't that right, Monte?"

All eyes swung to a stocky young man standing near the front of the crowd. His jaw was set stubbornly as he answered, "Durned right it is, Johnny Joe. Marshal Sweet said he planned on waiting for the circuit judge to come around and advise him on charges. If Mrs. Chamberlain or one of the others died, he said, then that would probably be a case of involuntary manslaughter. But otherwise, he wasn't sure."

Middleton frowned at the speaker. "Where's your badge, Deputy Ralston? Are you so ashamed of being here that you took it off? That should tell you right there how wrong all of this is."

"It's the badge that he was ashamed of," declared Johnny Joe, the gunman. "The badge that was only good for allowin' weasels and lowlifes to get protected while the wheels of the so-called law crawled along so slow it'd make any real man puke. Well, Monte finally saw the light when it came to this slicker we got here on the end of a rope, and he realized puttin' him there was the right thing. So he helped us stick Marshal Sweet in a cell while we dragged Fancy Shirt out and brung him here for what he deserves!"

Another rumble of agreement came from the crowd.

Mac looked around, his anxiety increasing as he could feel the tension growing tighter. He wished Roman would show up with this Marshal Sweet everybody was talking about, but so far there was no sign of them.

Doc Middleton fixed his gaze on Hiram Chamberlain and said in a pleading tone, "You may be the only one who can stop this before it gets totally out of hand. There's no need any more. I swear to you, your mother is alive and doing well."

Hiram looked tormented. "I believe you, Doc. I *want* to believe you. Only . . . what about the others who are terrible sick? It's a blessin' about my ma, but what if some of them don't make it?"

"I figured out an antidote to the poison," Middleton told him. "It's what I gave to your mother, and I'm ready to administer it to the others who are still sick. It should start taking effect by this afternoon. I'm confident they'll all be fine."

Hiram looked like he might be wavering. The two brothers, Johnny Joe and Billy Bob, didn't like that look.

"Don't let him get to you," said Johnny Joe. "It's real good about your ma and all—*if* he's tellin' the truth. We still don't know that for sure. But important as your ma was and is, this never was just about her. There's lots of other folks who suffered on account of this varmint. He poisoned our whole town! And even the doc admits some of those others ain't all the way out of danger yet."

"And for all that, even if somebody *does* die," added Billy Bob, "all the marshal—the law—is gonna do is call it involuntary manslaughter. Involuntary! You heard Monte say so. Does that sound like serious enough punishment for the snake behind it all? No! The only proper punishment is what we got right in front of us, and everybody here knows it!"

Once more the crowd roared.

Billy Bob's eyes suddenly bored into Hiram. "You need to make up your mind. If you don't have it in you to tie off that rope and haul back on it while we swat away this horse, then hand it over to somebody who does. It's time to get this done."

"One way or the other, by the rope or by this gun in my hand, if I have to use it," spoke up Johnny Joe, "this varmint is gonna get his sun set."

Suddenly, Mac's voice rang out. "Where I come from," he said for all to hear, "a fella who draws a gun and then only *talks* about using it don't amount to much of a threat." The words were accompanied by his own .45 appearing in his fist, leveled on Johnny Joe. "Me, on the other hand, once my gun is drawn I'm done talking. Now, you gonna keep yammering or you aim to try and do something with that smoke wagon of yours?"

Moving only his eyes, Johnny Joe slowly shifted his gaze to Mac. "Who in tarnation are you?"

Mac met his gaze, said nothing.

Several seconds ticked by.

Doc grinned. "He told you he's done talking . . . unless it's with that .45."

Billy Bob's mouth sagged open. Then he clapped it

shut and said, "Are you crazy? You see all the people around you? You figure you can get away with going up against all of us, chuckwagon man?"

"Maybe, maybe not," Mac said. "Guess it depends on whether or not this bunch is as gutless as the folks in town. But if they're not and any one of 'em tries more than shooting off his mouth, neither you nor your brother will be around to appreciate it. So why not call this off before it comes to that?"

Hiram Chamberlain suddenly yanked taut the rope he was holding and made three quick turns with it around his saddle horn. "You pull the trigger on Johnny Joe," he declared, "the shot will cause that horse to bolt and Fancy Shirt will end up swinging in the breeze just like he was meant to. So what will this stunt have gained you then?"

Mac seemed to consider for a moment. Then, calmly, he said, "Nothing . . . unless maybe if that rope don't hold."

He tipped the Colt up and triggered three shots in rapid succession. Pieces of bark and wood chips erupted from the tree branch over which the rope was draped as the bullets chewed into it, and then suddenly the rope was no longer there, its strands blown apart.

As predicted, the horse carrying the intended hanging victim bolted at the sound of the shots. With his hands tied behind his back, the sudden movement immediately unbalanced the man in the saddle and sent him toppling to the ground as the horse sprang away.

While the fall was undoubtedly jarring, it saved the man from more serious harm, possibly death. Johnny Joe was startled into momentary inaction by what Mac had done. By the time he did react, out of reflex more than anything, the horse had made its initial lunge and the man in the fancy shirt was already starting to fall off its back. For this reason, the shot that exploded from Johnny Joe's gun sent a bullet screaming toward where the man had been and ended up missing his toppling form by several inches.

Before Johnny Joe could adjust his aim, Mac's pistol roared again, and his bullet didn't miss. It slammed into Johnny Joe's left shoulder, twisting him halfway around in his saddle and jerking a sharp yelp of pain from his lips. For a moment, it looked as if Johnny Joe might also drop to the ground. Instead it was his gun that dropped as he let go of it and clamped his right hand over the blood-spurting shoulder wound.

As this was playing out, Mac immediately lowered his .44 and centered it on Billy Bob, who, after his own startled moment of inaction, was beginning to dig frantically for the gun holstered on one hip.

Through clenched teeth, Mac barked, "Leave it where it is or die with it in your hand!"

A fraction of a second later, both of Billy Bob's hands were high in the air, and the gun at his hip remained in its holster.

If not for some quick maneuvering from Doc Middleton, all of that still would have left a potential threat from Hiram Chamberlain. But the instant the intended hanging victim's horse bolted, Middleton whipped his buggy horse into a forward surge that caused it to collide with Hiram's mount. The latter reared up on its hind legs, issuing a whinny of surprise and anger. Hiram had all he could do to stay on the hurricane deck and get the agitated animal settled down. By the time he'd accomplished this, Mac—satisfied Johnny Joe no longer posed any danger—had swung his pistol around and leveled it steadily at him.

The rapid sequence of events left the lynch-happy crowd looking on in stunned silence. Mac briefly cut his eyes away from Billy Bob and raked his gaze over the faces in this pack, trying to read what might be going on behind their wide eyes and gape-mouthed expressions. Were they ready to accept that the moment had passed, that the lynching had been successfully broken up—or were they so bloodthirsty they were ready to swarm forward and still try to see it through?

But then, piercing the tense silence, came the swift rataplan of horses' hooves approaching from the direction of town. The boom of a shotgun shattered the air, followed by a gruff voice hollering, "Break it up! Break it up, you fools!"

Mac swung his gaze in the direction of these new sounds and saw two riders spurring their mounts hard. One was the familiar form of Roman, the other a heavyset man with a marshal's star glinting on his shirt and a smoking, skyward-pointed shotgun brandished in one hand.

Mac exhaled a breath he hadn't been aware he was holding.

CHAPTER 14

"I can't tell you strongly enough how grateful both my daughter Belinda and I are for the intervention of your brave men, Mr. Bradley. Had they not acted as they did, I'm confident I would not be alive to stand here before you now. Furthermore, though I believe the marshal of Torrence to be a decent and fair-minded man in spite of the outrageous amount he fined me for damages done, I am equally confident that his actions did not satisfy the ruffian element of his town. Had Belinda and I remained there, even after paying that fine, I highly doubt we would have been safe. And leaving without the escort I implored your men to grant us surely would have invited some members of that same element to follow and make trouble for us on the trail—perhaps even to the point of trying to finish their lynching of me!"

Norris Bradley frowned at the man who'd unleashed this torrent of words—a fancy-dressed individual who'd been introduced to him as Herbert Forrest. According to the bold, colorful lettering that decorated the wagon he and his daughter had rolled up in, he was actually "Professor" Herbert Forrest, a "renowned pharmaceutical chemist specializing in healthy, revitalizing elixirs for the human condition."

If Bradley had encountered a character making such claims under almost any other circumstance than Mac and Roman returning from town with him and his daughter in tow, the skeptical old rancher probably would have sent the professor packing without listening to a word he had to say. Even now Bradley wasn't feeling particularly tolerant of the ear-bending he was getting, but he'd seen the ugliness of a lynching as a young man, and the experience had left him with bitter disgust for the kind of cruelty that could be displayed by even so-called decent folks when whipped into an angry mob.

"And so," Forrest went on, "I now implore you, my good sir, to grant us a continuation of that same consideration. Without it, I fear we will be thrust right back into serious jeopardy. And though I myself may be somewhat deserving of rancor for my mistakes, surely my daughter is not."

By the time the professor paused to take a breath, Bradley's frown had pulled the corners of his mouth down even farther. "Whoa now," he said rather hurriedly, before Forrest started in again. "I follow you all the way through the business about my men lending a hand to break up that necktie party, and I'll even go as far as to say I'm right proud of 'em for that. But what you just said about imploring me to grant you the same consideration . . . You don't mean you expect me to let you continue with us on our cattle drive, do you?"

Forrest's expression became one of hopeful innocence. "As a matter of fact, yes, sir, that's precisely what I'm asking. Begging, if I must."

Bradley slashed the air in front of him with one hand. "No. Out of the question. It's the craziest thing I ever heard of." He turned his head and glared at Mac, who was standing nearby, watching and listening. "Did you and Roman lead this man to believe there was a chance I might agree to such a preposterous notion?"

The creases in Roman's forehead puckered a little deeper. "I don't recall nobody *leadin'* the professor anywhere except to our camp here," he said. "As far as that part, yeah, I guess me and Mac sorta thought it might be a good idea to look after the professor and his daughter for a while longer on account of those town rannies still havin' some bad intentions stuck in their craw."

Mac added, "It was plain that the marshal wanted the medicine wagon to clear out pronto so he could wash his hands of the whole works. He knew some folks weren't ready for it to be over so easy, but as long as any more trouble happened outside of his juris- diction, he didn't have to concern himself with it. So as soon as we picked up those supplies—which the storekeeper wouldn't have sold us if the marshal hadn't made him, so as to get rid of us quicker—we lit a shuck out of there."

"Didn't even get my tooth fixed," Roman grum- bled. "And there was a doc right there to do it, too."

Bradley blew out an exasperated-sounding breath. "That still doesn't address the issue of these people wanting to continue with us on our drive."

"The answer for that—the genesis for such a 'pre- posterous notion,' as you put it—rests solely with me," said Forrest. "The idea came to me when I heard your destination was Miles City up in Montana."

"What does that have to do with it?" Bradley wanted to know.

"Two things," Forrest replied. "First, it is far enough away for my daughter and I to get clear of this ugly Torrence business and have the chance for a fresh start. Second, traveling there in the company of you and your outfit would provide us some companionship and added safety for making such a long trip over open, rugged country with which we have no familiarity."

Bradley grunted. "At least you're smart enough to recognize that making a trip from here to Miles City ain't no easy thing. Besides whatever the land and the elements throw at us, there's always the risk of rustlers waiting to try and take our herd as word spreads on ahead that we're coming in. And a pack of renegade Injuns with their feathers ruffled about something ain't out of the question, either."

"I can well appreciate the hardships of the trail, Mr. Bradley," Forrest responded. "My daughter and I have lived a nomadic existence out of our wagon for more than three years now. All up and down the front range of the Colorado Rockies and across the base of Wyoming. That, I feel, has adequately conditioned us for the physical hardships that the journey to Miles City will present. As to the potential dangers you listed . . . well, even you admit they are only *potential* dangers. Ones you must feel confident you can deal with or you would hardly be venturing out to begin with. In your company, then, I feel my daughter and I could share in that same confidence for our own safety."

Bradley was shaking his head before the last words were out of the professor's mouth. "That's the whole thing right there. I don't *want* the responsibility for the safety of anybody else. I've already got my hands full getting my daughter and my crew and our cattle to Miles City all in one piece. That's more than enough."

As if on cue, Colleen came walking toward where the men were having their discussion. Accompanying her was Belinda Forrest. The coolness of the evening had prompted the blonde to wrap herself in a shawl.

Watching her approach, Mac couldn't help thinking to himself that this was a good thing. If she still had on that off-the-shoulder blouse underneath, the one she'd been wearing back in town, the resulting display of creamy flesh and overly generous bit of cleavage would have surely brought out the rooster in the Rafter B men.

"Father," said Colleen, without preamble, as the two women reached them, "have you heard the details of the outrageous treatment Belinda and her father received in that awful town?"

"I believe I've heard most of them, yes. That's what we're discussing here," her father told her.

Belinda spoke up, saying, "If not for the bravery of your men, Mr. Bradley, such a discussion would be impossible. Because my father would have met his end at the hands of those horrid men back there. Mr. Mackenzie and your son"—she tipped her head toward Roman, causing a spill of pale hair to drop down over one eye—"were nothing short of wonderful. Not only did they save my father from the noose, but then they insisted on escorting us safely out of town after that weak excuse for a marshal took all our money and hurried us on our way."

Colleen said, "Belinda is convinced—and, from everything she's told me, I believe she's right—that certain members of that lynch mob are still bloodthirsty enough and unsatisfied enough to very likely come after her father in order to try and finish what they started."

Bradley nodded. "Yes, we've been talking about that, too."

"Obviously, we can't let that happen," Colleen stated firmly. "We must continue to help keep them safe."

Bradley's eyebrows lifted. "Well now. That's a real admirable notion, daughter. But considering the little matter of about eight hundred longhorns our outfit is in the middle of driving north with still a long stretch to go, don't you think we've got about all we can handle looking out for our own interests? When and how, exactly, do you figure we can fit in seeing to the safety of these folks?"

"We take them with us," Colleen answered. "The cowards from Torrence who'd be quick to track them and jump them if they were traveling on their own would know better, after Roman and Mac already gave them a taste of what they'd run into, than to try anything if they were traveling with us. Belinda and her father talked it over on the ride out here to our camp. They agreed that Montana would be a good place for them. In Miles City, they'd have the chance for a fresh start with a clean slate."

"Before you go any farther," said Bradley, "you should know that the professor here already brought up the notion of him and his daughter coming along on our drive—and I said no."

Colleen's expression turned anguished. "Father! I can't believe that. I've never known you to turn your back on someone in a time of need—especially not someone in danger."

"Now doggone it, that ain't fair," Bradley protested. "I don't make a habit of turning my back on folks in need, and you blasted well know it. But it starts with those dearest and nearest to me. You're well aware that when we left Texas we left behind a certain situation of our own. That makes this drive to Miles City almighty important to the future of each and every person in our outfit. Important enough to come first, before we can afford to worry too much about others, no matter how much we may want to. Surely you understand that . . . don't you?"

"Yes. Of course, I do. But in this case, I don't see one as being exclusive of the other," Colleen insisted. "The professor's wagon can easily keep up with our herd. He and Belinda even have their own provisions. So they won't slow us down and they won't deplete our supplies. The only possible problem I can see resulting from having them travel with us is if those varmints from Torrence show up and try to start something. But once they realize that the Forrests remain under the protection of the men in our crew . . . well, I think it's safe to say their eagerness to make any more trouble will shrivel up quickly."

CHAPTER 15

Plaster of Paris casts had been around for years and were frequently used by doctors in larger cities, mainly to help in the mending of fractures and the like. They weren't all that common on the frontier, however, making the one Orson Brandenburger was sporting on his injured hand something of a novelty and Orson himself, by extension, a bit of a celebrity in some of the saloons and cafés where he stopped as he made his way south.

Flush with money from drawing his pay when he left the drive and having no particular destination in mind nor any big hurry to decide on one, the disgruntled cook was taking his time meandering through the small towns and settlements sprinkled along the foothills of the Colorado Rockies. Discovering that his cast generated a surprising amount of interest and friendliness toward him, his disposition had improved considerably in the four days since he'd bitterly parted ways with Norris Bradley's outfit.

It had gotten so that when he entered a new establishment like this one here tonight—the dingy, smoky Buffalo Wallow Saloon in a settlement called Bison

Horn—Orson made it a point to brandish his hand with a bit of a flourish in order to make sure folks noticed the cast adorning it. By the time he got to the bar and thumped the hand onto its top, as if to rest it there as he bellied up, he could feel the eyes following him and knew it would be just a matter of time before folks would be coming around, wanting to strike up a conversation about it and often as not offering to buy a drink.

In the past couple of days, Orson had concocted some colorful yarns about the dreadful thing had happened to require such special treatment. He'd recognized early on that nothing killed the interest in him quicker than explaining how he'd merely cut himself slicing bacon. So, to match the initial curiosity and keep the interest fueled, he'd come up with a range of imaginative encounters that amounted to nothing more than tall tales. Everything from being attacked by a mountain lion and having to reach straight into the beast's mouth and rip out its tongue and gizzard in order to kill it . . . to being forced into a knife fight with a descendant of the fabled Jim Bowie and suffering severe lacerations to his hand when he blocked his opponent's blade to keep it from cutting his throat . . . to rushing into a burning orphanage and receiving terrible burns when he used the hand to rip away flaming blankets from a tiny toddler trapped in the bowels of the inferno.

Orson had several new embellishments rolling around inside his head that he hoped he could use once he got some final details worked out. If not for the cast on his hand, undoubtedly a few folks would have balked at his outrageous claims. But something about the cast, some mystique, made anything related to the rather grotesque apparatus seem too serious to question.

Tonight, here in the Buffalo Wallow, Orson had used the burning orphanage tale, and it had gone down like candy. He hadn't had to buy a drink for himself in nearly three hours. What was more, there happened to be a little half-breed Arapaho gal on hand—available as part of the saloon's "entertainment"—who seemed particularly fascinated by Orson's cast. She had planted herself on his lap as he was washing down a plate of enchiladas with the latest mug of beer someone had put in front of him and had let it be known in no uncertain terms that she was intent on taking Orson—and his cast—to her room in the back and showing him a very special time.

It had been a long time since any gal, even the for-hire kind, had gone out of her way to show any interest in Orson, and he was ready to enjoy the experience. He could hardly get his enchiladas gobbled down fast enough.

"Take your time, my brave firefighter," the girl cautioned him. "You do not want to get, how you say, an upset tummy in the time that lies ahead for the two of us. There is no hurry. We have all night."

The bite of enchilada Orson was in the process of swallowing suddenly seemed to grow in size and he barely managed to get it down. As she spoke, the girl was caressing the cast on his hand. Caressing it as if . . . Orson felt beads of sweat pop out on his forehead, and it wasn't from the spiciness of the food. Somehow, even though he couldn't actually feel anything through the cast, the girl's lightly gliding hand felt good. Felt wonderful, exciting. His imagination raced.

If she could excite him like that caressing him through thick layers of plaster, what would it be like to . . .

"Hey, you. You in the derby hat."

Orson had been so lost in thinking about the girl, the touch of her hand, and on getting this meal finished so he could go with her to the back that he'd failed to notice the two new patrons who'd entered the saloon and were now standing directly in front of his table. He looked up, somewhat startled, and ran his gaze over them in a quick appraisal.

One of the men was average in size and appearance, unshaven, clad in dusty, well-worn trail garb, a pistol holstered on one hip. A type so common as to hardly rate a second look under normal circumstances.

The other man, the one who apparently had spoken, was a slightly different story. He was taller, dressed in a better cut of duds, though still dusty and showing recent miles on the trail, and wore his gun lower with its holster tied down.

"You talking to me?" Orson asked.

"You're wearing a derby hat and I'm looking right at you. Who do you think I'm talking to?" said the man with the tied-down holster. He had brittle, cruel eyes in an otherwise handsomely chiseled face.

Orson's expression hardened. He might not be the firefighting, mountain lion–slaying hero he was pretending to be, but he was still a hot-tempered German far from being in the habit of taking guff off any man.

"You're interrupting my meal and my conversation with this young lady," he grated, "and you have an unfriendly tone to boot. Whoever you are, that makes you someone I have no interest in talking with. Best be on your way."

"Best? You want to talk about what's best?" the tall

man sneered. "Then let's talk about that horse at the rail out front, the one wearing a Rafter B brand that we've been told you rode in on. Because you'd *best* have a mighty good answer for how you came by that nag, or I'm calling you out as a stinkin', lowdown horse thief!"

CHAPTER 16

"Me and Curly had finished buying the supplies we went into town for," Chance Barlow, the man in the tied-down holster, was explaining, "and decided to stop for a quick shot and a beer before heading back. Walking into the joint was when we spotted the horse tied out front with the Rafter B brand."

After casting yet another baleful look in Barlow's direction, Orson Brandenburger shifted his gaze to the man the gunman was addressing. The latter was a stocky individual running to fat, a once robust type gone to seed yet still projecting a commanding presence. He wore a wide-brimmed, high-crowned Stetson, cream in color, as pristine looking as the day it was first displayed in an Austin haberdashery. Seated on a folding canvas chair before a campfire, the man held a cup of coffee in one hand, and clenched between the fingers of the other was a fat cigar. The plain, blunt features of the man's bloated face showed no expression as he listened to what was being told to him.

Eager to take his turn at doing some of the telling, Orson spoke indignantly. "Based on that and nothing more, these men of yours barged into the establishment where I was enjoying a meal and the company of a young woman and blatantly declared me to be a horse thief! They refused to listen to my perfectly logical explanation and insisted on creating a highly disruptive and humiliating scene!"

Orson's head was still reeling from how fast Barlow's accusation—the mere mention of the words "horse thief"—had turned the saloon crowd that prior to then had been eating out of the palm of his hand into a sneering, suspicious-eyed horde. Continuing, he said, "It was only the mention of your name, Mr. Van Horne, and my recognition of it as that of an honest, highly respected man that made me agree to come here and meet with you."

"Here" was a small grove of cottonwood trees a mile outside the town of Bison Horn. Escorted in by Barlow and the man called Curly less than an hour after the sun had gone down and there was still grayish half-light to see by, Orson found himself at a well-laid-out campsite occupied by five additional men, all well-armed save for Van Horne, and all giving the impression of having been on the trail for some time.

In response to Orson's lament, Barlow snorted derisively. "Whether you'd've agreed or not, bub, you was coming to this meeting," he said. "Don't pretend it could have gone otherwise."

Caleb Van Horne took a puff of the cigar and blew a jet of smoke out one corner of his mouth. "Appears to me that Chance is right. Looks like it would have been smarter for you to agree to this meeting a little quicker."

Orson involuntarily touched the bruised, swollen area on the left side of his face where a heavy and unexpected punch had been delivered. "Smart or not, I wasn't inclined to hop to the demands of a couple strangers throwing around lies about me. If they'd have been more reasonable in their approach or, like I said, mentioned your name sooner—"

A man standing off to one side of Van Horne cut Orson short, saying, "I think it's time for me to say something here. This hombre . . . Burlenberger, is it?"

"Brandenburger," Orson told him.

"Brandenburger, then," said the new speaker. He was a wiry hombre, five-ten, late thirties, with a boyishly handsome face until you got to the eyes: a no-nonsense edginess lurking just behind the mildness, waiting to flare up at the right provocation. There was something about the way he carried himself, too, and the way a Colt .45 rode with quiet menace on his hip. The hint of something more behind his easy-going veneer.

"Bracing Mr. Brandenburger that way, roughing him up," the interrupter went on, "was uncalled for. That ain't the Ranger way."

Barlow grinned smugly. "Well now, there's a real simple explanation for that, Malloy. Me and Curly, we ain't Rangers."

"No, but I am. Since Brandenburger was showing no signs of being a flight risk, you should have taken the time to come and get me," said the man referred to as Malloy. He cut his gaze to Van Horne. "I understand that I'm part of this as arranged through Judge Ballantine and your influence with him, but I still operate under Ranger policy. There are certain things I made clear from the beginning that I won't be a part of."

Orson eyed Malloy with increased interest. "You're a Texas Ranger?"

Malloy nodded. "Am for a fact. Garfield Malloy's the name."

Van Horne blew another stream of smoke and

shifted impatiently in his chair. "Okay, let's get to the real meat of this matter. Brandenburger, if my boys were out of line in roughing you up, then you'll get my apology in due course. But first I want to hear the full story behind that Rafter B brand. And Malloy, if you've got some special Ranger way of getting to the truth of things, then have at it. And try not to take all night. I'm tired and want to get this over with."

"All right," said Malloy. His eyes came to rest on Orson. There was no mildness in them now, nor any particular hostility, either. Just a penetrating intensity. "Let's start with that Rafter B–branded horse. How did you come by it, Brandenburger?"

"It came from the Rafter B remuda. It was give to me by Norris Bradley himself—he's the owner of the Rafter B spread, you see—when me and him parted ways four days ago," Orson answered straightforwardly.

"Four days ago?"

"That's right."

Malloy frowned. "Mr. Brandenburger, I happen to know that the Rafter B ranch is down in Bellow County, Texas. That's a lot farther than a four-day ride from here."

"Well, of course it is. I know that. But I never said we was at the ranch when I was give the horse, did I?" Orson paused, looking a little smug. "That happened north of here, not far across the Wyoming border."

The other men around camp had all drawn in closer, clearly interested in what was being said.

"And what were you and Mr. Bradley doing up in Wyoming?" Malloy wanted to know.

Orson grunted. "He was firing me, and I was telling him to take his cattle drive and shove it! That's what we was doing." He held up his cast-encased hand. "I was cooking for the drive, that's how I got this. Then, when I ended up too crippled to cook, the ungrateful blackguard sent me packing. And good riddance to 'em all, says I. I never could satisfy that bunch of belly-achers anyway."

"So," Van Horne said, "you were part of Bradley's drive right from the start. Is that it?"

Orson's head bobbed. "That's right. He hired me at the last minute, just before they headed out. His regular cook got married all of a sudden and didn't want to trade taking his honeymoon for going on a long, dusty cattle drive. So I was obliging enough to sign on at a second's notice and work my tail off to keep the ingrates fed. And what do I get for my trouble? This"—once again Orson brandished his injured hand—"and a lousy kick out the door!"

Malloy and Van Horne exchanged looks. "Matches what we already know from back in Texas, about Bradley hiring a last-minute cook before he took off."

"Yeah, and something else," said Barlow, somewhat grudgingly. "Now that I've listened to him babble and looked this crusty old goat over a little closer, I recognize him from seeing him around Hart City. Wasn't very long ago he was bartending a while for Jules O'Roarke at the High Top. He got canned from there, too, way I recall. And it didn't have nothing to do with no hurt paw."

"So he's telling the truth, at least about not working for Bradley until only recently," muttered Van Horne.

"Seems like," agreed Malloy.

Van Horne turned his attention to Orson. He

said, "You say you were quick to recognize my name, Brandenburger. What is it you think you know of me?"

Orson blinked. "Why, pretty much what everybody knows, I guess. That you're one of the biggest cattleman down in the Panhandle. Certainly in Bellow County and the area close around. I mean, you can ride any direction out of Hart City and practically everything you see with four legs has got your Horned-V brand stamped on it, right?"

A mildly satisfied expression touched Van Horne's face. "Almost," he said. "Before I'm done, I aim for every four-legged critter—leastways the kind money can be made off of—to carry that brand. And as of a few weeks ago, that legally includes everything that *used* to carry the Rafter B mark."

"Not sure I'm following you," said Orson, looking puzzled.

"It's simple." Van Horne made an expansive gesture with the hand holding the cigar. "After the first of this year, it was discovered that Norris Bradley had fallen in serious arrears on the taxes he owed for the Rafter B. The court allowed him a reasonable amount of time to catch up. He wasn't able to, not even close. Learning of this, I took the opportunity to satisfy the tax burden and thereby took over legal ownership of the Rafter B. Not wanting to be unduly harsh, I gave Bradley and his people a month to settle their affairs and gather together their personal belongings before vacating the place. And then, while I was away on business and nobody was paying close enough attention, they vacated the place all right. Trouble was, when they did they took eight hundred head of cattle—*my* cattle—along with 'em!"

By the time he finished speaking, Van Horne's voice was harsher and had increased in volume. And listening, Orson's jaw had sagged steadily open wider.

"Sufferin' Virgin Mary," the former cook groaned. "You mean all the while I was traveling with a pack of cattle thieves?"

Van Horne grimaced. "No other way to put it. Those longhorns might still be wearing Bradley's brand, but they're technically mine and he's nothing more than a no-good rustler. Ain't that right, Malloy?"

"Like you said, that's what it comes down to," Malloy replied, though not looking particularly pleased with the pronouncement.

Orson's expression grew suddenly anxious. "I had no idea. I swear! You've got to believe me."

"Lucky for you, I do," Van Horne allowed.

"So do I," said Malloy. "But now, Brandenburger, you'll have the chance to prove your innocence even further with some added cooperation. As you can see, this posse has been formed to run down Bradley's bunch and retrieve Mr. Van Horne's property. Up until a short time ago, we figured they were aiming to try and sell the cattle in Denver. But as you know, they passed that up. What you can help with now, to get us back on track, is to reveal what they've got in mind instead. Where are they headed with those stolen longhorns, Brandenburger?"

Half an hour later, after he'd gladly given up Miles City as Bradley's destination, Orson was on his way back to Bison Horn, once again in the company of Barlow and Curly. In the interim, he had been invited to sit and have a cup of whiskey-laced coffee with the appreciative posse members before leaving their camp.

With that behind him, his mood was light as he rode off. Not only was he relieved to have gotten things squared with Mr. Van Horne and Ranger Malloy, but there was a spiteful part of him that relished knowing he'd also gotten a measure of revenge on those Rafter B varmints.

A lingering sour note, however, was the realization that his reception back at the Buffalo Wallow would almost certainly be negative, including from the half-breed soiled dove who'd earlier been so eager to take him into the back room. No explanation would be able to easily erase the "horse thief" accusation that had been announced for all to hear. For this, Orson still harbored a grudge against Barlow and Curly.

But their status with Van Horne and the Ranger—not to mention the fact they'd proven to be a couple of formidable hardcases strictly on their own—made Orson think better of seeking any more trouble with them. It wouldn't be hard to find other saloons where the novelty of his cast would get him the kind of attention he'd grown to crave. Orson smiled inwardly, and as he rode along between Barlow and Curly, in his head he once again began rolling around some ideas for new tall tales to explain the hand injury.

Some fanciful fabrication was the last thing on his mind, then, when Barlow's arm suddenly reached out, the knife in his fist flashing in the moonlight as it passed under Orson's chin and laid open his throat. The former cook made a single sound, like a subdued cough, as blood gushed down over the front of him. His shoulders slumped, then he crumpled and slipped slowly from his saddle, dead before he hit the ground.

"The old goat sure had a lot of juice in him, didn't he? Look how it's still pumpin'!" Curly Pierce marveled, gazing down at the fallen body.

"We ain't got time to hang around gawking," said Barlow as he swung down from his saddle. "We've got to get him buried. Van Horne told me on the sly to get rid of him and not leave any trace. Then be sure to bring the Rafter B horse back with us."

"Why's he so worried about the horse?"

"It's his property now. Remember? What's his, he wants."

"Can you believe that? All that money he's got, and he's worried about one lousy horse?"

"Just be thankful he didn't say to kill it and bury it, too."

"I suppose. I don't recall signin' on for no shovel work, though. Not even a little bit," Curly groused as he dismounted.

CHAPTER 17

Colleen's intervention on the Forrests' behalf finally wore down her father's resistance to them tagging along on the drive. There was a final question Bradley demanded must be addressed, though, before giving in entirely. That was the matter of what had gone wrong back in Torrence that resulted in the professor's elixir making so many people so sick, some of them nearly dying.

The only explanation Forrest could come up with was that he'd made the harmful batch with some recently purchased whiskey that must have been tainted. "A primary ingredient in my recipe, as is the case with almost all elixirs such as mine—not to mention many of the concoctions prescribed by licensed physicians, truth be told—is a strong dose of whiskey," he'd revealed.

He'd then gone on to admit, with great remorse, that the whiskey he used for the bad batch had been purchased, due to its bargain price, from a moonshiner outside of Laramie. Since he strictly followed the same recipe he had used dozens of times before with no problem and all the other ingredients came from supplies he had on hand that had previously been used without any problem, the cheap moonshine—which Forrest foolishly never tested or sufficiently sampled before introducing it into the mix—had to have been the source of the subsequent suffering.

In the end, the man's frankness and his sincere-seeming regret for the damage his carelessness had caused was enough to convince Bradley that the incident had been an accident—a near-tragic accident, to be sure—and therefore deserving forgiveness.

That had been two days ago. Now, on the morning of the third day, breakfast was finishing up and they would soon be on the move again. As it was turning out, the Forrests were so far proving to be no hindrance to the drive. In fact, the professor—after being given a few pointers—was actually being of considerable help. An experienced rider, he had begun assisting Colleen with the remuda by day and had also insisted on taking his turn at nighthawk duty. His daughter, Belinda, managed their team and wagon on her own and at evening camp made herself useful in small ways however and whenever she could. The way the men of the crew followed her with their eyes at every opportunity, there wasn't much doubt they found her to have sufficient worth merely by her presence.

Surely Belinda must have had some awareness of this, but if so, she didn't display it outwardly. Nor, other than to take the normal womanly measures to maintain her appearance, did she flirt or act in any manner to solicit it.

Still, her effect on the men did not go unnoticed altogether. When Colleen brought the mule team around and helped Mac get them hitched to the chuckwagon, she abruptly asked, "Do any of the men look at me that way?"

Mac immediately recognized what she was referring to. But he also recognized that the smartest thing for him to do was steer as wide around the answer as possible. In an attempt to do so, his response was to concentrate harder than necessary on the task at hand and mumble a vague, "What's that? Look at you how?"

"The way they look at Belinda, that's how," Colleen answered somewhat testily. Then added, "And that includes you—although you don't gawp quite as bad as most of the others."

"Gawp?" Mac echoed with a frown. "Ain't sure I'm following you."

"The heck you're not. Quit playing dumb, you're not fooling me one bit," Colleen snapped. "I'm talking about the way all the fellas gaze at Belinda, practically drooling, whenever she comes in sight. It's pathetic. They're like a bunch of humpbacked hounds panting after . . . well, you know what I mean. And don't pretend you don't."

Much as he didn't want to be, it looked like Mac was cornered. He tossed a couple sidelong glances, hoping somebody else might be headed his way to provide an interruption. But there was no such salvation in sight.

Colleen arched an eyebrow. "I expect an answer. And I'd appreciate it if you looked at me when I'm talking to you."

Mac lifted his eyes from the rigging and met hers. As always, he was struck by her fresh beauty. The just-rising sun caught her thick chestnut hair and framed it in shimmering gold. And her agitated state put an extra sparkle in her eyes and added a blush of color to her cheeks that made her features all the more appealing.

Mac sighed. "Doggone it, Colleen, what do you want me to say? Is this some kind of jealousy thing?"

"Jealousy's got nothing to do with it," Colleen insisted, a bit too forcefully.

Mac dragged the palm of one hand down over his face. "Okay. In the first place, how long have the fellas in this outfit—except for me, since I came along more recently—been on the trail staring at mostly nothing every day except the rear ends of a bunch of longhorns? Quite a spell now, right? Then along comes a gal looks like Miss Belinda. And she's right pretty, no getting around that. So ain't it kinda natural for a bunch of men like I just described to take particular notice of her?"

"Hmmph! If you mean it's natural for a bunch of men to act like drooling idiots, then I guess you'd know the answer to that better than me."

"Are you wanting to make conversation or looking for a reason to be insulting?" Mac wanted to know.

Colleen pressed her lips into a tight, straight line and didn't answer right away. Then: "I didn't mean to be insulting. At least not to you. But you avoided my original question. Do the men ever look at me the way they do her?"

Accepting he was cornered and there was no way he could avoid getting sucked deeper into this discussion, Mac said, "The answer to that is . . . not usually. Not from what I've seen. But it ain't that simple. You got to understand there are some good reasons why."

Colleen thrust out her chin. "Like what? Because

I'm not pretty enough for anybody to take a second look at?"

"Now, blast it, that ain't it at all," Mac was quick to respond. "How many times do we have to cover this business about you being pretty? Once and for all, I think you're pretty—no, I *know* you're pretty. Same as anybody who's ever laid eyes on you. And if you figure I've never taken a second look at you in the time since I joined this drive, well, then you ain't been paying very close attention."

Colleen's expression changed, softened. "I'm grateful for you saying so, Mac. I needed to hear that just now . . . And I *have* noticed you looking at me. And unless you're a lot dumber than I take you for, you know that I've been looking back."

The way the conversation had suddenly turned was causing Mac to feel uncomfortable in a whole different way. Trying to keep things from getting too far out of hand, he said, "As far as how the other fellas in this outfit do or don't look at you, you've got to stop and consider a couple things. First, you're the boss's daughter. That'd give any sensible hombre some amount of pause, whether you think it should or not. Second, over half the men in camp are relatives to you—your father and brothers. They sure ain't gonna look at you the way we're talking about, yet the four of them always being close by is another sort of roadblock to anybody else who might be inclined to pay you attention. You beginning to see what I mean?"

Colleen gave a faint bob of her head. "Yes. I guess I do." She gazed at him for a long moment before saying, "Thank you for sparing me the time, Mac. There's no one else in camp I could have had this talk with. I appreciate it. And I hope I didn't come across as being petty or mean-spirited where Belinda is concerned. I actually like her and we seem to be hitting it off well. It's just that . . ."

"No need to explain," Mac told her. "If talking to me helped, then I'm glad. We'll just leave it at that."

Colleen smiled. "Very well. But there is one more thing. Above all, make sure you understand that I don't mind you taking those second looks at me." She paused. "I don't mind at all."

CHAPTER 18

The descending sun was just getting ready to touch the western horizon when Mac reached the spot Shad Hopper had marked for their night camp. There was a meandering creek close by from which the stock could slake their thirst and then a wide, grassy expanse where they could rest and graze until it was time to get moving again in the morning. Mac figured the herd was a good hour or more behind, giving him plenty of time to set up and have a good supper waiting for the crew when they came straggling in.

Belinda Forrest had rolled her wagon up soon after he reached the campsite. She was quick to express her relief that the end of another long day had been reached.

"That wagon seat beats walking, to be sure, and probably spending hours in a saddle, too, I imagine," she said. "But I guarantee there are certainly more comfortable ways to pass the time of day."

As she said this, Belinda placed her hands at the small of her back and tipped her head from side to side as she arched her back, working out some kinks and aches. These actions caused a spill of wavy blond hair to fall over one side of her face and, at the same time, thrust her generous breasts even more prominently against the front of her blouse.

The whole thing was quite natural and not meant to be intentionally provocative, yet that was exactly what it was. Mac had to abruptly look away in order to keep from "gawping" as a result. The recollection of Colleen's word from their discussion only that morning made Mac feel immediately guilty on two counts: one, that he was reacting the way he was in the first place, and two, that by so doing he was somehow betraying Colleen.

Promptly focusing on the work he had to do as a means to shift his thoughts away from where they didn't belong, Mac began unharnessing his mule team and said over his shoulder, "There's a small grove of trees over there by the stream. Why don't you go ahead and sit over there in the shade for a while, relax and rest a bit. Maybe soak your feet in the cool water. We've got a good hour, maybe a little more, before the others show up."

"But what will you be doing?" Belinda wanted to know.

Mac answered, "I'll get the teams unhitched, leave them to drink and graze. Then I've got to start supper for the crew. You can bet they'll show up plenty hungry and not in any mood to wait very long for something to fill their bellies once they get here."

Belinda moved up beside him. "No, that won't do. Not at all. Let me see to the teams while you go ahead and start your meal preparations. I can't very well laze about like some pampered princess while everyone else continues working. As it is, I feel like I've already contributed too little ever since Mr. Bradley allowed us to join your group."

"You've done everything asked of you," Mac pointed out. "You've taken care of your team and wagon while your father pitches in elsewhere."

"That's just it. Father is pitching in, contributing something to the overall drive as a means of payback to show our gratitude. Yes, I've been handling our team and wagon. But that doesn't benefit anyone else." Belinda reached out and gripped Mac's wrist, stopping him from continuing to unfasten the rigging. "And I certainly won't allow you to see to my team as well as your own. That would make me riding ahead with you today only added work for you. That's the last thing I want. So let me take care of the animals. It's the least I can do."

"Okay. Your horses are your own business. But," Mac said stubbornly, "mules are whole different critters. Especially this pair of ornery knotheads. They may look mild as milk right at the minute. But right when you least expect—"

"Leave them to me," Belinda cut him off. With the grip she had on his wrist she tugged his hand off the leathers then reached with her free hand to take them instead. "Believe it or not, I've handled mules before. I even know the kind of salty language it takes to get their attention. So promise me you won't be shocked if I have to cut loose with a whole string of unladylike words."

Mac gave in with a wry grin. "I promise. But I can't speak for the mules. Them, you might shock. They're only used to sweet, gentle, coaxing words spoken in a soothing voice."

Belinda laughed. "Yeah, I bet. You just go on about your cooking. Leave these jug-eared wastes of good hay and oats to me."

Mac held up his hands, palms out, in a gesture of surrender. Then, still grinning, he made his way around to the side of the chuckwagon. From where a horsehair rope held it lashed to the outside of the box, he took an ax. He carried it with him as he strode toward the grove of trees he had pointed out to Belinda earlier. Behind him, he could hear her talking to the mules—her velvety voice gentle and pleasant to start with, even as it warned them in no uncertain terms what kind of tongue-lashing they were in for if they gave her cause.

Half an hour later, Mac had two cooking fires burning strong, fueled by the wood he'd chopped, and he'd begun laying out the makings for supper on the fold-down table at the rear of the chuckwagon. Belinda had unharnessed the two teams without any problem, and the animals were now down by the creek where they'd be left to drink and graze on their own until the rest of the outfit arrived, at which time they would be rounded up and put in with the remuda until needed again in the morning. Finished with them for the time being, Belinda had muttered something about "freshening up" before disappearing into the medicine wagon and not yet reemerging.

As he continued with his meal preparations, Mac's mind strayed to wondering what the blond beauty might be doing in there by herself. After a few minutes of this, the realization came suddenly that what was really on his mind was wishing she was out here talking with him instead of being hidden away. Then,

on the heels of that, almost as suddenly, came another
pang of guilt for having that wish and knowing how
much it would hurt Colleen if she knew he harbored
such a thought.

It was clear Colleen was developing some deepening feelings toward him. And under different
circumstances—namely, if he wasn't a fugitive on
the run with murder charges hanging over his
head—Mac could easily fall for her, too. What red-
blooded male in his right mind wouldn't?

But being wanted for murder made him undeserv-
ing, for Colleen's sake, to entertain such a possibility,
not even for a little while. As far as that went, he
didn't have the right to feel any longing for Belinda's
company, either. Until he could somehow manage to
clear himself of those false charges—which would
have to start with finding the gumption to return to
New Orleans in order to face up to them—he didn't
deserve to be in the company of any decent woman.

With his mind wandering down that melancholy
path, Mac's mood was turning more sour than at any
point in weeks. Looking up from the biscuit dough he
was kneading, however, he happened to cast a glance
off toward the northwest and spotted something that
suddenly soured his mood a whole lot worse.

Continuing to work the dough, careful to show no
outward reaction, Mac turned his head slightly and
called over his shoulder, raising his voice no more
than necessary to be heard in the medicine wagon.
"Miss Belinda? Could you come out here and give me
a hand for a minute, please? As soon as possible."

After a moment, the rear door of the enclosed,
gaudily painted wagon opened and Belinda stepped

out. As she walked over to Mac, he could see she had brushed her long, pale hair into a glossy luster, and it appeared her face was freshly scrubbed. An expression of curiosity touched by a hint of concern was on her face.

"What is it, Mac? Is something wrong?"

"I'm not sure yet," he told her. "Step over here on the other side of me. Don't show any sign of alarm. Listen close and don't give any sudden reaction to what I tell you."

Belinda did as instructed, moving around to Mac's side nearest the chuckwagon box. But she couldn't quite keep the concern on her face from deepening somewhat.

"What's going on?" she wanted to know. "I must say, the way you're acting is a little frightening."

"That's the last thing I want you to show. Try to stay calm," Mac said, continuing to work the biscuit batter. "Start taking some airtights out of the cupboard there. It doesn't matter what, just do it slow and examine each one like you're looking for something I asked for. As you're doing that—and, again, it's important you not display any big reaction—glance off toward the west and tell me what you see."

Belinda began pulling some airtight cans down from the chuckwagon cupboard Mac had indicated. She did it slow, examining them one by one as she did so. On the third one, her eyes flicked to the high, grassy ridge that lay to the west. She gave an audible intake of breath but otherwise showed no emotion.

"There are three men up there on horseback," she said, a faint raggedness to the words. "Do they mean trouble for us?"

Mac said, "I don't know yet. Right now they're just sitting and watching."

"Do you think it's some of the men from Torrence?" Belinda asked.

Mac shook his head. "No, we were rid of those lowlifes a long ways back. If they came after your father at all—and as far as I know nobody in our outfit ever spotted hide nor hair of any of 'em—they must have seen that him and you had fallen in with us and decided it was smartest to leave things be. Besides, those hombres up there on that ridge are Indians."

Belinda's breathing quickened. "Are they getting ready to attack?"

"I don't think so. Not just yet anyway," Mac said, trying to keep his tone as reassuring as possible. "I don't have a whole lot of experience with Indians, but from what I do know, if they meant to attack, I figure they would have done it by now. And in that case, we likely never would have seen 'em until they were right on top of us."

"I—I guess that's good news," said Belinda, trying to sound brave.

"Matter of fact, there's a good chance they're more interested in our horses and mules than they are in us," Mac told her.

One corner of her lush mouth lifting in a wry smile, Belinda replied, "I never thought I'd be glad to hear I was looked on less favorably than a mule, but in this case I am very willing to settle for that."

A corner of Mac's own mouth quirked upward briefly. He was glad to see this gal had enough spunk to maintain a sense of humor even in a tense situation. Then, sticking to the more serious side of things, he said, "Does your father keep any weapons in your wagon?"

"He has a pistol that he wears under his jacket sometimes. I think he has it with him today."

"No long guns? No rifles in the wagon?"

"No. None that I . . . Oh wait. Yes, I think there's an old shotgun in there somewhere. I'd have to do some digging to find it." Belinda's brow furrowed. "But don't you have your own gun?"

"Yes. I have a handgun in my belt and a Winchester up under the seat. But in a case like this, the more firepower at our disposal the better."

"Will that old shotgun be of any help?"

"Won't hurt," Mac allowed. "Stop taking down those cans now. Set aside the last one you brought down, like it was the one you were looking for. Put the others back. When you're done, I'm going to ask you to return to your wagon. When you get there, find that shotgun right away and make sure it's loaded."

Belinda frowned. "I'd rather stay close to you. I'd feel safer."

"In case I get busy, you'll have protection inside that enclosed wagon."

"Now you're scaring me again."

"It's okay to be scared as long as you don't let it freeze you and you use your fear to take precautions and make smart moves. That's why I'm asking you to—"

Mac stopped short, suddenly focusing intently on listening instead of talking. A faint but rapidly increasing sound had reached his hears. Coming from the south, rising and falling from somewhere back among those choppy hills—the swift rataplan of a horse's hooves running hard.

It sounded like the approach of a single horse, yet

Mac's first thought was that it might be more Indians sweeping in from a different direction from those up on the ridge. He quickly wiped his gun hand on the front of his apron, then drew the Smith & Wesson from his belt. Shifting his body, he stood so that he was blocking Belinda, standing between her and the advancing rider or riders. Over his shoulder, he said, "If I give the word, race to the front of the wagon and bring me the Winchester from the boot under the driver's seat. Otherwise stay close and still behind me."

CHAPTER 19

Tense seconds that seemed to pass like minutes ticked by as Mac and Belinda stood poised, watching for the first sign of whoever was approaching.

Then, in a sudden, strained whisper, Belinda said, "Look—up on the hill."

Mac cut a quick glance toward the grassy ridge. It was empty, the three mounted men who'd been planted on its crest as still as statues earlier now were gone.

"What does that mean?" said Belinda.

"No way of knowing," Mac answered. "I hope it means they're not in cahoots with whoever's coming in so they're making themselves scarce because of his arrival. Continue keeping a sharp lookout, though, in every direction."

No sooner had he gotten the words out than the rider coming from the south finally burst into view. It was a single horseman, pushing his mount hard. The haze of dust swirling around him made his features indistinct, but the wide-brimmed hat on his head, its front pressed up flat against the crown by the rush of motion eased Mac's concern that this might be another Indian.

"Is that one of the men from our outfit?" asked Belinda.

"I think so," Mac replied.

A moment later the rider was close enough to be identifiable. It was indeed one of the Rolling B wranglers—leathery-faced Laird Nolan. He reined to a sharp halt just a few yards short of Mac and Belinda. Both rider and horse were breathing hard, and Nolan's face was streaked with dust and sweat.

Nobody spoke for a minute, waiting for the thickest part of the boiling dust cloud that had built up in Nolan's wake to roll on past. Then Mac said, "Can't say we're sorry to see you, Laird, but what's the big rush? You came tearing in like your tail was on fire."

"Ain't my tail that I'm worried about," Nolan responded, puffing slightly. He lifted the canteen that hung at his knee, unscrewed the cap, and took a big swig. Lowering it, he passed the back of one hand across his mouth, then added, "It's my hair."

"Your hair?" Mac echoed.

"My scalp, to be exact. That's what Mr. Bradley sent me ahead to warn you about." Nolan seemed to hesitate, his brow puckering as he looked past Mac to Belinda standing behind him. "Don't mean to alarm nobody more than necessary, but we seem to have stirred up some Injuns in the area. Mr. Bradley wanted to make sure you knew so's you could keep an eye peeled until him and the rest get here."

Mac nodded. "Appreciate the warning. But somebody beat you to it."

"What do you mean?"

"I mean we had visitors. Until you came thundering

up, that is." Mac raised a hand and pointed toward the ridge to the west. "Up there. Three mounted Indians were sitting their horses, just watching, for a good long stretch."

Nolan grimaced. "Blast it. If they're strung out this far, that must mean there's a fair number of 'em. More than we were hoping."

"Strung out how far? All the way back to the herd, you mean?"

"That's right. Mile and a half, maybe two."

As he'd advised Belinda to do, Mac had been tossing frequent glances in all directions, now more than ever on the lookout for any more Indian signs. Returning his gaze to Nolan, he said, "You mentioned something about stirring the Indians up. What happened?"

"It was young George, he's the one who brung it on." Nolan's face scrunched into a forlorn expression. "He didn't know no better, I reckon. Heck, any of the rest of us might've even done the same. But it fell to him and he stepped in it good."

"Get to the point. What is it he did?"

Nolan took another long pull from his canteen. Then, lowering it, he said, "The long and short of it is that he shot a buffalo. He was sort of off by himself a ways, out on the west flank of the herd, see, chasin' back in some independent-minded critters who was tryin' to roam clear of the others. That's when he saw this lone buff standin' down in a shallow draw. The way George told it, all his life he'd been hearin' stories about what good eatin' buffalo was supposed to be. So, havin' the chance right there in front of him, he figured some nice fresh buff meat would go good in one of your cookin' pots and be a welcome change for the whole crew. Once he decided that, he didn't waste no time puttin' his Henry rifle to his shoulder and plunkin' that buff right through the brain."

"Don't seem like a particularly unreasonable thing to do," Mac allowed.

"No, it don't," Nolan agreed. "Like I said, any of the rest of us might've done the same. Fact is, when me and Sparky heard the shot—thinkin' George had probably popped at a coyote or maybe a rattler, but decidin' we'd better go and check for sure—our first reaction upon spottin' the fallen buff was that it was a right fine thing. We hopped down from our saddles and was excited to commence helpin' George get that rascal skinned so's we could hide-wrap some fat, juicy cuts and fetch 'em to you for cookin'."

It wasn't hard for Mac to guess what had happened next. "And that's when the Indians showed up, right?"

Nolan rolled his eyes. "Boy, did they ever! Kiowas, is what Mr. Bradley figures they are. But knowin' their tribe was the least of our concern when me, Sparky, and George first looked up from our skinnin' and saw a whole heap of 'em bunched together on a hill lookin' down on us. And then, once they knew we'd seen 'em, they didn't waste no time lettin' us know they was powerful agitated about what we was up to. They cut loose with howlin' and wailin' and cussin' in some kind of Injun lingo the likes of nothing you ever heard before! And all the while they was shakin' their fists and spears and tomahawks at us, makin' it plenty clear—even if we didn't understand the language— what they was itchin' to do to us if they got half a chance."

"But they never actually tried anything?"

Nolan shook his head. "No. Roman and Mr.

Bradley heard the commotion and rode over to join us. Seemed like the sight of all five of us, heavily armed and facin' up to 'em, was enough to hold the rascals at bay. That sure didn't stop 'em from keepin' up with the howlin' and cussin' at us, though."

"So everyone is still okay? My father?" Belinda asked.

"Oh yes, ma'am. Your pa is fine," Nolan told her. "So far, no harm has been done nowhere . . . Well, except to that buff what started it all."

"How many Kiowas, total, you figure we're talking about?" said Mac.

"Mr. Bradley reckons not more than a dozen," Nolan replied. "Once we started the herd movin' again, our rifles propped on our hips in full display, the redskins stopped their caterwaulin' and began just keepin', silent-like, up on the hills and ridges. Some of 'em would fade back out of sight for a while and then reappear again farther down the line. But it never looked like they added any more in number. I don't know what to make of the three you say you saw."

"Waiting for night, probably meaning to hit the herd in the dark and take some cattle as payback for the buff George shot," Mac mused.

"Uh-huh. That's the way Roman and Mr. Bradley are figurin' it, too."

"What about Shad Hopper? Was he around during any of this?"

Nolan shook his head. "No, he's still scoutin' up ahead somewhere. Mr. Bradley was kinda hopin' he'd be here with you."

"I wish he was," Mac grunted. Then, eyeing Nolan hopefully, he said, "What about you? You supposed to report back to Bradley or stay here with us?"

"I'm to stick here. Unless something more happens, the rest of the outfit should be along in about an hour."

Mac nodded. "Good. In that case, the first thing I'd advise, since you're mounted, is to go round up our wagon teams, the mules and horses down by the creek over there. Bring 'em back and picket 'em along with your horse right here close to the wagons so none of 'em will be as likely to tempt those Indians we saw into making a try for 'em."

"Good idea."

"After that, you just hang close and keep watch while I get back to making supper."

Belinda's eyes widened. "You can think of eating at a time like this?"

"Body's got to eat to keep its strength up," Mac replied with a shrug. "With those Kiowas lurking close, the lot of us are going to be in for a long night. Apt to need all the strength we can muster to make it through . . ."

CHAPTER 20

"Four of us, paired up, on nighthawk duty in four-hour shifts. That'll have to include you, too, Mac. And when any of us is taking our turn in camp, we'll sleep with our boots on and a saddled horse close by our bedrolls." Norris Bradley paused, his eyes sweeping over the faces of those gathered around him. "Any questions?"

It was full dark now. The herd was bedded down for the night, grazing quietly in the still, rapidly cooling air. A three-quarters-full moon hung in a cloudless, star-studded sky. Supper was finished, and everything was cleared away save for some final cups of coffee gripped in the hands of a few. Expressions on the faces of all clustered at the central campfire, men and women alike, were somber, made even more so by pulsing, deeply etched shadows thrown by the flickering flames.

"What about Shad?" asked Henry Bradley. "He's still out there somewhere—alone."

"You think I don't know that? But what I'm also aware of is that if there's anybody who knows how to take care of himself, it's Shad Hopper." The elder Bradley's response was firm and confident-sounding yet there was a tightness around his mouth that suggested he was harboring more of a concern than he wanted to let on.

"What if he stumbles into some of those Kiowas?" insisted Roman. "We know they're there, because we had the chance to spot them while it was still daylight. But if Shad is returning to camp, in the dark, what reason would he have to expect there are any riled-up redskins between him and us?"

His father's expression shifted, took on a deepened look of resolve. "Your concern is commendable, but you and your brother are mighty quick to dismiss the abilities of the man we're talking about. One of the main reasons Shad is the one doing the scouting for us is because of his experience. He's sharp and alert and on the lookout for any and all things that could affect our drive—more than just marking the trail and finding water and picking the best spots for night camp. Him stumbling accidentally onto a pack of renegades dogging us and our herd? Not likely."

Bradley paused and his mouth spread in a sly smile. "Tell you what. Anybody looking to relieve themselves of some money, I'll give you odds on a little bet. I say that Shad not only is aware of the Kiowas lurking out there, but right about now, the old fox is probably scouting them, aiming to learn more about who they are and what they've got in mind. That means when he does show up in camp, he'll be the one filling us in on a whole lot more than the other way around. Any takers?"

The challenge caused some shuffling of feet and a

couple of sidelong glances were exchanged, but nothing more.

Bradley issued a satisfied grunt. "What I thought. Okay, so we'll trust that Shad can take care of himself. What that leaves is for us to hold up our end and do the same for ourselves. So two pair of nighthawks need to get out there guarding the cattle right away. In four hours, you'll be relieved. At the first glimmer of gray in the eastern sky, we'll start on the move again. Breakfast will be coffee and leftover biscuits, nothing more. Mac, you'll keep the chuckwagon with the herd when we move out, no going on ahead. The same, obviously, for the Forrests' wagon. After we've covered some distance, hopefully we can stop for a decent nooning. That will depend primarily on what the Kiowas have in store for us. Now, who's ready to take the first nighthawk turns?"

"I will," Roman spoke up promptly. "I'll take Mackenzie with me. We'll cover the west and north perimeters of the herd."

Only after he'd spoken did he look over at Mac to see if there was any objection. Mac met his eyes and gave an okay-by-me shrug.

"Me and George will take east and south, then," said Henry.

His father nodded. "Good enough. I'll pair up with Professor Forrest, and we'll relieve Roman and Mac when it's time. Sparky and Laird will take over for Henry and George." His gaze sought out Colleen and Belinda. "I hope you gals got no problem pairing up in a kind of way, too. I'd feel better if the both of you bunked tonight inside the medicine wagon. In case any trouble breaks out, you'll have some added protection."

"Whatever you think best, Mr. Bradley," Belinda said.

Colleen didn't look quite so eager. Nevertheless, she said, "If that's the way you want it, Father. But I'll have a loaded rifle in there with me, and if any trouble breaks out, I'll be putting it to use—not staying hidden away like a helpless damsel in distress from some stupid dime novel."

Bradley regarded her for a long moment, then was unable to suppress a soft chuckle. "I wouldn't expect anything less from you."

A short time later, Mac and Roman were mounted and holding their horses to a slow plod as they rode stirrup to stirrup, skirting along the western side of the cattle herd. In the wash of moon and starlight, the shadowy mass of longhorns seemed relaxed and peaceful tonight, no signs of restlessness in any of them. As the drive wore on, they also were growing weary from the long, grueling days so that by the time they were allowed to settle at night they were mostly too tired to be proddy or troublesome.

Mac and Roman rode in silence for a while. As they worked their way north, following the irregular outline of the herd over gently undulating terrain, the glow of the camp's dying fire fell from view. Their eyes had grown accustomed to the dark by then. That fact and the illumination thrown from above combined to provide a relatively clear view of things. Drifting from the opposite side of the herd, they could hear the faint strains of George, who had the most pleasant singing voice in the outfit, crooning to lull the cattle even more.

This caused Roman to remark, "I'm glad you're not one of those who figures nighthawkin' duty just automatically calls for trying to soothe the critters with a lullaby."

Mac grinned. "I've been known to warble a tune now and then when I was nighthawking on my own. Had you ever heard what came out, then you'd *really* be thankful I ain't so moved tonight."

"I'll take your word for it."

"If I had as good a voice as George's, though, I wouldn't hold back."

Roman twisted his mouth wryly. "Yeah, the little squirt has a talent for singing, no denying that. It's just too bad his brain don't work as good as his voice. If it did, maybe he'd've thought twice about shooting that buffalo and we wouldn't have those redskins breathing down our necks."

"I reckon George ain't the only one in our outfit— including me, I'll admit—who'd see a lone buffalo as an awful tempting target for the sake of bagging some fresh meat. Figuring there might be a passel of Kiowas close by to raise a fuss about it ain't hardly something a body would expect."

"Maybe so," Roman replied in a sour tone. "But that don't change the fact trouble was brought on because of George doing what he did."

"I think your pa's got a pretty good grip on handling whatever trouble comes of this," Mac pointed out. "We make it through the night without letting any cows get snatched away, I got a hunch whoever the leader of that Indian pack is will show himself tomorrow and try to strike some kind of deal—claim the right to a few head of cattle to make up for the buff we stole from his hunting ground."

"Be a cold day in Hades before that happens!"

Mac shrugged. "Saw a similar situation on another drive I was part of where the trail boss in that case figured it was better to strike a deal and give up a few cattle willingly rather than risk losing even more cows, possibly some human lives to boot."

"And you're saying you think that was a good idea?" Roman's question was accompanied by a dark scowl.

With a slow wag of his head, Mac responded, "Wasn't my place then—or now—to think one way or the other. I'm just saying, that's all."

"Never mind that whole business," Roman growled, reining his horse to a halt. "Like you said, my old man is gonna handle it, and what me or you think ain't likely to make a difference how he decides."

Mac brought his paint to a halt, too. Waited for the rest of it.

Roman eyed him for several seconds before speaking again. "Why do you think I suggested you and me pair up for this little exercise?"

"Didn't know there *was* any particular reason, other than having shown we can work together, in spite of hard feelings between us at the start."

"Yeah, well maybe those hard feelings ain't so far gone. Maybe because one of us is turning out to be a lowdown snake after all, only just a snake of a different stripe."

Mac didn't know what this was all about, but what he did know was that Roman's hostile tone was bringing his blood to a quick simmer. "You're not making a lick of sense," he said. "How about you spit out whatever it is that's stuck in your craw?"

"There's a lot about you that sticks in my craw," Roman grated. "Starting with the way everybody is so quick to label you such hot stuff when it comes to everything from using a frying pan to handling that stupid ancient gun you carry stuffed in your pants. But what's at the head of my craw-sticking list right at the moment is something else that it's plain to see you're having trouble *keeping* stuffed in your pants!"

"I hear noise coming out of your pie hole, only there's still no sense to any of it. You want to chew it a little finer?"

"Aw, come off it. You ain't that dumb." Roman's lips peeled back in a sneer. "You think I ain't noticed you cozying up to my little sister every chance you get? Leading her off to private little corners of the camp where just the two of you can make cow eyes at one another?"

"I admit that Colleen and I have become friends," Mac said. "But that's all there is to it—us being friends."

"And I'm supposed to believe that?" Roman scoffed. "My sister and I may not see eye to eye on many things, but that don't mean I'm blind to the fact that she's grown into a mighty attractive young woman. Too good for a saddletramp drifter like you, that's for sure."

"Can't say I like hearing those words spouted by you," Mac replied, "but it happens I agree with 'em. Colleen deserves far better than I could ever offer her, no doubt about it. That's why my aim has never been any higher than merely friendship."

"Uh-huh. I bet." Roman's sneer grew even nastier.

"But what friendship means to your kind and what it means to any gal you can sweet-talk and then leave ruined in your wake are two mighty different things, ain't they?"

Mac went rigid in his saddle, his eyes suddenly blazing in the dimness. "That's a dirty lie! I've never done a woman that way and don't have any thoughts like that toward Colleen! You take those words back, or I swear I'll pound an apology out of your hide."

Roman raised one hand in a cautionary gesture. "I'm warning you, mister. You ain't gonna catch me again with a sucker punch, like happened last time. And without that, I can whup you to a frazzle."

Mac swung down from his saddle. "Talk's cheap. Climb out of those stirrups and let's see you back it up, if you got the guts. I'll even give you first swing just so I can quit hearing you whine about a sucker punch that never happened in the first place."

"You're right about one thing—talk being cheap," Roman said, ignoring Mac's challenge and showing an inclination to goad him some more instead. "About as cheap as your Mr. Noble act when it comes to women. You got nothing but pure thoughts for my sister, eh? What about Belinda Forrest, then? Luring her ahead of the drive with you today, setting it up so's just the two of you could be all alone for a whole hour or two, with nobody else around for miles. You claiming your intentions were all pure and noble in that case, too?"

"It was Miss Belinda's notion to ride ahead with me. She wanted to get clear of the dust and the bawling of the cattle for a while."

"Oh, yeah. And I bet you resisted real hard, didn't you?"

"No, as a matter of fact I didn't. I'll even go as far as to admit I kind of liked the idea." Mac paused. A sudden realization hitting him. "I see now what this is really about. You're jealous, and acting like a blamed fool over it. Talk about me cozying up to Colleen— ain't that exactly what I've seen you trying to do with Miss Belinda? Only going at it about as crudely as a humpbacked old hound dog panting after she-hound in heat."

"Just like every other man in camp. So what of it?" Then, neither expecting nor waiting for an answer from Mac, Roman provided one himself. "I'll tell you what of it—I saw her first, that's what! I saw her and I'm claiming first rights."

Mac's jaw dropped. "You're *claiming* her?"

"That's right. I made it clear to my brothers and to Sparky and Nolan. Now I'm telling *you*. It's just a matter of time before I have my way with that blond hellcat. So you stay out of the picture, or I'll break you in half!"

Mac felt anger surging in him once again. Having ultimatums hurled at him went mighty hard against his grain. Through clenched teeth, he said, "Ain't like I had any particular designs on Miss Belinda, one way or the other. But no matter, you can't *claim* her—or any woman—like some wild mustang you broke and branded. What kind of sick reasoning boils inside that head of yours, anyway? The filthy thoughts and motives you're accusing me of are really your own, ain't they? Any decent woman comes within half a mile of you ought to be warned off same as if they was at risk from a hydrophobia skunk!"

Now it was Roman's eyes who blazed. "You saying you'd do that? Warn Belinda against me that way?"

"Why shouldn't I?" Mac said with disgust. "It'd be no more than you deserve!"

"You want to talk deserves, Mr. High and Mighty? Then it's past time you got yours!"

With that, Roman launched from his saddle and landed on Mac with fists hammering furiously.

CHAPTER 21

As Roman slammed into him and drove him off his feet, Mac mentally cursed himself for being caught by surprise. Moments ago, he had been braced and ready to fight. Shoot, he'd been the one *asking* for it. But Roman, seeming only intent on spouting hot air and making jealous accusations, had lulled Mac into relaxing his guard . . . and now he was paying for it.

They hit the ground hard, tangled together, Roman mostly on top. It was an ironic reversal of their first encounter and one Roman seemed bent on taking full advantage of. He spread his legs wide, straddling Mac, pinning him in place while continuing to relentlessly rain down blows with fists, forearms, and elbows. Mac got his own arms up, forced to concentrate on defense, trying to protect his face and head. He found very few openings for striking back, and too many of Roman's punches were slipping through, landing with jolting effect.

Roman's pressing weight made it hard for Mac to breathe, and his head was reeling from the punishment he was absorbing. He desperately needed to do something and do it fast. In his estimation, Roman was the type—especially in his current enraged state—who wouldn't stop at simply defeating a foe but would continue to pound and stomp mercilessly even after he had his man beat.

With a frantic surge of effort, Mac arched his back and thrust his middle upward as high as he could, lifting Roman's body at the same time. Then Mac suddenly dropped his weight back down and instantly twisted, rolling onto one hip before Roman could fully straddle him again. Simultaneously rolling his shoulders, Mac angled one arm upward and hooked one of Roman's arms in the crook of its elbow. Completing his roll, Mac gave the captured arm a savage jerk, out and down, pulling Roman along with it so that he was toppled from remaining on top of Mac.

Sprawled face-to-face on their sides now, the two men immediately began flailing at one another, throwing fists, knees, and feet. Freed of Roman's smothering weight, even though his head was still ringing, Mac felt surprisingly revitalized. Landing a couple solid shots with his fist and feeling his knee sink deep into Roman's gut energized him all the more. Suddenly he was the one raining blows relentlessly.

Seeking to escape this onslaught, Roman pushed away and scrambled to his feet. He stumbled a step or two, then quickly turned back to face Mac. The latter had also gained his footing and came lunging in pursuit—at least, that's what he attempted to do. But all those blows he'd taken to the head had disoriented him more than he realized, resulting in a jerky half-stagger as he started forward. This gave Roman just enough time to get set and be ready with a well-timed right cross that crashed hard against the side of Mac's jaw.

Mac spun around ninety degrees, his knees half buckling. But he stayed on his feet. Not only that, but in the curious way that sometimes occurs in the middle of a slugfest, the blow somehow injected a spike of crystal clarity rather than knocking him closer to unconsciousness. So when Roman advanced to follow up on his right cross and Mac turned back to meet him, the vague disorientation that had caused the earlier stagger was gone and this time it was Roman who stepped into a perfectly timed right.

For the next half minute, they stood toe-to-toe, trading punches, neither man gaining, neither retreating. The grunts of wearying effort and the meaty smacks of connecting fists filled the night.

Then a gruff voice cut through it all. "Stop it, you blasted fools! What's the matter with you?"

Suddenly the towering form of Shad Hopper wedged between them, shoving them apart. Gripping each man by his shirtfront, holding them at arm's length, Shad shook them violently, like rag dolls.

"Where are your brains?" the trail boss demanded. "With a cluster of proddy Kiowas squattin' out there in the night, you two got nothing better to do than knock knots in each other's heads?"

His breath coming in puffs, Mac backhanded a trickle of blood from the corner of his mouth and said, "You know about the Indians?"

"I just said so, didn't I?" growled Shad. "I'd be a mighty poor scout if I missed a kind of important detail like that."

"You know what they're up to?" Roman asked.

Shad gave him a look. "'Spect I know a sight more about what they got in mind than you do. I been skulkin' around their camp for near two hours, listenin' in on their pow-wowin'.'"

"What *have* they got in mind?" Mac wanted to know.

Shad pinned him with the same withering look he'd given Roman. "Oh, so *now* you're gonna get around to wonderin' about that, eh? Ain't that the main thing you was supposed to be thinkin' about the whole time—the main reason you two lunkheads are out here nighthawkin' in the first place? Shouldn't that have come ahead of scrappin' like a couple schoolboys? What if it had been two or three Kiowas, instead of me, who'd slipped up on you just now while you was dukin' it out rather than payin' attention the way you should have been? Instead of me standin' here holdin' handfuls of your shirts it could have been them holdin' your scalps!"

The shoulders of both Mac and Roman sagged and they averted their eyes from Shad's blistering glare. Then, abruptly, he let go of their shirts and shoved them away from him.

"Come on, let's head for camp," he muttered. "No call to worry about those Injuns botherin' the herd tonight. I'll give the lowdown on what I overheard once we've got everybody gathered together."

"Strong Wolf, the leader of this bunch that has begun doggin' you, is a young hotblood tryin' to earn a higher notch in the peckin' order of his tribe," Shad explained a short time later. "The elders, so far, have been keepin' him in his place—all except for the handful of other hotbloods who've jumped the reservation with him. What Strong Wolf now figures he's got, with this herd of ours passin' through, is an opportunity to put on a big show that will gain him some of the stature he's so eager for. Claimin' justification on account of one of ours wastefully killin' that buff, he's plannin' to demand some cattle, as many as a dozen, as payback to even things out. If he succeeds and is able to go struttin' back to the reservation leadin' a string of prized longhorns he bargained away from us White Eyes, he don't see how the old chiefs can dispute he has some mighty powerful medicine brewin' in him and deserves a spot on the leadership council."

Every eye in camp remained locked on Shad. Henry and George had been called in from their nighthawk duty, and the women were rousted from the enclosed medicine wagon, so everyone was present. The central campfire had burned down to mostly just glowing coals with a few weak flames licking up here and there, providing muted illumination that painted the circle of faces with splashes of pale orange.

When Shad finally paused to unhurriedly relight his pipe, Norris Bradley cleared his throat and asked the question that likely was on the minds of everybody else. "What happens if we *don't* bargain? What if we're not willing to give up any cattle?"

Shad puffed some smoke, then said, "Wasn't something Strong Wolf spoke on. Leastways not while I was listenin'. He seems pretty confident he can get you to deal."

"Then they all must have been chewin' locoweed," Roman fumed. "No way we're going to hand over a dozen head to balance out one mangy buffalo!"

"That does seem awful lopsided," Bradley pointed out.

"Yeah. From a white man's way of lookin' at it, I reckon it does." Shad puffed some more smoke. "For an Injun, though, the buffalo—which the white man has now slaughtered to near extinction—provided practically everything they needed to live. Far more than just meat. They made use of every last morsel of a buff—the hide for blankets and clothes and moccasins, the bones for everything from sewing needles to spoons and bowls and arrowheads, the gut for bowstrings and thread. They even ground up the horns to make potions." His eyebrows lifted and he seemed to gaze off at something far away before adding, "A longhorn, on the other hand, they don't count for much except some stringy meat and a hide that's only worth a few leather goods. In other words, Injuns don't hardly hold a cow and a buff as an even trade."

Herbert Forrest regarded him closely and said, "By your tone and the look on your face, you almost sound like you agree with the red devils."

Shad met his gaze until Forrest looked away. Then, removing the pipe from his mouth for a moment, the old trail boss replied, "Don't matter whether I agree or not. All I'm doin' is reportin' what I overheard and how I figure Strong Wolf came up with the terms he gonna try and get."

Bradley said, "But even by the reasoning you just laid out, Shad, a twelve-for-one trade seems mighty high, don't you think?"

"Red man or white man alike, ain't that the way negotiatin' goes? One side starts high, the other starts low, and they try to meet somewhere in the middle?"

"So you're saying that's how this could go—that

Strong Wolf might be willing to give ground and maybe settle for fewer cows, perhaps a half dozen or less?"

Shad put his pipe back in his mouth and clamped it between his teeth. "Likely. Don't know that you can push him down too low, though."

"That almost sounds like something Mackenzie was telling me about earlier," said Roman. "How the head of another drive he was on did some similar bargaining with some Injuns."

Bradley looked at Mac. "That right?"

Mac nodded. "It is. In that case, though, it was just a matter of some hungry Indians angling for a kind of payment for us passing through their land. We gave 'em a few to settle the matter."

"From tales I've heard," Shad said, "that kind of thing ain't uncommon."

"I don't care how common it is or ain't. It's plain thievery any way you cut it." Roman glared as if challenging anyone to disagree with him. "Surely you ain't thinking about giving in like that, are you, Pa?"

Bradley settled his gaze once more on Shad. "I'll repeat my original question. What if we refuse to hand over any of our cattle? What do you think Strong Wolf's reaction would be?"

Shad just scowled, pondering for several seconds before working up a response. "Keep in mind, nobody can ever be certain how an Injun will react to a given situation. But Strong Wolf, based on what I overheard, ain't ready to go full renegade and start killin'. That would only lower him more in the eyes of the elders he's tryin' to impress and end up bringing the Army in to chase him down. That ain't what he's after.

"On the other hand," Shad continued, gesturing with his pipe for emphasis, "he's still got to do something to try and save face with the other hotbloods he's got followin' him. If you won't bargain with him, he ain't likely to just walk away empty-handed. And while I said I don't figure he's primed for killin', that don't mean he'll balk at hittin' us in some other way. I expect him and his braves will for sure continue to hang close and pluck away any strays if they can. On top of that—to prove he ain't somebody to be easily brushed off—I wouldn't be surprised if he ordered some cows shot from ambush, just for spite."

Bradley's expression hardened. "In other words, he may take a heavier toll that way than if I bargain with him straight up."

"That's the general idea."

"And it's a totally unacceptable idea!" Roman insisted. "And this dog-eating fool has the gall to think he can get away with it? I say the only deal we offer is payment in lead!"

"Uh-huh. That's real bold talk," Shad said with a sour twist to his mouth. "Tell me . . . how many Kiowas did you see durin' the course of the day?"

Roman frowned, appearing somewhat puzzled. Then he said, "We saw plenty of the red devils. But we figure there ain't more than ten, maybe a dozen all told. After their first bit of whooping and carrying on following George's shooting of that buff, we kept seeing 'em scattered at different places up on the hills and along the ridges."

"Too far away for an accurate shot, right?"

Roman's frown deepened. "Can't be sure. Nobody tried. Pa said—"

"I'm *tellin'* you they was too far," Shad cut him off. "They're clever enough to know. And I'll tell you something else. They take a notion to start peckin' away at our cattle, you won't see hide nor hair of 'em any more at all. You'll only see the carcasses of the cows they decide to drop and notice the absence of the ones they've led away."

"You make 'em sound unstoppable, like phantoms or something," said Roman. "You make it sound like we've got no choice but to give in to 'em."

Shad wagged his head. "Ain't meanin' it that way. They're stoppable, if your pa wants to make that call. All I'm sayin' is that it will come at a cost and it sure won't be as easy as plunkin' 'em off the ridgelines like tin cans lined up on a fence."

"What about hitting them in their own camp, then?" Roman suggested. "You were just there, Shad, you know how to find it again. What if you led some of the rest of us back and . . . well, we can settle this whole matter before they ever—"

"No!" Bradley's voice cracked like a whip. "We're cattlemen, not Indian slaughterers. We'll fight them if we have to, but not that way."

Nobody said anything for several moments. Now all gazes rested on Bradley. In the weak illumination, his expression was clearly torn by indecision.

Finally, in a low, measured tone, the ranch owner spoke again. "I'll meet with Strong Wolf in the morning. I'll listen to what he has to say. If he's willing to negotiate reasonably . . . well, we'll see. I need to think on it some more. In the meantime, the rest of you go ahead and try to get some sleep. Henry, you and George go back to standard nighthawk duty. Stay sharp. Everybody else do like I said before. Women, back in the medicine wagon. Men, stay armed and keep a mounted horse close by. It'll still be a cold breakfast eaten in the saddle, and we'll roll out at first light. That's all."

CHAPTER 22

Out of habit, Mac woke ahead of everyone else. He rolled out of his blankets a bit more stiffly than usual, courtesy of the scrap with Roman, and when his mouth stretched in a yawn there was a faint crackling in one hinge of his jaw where he'd taken a particularly hard punch. But he stood up straight and squared his shoulders, determined not to let any ill effects show.

In keeping with Bradley's announcement of a limited breakfast, Mac stirred up one of the cooking fires just hot enough to brew an oversized pot of coffee. Along with this, he laid out a spread of leftover biscuits on the drop-down table. That done, he went to fetch his mule team from the remuda. By the time he was leading them back, the first streaks of pale gray were reaching above the eastern horizon and the others were starting to crawl out of their bedrolls.

In less than half an hour, everybody was ready to roll. The coffee and biscuits having disappeared quickly, Mac rinsed the pot, stored it back in the wagon, and closed up the drop-down table. Then he kicked out the fire and got ready to climb up in his seat. On the way, he paused to pat the neck and speak a few words to his paint, who he'd decided to keep saddled and tied to the wagon until he saw how things played out this morning.

"Don't worry, fella," he told the animal, "with any luck I'll have you shucked of that saddle and running back with the others in no time."

Before he reached the front of the wagon, Roman came trotting up astride a tall roan. There was a mouse puffed up under one eye and some abrasions along his jawline. Looking down at Mac, he cocked one eyebrow and said, "I was hoping to see you limping around a little worse for wear this morning."

"Sorry to disappoint you, but I feel fit as a fiddle," Mac replied.

Roman grunted. "Yeah. A fiddle that's been dropped and kicked across the dance floor a half dozen times maybe. I know, because I was on that same dance floor and feel the same way."

"Reckon we deserve it," Mac said, "carrying on like we were in the face of the Indian trouble."

"Could be," Roman allowed. "But that don't change nothing about what I told you. You make sure you remember, you hear?"

"I hear. But your words and suspicions are just as empty as they were last night. Anything else?"

Roman's mouth suddenly stretched in a crooked grin. "Yeah, as a matter of fact there is. That tooth that's been bothering me, the one we never got took care of back in Torrence . . ." He reached into his vest pocket and withdrew a small, bloody lump that he held up between thumb and forefinger. "One of the punches you landed last night knocked it loose. Never let it be said I don't express gratitude when it's due . . . so thanks for that, anyway."

With that, he wheeled away and took his place in the formation his father had ordered, consisting of Bradley and Shad riding up front, the two wagons coming along behind them, then the herd and the remuda following. One additional change was that Colleen was not left back with the remuda but rather was moved up near the point and her brother Henry took her place at the rear with the horse pack. Mac was glad to see this. Bradley had once again ordered that in the event any conflict broke out with the Kiowas, the two women were to immediately take shelter in the enclosed medicine wagon.

"Move 'em out!" Bradley ordered as soon as he was satisfied everybody was where he wanted them to be. Urged on by yips and curses and more than a few rump slaps from coiled lassos, the herd lumbered into motion. The first shimmering slice of the sun was just breaking into view.

The Kiowas didn't show themselves until after the sun was fully risen. When they appeared, it seemed all at once, almost like they materialized out of thin air. First, half a dozen riders crested a rounded hill to the west and checked their ponies sharply, then became as motionless as statues. Seconds later, a half dozen more swept down from the east onto a flat expanse directly ahead of Bradley and Shad. When they too fanned out and then reined up in a perfectly still line, the two cattlemen did the same and Bradley signaled for the wagons and the herd coming up behind to also be brought to a halt. Once this was accomplished, there was a brief pause waiting for the dust cloud stirred up by the cattle to fade away.

From his wagon seat, Mac appraised the six braves positioned directly ahead. It wasn't hard to pinpoint the leader, the one Shad had identified as being called Strong Wolf. Centered in the line of horsemen, he was young, not more than twenty-five. He was trim and broad-shouldered and held himself with an unmistakable bearing. His chin was held high, jaw set firm, and quick, alert eyes intently scanned those before him.

From Mac's perspective, slightly to their rear, he could see Shad and Bradley also holding themselves rigid in their saddles, and he judged their eyes were meeting Strong Wolf's gaze with equal intensity. Once again, Mac felt a wave of confidence in the two men handling this matter for their side.

Abruptly, Strong Wolf heeled his pony a half dozen steps forward before reining it short once again. The other braves stayed where they were. In one hand, Strong Wolf held—in a nonthreatening manner—a brightly feathered lance. This he raised slowly and then thrust it downward, burying its tip in the ground just ahead of his pony's right shoulder.

"He wants to parley," Shad said without turning his head but loud enough to be heard not only by Bradley but also by both Mac and Roman, who had ridden up between the two wagons.

Unbuckling his gunbelt and handing it over to Bradley, the trail boss said, "I'll go this first round alone. It'll show you in a position of power if you hang back until I return with a report on what he's got to say. In the meantime, everybody stay sharp and keep your rifles ready but do not—repeat, *do not*—do anything stupid."

Shad then rode forward and pulled up abreast

of Strong Wolf, the feathered lance thrusting up between them. With considerable hand gestures and bursts of guttural language that Mac could barely hear and wouldn't have understood even if he did, the two men talked. It didn't last long, even though just looking on and waiting made it seem so. Shad swung his horse around and came riding back, his expression grim. Strong Wolf remained where he was.

"Well?" said Bradley. "What's his demand? How many cattle does he want to let us pass with no more bother?"

Shad thumbed back the brim of his hat and puffed out his weathered cheeks, expelling a hiss of air before he answered. "Things have changed considerable from the talk I was hearin' last night. And not one bit for the better."

"What does that mean?" Bradley's voice was on edge, irritable. "You mean he's expectin' us to give up even more than a dozen head?"

"Cattle have kinda fallen off the bargainin' table altogether," Shad said with a grimace. "You see, Strong Wolf had hisself a dream last night. A vision, to his way of thinkin'. It showed him a different way to rise to a high, special rank in his tribe and it ain't got nothing to do with how many cattle he can haul back."

"Blast it, get to the point, man. What is he asking for?"

Shad's gaze drifted past Bradley and came to rest on Belinda where she sat on the seat of the medicine wagon. "In his dream, Strong Wolf saw a golden-haired woman at his side. His vision told him that if he were to take her for his bride in a full tribal ceremony then him and this golden princess would become held in the highest regard and would enrich the tribe by producing many golden-haired warrior offspring. In other words, he wants Miss Belinda."

CHAPTER 23

Belinda's startled gasp pretty much spoke for everyone within earshot of Shad's words.

"That's madness," Bradley exclaimed. "He can't seriously expect us to give even a moment's consideration to—"

Shad cut him short. "Yes, he can. He can and he does. Tradin' squaws and horses amongst Injun bucks ain't at all an uncommon thing. Strong Wolf's openin' offer, after some closer examination takes place, is three of their finest ponies—on top of the buff that George already killed—in exchange for the golden woman. His way of lookin' at it, that's a mighty big compliment as far as a startin' bid."

"I don't care how he looks at it," Bradley huffed. "You naturally told him no, right? That such a thing is out of the question?"

"No, I didn't tell him that," Shad replied. "I told him I would bring his offer back and see what you had to say."

"Why waste time about it? Why drag it out? You know good and well what the answer is going to be."

"Hear me out," Shad said. "Yeah, of course I know

what the answer has to be. But there's a right and a wrong way to go about deliverin' it. There's a kind of ritual I recommend we follow. If we don't, if we flat out say no right off the bat, we'll insult Strong Wolf's generous offer and threaten makin' him lose face in front of his men. Before he lets it come to that, I expect he'd turn this whole thing into a lot bigger problem than we want."

"Why should I care if we insult him?" Bradley said. "His offer is insulting to me and to all of us. What's the difference?"

"The difference," Shad said, working hard to keep his voice calm and level, "is tryin' to settle this without any bloodshed or without gettin' a whole bunch of cattle wastefully butchered. Now, if you don't care about that, then we can go ahead and tell Strong Wolf to shove his offer and we'll see what commences. Or you can try it my way, go through the negotiatin' ritual, and in the end I believe come to a better conclusion."

From where he sat his saddle, Roman said, "I been giving these dog-eaters a good looking over, high and low. Ain't none of 'em got any rifles or firearms of any kind. Just bows and spears and such. That being the case, even though they outnumber us, why do we need to pussyfoot around and worry they might cause trouble? We could handle them easy."

"That's ignorance talkin'. We covered that kind of thinkin' last night," Shad reminded everybody. "You might spring a sudden attack and cut down quite a few by surprise, but you wouldn't get 'em all. And if you went on the chase for the rest, that's all you'd do—chase. They'd make fools of you out in the open. And while you was chasin' and not catchin', they'd

circle around and peck away mercilessly at the herd
with those arrows and lances you hold in such low
regard—and maybe knock off a few of their pursuers
as well."

"I swear, Shad," Roman said with a scowl. "Sometimes I have trouble telling which side you're on."

The old trail boss bristled. "I'm on the side of
gettin' this herd to Miles City with the least amount of
injury or loss of life—that's both cattle *and* people—
possible. If that ain't clear enough, you smart-mouthed
pup, I'll be glad to pound the message in a little
deeper as soon as we finish this Kiowa business. Until
then, I'm reportin' to your pa, and unless he says otherwise, I'd advise you to keep your mouth shut and
your ignorant comments to yourself!"

"That's enough, both of you," Bradley snapped.
"Don't we have enough trouble without quarreling
amongst ourselves?" He brushed his gaze across Shad,
then twisted around in his saddle and stared pointedly
at Roman for a long moment. Turning back, he said,
"All right, just what is this 'ritual' you think is so important for us to go through before announcing what
we already know we're going to conclude?"

Now that he was given the go-ahead, Shad suddenly
appeared somewhat apprehensive. His gaze shifting
once more to Belinda, he expelled another breath
before saying, "This is gonna be the hardest part. It's
gonna need some direct involvement from you, Miss
Belinda. I hope you can be brave and trust me in what
I'm about to ask."

After a moment's hesitation, Belinda said, "What is
it? What do you need from me?"

"I need you to walk back out there with me—and

Mr. Bradley should come this time, too—and be present for the rest of the negotiation."

Beside Belinda, Colleen said, "You can't be serious! You can't expect her to do that, Shad!"

From his saddle, Roman blurted, "No way that's going to happen!"

Bradley stared at Shad plaintively. "That's a pretty big thing to ask, Shad. Not me, I don't mean. Of course, I'll go. But the girl—is it really that important?"

"I wouldn't ask if it wasn't. It goes to insultin' Strong Wolf if we don't play it out proper."

"I say it's out of the question," Roman interjected again. "Too bad if we insult the heathen."

"And too bad is exactly what might result if it comes to that," Shad snapped in response. "And if you keep snarlin' behind my back, you're gonna ruin the whole works anyway!"

"Roman, keep quiet," Bradley ordered his son.

Belinda spoke abruptly, her voice, though quiet, cutting cleanly through the more boisterous tones. "Very well. If it's necessary, I . . ." She paused as abruptly as she'd started and turned her head to look over at Mac. "What do you think, Mac? Is it important that I be part of it?"

Caught off guard by the question, Mac was momentarily at a loss for words. But he found some quickly enough, saying, "I have full faith in Shad Hopper, ma'am. If he says it's the right thing, I believe it must be."

Continuing to look at him, Belinda said again, "Very well." Then she added, "But will you go forward with us also? I'd feel better if you did."

"Okay . . . if it don't make for a problem." Mac glanced questioningly at Shad.

"Shouldn't be no harm," Shad said. "Let's get on with it. Leave your gun with the wagon, Mac. You'll have to shuck your gunbelt, too, Boss."

Mac did as instructed. As he climbed down from his seat, he was keenly aware of Roman glaring at him with seething contempt. That didn't bother him—he would have expected nothing less. What did bother him, though, was the look on Colleen's face as she watched him take Belinda's elbow and walk with her away from the wagons. Mac badly wanted to say something to her, to address her forlorn expression, but now was obviously not the time.

Shad and Bradley dismounted as they were joined by Belinda and Mac, and together the four of them proceeded toward where Strong Wolf awaited. As they approached, three of the riders from up on the hill broke away from the others and came galloping down to join those on the flat. Mac guessed the horses they were riding likely were the ones Strong Wolf would be offering in trade.

As they walked, Shad spoke quietly to Belinda. "It is important not to show any fear or act repulsed in any way by him. He'll want to examine you some. There'll be no inappropriate touchin', but he'll likely run his fingers through your hair, maybe check the sturdiness in your arms and shoulders. And he'll probably want to see your teeth. Can you bear up under that? Like I said, it's important you do."

"I understand. I think I'll be all right," Belinda told him.

They reached the point where the lance was thrust in the ground and halted. By then Strong Wolf had also dismounted and stood with his arms folded across his chest, waiting. The three horseman who had come down from the hill had advanced and likewise dismounted, holding their ponies steady and close behind him.

Shad spoke first. As he did, he made gestures toward Bradley, Mac, and Belinda, introducing each of them. Strong Wolf nodded accordingly. Then he spoke. He did not introduce the three braves but rather made several sweeping gestures meant to extol the fine features of the ponies they had ridden up on. When he was done speaking he again folded his arms and resumed his waiting stance.

Shad turned and spoke quickly to Belinda, Mac, and Bradley. "Okay, Boss, those are the three ponies he's offering in trade. It's time for you and me to give 'em a good lookin' over, like we'd really consider makin' the deal if they're up to our standards. In the meantime, Strong Wolf will be takin' his look-see at Miss Belinda. I told him Mac is her brother and will allow no improprieties."

"I'll back that up," Mac said.

"I doubt he'll test you. But if he does, object quick and in a loud, clear voice. But don't make no move toward him," Shad advised.

"Understood."

Shad and Bradley moved around Strong Wolf and went to begin their examination of the ponies.

For the first time, Strong Wolf looked directly at Belinda. He stood without moving and let his eyes travel slowly up and down her body, pausing notably at her breasts and hips. His expression showed nothing. After studying her face for several seconds, he finally stepped closer and reached out to touch her hair. He lifted it gently and let it sift through his fingers. His expression remained unchanged and all the while Belinda stared straight ahead, her own finely chiseled face an emotionless mask.

Slowly, Strong Wolf circled the girl, continuing to look her up and down. When he was again standing in front of her, he reached out with both hands and took her by the shoulders, squeezing them for muscle tone. He did the same with her upper arms. Then he opened his mouth wide, stretching his lips to show his teeth as a signal for her to do the same. After Belinda had complied, Strong Wolf stepped back and again folded his arms. His examination was apparently done. Whatever his conclusion, his expression showed nothing.

Mac felt a tenseness leave his body that he hadn't realized was gripping him. Even though this matter was far from over, he was glad at least this step was complete. Each time Strong Wolf had reached to touch Belinda it had been difficult for Mac to restrain himself from objecting. He couldn't imagine how hard it must have been for Belinda.

As if bidden by these thoughts, a slight commotion back by the wagons and the rest of the outfit caused Mac to glance around briefly. He saw Herbert Forrest, Belinda's father, standing beside Roman. Both men had dismounted from their horses and Roman had his hand on Forrest's chest, holding him back, while the two were having what appeared to be a somewhat heated exchange of words. They were far enough away so that Mac couldn't hear what they were saying, which was a good thing, because it meant they weren't making enough noise to draw undue attention from Strong Wolf or his braves.

Mac was able to guess what was happening. Forrest, from back where he'd been helping tend the remuda, must have seen his daughter advance with Mac and the others to palaver with Strong Wolf. Since there'd been no chance to tell Forrest about the Kiowa leader's dream vision that made Belinda a critical part of the bargaining, he naturally must have been alarmed and came rushing up to find out what was going on. Roman had been there to intercept him, and as Mac watched, Colleen came hurrying over to also help calm things down.

Mac brought his focus back to the matter more directly at hand, not wanting his own distraction to redirect the attention of Strong Wolf or any of the other Kiowas and give them reason to wonder what that other ruckus was about. Luckily, Strong Wolf was still busy enough appraising Belinda's charms—even though he'd completed his official examination—so that he wasn't easily drawn away from that.

The completion of examining the Indian ponies couldn't have been more timely. Done with that, Shad and Bradley came back around to stand with Mac and Belinda, once again facing Strong Wolf.

Wearing a guarded smile, Shad said in a low voice to Mac, "Since all blasted redskins take a heap of pride in not lettin' any feelin's show, I can only guess that Strong Wolf's once-over of Belinda was satisfactory, eh?"

"Didn't seem to have any complaints," Mac answered.

"That's too bad. Because now comes the part where I tell him how honored we are by the fine display of horseflesh he's offerin' and how purely sorry we are for the slain buffalo . . . but, all the same, we ain't in the market for more horses, and our golden woman ain't in the market for a husband." Shad heaved a sigh. "From there, we'll see if all this rigmarole I've put us through was worth it and if I can lay some more on thick enough to shift him around to considerin' another way to make up for that buff."

CHAPTER 24

It didn't take long for Strong Wolf's stone-faced expression to finally crack. It started as soon as Shad went into his spiel, despite its highly respectful tone meant to provide face-saving for the Kiowa leader in front of his men. The careful wording of the rejection didn't seem to make much difference, either. Strong Wolf was mad and he didn't hold back from showing it.

His thick brows knitted together fiercely, his face darkened even more, and his mouth twisted angrily as he hurled a flurry of guttural words directly at Shad. The still-mounted braves looking on grumbled a little among themselves but left it to their leader to be their voice and to determine whatever action would come next.

Shad stood calmly under the barrage of Strong Wolf's heated response. When Strong Wolf finally paused, Shad began speaking again—in the same calm, respectful tone he had used before. As he talked, he made frequent hand gestures. First he held up three fingers, at which Strong Wolf violently shook his head. Then Shad talked some more and pretty soon held up four fingers. Watching, Mac realized that Shad

had now started trying to reach a new agreement by offering heads of cattle in return for the slain buffalo. But Strong Wolf was just as quick and firm to reject the offer of four as he had been three.

After Shad talked some more and then got another rejection when he raised five fingers, he turned momentarily away from the haggling and came back to where Bradley, Mac, and Belinda still stood.

"As you can see," he said to the ranch owner, "he's gonna be stubborn about holdin' out for as many cows as he can get. But at least he's listenin' and appears to be willin' to move on to some kind of deal that don't include the golden woman."

"That's a relief," Bradley replied. "But how many head do you figure the red devil will demand before he's satisfied? You said he was throwing around the figure of a dozen last night. Dang, I'd hate to have to give up that many!"

Shad's mouth stretched into a grimace. "I can appreciate that. But now he's worked up a whole extra notch from last night. He's even madder on account of bein' disappointed for not gettin' what he saw in his dream. Might have an even higher number in mind now."

"That's preposterous! We've got to hold the line at some more reasonable level than that," Bradley insisted.

"I'll dig in my heels, do everything I can," Shad said. "But when I go back to hagglin', it might be a good idea to take Miss Belinda back to her wagon. Better yet, when you get there, ma'am, how about goin' inside out of sight? I figure you bein' where Strong Wolf can see you is just sort of tantalizin' him—

remindin' him what he can't have—and makin' him all the more stubborn about strikin' some other deal."

"I'll happily return to the wagon and do as you say," said Belinda.

"Hold on a minute," spoke up Mac. He tipped his head in the direction of Strong Wolf. "What's going on there, Shad?"

When Shad had retreated to confer with Bradley, one of the mounted braves behind Strong Wolf had stepped forward to likewise confer with his leader. Upon closer examination, this second individual appeared somewhat older than the others in the group. He wore a necklace of various animals' teeth around his neck and his wrists were adorned with bracelets of eagle feathers. As he spoke with Strong Wolf, their heads tilted close together, the man raised his arm and began pointing with a fair amount of vigor in the direction of the medicine wagon. It was this activity that Mac was calling attention to.

After Shad had turned his head to study these goings-on for a minute, he turned back to say, "That older gent appears to be actin' as a sort of shaman to this pack of hotbloods. Calls hisself Spotted Owl. He ain't no full-fledged medicine man but lays claim to havin' it in his blood and is aimin' to be one some day. I heard him doin' some of the talkin' in their camp last night but never got a really good look at him before now. He didn't say much then, but at least he seemed to be the one other voice that Strong Wolf was willin' to do some listenin' to."

"So what's he carrying on about now?" Bradley wanted to know.

"Can't say. Let me go find out," Shad told him. Over his shoulder he added, "Since they seem to have taken some interest in your medicine wagon, Miss Belinda, maybe you should stick around a mite longer after all, in case they got a question you can help me answer."

Shad returned to where Strong Wolf and Spotted Owl stood talking. He joined them, listening as Spotted Owl addressed him now. The would-be medicine man's tone was stern, not exactly friendly, but neither was it as agitated as Strong Wolf's had been. In the course of the conversation, several more gestures were made toward the medicine wagon.

"They're mighty interested in what-all is bein' carried in that brightly painted wagon," Shad reported when he came back to the others. "They can't read none of the words or any of the highfalutin promises, but they sure enough understand the big pictures of the bottles with bubbles comin' out of 'em. They want to know if we got some firewater we'd be willin' to offer as part of our deal?"

"Certainly, we wouldn't be willing to do that!" Bradley protested. "Especially not a concoction we know to be poisoned."

"That's all been dumped out," Belinda was quick to say. "We destroyed all of that back in Torrence. We're carrying no whiskey of any kind now, tainted or otherwise."

"I already told 'em it ain't firewater, that it's medicine. But they're still interested," Shad said. "The thing I'm wonderin' about is what I see advertised there on your wagon. The big push is for your pa's Elite Elixir— that's the stuff with the whiskey in it, right?"

"Yes," Belinda replied.

"But you also advertise something called Tummy

Tonic . . . 'for the pleasure of youngsters and the relief of elders', it says. What's that all about?" Shad wanted to know. "If it's for kids, it doesn't have alcohol of any kind, does it?"

"Why, no," said Belinda. "It's basically an old-fashioned vinegar fizz made with sugar water colored by food dye. My father bottles it with just a touch of soda and vinegar so that, when you shake the bottle, it fizzes. The kids get a kick out of that, and adults with upset stomachs or maybe even a trace of ulcers get relief from the fizziness, because it makes them burp. It promises no long-lasting cure, but it tastes good and is fun to drink."

"Does your pa have any of that on hand?"

"Yes, I think so. I believe there are a few cases in the back of the wagon."

Shad and Bradley exchanged looks.

"Do you really think the Kiowa would go for something like that?" Bradley said.

"Durned if I know. But they're almighty curious about whatever those pictures on the wagon represent, I know that much," Shad stated. "We won't be lyin' to 'em about it. So I say we give 'em a taste and see what they think. It's worth a try."

And so it came to pass that the unlikely combination of five longhorns and three cases of Professor Forrest's Tummy Tonic was what it took to compensate for the slain buffalo and provide Strong Wolf with a face-saving novelty that resulted in him proclaiming the Rafter B outfit could continue on through Kiowa land unhindered. Mac made an initial hurried trip to fetch a half dozen sample bottles of the tonic for Strong Wolf and some of the others to try. To a man, they liked it right off. When Shad showed them how to shake the concoction and make it fizz, they liked it even better. And when the fizziness started causing loud burps to erupt from some of the braves, the accompanying laughter signaled that a deal was all but done.

With the aid of Roman and Professor Forrest himself, two full cases of the tonic along with the balance of the one Mac had taken the sample bottles from were brought from the medicine wagon.

Considering what a hit the Tummy Tonic was—with himself as well as with the rest of his braves, even Spotted Owl—Strong Wolf accepted with only a token show of reluctance.

In short order, the five head of cattle had been culled out from the main herd and the cases of tonic—minus a bottle gripped in the fist of each brave—were loaded onto three of the ponies. Thus satisfied, the Kiowa pointed their ponies and newly acquired cattle west and were soon fading over the crest of a hill.

Watching them go, with Mac and Bradley and the others grouped around him, Shad wagged his head slowly and said, "I'll be damned. That's all I can say . . ."

"I'd like to think," said Professor Forrest, "that my Tummy Tonic has truly settled more than a few upset stomachs in its time. But in my wildest dreams I never envisioned it would help settle a potential Indian skirmish."

"Your wildest dreams?" echoed Belinda. "In *my* wildest dreams—or maybe I should say nightmares—you think I ever envisioned me and my blond hair on a sales block with a dead buffalo and three horses being offered as payment? Come to think of it, I don't know what's worse . . . that, or being replaced in the end by a handful of cows and some cases of Tummy Tonic!"

The men all regarded her uncertainly for a long moment before her lush mouth finally curved into a wry smile and they were able to breathe a little easier again.

"Professor," Bradley said, "I don't know if you're aware of it or not, but you have one remarkably brave daughter. Without her willingness to endure some very tense moments as part of the initial negotiating, this whole thing might have turned out a lot worse—fizzy water or not."

"Yes," said Forrest, "it seems I'm learning more about my daughter every day."

"Well, the main thing is that it all worked out okay," said Belinda. Then, eyeing Shad, she added, "I mean, that is if Strong Wolf can be counted on to keep his word."

Shad nodded. "Oh, I think Strong Wolf's word is good. But that don't mean we should tarry as far as gettin' on through the rest of Kiowa territory. It ain't even noon yet. We've got a lot of day left, we ought to use it coverin' some miles."

"Now you're talking my language," spoke up Bradley. "It's time to remember we've got a cattle drive to push along."

"You do that," said Mac with a sudden grin. "You push them critters through the remainder of the day, and I'll roll my chuckwagon on ahead. Then tell the rest of the crew that when y'all make it to night camp, I'll have some well-earned buffalo steaks waitin' for supper!"

CHAPTER 25

"You and me need to talk, Van Horne. The way we're going about things is making less and less sense. So the only thing I can figure is that there must be something going on that I'm not privy to. I reckon it's time I was."

Caleb Van Horne, once again seated on his folding canvas chair in the shade of a flat-faced rock cliff, released a slow trickle of cigar smoke from the corner of his mouth as he looked up at the man standing before him. When all of the smoke was exhaled, he said, "I don't know what you're talking about, Ranger Malloy. But what I do know is that I'm not used to being talked to in that kind of tone, and I don't like it very much."

Garfield Malloy set his jaw firmly. "I'm trying not to be intentionally disrespectful, and I waited for a time when your men are all busy elsewhere so as not to brace you in front of them." He made a catchall gesture to indicate the other posse members scattered about, watering and picketing their horses and setting up camp on this flat, grassy apron where a pool of spring-fed water lay between some low, ragged rock outcrops. "But enough is enough, and I feel I'm due some answers."

"And I feel," replied Van Horne, "that you appear to be forgetting the arrangement you are here under."

"I haven't forgot. You've made sure to remind me often enough," Malloy said. "I thought it was a strange deal from the start, but I'm not usually the type to question orders."

"Then don't start now. This undertaking has the full backing of Judge Horace Ballantine and your commanding officer. What more do you need to know?"

Malloy frowned. "For starters, it's never been clear to me just what my role is supposed to be if and when we do catch up with the Rafter B outfit. We're a long way from my Texas jurisdiction, and getting farther all the time."

"The reputation of—and respect for—the Texas Rangers organization has grown far beyond just the borders of our state." Van Horne puffed another cloud of cigar smoke. "As a proud Ranger yourself, you ought to know that as well or better than anyone. I was there the day Judge Ballantine explained why you were assigned to accompany me and my group in our pursuit. No, you may not have any *official* jurisdiction where this chase has taken us, but the presence of you and your badge will nevertheless still have an impact—hopefully on Bradley and his bunch, if they're smart, and lacking that then at least with any local law enforcement we may need to involve."

"That made a certain amount of sense when we were passing near Denver or some other larger towns, even back when Cheyenne was fairly close," Malloy allowed. "But out here in the middle of nowhere—

which is pretty much how it's going to be the rest of the way between here and Miles City—there ain't likely to be much in the way of local law that we *can* involve."

"Then it will fall to us to do whatever it takes to settle with that pack of Rafter B thieves ourselves." Van Horne paused to remove the fat cigar from his mouth and then added, his eyes boring directly into the young Ranger for emphasis. "In which case, *your* involvement and subsequent testimony will assuage any concerns that might arise about the legality or harshness of our actions."

"You almost make it sound like you're looking forward to taking some harsh action."

"If that's what it comes to, it's certainly not something I'd have any regrets about," Van Horne said indifferently. "Norris Bradley is a thieving piece of scum in possession of thousands of dollars' worth of my property. I want him caught and punished to the fullest extent."

"'To the fullest extent of the law' is how the rest of that usually goes," Malloy reminded him. "That implies due process and punishment determined after a court trial."

"Due process can mean different things in different places under different circumstances," Van Horne was quick to retort. "Are you telling me you've never gone after a lawbreaker and brought him back over a saddle instead of apprehending him and handing him over to a court?"

"Only times where I had no other choice."

"That's exactly what we're talking about here. What part didn't you understand when I said your presence would have an impact '*if Bradley was smart*' when we catch up with him? If he is, then we round up him and his crew—along with *my* cattle—and turn him over for the kind of due process you seem so worried about. Otherwise," and here Van Horne once again added emphasis to his words, this time by jabbing his cigar in Malloy's direction, "due process turns into whatever it takes to reclaim what's rightfully mine. You'd better be straight on that."

"I am," Malloy said, a hint of bitterness in his voice. "But that brings me to the next thing that's bothering me."

"Now what?" Van Horne groaned in exasperation.

"If we're so hell-bent on catching up with the Rafter B bunch, why aren't we pushing harder to do it?" Malloy wanted to know. "Like I told both you and your man Barlow earlier this afternoon, by my reckoning they can't be more than a day and a half ahead of us. Yet here we are, calling a halt to make night camp with nearly two hours of daylight left. We could gain valuable ground in those two hours. And if we got an early start tomorrow and rode hard, we might even close on them by tomorrow night. What am I missing? What are you holding back for?"

Van Horne didn't answer right away. He shifted his considerable weight in his chair and tapped a length of ash from his cigar. Then he said, "Malloy, I'm not a man given to making apologies. And I'm not making one now. But I will say that I should have included you in a decision I made a while back. You didn't deserve to have been left out, and now your powers of observation are causing suspicion that could have been avoided."

Malloy made no reply but merely stood waiting to hear more.

"We've slowed down," Van Horne explained, "because I'm waiting for some men to catch up with us before we close on the Rafter B bunch."

"What men?"

"Frankly, I don't know their names. When they arrive, you and I will be introduced to them together. They're acquaintances of Chance Barlow, you see. From the Cheyenne area."

"You're talking, but you're not telling me much," said Malloy.

"It was after we interrogated that cook who got fired by Bradley and told us the Rafter B crew and my herd were well on the way to Miles City," Van Horne said. "In other words, up through the middle of nowhere as you put it a few minutes ago—where people tend to be so scarce we aren't likely to be able to solicit help from local lawmen or anybody else. With that in mind, it occurred to me that if the Rafter B bunch decided not to be intimidated by you and your badge and chose to make a fight instead, we weren't particularly well matched."

Malloy cocked an eyebrow. "I don't know how fast his gun hand is, but Barlow has all the markings of a hardcase. And Curly Piece ain't far behind. Don't tell me you keep their like around for stimulating conversation."

"No, of course not. They're hired intimidators to be sure," Van Horne freely admitted. "It's only smart for a man in my position to keep a certain amount of protection close at hand, to dissuade others from trying to crowd in on what I've scratched and clawed so hard to gain. Barlow and Curly fill those roles. Yes, they're decidedly rough around the edges, but they're not wanted by the law, and they're smart enough to keep it that way or they'd be of no value to me."

"But you don't think they're enough to handle Bradley's crew?"

"Not necessarily, no. Not by themselves. There'd be you, too, of course. But the rest of the men I brought along on this so-called posse," Van Horne said, "are just wranglers—men I chose when I had visions of driving the stolen herd back to Texas. They're rugged enough in their own way, but they're not gunfighters."

"Ain't the same true of Bradley's men?"

Van Horne frowned. "Maybe, maybe not. The oldest son, Roman, is known to be something of a hothead and not averse to pulling a gun. And their ramrod, Shad Hopper, is a rough customer with plenty of bark still on him. Plus, you've got to keep in mind, the lot of them have now made themselves outlaws, desperadoes. Desperado—that's another way of saying a desperate man. And when desperate men get cornered, they can be dangerous. That's why, when Barlow and Curly escorted that old cook back to town the other night, I had Barlow send a wire to some hombres he knew to be in the Cheyenne area—men cut from the same cloth as him and Curly—and inform them I'd pay top dollar for a few days of their service."

"Hired guns, in other words," Malloy said distastefully.

Van Horne scowled through another puff of cigar smoke. "That's one way of putting it. In a manner of speaking, aren't you also a hired gun? As long as the gun is put to use for a legal purpose, isn't that all that really matters? And on the subject of guns and gunmen, are you forgetting that little incident the good people from the town of Torrence told us about when we passed through there recently—how a couple of Rafter B riders shot it out with some local trouble-makers? From the descriptions given, it sounded pretty clear to me that one of the Rafter B men was Roman Bradley. But the one who shot the lynch rope was a stranger. Since he could shoot like that, who's to say that Norris Bradley didn't sign on a hired gun?"

Malloy gritted his teeth, liking what he was hearing less and less. "You'll have to excuse me if I hold off judgment on that. All I know right now is that we're dragging our feet, waiting for those gents to show up. How do you know for sure they're even on their way?"

Van Horne's scowl turned into a smug smile. "Because Barlow used my name. For the kind of pay my name represents, you can be sure the sort of men we're talking about are on their way."

"I can't stop what you've gone ahead and set in motion." Malloy's teeth remained on edge. "But you'd better know that I'll do everything in my power to prevent those gunnies from turning unnecessarily trigger happy when the time comes to face Bradley and his bunch."

"You do what you feel you have to, Ranger," Van Horne said icily. "Just remember that I'll settle for nothing less than retrieving my property and seeing to it Bradley and his Rafter B thieves are sufficiently punished. We'll continue closing the gap on them, but I'm not prepared to make our final move until our posse has been reinforced."

CHAPTER 26

"I made up my mind to hate her . . . but in the end wasn't able to. When Father suggested we share the medicine wagon together, I wanted to refuse in the worst way. But with the Indian trouble already in our laps, I couldn't very well add to it by making a scene. It was during the time we ended up spending together that I began to see she's mainly just a down-to-earth girl not too different than me, hardly the flirtatious tart I had myself believing her to be. And then, when Shad asked her to be part of the initial negotiating and she walked out there so bravely and stood face-to-face with Strong Wolf . . . Well, how can you not find that pretty admirable?"

"Yeah, that was a bold move right enough," Mac allowed when Colleen paused.

"And for you, too. Right there in the thick of it once again."

"My part didn't amount to much," Mac down-played. "All I did was stand around until it was time to go fetch some of that fizz water."

"Nevertheless, you were there to do whatever was needed." Colleen frowned briefly before adding, "I have to admit, though, that when Belinda asked you to accompany her, I got jealous again for a moment and I was ready to dislike her—and you, too—all over again. But thankfully, the seriousness of the moment caused me to realize how selfish and petty it was for me to feel that way. I told myself I simply had to accept what was and that I had no right begrudging you and Belinda being attracted to one another. That's what I came over here to tell you, what I wanted you to know."

"Whoa. Back up a minute." Mac frowned in surprise. "Jealousy? Me and Miss Belinda being attracted to one another? Where in blazes is that coming from? You're starting to sound like your brother."

"And why not?" Colleen said indignantly. "We both have eyes to see what's going on, don't we?"

Mac lifted the drop-down table at the rear of the chuckwagon and pushed it up, slamming it into its closed position. "Trouble is," he said over his shoulder as he twisted the tabs that locked the folded-up surface in place, "a person can sometimes see a thing yet still make it out to mean something altogether different than what it really is."

The Rafter B outfit was once again settled into night camp. The buffalo steak supper Mac prepared was well received in spite of the problems that had been experienced as a result of acquiring the fresh meat. With the hearty meal resting in their bellies and the long day that had started out in such a bizarre fashion finally at an end, everybody was more than ready to relax and grab some sleep without the tension of the previous night.

George and Henry, having slept not at all due to shouldering extended nighthawk duty for that period, were already nestled in their bedrolls. Laird and Sparky were out taking the night's early turn with the herd. Everyone else was occupied with personal tasks before getting ready to turn in themselves.

Mac had just finished cleaning up after the meal and storing his various cooking utensils, when Colleen wandered over to make conversation. Mac was happy for her company, largely because he kept remembering the look on her face when he'd accompanied Belinda out to meet with Strong Wolf that morning. He'd been hoping for a chance to talk to her about that. What was more, it had also dawned on him that Colleen seemed to have been avoiding him for some time even before then—ever since he'd admitted that he was prone to taking "second looks" at her. He'd thought at the time she was flattered. Reflecting back, he was left to worry that she might have been made uncomfortable by the admission, instead.

And now, out of the blue, here she was talking about jealousy and some perceived attraction between him and Belinda.

Responding to Mac's counter to her statement, Colleen said, "I suppose it's possible to be confused about certain things. But on the other hand, when something is as plain as the nose on your face, I hardly see any need to waste time trying to deny it."

"It's always worth denying a falsehood," Mac insisted. "And that's what any notion there's something going on between me and Miss Belinda is—false."

"Then why were you and Roman fighting over her?"

Mac scowled. "Is that what he told you?"

"No, he's been as closemouthed as you about any trouble between the two of you. But when both of you came in from nighthawking all bruised and dusty from rolling around on the ground, it was pretty clear what had been going on. Shad's report on what the Kiowa were up to, however, made everybody focus on that instead." Colleen paused, then added, "Later, though, I overheard Shad and Father talking, and I heard Shad say how he'd broken up the fight but before he got you pulled apart he heard enough to know it was over Belinda."

"It was about Belinda—but not *over* her. There's a difference," Mac said. "Plus, that was only part of it."

"You're talking in riddles."

Mac heaved a frustrated sigh. "Look, you know your brother has had a chip on his shoulder where I'm concerned since we first laid eyes on each other. You even warned me about it. I thought it was over, but I was wrong. The thing is, Roman has his eye on Belinda for himself, and he's powerful jealous about anybody else getting in his way. He's warned off all the other fellas, and the other night was his way of warning me."

Colleen gnawed her lower lip. "I have to admit that sounds like something Roman would do."

"Before he got real forceful about warning me off Belinda, he warned me against carrying on with you, too." Mac grimaced and added, "Listen, maybe I shouldn't tell you this, but your brother has a real coarse way of looking at women. And he seems to reckon that every other man sees it the same."

"Back home," Colleen said haltingly, "there were two or three instances where Roman had some trouble with girls. I never knew the exact details, Father worked things out so it was kept kind of hushed, but I found out enough to know that the girls involved all claimed that Roman got too forward when they tried to resist his advances."

"Look, I didn't mean to speak of it," Mac said, regretting the troubled expression he'd caused to be on Colleen's face. "But Roman's real set on going after Belinda. I don't see things getting out of hand, partly because I figure she's the kind of gal who can take pretty good care of herself. Especially with everybody—including her pa and yours—close around like we are. My main concern right now is that me and you are straight on the fact that I got no interest in her other than as a friend."

Colleen gazed up at him, her expression softening. "All right. I believe you . . . but I wonder some about her interest in you. You may be too naïve to see it, but there's no getting past how she asked for you to be by her side when she went to face Strong Wolf."

Mac felt the heat of a blush warming his cheeks. "I don't have an answer for that. When we first spotted those Kiowa up on the ridge the other day, Belinda said she felt safer being close to me. Maybe it's as simple as that. You know, going back to when I helped save her and her pa from that lynch mob in Torrence."

"But Roman was there, too," Colleen pointed out, "and she doesn't seem so reliant on him."

Mac didn't have a response for that, either.

Colleen smiled faintly. "Like I said, I think maybe you're a little naive . . . I hope not too much for your own good."

CHAPTER 27

The crack of a hard slap was loud and unmistakable.

Mac froze in his tracks. The sound had been too clear and too sharp for him to ignore. But where had it come from?

Mac was near the north edge of the camp, making his way toward the fringe of trees just ahead. The central area of the camp lay directly behind him, the chuckwagon off to his left, the medicine wagon on his right.

Turning his head, Mac looked back at the camp. Nobody was stirring. All were motionless lumps in their bedrolls. The fire was burned down to mostly coals, a few stubborn flames licking through now and then. It provided little in the way of illumination, and in the night sky, long fingers of dark clouds reaching in from the west blotted out thickening segments of the stars. Mac's eyes were well enough adjusted to the dark, though, so that he would have spotted any motion. His own reason for having reluctantly left his blankets under the chuckwagon had to do with nature calling too insistently to wait until morning.

So who else was prowling around at this wee hour? And what had brought about the slap?

The answer came, indirectly, from a sudden exchange of unseen yet nearby voices. Harsh whispers straining not to be too loud.

"Blast it, woman, if you ever hit me like that again, I guarantee I'll make you sorry."

"How can you make me any sorrier? I'm sorry every stinking day for what we've become and how we're living! Expecting me to put up with your mauling and manhandling on top of it is too much."

"Too much! I haven't laid a hand on you in days. There are certain obligations a wife has to her husband, in case you've forgotten. And you also seem to have forgotten how you used to not only have no objections but, in fact, were often the one who—"

"Stop it! That was a million years ago. I'm not the girl I was then."

"Girls like you never change, Brenda. Do I have to remind you exactly what kind of girl that is?"

"Shut your dirty mouth!"

"You'd better hold it down or you'll rouse the whole camp."

"Maybe I don't care. Maybe I'd like that. I would, if I thought it would change things."

"What kind of change? You looking to trade me for one of those stupid cowboys who drool all over themselves every time you walk by? Maybe the young cook you seem so enamored of? Or maybe that stud Roman who lusts for you so openly it's pathetic?"

"At least it would be something different."

"If you wanted something different so bad, maybe

you should have gone off with that Indian buck, Strong Wolf. He'd have given you—"

Mac heard the sound of another slap, at least an attempted one. This one didn't land near as solidly. The sounds of a struggle followed quickly, bodies thrashing against each other, the medicine wagon shifting somewhat. Then it stopped and everything went quiet for a moment.

Mac fought the urge to bolt toward the wagon. He would have if he had any business overhearing what he did. The voices from inside were obviously those of the Forrests—Herbert and Belinda, even though he had referred to her as "Brenda."

What else was obvious from the rapid-fire exchange of words was the fact they seemed to be married—not the father-daughter charade they were putting on for everybody. This startling revelation, the duplicity of it, was also what held Mac in place.

What in blazes was going on? And why?

The momentary impulse Mac had felt at first to rush ahead like some kind of cockeyed white knight bent on "saving" Belinda/Brenda from distress, was further quelled by the sounds that now began coming from inside the wagon. Voices lowered, murmuring, then whispering and moaning softly. Not moans of pain or grief, but rather of . . . pleasure. Sounds that clearly meant the two people inside the wagon, the man and wife, were no longer angry or at odds with one another.

Mac suddenly felt highly uncomfortable and . . . dirty. He hadn't meant to sneak about and eavesdrop. The exchange of voices had been so sudden and quick there'd been no chance to withdraw—nor any compunction to, once he realized the unnerving secret being revealed. But he had no decent cause for remaining and listening any further.

His original reason for leaving his bedroll no longer seeming so urgent, Mac turned and went back to the chuckwagon. Wrapping himself in the still-warm blankets underneath was a welcome relief. Also welcome was the fact he was far enough away from the medicine wagon to no longer be able to hear anything coming from inside it. Despite his rule about always grabbing sleep whenever you got the chance, no matter what might be weighing on your mind, Mac got very little restful slumber for the remainder of the night.

By dawn, the air was cold and damp with the threat of imminent rain.

As Mac dished up breakfast to the hungry crew, he warned sourly, "Eat hearty, everybody. By the look of that sky, come noon you might have to settle for rainwater and soggy corn bread."

The rain started falling just as the herd began to move. It didn't come down too heavily at first, just a light, steady drizzle. But as the morning progressed, the drizzle soon became a downpour. A gusting wind whistled in out of the northwest, whipping the rain into slashing sheets that battered and soaked man and beast alike.

But the outfit kept moving. The drovers wrapped themselves in slickers with the collars turned up high and their hats tugged down low so that only narrow slices of faces were left exposed, all the while pushing bawling, complaining cattle who bit and butted one another in their irritation even as they continued plodding on.

Rolling ahead with his mule team and chuck-wagon, Mac felt a gloomy kinship with the change in weather. It suited the unsettled turmoil that continued to turn and twist in his mind. He wished he hadn't overheard the things he had last night. More than that, he wished he could decide what he should do about it.

His own secret was one strictly of self-preservation, hiding and running to escape a terrible injustice done him. Other than maybe someday returning to New Orleans and striking back against those who had wronged him, he sought to do no harm to anyone in the course of his flight.

Yet how could he know that was the case with the Forrests? How could he be sure their act wasn't part of some larger scam, some possibly illegal trickery through which they sought gain?

The rain continued to slam down.

Mac wished it would either flush an answer out of his head . . . or wash away his fretting about it.

It was past noon when he reached the marker Shad had placed for the midday stop. Mac had almost begun to fear that, in the driving rain, he might have missed the indicator stake. But then, when he spotted it, he saw why the scout had extended the distance and the extra time it took to reach it. The spot he chose was in the V of some tall rock spines running at angles that formed an effective wind block. Setting up his chuckwagon tightly within this V wouldn't keep Mac and his gear entirely dry, but at least it would diminish the lashing sheets of rain well enough that he could build a cooking fire and fix a good hot meal for the cold, bedraggled crew soon to arrive.

Using pieces of dry wood and buffalo chips he kept stored in the possum belly—a canvas hammock slung under the wagon for just such situations—Mac got his fire going first. Then, after dropping down the fold-out table and clamping two seven-foot poles to each outside corner, he rolled out a canvas tarp from the rear edge of the wagon canopy's highest point and attached it to the tips of the poles, thus creating an extension of the canopy that provided protection for his meal preparation.

It felt good to be caught up in this work. In a strange way, Mac was even somewhat grateful for the weather conditions that made it more challenging, forcing him to be more focused than he'd otherwise be under standard conditions. It kept him from thinking so much about the Forrests and what might be behind their deception.

When the others showed up, wet and miserable and additionally surly due to the extended time they'd had to wait before coming within sight of the chuckwagon, the planning and work Mac had put into fixing a decent meal in spite of the weather quickly took some of the edge off their attitude.

"I swear, Mac, you're more wizard than cook," declared Norris Bradley, around a mouthful of thick stew and the bite of decidedly un-soggy corn bread he'd crammed in after it. "How you managed a meal this good under these conditions, I'll never know."

"A lot of the credit goes to Shad for finding and marking this spot," Mac explained. "If I'd had to set up out in the open, in that driving rain, believe me, it would have been a different story. I'd've been lucky to even get a fire going for some hot coffee."

"Where is Shad anyway?" asked Colleen, who hunkered close to her father, wrapped in an oversized slicker that flowed down around her like a tent. "I know he's scouting on ahead, but in weather like this you'd think he would swing back long enough to take in a hot meal."

"You know how stubborn and dedicated Shad can be," her father replied. "He's probably getting by on jerky and canteen water until he's covered what he considers a sufficient stretch ahead. I suspect he won't miss supper tonight, though."

"In that case," said Mac, "I hope either this rain lets up by then or he finds another decent spot to mark so I can have a good feed waiting for him. He'll be soaked to the bone and well deserving by then."

After spooning in another gulp of stew, Bradley gave his daughter a sidelong look. "Speaking of being soaked to the bone, I wish you'd accept the Forrests' invitation and go sit inside their wagon for a while so you can do some drying out while you've got the chance."

"This slicker keeps me dry enough," Colleen argued. "Besides, there's not room in there for everybody, and I'm no better than any of the others who've been out in the rain just like me. I don't expect special treatment."

Bradley scowled. "Well, doggone it, maybe I want special treatment *for* you. I *am* the boss around here, you know, and you're my daughter."

Colleen smiled. "Remember that after we make it to Miles City and you get your money from selling the herd. *Then* you can pamper me with all the special treatment you want. You're my witness, Mac."

Mac held up his hands, palms out. "Leave me out

of it. I'm just an innocent bystander caught between my boss and his daughter. I can't win either way."

Further debate on the matter was interrupted by a horseman coming around one end of the rocky spines and trotting into the camp. It was Shad Hopper.

Swinging down out of the saddle, rivulets of rainwater sluicing from his slicker and the brim of his hat, he dragged the palm of one hand down over his face, wiping away the beads of water there, and declared, "Whooee! There better be some coffee left in that pot or I'm gonna be raisin' me a powerful ruckus."

Mac grinned as he reached for the pot and an empty cup. "You can have the rest of this pot and as many more after that as you want. Got plenty more stew, too!"

"Son, you are pure singin' me a hymn. Keep right on, just as long as you pass me that cup and a plateful of what you're singin' about."

After he'd gulped some scalding coffee and spooned down several bites of the stew, Shad said to Bradley, "Well, Boss, I got some good news and some bad news to report. It starts by tellin' you there's a river about five miles ahead. Between here and there is a patch of nice thick grassland where the herd can graze for several days. That's the good news. The bad news is that they're gonna have to be grazin' there for a spell, on account of that river is rippin' and roarin' and there ain't gonna be no gettin' our cattle across until it calms down considerable."

A frown pulled on Bradley's face. "How long you figure it's going to hold us on this side?"

"At a guess, I'd say two, maybe three days." Shad drank more of his coffee. "Way I figure it, this storm we're gettin' down here now started a lot sooner up in the high country to the north. Way it looks, it must have busted up some ice jams still left from winter in a couple channels somewhere up there. So, in addition to the rain that's comin' down, you got a release of backed-up water and even some chunks of ice flowin' into the river. Even if we tried to fight the current, some of those big ice shards would carve and slice our cows' legs to ribbons."

Nobody spoke for several seconds.

Shad mopped more water from his face and said, "When this rain lets up, we can move closer and bed the herd in that grassy patch I spoke of. We can keep an eye on the river from there and be ready to cross as soon as it goes down enough. Meantime, with the wind whippin' and slashin' like it is, I say right here is as good a place as any to hold for a while."

CHAPTER 28

"In a way, I'm actually glad someone found out the truth. And if it had to be, I'm glad that someone was you, Mac." Belinda's tone was plaintive, her averted eyes glistening on the verge of tears. "Now that we've been exposed for living a lie, I realize you owe neither me nor Howard—that's my husband's real name, Howard Faust—any favorable consideration. But I hope you'll try to be a little bit understanding, anyway."

"It might help me understand," Mac said, "if you told me the truth." Even though he fought hard to keep his voice stern, he could feel a faint weakening upon seeing the hint of tears. At the same time, he warned himself to remember that this woman had already proven herself an accomplished actress and a skilled manipulator, especially of men.

The two of them were off on their own again, two or three miles out ahead of the rest of the outfit. The storm had lasted through the rest of the previous day and into the night. The wind finally let up at sunset, and the rain finally stopped sometime after midnight. The outfit had stayed camped within the rocky spines, with the herd bedded nearby, until the break of this new day under a clear sky. Over breakfast, Bradley and Shad had decided they would move the herd to the grassy area Shad had picked out. There they would camp again and wait for the rushing current to subside enough to allow a crossing.

With the water barrels that were lashed to the sides of the wagons replenished by captured rainwater and a prolonged layover in the offing, it was further decided that this would be a good opportunity to do some much-needed laundry. Belinda had volunteered to get a start on this task and for that reason had once more driven her wagon ahead, along with Mac's, to get set up at the new campsite.

Upon arriving at the grassy area and choosing a spot on the perimeter nearest the river, Mac had made up his mind to confront Belinda with what he'd overheard two nights earlier. He had plenty of time to start preparing the noon meal, so he was giving her a hand getting her tub and washboard set up and stringing some lines between the two wagons on which to hang the clothes for drying.

Having not yet told anyone else about what he'd learned, still wrestling in his mind as far as whether or not he even should and who it would be if he did, it had suddenly struck Mac that one possibility might be to start with Belinda and see what she had to say for herself.

Which was where things now stood.

"The truth," Belinda echoed woodenly. "That seems so far away and long ago."

"If you ponder on it, I got a hunch you can recall."

Belinda leaned back against the wagon and folded her arms under her breasts, lifting them and causing them to push hard against the front of her blouse.

Mac couldn't tell if the act was intentional or not, but either way it was mighty hard not to stare.

"The truth starts with the man you know as Herbert Forrest, but back in Chicago where he grew up, he was Howard Faust," Belinda began. "He is a very intelligent, well-educated man. At his parents' urging, he even attended medical school for three semesters. But Herb—that's what I've grown used to calling him now—was too adventurous and high-spirited to live such a conventional, well-planned life. He left medical school and headed west, the Southwest to be exact.

"He traveled through Arizona, New Mexico, some of Texas. Along the way he joined a traveling medicine show. Maybe it was some leftover appeal from his training for the real thing, I don't know. But, ironically, apart from what he was *supposed* to be studying in medical school, he'd learned a range of impressive magic tricks. So that became his act in the show."

Belinda paused to brush back blond hair from the side of her face, then went on, "In time, Herb bought out the original owner of the show and took over the running of it himself. It got quite popular and grew to include acts such as a sharpshooter, a trick rider, and a strongman. In a nowhere little town west of Tucson, I hired on as an assistant to Herb's magic act. I stood around in a skimpy costume, handed him his props, and lay inside a box that he pushed swords through. Before long, we fell in love—or thought we did—and got married. Herb's really not that much older than me. I look young for my age and Herb started getting gray streaks making him look older. Once we were married, Herb talked me into doing an exotic dance act at the close of the late performance in some of the rowdier towns where the law wasn't so strict. It was very popular, always drew big crowds and made us some of our best money . . . but in the end, it's what led to everything falling apart.

"It happened one night in a New Mexico border town. After the show, a liquored-up young cowpoke barged his way backstage and insisted I put on a private show just for him. He wouldn't take no for an answer. He drew a gun and used it to club down Jerome, the strongman for our show, who tried to run him off. Then Herb stepped in and grabbed the man's gun arm. The gun went off and the cowboy took the bullet just an inch under his heart, killing him instantly."

"Sounds to me like a pretty clear-cut case of self-defense," said Mac.

Belinda's mouth twisted wryly. "You'd think, wouldn't you? But the drunken cowboy turned out to be the son of a local big shot, a cattle baron who owned half the town and most of the surrounding countryside. No way he was going to leave it that his son fell victim to a bawdy dancer and a pack of show folks without somebody being punished to the hilt. He hired a fancy lawyer and got all of his son's drunken friends to swear that I had lured the boy backstage after the show, promising him anything he wanted but all the while only setting him up to be rolled by Jerome and my husband for the wad of bills he had on him when he died. It was all a big lie, of course, but all of a sudden, the big shot's son, instead of being a would-be rapist, was a young innocent who'd foolishly fallen for one of the oldest tricks in the book. And rather than us being the victims who'd only acted in self-defense, we were charged with murder."

Belinda stopped abruptly. Toward the end, her words had been coming in an angry rush and her eyes had taken on a fierce glare even though she was gazing off at seemingly nothing.

Mac's expression had turned grim, as well. The exact details of what had just been described to him were different from his own situation yet, at the core, were painfully matched. A trumped-up murder charge by corrupt persons of influence resulting in desperation and ruination for someone of lesser status.

"Was there a trial?" Mac asked.

Belinda shook her head. "No. But it was a foregone conclusion what the outcome would have been. My husband surely would have been sentenced to hang, and Jerome and I . . . prison somewhere, I suppose, who knows for how long." She took a breath then let it out quickly. "But it never came to that, thanks to the others in our show troupe. Bless them. At great risk to themselves, they broke us out of jail the night before the trial was scheduled to start. We all fled, scattering to the four winds. Scattering and never encountering one another since. That was more than two years ago. I'll be eternally grateful for their brave loyalty, and I'll be eternally sad if I never meet up with any of them again."

Neither of them spoke for several seconds, until Mac thumbed back the brim of his hat and said, "That's quite a tale."

Belinda regarded him. "I suppose I couldn't blame you if you didn't believe a word of it."

It was all Mac could do to suppress a bitter smile. He wondered how she would react if he told her that he was probably more prone to believe her because a very similar thing had happened to him.

"The rest of it, the past couple of years," Belinda said with a fatalistic sigh, "have been spent on the run. The sheriff from that border town sent out Wanted posters from the Rio Grande to the Dakotas and who knows how wide to the east and west. And the cattle baron added a fat reward that seems to increase every time we run across one of those dreaded posters. To counter the descriptions given, Herb and I changed our names and altered our look—him growing a beard that came in gray, me changing my hairstyle. It was Herb's idea to adopt the guise of father and daughter, reasoning that any man-woman couple traveling together might draw attention and suspicion due to those Wanted posters. But an older man, a father accompanied by his daughter, would seem more innocent, less likely to do so."

"I'm surprised you'd go right back to running another medicine show. I'd think that would also risk drawing attention from somebody who'd possibly make the connection to that border trouble," Mac said.

"We didn't resort to the medicine show right away, for the very reasons you say," Belinda explained. "But we quickly found out we weren't very good at making a living any other way. And then Herb decided that starting up another show—a vastly different one, just a so-called professor offering products for good health—would be safe exactly because no one would figure anybody in our position would return to something so obvious."

Mac's eyebrows lifted. "Gotta say, that's kind of clever thinking."

Belinda gave a one-shoulder shrug. "Like I said before, my husband is a highly intelligent man. And, admittedly, it's worked out well enough for us, money-wise. We don't draw big crowds like we used to, but neither do we have the overhead or the other troupe members to split with. Until the recent incident in Torrence, we haven't had any trouble."

Mac glanced southward, the direction the rest of the outfit would be showing up from. He didn't want to spend too much more time on this conversation and keep Belinda from having the laundry sufficiently far enough along to avoid triggering another round of suspicion and jealousy from Roman. Or, for that matter, from Colleen.

Now that he had some explanations for the things he'd overheard, he still had to decide what to do about them. He had no particular desire to hold the Forrests, as he continued to think of them, accountable for their duplicity or past deeds. He was willing to let that be the worry of someone else. His main concern, from the beginning, had been to make sure their motives were not aimed at harming the Rolling B outfit.

Mac now felt satisfied the couple posed no threat. Despite constantly reminding himself that Belinda was a skilled manipulator, he tended to believe her tale.

Reading the indecision on his face, Belinda said, "So what now? Are you going to tell the others? Turn us in when we get to Miles City so you can collect that fat reward?"

Mac met her eyes and held them until she averted hers. "I'm not a bounty hunter," he told her. "If what you've told me is true, then you'll continue looking over your shoulder for a long time to come. But you won't have to worry about me."

Belinda's eyes swung back, hopefulness in them now. "You mean you . . . you're going to keep this to yourself?"

"All I cared about after I stumbled on your act—you and your father or husband or whatever he's supposed to be," Mac grated, "was that it wasn't meant to cause trouble for Norris Bradley or any of his crew."

"No! No, never," Belinda insisted. "You helped us, you saved Herb's life. Why would we ever want to make trouble for the Rafter B?"

Mac's eyes bored into hers some more. Then he said, "I'm going to take you at your word and this can end right here, between just you and me. But if I'm wrong, if you make a fool out of me for believing you . . . Then I'll come after you and your husband with a vengeance that will make bounty hunters look like a pack of rosy-cheeked choirboys."

CHAPTER 29

"Are you certain it's them?"

Garfield Malloy tapped the pair of field glasses suspended from around his neck by a leather thong and said, "The herd is bedded down in a grassy flat and I could see the Rafter B brands on their rumps plain as I'm looking at you right now. The outfit is camped only a short way beyond and a swollen, flooded river is just past the camp. None of them are going anywhere until that river eases up considerable."

Caleb Van Horne's fleshy face rose and fell with a nod. "It's a good thing you took a notion to scout ahead this morning, Malloy, else we might have ridden right into them without warning."

"The storm slowed them and then the river stopped them," mused Chance Barlow, sitting his saddle next to Van Horne. "That gives us a real opportunity. We've got them in a box."

"I'm thinking the same thing," said Malloy, even though it went against his grain to be in agreement with the handsome gunman about much of anything.

"A box, perhaps. Trouble is," Van Horne muttered,

frowning, "we are still lacking a sufficient lid to seal the box."

Barlow's thick brows pinched together. "We got us eight men, Boss. Nine, countin' you. We swoop in on 'em real sudden and surprisin'—and them with nowhere to run or scatter—seems to me would give us a pretty good chance of bein' a strong enough lid to seal the deal."

"The element of surprise and having them backed up against that river really works to our advantage," Malloy added.

Van Horne scowled. "Does it? Haven't either of you ever heard how a cornered animal—or a man with his back against the wall—can be the most dangerous kind?" He aimed his scowl directly at Malloy. "How many men did you count in that camp?"

"Nine. And one woman," the Ranger answered. "The medicine wagon we heard about from those folks back in Torrence is there, too. So the pair that goes with the wagon must have continued on with the Rafter B outfit after their trouble in that town. And the woman I saw must be the daughter of the snake oil salesman they came near to lynching."

"Plus we know that Bradley's daughter lit out with 'em when they left Texas," Barlow said. "She'd still be somewhere in the mix, too, so that could mean as few as eight men we'd be goin' up against."

"What about more out working the cattle? Keeping strays gathered in and such?"

"I didn't see any. But I suppose there could have been one or two out on the fringe, involved in something like that I didn't notice," Malloy allowed.

"Still wouldn't be bad odds, not with us havin' surprise and all on our side," Barlow pressed. "Can't count for much out of Bradley, he's an old man. And, accordin' to the way we heard it, the medicine wagon fella didn't manage much of a fight even when they was about to string him up."

"You can't count for much out of me, either. Not when it comes to gunplay," Van Horne said rather stiffly. "And I'll remind both of you—again—that, apart from you two and Curly Pierce, neither are the rest of our men experienced gunhands."

"They're experienced enough to understand what part of a gun is the business end," Barlow countered. "We hit that bunch and mow 'em down before they can blink, wouldn't be no need for a lot of lead swappion'."

Malloy bristled. "Now wait a minute. I won't be part of anything like that. I'm here to help retrieve stolen cattle, apprehend the rustlers responsible, and return them to Texas for trial. If they resort to armed resistance, then naturally I'll respond in kind. But ambushing them without giving them the chance to surrender? No, I refuse to allow that."

"Then what good are you to us?" Barlow snarled. "If you think I'm gonna say please and thank you and not clear leather until somebody is already throwin' lead my way, then you got another think comin', mister!"

"Knock it off!" Van Horne bellowed. He glared at the men on either side of him. Then, as both reacted by clamping their mouths shut, he shot a glance at the other mounted posse members holding their places a few feet behind, as if making sure they saw and understood that, despite the spurt of bickering, he remained the one in charge.

Swinging his gaze back first to Barlow and then Malloy, he said, "This argument is pointless. Because we'll be pursuing neither of your ideas. Not a bloody ambush, not an attempted apprehension. My proposal, which is what we *will* follow, is to take no action at all for the time being. You see, the beauty of having our quarry in a box, as each of you was so eager to point out, is that Bradley and his bunch aren't going anywhere until the river allows them to.

"In the meantime, since that gives us no reason to be in a rush, we will await the reinforcements we know to be on the way. When they arrive—which should be practically any moment—we will then be assured of not only having superior odds but also of having superior firepower. Such a display *should* be enough to encourage Bradley to give in with little or no resistance. If he's too foolish to see that . . . well, then what results will most likely turn bloody, but no one can accuse it of being a merciless ambush."

He paused, his eyes again sweeping back forth between Malloy and Barlow. Neither said anything.

Taking a fresh cigar from under the lapel of his jacket, Van Horne waved it with a flourish. "Very well. Let's pick a spot to pitch camp. I can't wait to get out of this saddle."

CHAPTER 30

Belinda Forrest, aka Brenda Faust, had been whipsawed by extremes of emotion all day long, ever since Mac stunned her with his knowledge of the truth about her and Herb and demanded an explanation.

The crush of uncertainty caused Belinda to do something that may have only made matters worse. On impulse, she had resorted to the one thing she *did* feel certain of, the thing she'd learned at an early age—even before Herb came along to help her refine it—could be used to her advantage in almost any situation. That thing was her feminine wiles—the face and body that few men seemed able to resist.

Mac had scarcely finished issuing his warning against doing anything that would make him regret giving her a break before she gave in to the impulse. Gave in to a notion of how she might attain, if not an actual advantage, at least a portion of control over the way things stood between them.

Placing a hand on his forearm, her fingers tightening, stopping him from turning and walking away, Belinda had said, "Wait, Mac . . . There's more I want you to know."

He said nothing, just looked at her. Waiting for her to go ahead.

"I'm not pleading innocence, not claiming I didn't have my eyes wide open when I got involved with Herb and the way of life he represented," she'd said. "It seemed exciting and even kind of glamorous at first—far better than any options my future appeared to hold before he came along. And for several years, it was. We traveled, lived expensively much of the time, saw things and places I never dreamed I would. Whether I ever truly loved Herb, I can't say for sure. I was young, my head was in a swirl . . . I thought I did."

Belinda had paused to heave a big sigh, doing it with some practiced dramatic flair and making sure her bosom rose and fell enticingly. Then she'd continued, "Eventually, however, that life—even before the murder frame and that whole dreadful business—lost all appeal to me. I wanted to settle down somewhere and live a more normal life. Put down roots, like people say . . . But of course, that held no appeal whatsoever for Herb. That adventurous, high-spirited streak in him was far from being ready to settle down. And probably never will be, I've come to realize. I guess that realization is what brought me to question whether or not I was still in love with the man I'm married to . . . or if I ever had been."

"Did you tell him this?"

Belinda responded with a quick shake of her head, golden hair snapping from side to side. "No, I didn't dare. I was scared to."

"Scared? Why?" Mac had asked, seeming to take a genuine interest, just as she'd hoped he would.

"For one thing, if I were to leave Herb . . . where would I go? What would I do? Choices for getting by—decent ones, that is—are mighty slim for a lone woman on the frontier. And going back home was out of the question. Plus, Herb is extremely possessive and jealous. I didn't know how he might react if I told him I wanted to leave—but I feared it would be quite ugly."

Mac had shifted his feet and looked uncomfortable. "Look, I'm sorry you got yourself in a fix like that. But why tell me about it? What difference can I make?"

That was exactly the response she'd been hoping for! Belinda had squeezed Mac's arm harder and then turned her body fully toward his, pressing herself tight against his shoulder. "You can make all the difference, Mac, if only you're willing! I know, from things Colleen has told me, how you're planning on going to California as soon as the Rafter B herd is delivered in Miles City. You, too, have some kind of past you want to get away from. Oh, I know you've never said as much—that you've been terribly mysterious. Colleen thinks a sweetheart somewhere hurt you deeply. We gals have a way of sensing those kinds of things, don't you know."

When Mac tried to protest, Belinda had forged ahead. "It doesn't matter. You don't have to tell me. I'll never try to get you to say more. But don't you see, Mac, that makes us two of a kind! I want to get away, too. Far away! It's a long way to California, Mac . . . with a lot of lonely nights between Miles City and there. If you took me with you, together we could make those nights a lot less lonely."

She'd wanted to savor the look on his face right then—much like hers, she imagined, when he had confronted her at the start. But it was more important to keep making her case while she had him rocked back on his heels. "I've seen the way you look at me,

Mac. And if you've been paying attention, you must have noticed me noticing. There's a gentleness, a kindness about you. Yet there's also a harder side, the side you displayed when you came to the rescue of Herb and me and again when those Kiowas first appeared up on that ridge. Those are qualities any woman would find attractive. Qualities that I know would get both of us safely to California. Once there—"

That was as far as she'd gotten. It was at that point that Mac had taken her by the shoulders, pushed her back to arm's length, and held her there as he said, "Stop it, Belinda. Don't humiliate yourself any further, you're better than that. I don't know how much of what you just told me is true, but either way, I don't care. I won't allow myself to. If you really want to get away from your husband after we make it to Miles City, I'm sure you'll find a way. But it's not going to be by using me."

And with that, he'd let go of her shoulders, turned, and walked off.

Belinda had stood very still for several minutes, just leaning against the side of her wagon. Rejected. Something she'd had very little experience with, when it came to men. Not that she'd thrown herself at that many, but when she had it had always been eagerly received. The reverse was an empty, bitter feeling. What was worse, not only had she failed to gain the edge she was hoping for, but she likely had given Mac cause to trust her less and therefore be less inclined to keep her secrets.

In the hours that followed, the laundry task she'd volunteered for had given her something else to concentrate on rather than just the fretting that continued to churn inside her. It also gave her a reason to be off alone, away from the others, so that her mood didn't draw unwelcome attention or questions. When Colleen had offered to assist her, Belinda had played the martyr to the hilt, insisting that no, she'd had the easiest go of it for these past several days while Colleen and the rest of the crew had been hard at wrangling. It was only fair that Colleen and the others take the opportunity to relax and rest up a bit and leave Belinda to handle this chore.

After the midday meal, everyone had proceeded to do exactly that. Some napped, some attended to things like saddle mending or gun cleaning and oiling, minor tasks they'd been letting go after long hours in the saddle pushing cattle.

After a while, a card game started up. When Professor Forrest joined in, it wasn't long before he decided to turn it into a display of the various card tricks that had been part of the magic act he'd performed years past in the earlier version of his medicine show. In due time, everyone in camp—including Mac and even Norris Bradley—were gathered around to be awed and mystified.

While this was going on, Belinda continued to work with the laundry. Most of it was dry by now, so she was removing it from the lines and sorting and folding the array of shirts and trousers. She continued to be glad everyone was otherwise occupied and leaving her alone. A collapsible table had been set up, one normally used for sales displays of elixir and tonic when the medicine show was in a town, so its surface provided a place to lay out the stacks of clean clothes.

Belinda had chosen the spot for the table to be on the back side of the tall, enclosed wagon so that she was in its shade. The now-descending sun had grown quite warm during the course of the afternoon. And while working back there kept her out of sight from those out in the center of the camp, she could hear them reacting to the show her "father" was putting on for them. She smiled wryly to herself, knowing how much enjoyment he also would be getting from being the center of attention.

Concentrating on her task, the murmur and sporadic applause drifting from the center of the camp, Belinda had no awareness of anyone else being near until Roman Bradley spoke directly behind her.

"Darn shame to have the prettiest thing in camp hiding back here all alone," he said.

Belinda whirled, catching her breath. When she saw who it was and saw his disarming grin, she quickly relaxed. "My goodness! You gave me a start."

"Sorry, I didn't mean to," Roman said, taking a step closer. "After the hardships you've had to put up with, gettin' dragged along on this cattle drive and all—not to mention that nasty business with those heathen Injuns the other day—the last thing I wanted was to unsettle you anymore."

"No harm done," Belinda replied, smiling. "It's just that I thought everybody was being entertained by my father. I didn't expect anyone to come around paying attention to the camp washerwoman."

"Fella'd have to be loco not to pay attention to you, Miss Belinda," Roman told her.

Belinda pushed blond hair back off her sweat-moist forehead. "That's a very gallant thing to say. Especially the sight I must look at the moment, after wrestling with dirty, dusty range wear most of the day."

"In my eyes, you look just fine. Matter of fact, about as fine as any gal I've ever seen," Roman said earnestly.

"I hope that don't sound too forward, but I been holdin' those words in for a long time without ever havin' no good chance to say 'em before. Now that there's a chance, what with it bein' kinda private-like back here and nobody else stumblin' around close like they usually always are . . . Well, I didn't want to hold off no more."

Belinda regarded him. "I'm glad you didn't, Roman."

Her mind was racing. She was feeling that impulse again. Maybe the rejection by Mac, so fresh and raw in her mind, was spurring her into recklessness. The things she had told Mac about no longer loving Forrest and wanting out of the life he was so enamored of, had all been true. Including being afraid of his jealousy and being equally afraid to strike out on her own, not knowing how she would get by. But now, suddenly, here might be an answer to all of that—an even better answer than attaching herself to an aimless drifter going nowhere except vaguely in the direction of California.

Roman took another step closer. "I'm a fella who don't have much use for slingin' fancy words or whisperin' sweet-sounding things to get a gal's interest. I don't like games. I'm an hombre who, if he sees something he wants, believes in going after it straight on . . . When you say you're glad I didn't hold off comin' back here to have some private time with you, are we speaking the same language?"

Belinda smiled. "My goodness. You do go straight to the point of a matter, don't you?"

Roman was standing mere inches from her now. "Like I said, I ain't much for playin' games. I've been watchin' you for days, watchin' close. But I don't have to tell you that. You've known. An all-over woman like you knows that all men are watching her. They also know that only a few have the guts to step past just the watchin' and make it mean something."

She turned to face him full on. She could feel the heat of his nearness and she could feel something more—a sudden excitement building in her that she hadn't felt for a long time. This was no longer just a calculated response on her part. He was strong and bold and handsome, and in the moment, she was feeling bold and daring, too.

Belinda lifted both hands and placed her palms on his chest. "Yes, Roman," she said. "I've been very aware of you watching me. And I've definitely hoped you would 'step past' just the watching."

Suddenly his arms were around her, strong and demanding, pulling her hard against his body as his mouth covered hers with an urgent hunger. They stood like that for a long time, holding both the embrace and the kiss. How much longer it might have lasted or what would have come next was never answered.

Instead, what did come next was a harsh voice shouting, "What in blazes is going on here? Get your filthy hands off her!"

CHAPTER 31

Belinda and Roman sprang apart as if jerked by invisible wires. Their faces snapped around, eyes darting in the direction of the harsh voice. Their startled gazes locked on Herbert Forrest standing at one end of the medicine wagon, his own face purple with instant rage.

"Herb? Father!" Belinda exclaimed.

"I asked a question—what's the meaning of this?" Forrest moved forward, edging around the corner of the wagon. "You unfaithful slut, how many other men have you thrown yourself at behind my back?"

"Now hold on a minute," Roman said. "You got no call to—"

"You shut up," Forrest cut him off. "I'll deal with you soon enough, but in the meantime, I told you to get away from her!"

The loud exchange of voices had captured the attention of everyone else in camp. Forrest had excused himself from those he'd been entertaining to go fetch a fresh deck of cards from the wagon, something he'd assured all would be just a short break in the action.

But that changed when he happened to take a casual peek behind the wagon to check on how Belinda was doing.

For his part, Mac was over by the chuckwagon when all the hollering broke out. He'd reluctantly left the display of card trickery a few minutes earlier because it was time for him to start making supper preparations. From his vantage point, he was closer than the others to the now enraged Forrest yet was still positioned at an angle that left him unable to see what was taking place behind the wagon. But when Mac heard the startled voices of both Roman and Belinda responding to Forrest's angry demands, he had a gut-clench feeling that he knew what it was.

As Forrest advanced around the end of the medicine wagon, Mac shoved away from his drop-down table and hurried toward him. In his peripheral vision, he saw the others from the middle of the camp starting to flow that way, too, though not with as much urgency.

"You need to take it easy, Professor," Roman said, taking a step to meet Forrest and at the same time placing himself partially in front of Belinda. "It was just a little ol' kiss. How much harm can there be in that?"

"Too much!" Forrest replied sharply. "I know what I saw with my own two eyes. It was a kiss on its way to becoming a whole lot more."

"Father!" Belinda wailed.

"Slut!" Forrest said again, fairly spitting the word as he continued forward.

"Now, blast it, there ain't no call for that." Roman glowered. "What kind of way is that to talk to your own daughter?"

Mac came up beside Forrest. "What's the trouble

here?" He tried to make his tone somewhat light, wanting to break up the tension, not add to it. As he spoke, he got his first good look at Belinda and Roman—the still-flushed cheeks, the body language that bespoke of alarm as well as a trace of guilt. It was more than enough for him to put two and two together and conclude what Forrest had blundered upon.

As far as his attempt to break the tension, it didn't go very far. In almost perfect unison, both Roman and Forrest barked at him, "You stay out of this, Mackenzie!"

"No!" Belinda countered. "Go ahead, Mac. Say something, do something. Don't let this turn ugly over such a minor thing."

"Minor?" Forrest echoed, his voice quaking with anger. "You call throwing yourself into the arms of an uncouth, unwashed cowboy you've only known for a matter of days a minor thing?"

"He saved your life, Father," Belinda reminded him.

"Yes, and right about now he's no doubt regretting it," Forrest sneered. "If he'd let me swing, he probably figures he could have gotten his paws on you all the sooner!"

By now, Bradley and the others were swarming around both ends of the medicine wagon to see what was going on. Bradley himself was crowded up close to Mac and Forrest. "What is all this? What happened?" he demanded.

"Him! Your son," Forrest answered, thrusting out one arm and pointing an accusing finger straight at Roman. "He snuck back here like a thief in the night, back here where he thought no one could see, and was taking liberties with my daughter. If I hadn't happened along when I did, no telling to what extent he might have forced himself on her."

"No, Pa! That ain't the way it was at all," Roman protested. "There was no force involved, I swear."

For a second, Mac was surprised by the way Roman's tone turned so suddenly plaintive, almost pleading. And then Mac remembered what Colleen had told him about Roman's past trouble from being too forceful with women and how the elder Bradley had helped hush it up. The stony, unforgiving stare on the old man's face now was an indication that he, too, was remembering those past incidents. And a quick glance over at Colleen showed that she couldn't help but think the same.

Roman turned to Belinda. "Tell 'em," he urged her. "Tell 'em how it was."

"Quit badgering her," Forrest ordered him. "Haven't you taken enough advantage of her? You, the big cattleman's son, thinking she ought to be so indebted to you over what you did to help me that she'd *have* to give in to you and your filthy lust."

"That's a lie! You've got a dirty, twisted mind," Roman responded, his anger flaring once again. "If you was my age and size, I'd pound those accusations back down your throat."

"There'll be none of that," Bradley warned.

"Am I supposed to just take it?" Roman wailed, turning back to his father. "I didn't do nothing out of line!"

"Oh, sure. You think everyone here is blind to the way you've been acting around my daughter ever since we joined your drive?" Forrest's sneer grew wider and nastier. "Or—since you're daddy's boy to the big he-bull of the outfit—are you counting they'll all conveniently forget that part? Most of them were so busy drooling themselves that maybe they *didn't* notice."

Bradley's eyes turned flinty. "You're out of line, mister. None of my men have acted inappropriately toward your daughter. But she *is* an attractive gal. You can hardly blame them for noticing."

Forrest snorted disdainfully. "Now I see where the younger stud gets it from. You're an old he-bull in more ways than one—is that it, Bradley?"

"Father! You're being ridiculous!" Belinda exclaimed.

"I don't need any advice from a tramp like you," Forrest barked back sharply. "Parading around camp, twitching your hips, making sure your blouse slid off your shoulders every chance you got . . . You've been practically begging for it. I should have reined you in long before this."

Belinda's eyes narrowed and fire flashed from the slits. "I'm a woman grown! I'm not your property—nor any man's—to be 'reined in' like some piece of horseflesh."

"We'll see about that," Forrest said. "Get in the wagon! At least have the decency to hide your face in shame, now that you've stirred up all this trouble. I'll be in to deal with you in due time, after I've finished up here."

"She doesn't have to go anywhere she doesn't want to," Bradley said. "And you won't be *dealing* with her—not the way you make it sound—not later, or any time as long as she's in the presence of me and my outfit."

"That's for sure. I personally guarantee it," Roman said through clenched teeth.

"In the spirit of helping simplify things," Forrest

stated, his gaze locked on Bradley, "you can consider our remaining with your outfit terminated as of this moment." Then, his eyes turning to Belinda, he added, "And you—I told you to get in the wagon! Start getting ready to leave."

Colleen, who had moved around on the opposite end of the medicine wagon, stepped forward to stand beside Belinda. "Apparently you don't hear too good, Professor. I think your daughter made it clear she's not someone or something to be ordered about. And she certainly has no reason to crawl inside that wagon and hide her face in shame."

Forrest rolled his eyes in exasperation and then settled his gaze once again on Bradley. "Don't you have any control over the behavior of this litter of whelps you drag around with you?"

"I'd be real careful how you talk about my 'whelps,' mister—especially my daughter," Bradley advised.

Abruptly, her shoulders sagging, her voice sounding distant, defeated, Belinda said, "This has gone far enough. Too far. There's no use, it's . . . Never mind." She made a dismissive gesture toward the stacks of clean, folded clothes. "You Rafter B people, gather up your belongings from the table please, so we can pack up our own stuff and get ready to go."

For a moment, no one else spoke. Until Roman blurted, "No. No, that ain't right. You don't want to go with him and you know it. The way he talks to you, treats you? What do you think he'll do when he gets you away from us?"

"I'll be all right. You don't have to concern yourself over me," Belinda told him.

Roman's eyes shifted to his father. "We ain't gonna stand by and just let that happen, are we, Pa? You heard the things he said to her, how he threatened to *deal* with her?"

"Roman's right," Colleen joined in. "We can't allow him to haul her off like . . . like a dog!"

Bradley spread his hands under a pained expression. "What do you suggest I do—hold her captive against her will? You heard her say that she'd be all right, that she was ready to go with him."

Colleen swung her eyes to Mac, saying, "Mac. Do something, can't you?"

Before Mac could respond, Forrest wheeled on him with a venomous look. "Ah, yes. Yet another whose gaze—albeit a bit more slyly cast than rambunctious Roman here—has devoured the movements of my daughter as hungrily as the gluttonous cowhands gulp down his pathetic chow. *He's* the one who's going to provide a calming, sensible voice to all of this?"

"Father! Must you insult and take issue with everyone?" Belinda pleaded. "Let's just leave and get this over with."

"No, I won't allow it!" Roman declared, shifting his stance again so that now he stood directly in front of Belinda.

Belinda placed a hand on his shoulder. "Please . . . It's no use."

Roman reached up and put his hand protectively over hers. As soon as he did this, a visible tremor of heightened anger passed through Forrest. "Get your hands off of her! I'm not going to tell you again!"

As he bellowed this, his hand flashed up, reaching behind the silk lapel of his vest, then reappearing a moment later with a short-barreled, nickel-plated revolver gripped in his fist. Extending his arm, he aimed the gun directly at Roman.

Roman kept his hand where it was. His expression turned flat and cold, with no trace of fear. "You cock the hammer of that smoke wagon on me, you crazy old coot," he grated, "I'll kill you where you stand."

"Stop this before somebody *does* get killed!" Colleen demanded.

"She's right, this is getting way out of hand. Put that gun away," declared Bradley. Then, taking a tentative half-step toward Forrest, he held out one hand and added, "Better yet, give it to me."

Wild-eyed, his rage appearing not the least bit abated, Forrest swung his revolver toward the ranch owner. "Take another step, I'll give it to you, all right. I'll give you the part you don't want!"

With Forrest's attention suddenly diverted away from him, Roman—his own anger still on full burn over having had the revolver pointed his way to begin with—didn't hesitate.

Mac saw it in his eyes, saw what was coming, and knew in his gut it would only take this whole thing the rest of the way to disastrous results. He saw and at the same time he knew there wasn't a thing he could do to stop it, even though he tried by shouting, "No! Don't!"

The words didn't have the least effect on Roman's hand dropping, his fingers closing on the grips of his .45, and the big gun rising up out of its holster. As fast and determined as Roman was, however, there was no getting past the fact that Forrest *already* had his gun drawn. Whether Roman's movement in his peripheral vision or Mac's shout alerted him, the professor managed to once again jerk the shiny little revolver around and do it faster than Roman was able to clear leather and set his own sights.

The revolver barked, surprisingly loud, and the bullet it spat tore into Roman's right side. Roman jerked partway around, hissing out a cry of pain, his .45 discharging with a roar that sent a round punching harmlessly into the dirt.

Mac's Smith & Wesson seemed to have leaped into his hand as if by its own volition. He'd been unable to stop Roman from going for his gun, and he hadn't been fast enough to prevent Forrest from taking his shot. But now, as he saw the professor clearly getting ready to fire again at the hunched-over form of Roman, this time there *was* something he could do. Had to do. No other choice.

Since calling out again would have been an even more useless waste of breath than the first time, all that was left was to beat Forrest to triggering another round and killing Roman. The Model 3 bucked in Mac's fist, and the .44 caliber slug exploding from its barrel slammed hard into Forrest, knocking him to the ground and stopping him from getting off a second shot.

CHAPTER 32

"If he hadn't moved, I'd've only got his arm. That's what I was aiming for," Mac said in a tight voice. "But at the last second, he leaned forward—lunged, sort of, as he was getting ready to shoot again. That shifted him right into my line of fire."

Kneeling beside the body of the fallen man, Norris Bradley reported, "Your bullet went into the side of his chest. Deep, might've clipped the heart. At any rate, it killed him. Quick and clean."

"Damn," Mac said under his breath.

His gaze lifted from the man he'd shot and went to Belinda, who remained standing where she'd been when the bullets started flying. Colleen had moved up to stand beside her. Belinda's face was ashen, pinched by shock and anxiety. When she heard the words "killed him," she closed her eyes and lowered her head, bringing her forehead to rest on Colleen's shoulder.

"What about Roman? How is he?"

Bradley's question caused Mac to shift his gaze over to where Roman lay on the ground with his brother Henry and Sparky Whitlock kneeling on either side of him. Without looking around, Henry said, "He'll be okay. Took a deep bullet burn on his side. Gonna be mighty sore for a few days, but it could've been a whole lot worse."

"It hurts like blazes! You were sure right about that much," proclaimed Roman.

Bradley straightened up. He glared down at Forrest. "Darn fool went plumb out of his head. I don't get it. As a father, I can understand being protective of your daughter and all . . . But to pull a gun and start shooting? Over a kiss?"

"That's all it was, Pa," Roman insisted. "And like I said before, wasn't nobody forcin' nobody."

Mac took a deep breath, exhaled through his nostrils. Then he said, "The way Forrest acted didn't come from being a father."

Bradley scowled. "What's that supposed to mean?"

Belinda lifted her face from Colleen's shoulder and gave Mac a pleading look. "You promised."

"I promised nothing," Mac replied with a shake of his head. "I said I'd keep your secret as long as no harm was done. One man's dead, another is wounded. I'd say that pretty much breaks the bargain. And if you hadn't been in such a hurry to fling yourself at Roman—the way I'm guessing you did, same as you tried with me earlier—it wouldn't have come to this."

Now everybody was looking at him. Even Roman, pushing himself up onto one elbow.

"What the devil are you talking about, Mac?" Bradley said, growing more impatient. "What secret? What bargain?"

Mac heaved another sigh. "First things first," he said. "Somebody throw a blanket over Forrest. Henry, Sparky—help Roman to his feet and steer him over to the chuckwagon where there's stuff to treat that wound. While we're doing that, I'll tell you all what I guess I should have spilled to somebody before this."

"Fair enough," allowed Bradley. "I'll take care of covering up the professor. You boys get started on Roman's wound. I'll join you in a minute." He cut his gaze to the two women. "Colleen, I think it might be best if you took Belinda to her wagon and sat with her for a spell. I'll come by directly and we can talk about . . . well, what else needs to be done."

Roman's wound turned out to be exactly as Henry had described, a bullet track through the meaty area above his belt and just below his ribs. Mac cleaned it first with soapy water and then sloshed it with whiskey, which got a louder yelp out of the patient than when he took the initial hit. Some additional whiskey, poured down his throat this time, helped settle Roman down. After the bleeding was stopped, some healing salve was smeared the length of the gash and then several wraps of clean dressing were wound around Roman's middle.

As Mac administered this treatment, he talked. He told all assembled around him—Bradley, Roman, Henry, Sparky, and Laird Nolan—how he had learned the truth about the Forrests actually being husband and wife rather than father and daughter; how he'd wrestled with what to do with the information; how he'd finally confronted Belinda and then agreed to keep their secret as long as they appeared to pose no threat to the Rafter B.

"Obviously," he concluded, "right about now I'm wishing I would have done different. Told somebody. Something. If I had, maybe what happened here this afternoon wouldn't have taken place. If Roman had known Belinda was a married woman . . ."

"Don't beat yourself up over that one," Roman responded. "Ain't nothing I'm necessarily proud of, but I haven't let the fact any gal was wearing a wedding ring stop me in the past when I thought I had a chance with her. I might have been a little more on guard when Belinda all of a sudden seemed so willing . . . but no, I'm afraid it wouldn't have made much difference in the long run." He quickly added, "But that still don't mean I forced anything on her."

"I can vouch for that," Mac said. "She wanted badly to make the break with Forrest. Once I discovered their secret and she'd opened up to me about everything behind it, she was afraid he might think she'd cooperated too easily. She was afraid of him in general and got even more desperate to get away. All me or Roman represented were ways she might accomplish that—provide her a way out and at the same time protection against Forrest's jealousy and any attempts he might make to force her to stay."

He gave a sorrowful shake of his head. "I didn't see that part in time. After her and I talked, she seemed nothing but relieved and grateful that I'd agreed to keep their secret. I was dumb enough to expect she'd wait until they got to Miles City before she tried to figure out another method to get away from the professor."

"Well, she's rid of him now. Permanent-like," said Bradley.

"Yeah, and don't think that don't eat at me," Mac said. "It ain't that I've got any problem with having killed that gun-waving fool. But knowing it played right into Belinda's scheme after all, that's what galls me."

Now it was Bradley who heaved a sigh. "Like Roman said, don't beat yourself up over it. None of it. Flapping your gums about somebody else's business, even if it's not exactly on the up and up, don't come easy to anybody who's on the level themselves. Even if you'd told me—or anybody—what you found out about the Forrests, what would it have changed? We likely wouldn't have cast them off on their own, not under these circumstances. So what happened today still could have happened."

"Especially where I was concerned," grumbled Roman. "I hate to admit it, but if you'd tried to tell me that Belinda was married and I ought to steer clear—coming from you, you think I would have listened? More likely, I would have accused you of trying to trick me out of the way so you could continue making your own play, and I'd've charged after her all the harder."

Mac grinned wryly. "Yeah, you probably would have at that."

Roman's brows pinched together. He looked ready to say something more, but hesitated. He tossed a quick glance to each of the others pulled in close around, then turned his gaze back to Mac.

"Look here. Mackenzie . . . Mac . . . I ain't done nothing but give you a rough way to go ever since you first showed up. Everybody here knows it. Just like they know I can be kind of a miserable jackass all the way around. But you never did a thing, really, to rate the way I treated you. All the rest of the outfit took to you like ducks to water, and that just burned me all the more . . . And now, blast you, you've gone and saved my life."

Roman cleared his throat. "Guess what I'm tryin' to say is—Thank you. Thanks for savin' my hide. And for what it's worth, you can look for me not to be such a no-good skunk from here on out. Leastways, not any more so than I naturally am to everybody."

"In other words," Henry, Roman's brother, said dryly, "don't expect too much of a change, Mac."

Roman grabbed a wadded-up, bloody piece of cloth that had been used to clean his wound and threw it at Henry, who managed to duck. Everybody had a bit of chuckle over the exchange, and it helped momentarily ease the tension still hanging in the air following the shooting.

Until Bradley turned serious again, saying, "Now that we're all caught up on everything, the rest of us need to make some decisions same as Mac was wrestling with. We can't dump the girl and leave her on her own out in the middle of nowhere. So if we take her all the way to Miles City with us, what do we do with her once we get there? Knowing she's a fugitive with Wanted papers on her, I mean."

Roman's eyebrows went up. "Aw, come on now, Pa. You ain't sayin' you think we should turn her over to the law, are you?"

"I ain't saying nothing. I'm asking what the rest of you think. If she's telling the truth about everything she told Mac, there's supposedly a sizable bounty on her."

"*If* she's telling the truth," said Henry. "Even if she is, that was a long time ago and clear down on the border."

"Besides, it was the professor who did the shootin'

down there," pointed out Sparky. "Miss Belinda was just an . . . ah . . . just a complish, or whatever you call it."

"An accomplice," Nolan said.

"Yeah. One of those," Sparky agreed. "Heck, on account of that, they probably don't even want her all that bad. And the reward on her alone might be too puny to bother with."

"Especially since we got plenty of, er, our own fish to fry," said Roman somewhat obscurely.

Bradley looked at Mac. "What do you think?"

"I already made my decision," Mac told him. "Bounty money don't have no appeal to me and something that happened down on the border two or three years ago don't rate as any big concern of mine."

Bradley gave a measured nod. "All right. Sounds like we're in agreement then. We take the girl—Belinda or whatever her name is—as far as Miles City and there we part company. Leave her to her own pursuits." His eyes settled on his oldest son. "No matter how doggone pretty she is, she's proven herself to be a brand of poison that nobody with a lick of sense would tamper with—especially not a second time. Is that clear, Roman?"

"You don't have to tell me, Pa." Roman did his best to look both sincere and innocent. Placing a hand gingerly over the dressing wrapped around his middle, he added, "Even if I was inclined to slip a little, in a moment of weakness you understand, I got me a pretty strong reminder against it right here."

Further discussion was interrupted at that point by the sound of horses approaching at a gallop. All heads turned to look and what they saw was Shad and

George—the two members of the outfit who'd been absent for much of the afternoon—riding up.

Reaching the center of the camp, they reined up sharply. It didn't take but a second for Shad's gaze to fall on the blanket-covered form of Forrest sprawled where he had fallen.

"What've we got here?"

As Bradley and the others peeled away from the chuckwagon and approached the new arrivals, the ranch owner answered, "You're looking at the late Professor Herbert Forrest."

Shad's eyes cut to Roman, shirtless and bandaged around the middle. "What happened to you?"

"Before he turned late, the professor shot me," Roman answered.

"So you kilt him?"

"Not me." Roman jerked a thumb. "Mac took care of that chore, savin' me from a second helping of lead the professor was ready to dish out instead of healing elixir."

Shad slowly scanned all of the men standing before him. Then, turning to George mounted at his side, he said, "Ain't it a fright how we can't leave this rowdy crew for even a couple hours without 'em findin' a whole new raft of mischief to get into?"

George, looking a little unnerved, made no comment.

Turning back to the others, Shad leaned forward, resting one thick forearm down on his pommel. "Here's the thing, though, lads," he announced. "Comes to stirrin' up mischief, me and Georgie here might have outdone the lot of you without half tryin'."

Knowing Shad well enough to sense there was something serious underneath the ramrod's touch of levity, Bradley cocked an eyebrow and said, "What do you mean? Stirred up mischief how?"

"Well, it ain't so much that we stirred it up. Not yet anyway." Shad straightened in his saddle again and cocked his head to one side. "But we sure found a whole passel of it waitin' for us. Little more than a mile off, you see, we spotted the camp of some hombres who look to be just kicked back, kinda relaxed, sort of like they're waitin' for something. I figure they must've been doggin' our trail for a while. I make 'em for a pack of no-good, lowdown rustlers . . . and that means what they're waitin' for is the right time and place to hit our herd."

CHAPTER 33

"Don't make sense no other way," Shad insisted. "Why else would they be stopped and camped so early in the day, hangin' back and not comin' on ahead to announce themselves, let us know there was somebody else in the area? We're stopped on account of the river, they're stopped because we are, and they ain't ready for us to know they're on our tail. To me, that adds up to them meanin' us no good."

"What were you and George doing back that way so's you happened to spot 'em?" Roman asked.

"Hunting," came the answer from George. "We figured as long as we were going to be stopped for another day or two, it'd be a good chance to try and bag some fresh meat for Mac to cook up or maybe even have time to make some antelope jerky out of."

"Antelope are thick through here," Shad added. "Leastways they seemed to be back when I was scoutin' before that storm hit. I spotted all kinds of 'em then. Don't know where they got to, but we sure didn't have no luck findin' any today."

"Well, if that pack of hombres back there are what you think they are, then I'd say your luck was pretty good regardless," said Mac. "Giving us warning they're there gives us a chance to plan for them and not get caught by surprise."

"Agreed," said Roman. "In fact, I'd say it puts us in position to be the ones springin' a surprise."

"I kinda like the sound of that. What do you think, Boss?" Shad directed the question to Bradley.

The ranch owner looked thoughtful. "Mighty tempting notion. How many are in that bunch?"

"We didn't have good enough cover to get in very close." Shad scrunched up his face. "Seven or eight, I'd say. For sure less than ten."

"That's about what I made out, too," George said.

Roman's head bobbed. "Nothing we can't handle. Especially with surprise on our side."

"Just before daybreak would be a good time for that kind of visit," Shad suggested. "Give us enough light to see by and catch them rascals snorin' nice and deep, not expectin' a thing. We could have the drop on 'em before they got the sleep blinked out of their eyes."

Bradley didn't say anything right away. His gaze drifted to the south, the direction the men under discussion were camped. When he brought his eyes back to those gathered around him, he said, "That's the way we'll do it then. If it turns out they have some legitimate reason for being where they are, we'll owe 'em an explanation and an apology for rousting 'em a little roughly. If they're up to what we think they are, we'll owe 'em something else."

Ahead of executing the planned raid on the suspected rustlers' camp, there was plenty for the Rafter B men to do before what little remained of the afternoon faded into dusk. For starters, while Mac returned to the chuckwagon and commenced trying to make up for the interruptions and delays to his supper preparations, Bradley and Roman told Shad and George about the Forrests and how their secret had culminated in the shooting. As they were doing that, Nolan and Sparky picked out a spot on a grassy slope overlooking the river and dug a grave.

Before the meal was served, while there was still some light left, everyone convened at the graveside. Forrest's body, wrapped in clean white linen, was lowered down. Colleen stood close to a quietly sobbing Belinda, one arm slipped around her waist. Bradley spoke briefly and impersonally, a few words about ashes and dust and a soul consigned to the mercy of the Lord. When he asked Belinda if she wanted to say anything, she shook her head mutely.

When everyone else filed back to camp, Nolan and Sparky stayed behind to finish burying the body. Colleen accompanied Belinda once more to her wagon. The men made their way to the stew pot being kept warm on the edge coals of Mac's cooking fire. Not surprisingly, when the fare was dished out, everyone ate more sparingly than usual.

Afterward, while Mac was cleaning up, the others drifted off to their individual pursuits. Darkness had settled in. Everyone was quieter than usual, partly due to the memory of recent violence and death riding fresh on their minds, partly due to the looming possibility of more soon to come when they paid their visit to the camp of suspected rustlers.

"Going in, we'll give them the benefit of the doubt," Bradley had instructed. "But I want you all to try and get some rest between now and then so you're sharp when the time comes. If they're looking for trouble, we won't hesitate to feed 'em lead for breakfast."

Mac was finishing things up for the night when Colleen emerged from the medicine wagon and walked toward him. She looked weary but still strikingly pretty as she passed through the pool of illumination thrown by the central campfire. Mac was glad now that he'd set aside a couple bowls of stew in case the women developed some late signs of hunger.

"You look kinda beat," he said as Colleen reached him.

"Yes, that's how I feel." She brushed some strands of hair back from the side of her face. "If it's not too late, I think it would help if I had something to eat. Neither Belinda nor I were hungry when we came down from the slope, and she still isn't . . . but I could sure use something."

Mac produced a spoon and one of the bowls of left-over stew. "Here. Thought you might get hungry and come around eventually."

"Oh, bless you." After she'd taken a couple of bites, Colleen said, "Kind of ironic, isn't it, to be feeling beat at all after having one of the easiest days we've had since starting on this drive? Only required to bring the cattle a short distance from those spiny rocks to this big patch of graze and then having the rest of the day not needing to do much of anything. Just wait for that stupid river to go down."

Mac grunted. "Would have been nice to keep not needing to do much of anything."

"It all changed so fast and so drastically it seemed unreal." Colleen said, chewing another bite of stew.

"One minute Professor Forrest was amazing us with his card tricks and everybody was in such high spirits—an instant later, he was a madman making accusations against my brother and spouting vicious things to the woman we all thought was his own daughter."

"Not all," Mac said sourly. "I knew better. But because I agreed to hold back what I knew . . ."

"Quit blaming yourself. The deceit and jealousy were festering there long before you were any part of it. They were bound to blow up sooner or later, no matter who else you might have told."

Mac gazed down at her. "As long as *you* don't blame me."

Colleen met his eyes. "Why should I blame you?"

"A little while back, you called me naïve," Mac reminded her. "What else was I being when I put my trust in Belinda? Even after she made a play for me to try and seal the deal. I should have seen then that she was only in it for herself and not capable of honoring any deal if she saw gain in breaking it."

A corner of Colleen's mouth lifted in a faint smile. "And while I was warning you about being too naïve, who was the one who changed her mind and proclaimed Belinda to be just a down-to-earth gal like me and oh-so-brave for facing that nasty old Indian chief? Let's face it, after she won me over, she had everybody in the whole outfit eating out of her hand."

"Right up until Roman tried to take his own personal nibble and almost got killed over it."

"But didn't. Thanks to you."

"Yeah. And I was the one who ended up killing a man. Another one. Kind of a bad habit I seem to have picked up lately. Something else you pointed out not so long ago."

"And something else you ought not blame yourself for, in spite of me and my sometimes overly idealistic remarks. The times you've killed, it's either been in self-defense or for the sake of someone else. Those aren't grounds for blame, especially from yourself."

Mac regarded her for a long moment. Then he said, "You have a way of somehow always making a body feel better."

"That's not a bad thing, is it?"

"Not at all. You're even extending comfort to Belinda at a time when . . . well, when her actions have been what you might call questionable, at best."

Colleen shrugged. "Right at the moment, I figure she's suffering enough. Maybe she no longer had romantic feelings for Forrest, but he'd still been a major part of her life for a long time. And even if she'd wanted to part ways with him, I highly doubt she wanted him dead. Especially not in such a sudden and violent way."

"He brought it on himself."

"I know that. And I'm sure she realizes it, too. What's more, I expect she's feeling her own share of blame and guilt. That's why I said I figure she's suffering enough. Being there for her to lean on a little bit, particularly in this early stage, until some of the shock wears off . . . it seems the least I can do."

"That's an awfully kind outlook," Mac told her. "Just don't *you* get caught being too naïve. Sorry if it sounds cold—but that woman's proven herself to be a manipulator and user."

Colleen smiled. "Thanks for your concern. But I know what I'm dealing with, I assure you." She scraped the last of the stew out of the bowl then held it and the spoon back to Mac. "Especially now that I've been fortified by some more fine Mackenzie chow, I promise not to let myself get used."

"Fair enough," Mac allowed.

"Now you give me a promise in return."

"About what?"

"When you and the others go out in the morning to brace that camp of men you suspect of being rustlers . . . you look out for yourself and my father and brothers and make sure to bring yourselves all back in one piece, you hear?"

Mac cocked an eyebrow. "Gee, thanks for reminding me. Might not have thought of that otherwise. We'll be back just fine. I'll make sure you haven't eaten your last bite of Mackenzie chow."

CHAPTER 34

"You in the tent! Roust yourself on out of there! Come out with your hands empty and in plain sight."

Inside his one-man tent Caleb Van Horne was jarred awake by the harsh demands. His mouth twisted into a grimace, and his eyes opened under an instant scowl. Blinking, he could see a sliver of murky, pre-dawn gray leaking through the slit in the flap covering the tent's entrance. *What the hell?*

"Get a move on!" the voice called again. "And in case you got a notion to try any tricks, you should know that all your men out here have been disarmed and are under our guns."

Van Horne pushed back his blankets, an annoyed growl rumbling deep in his throat.

Chance Barlow called from outside the tent. "You need to do what he says, Boss. They got the drop on us out here. About half a dozen guns, and they mean business."

A handful of seconds later, the tent flap was pushed open and a stooped-over Van Horne emerged. He straightened up, pushed lank strands of thinning hair back off his face, and glared at his surroundings with a highly agitated look on his face.

Before Van Horne could say anything, the man belonging to the voice that had rousted him stepped forward out of the shadows off to one side of the tent and let out a surprised whoop. "Well, I will be damned!" exclaimed Norris Bradley. "Look what we got here, boys!"

"You!" Van Horne croaked, looking somewhat aghast at the sight of Bradley.

The fire in the middle of the camp that had been allowed during the night to burn down to a few weak coals had been freshly stoked and fueled so that it was now crackling and burning steadily brighter, helping to illuminate the feeble light ahead of daybreak. Van Horne swept his eyes desperately away from Bradley and completed his appraisal of the situation he had woken to. In the pulsing golden glow thrown by the heightened flames, he saw a deeply alarming sight. All of his men—the wranglers as well as Barlow, Pierce, and the ranger, Malloy—were lined up, on their knees. Each man held his hands at shoulder height and all were minus their gunbelts. Gathered around them in a loose semicircle were shadowy-faced men holding rifles trained on the kneelers.

Van Horne's gaze came back to Bradley, who was also holding a rifle, this one aimed at the wealthy man's ample gut. "What do you want? Where did you come from?" Van Horne asked in a whispery gasp.

"Where did I *come* from?" Bradley echoed through bared teeth. "You know good and well where I came from, you cheating, conniving son of a she-dog! I came from the Texas ranch—the Rafter B—that you and your pack of corrupt, double-dealing cronies drove me off of!"

"I—I don't know what you're talking about," Van Horne stammered. "I didn't have anything to do with the Rafter B until you defaulted on your tax payments and the ranch became available for purchase. You can't blame me, as a landowner and businessman looking to expand my own interests, for taking advantage of that kind of opportunity. If not me, somebody else surely would have."

"But it *wasn't* nobody else," said Bradley, still through his teeth. "It was you and those other snake-low varmints you've got in your pocket—your bought-and-paid-for judge, the tax assessor he brought in, maybe even the banker for all I know—who swung everything your way and robbed me out of a lifetime's work!"

Van Horne started to show signs of regaining some of his typical bluster. "*I* robbed *you*? You're the one driving a herd of stolen cattle, mister. *My* cattle from the ranch *I* now own! Aren't you overlooking that little detail?"

"I ain't overlooking a thing where you're concerned, you pampered bag of guts." Bradley took a sudden step forward and thrust the muzzle of his Winchester hard into the soft bulge of Van Horne's belly. Van Horne did an awkward hop backward, emitting a whimper of surprise and pain. "On second thought," Bradley grated as he ground the rifle muzzle in deeper, "maybe I did overlook something before we left Texas. Maybe I should have taken time to empty that gut bag. Maybe I should have left the pus that fills your insides smeared all over the land you were so desperate to claim!"

"Pa! Don't get too carried away," called Roman from where he stood holding his own rifle at one end of the semicircle.

When Bradley appeared undecided, Shad Hopper, at the other end of the partial circle, added, "Boy's right, Boss. We already got rustlin' charges hangin' over our heads. Is that egg-suckin' weasel worth gettin' murder added on, too?"

Bradley heaved a sigh and pulled his rifle back some.

Swallowing hard, Van Horne said, "At least somebody in your outfit has a morsel of good sense."

Shad glared at him. "Don't get too cocky, fat man. We did that for him, not you. Put to a vote, be a good chance the majority of hands here would raise in favor of goin' ahead and buryin' your worthless hide in a gully somewhere out yonder."

Van Horne gave no response, merely pressed his flabby lips tightly together.

From the center of the row of kneeling men, however, someone else decided to speak. "Before this gets too far out of hand," said Ranger Garfield Malloy, directing his words toward Bradley, "I have something to say that I believe you'll find worth hearing."

Standing directly behind Malloy, Laird Nolan shifted his right leg and nudged the back of the Ranger's head. "Anybody wants to hear anything out of you, we'll let you know. Otherwise, keep your trap shut!"

Bradley cut his eyes to Malloy and studied the earnest expression on his face closely for several seconds. Then he said, "All right. Speak your piece. Make it quick and to the point."

Malloy nodded. "If you'll allow, I need to reach

into my shirt pocket. I have something there that will help explain."

"Go ahead. Real slow. Reckon I don't have to remind you that you've got seven rifles trained on you, should you try any funny business."

Slowly, Malloy reached into his pocket and withdrew a small, shiny object. When he extended his arm and displayed it in the palm of his hand, it was revealed to be the distinctive star-in-a-circle badge of the Texas Rangers.

"My name's Malloy. Garfield Malloy," he said. "Here are my bona fides. I'm a Texas Ranger from down in Bellow County."

A faint stirring passed through the Rafter B men curved around him.

Bradley, however, didn't appear overly moved. "That's real interesting, Ranger Malloy. Generally speaking, I have a high regard for the Rangers and anybody packing one of those badges. In your case, though, I got me a couple reservations. Big ones. For starters, I ought not have to tell you that you're a long stretch from Texas. That means a long stretch out of your jurisdiction. In the second place, any man traveling in the company of that lowdown cur Caleb Van Horne and hired scum the likes of Barlow and Pierce . . . Well, Ranger star or not, any regard I might have for such a man sinks real low real fast."

"I'm on assignment. I go where I'm ordered," Malloy replied somewhat indignantly.

"Ordered by who?" Bradley demanded. "You telling me your captain sent you all the way up here to Wyoming Territory, maybe into Montana? With authority to do what?"

"It was arranged through Judge Horace Ballantine. I'm to act as a special liaison between this civilian posse led by Mr. Van Horne and the nearest local law officials when we catch up to you and the stolen herd."

"Ballantine!" Bradley spat out the name like it was a bad taste in his mouth. "I should have known. That greedy, underhanded polecat has been in on this whole crooked grab of my ranch from the start."

Malloy squared his shoulders. "Judge Ballantine is a highly respected jurist of many years standing. I hardly think—"

"I don't care what you think," Bradley cut him off. "I just got done telling you what Ballantine *really* is. If you think otherwise, you're either a fool or as corrupt as him. Either way, that makes your opinion or any standing you might have as an officer of his court meaningless to me."

"Do you deny," Malloy pressed stubbornly, "that the herd of cattle you've been pushing all the way up from Texas is stolen property you have no legal right to?"

Bradley's eyes blazed. "Oh, they're stolen property, all right. They became that when your precious Judge Ballantine ruled they belonged to Van Horne after he paid the phony, trumped-up back taxes that Ballantine and his crooked tax assessor rigged against me. All I'm doing is reclaiming what's rightfully mine."

"If there's any truth to that, then it's something you ought to be presenting in a court of law—not going about things this way," Malloy declared.

Bradley laughed in his face.

"It's no use. Don't you see?" wailed Van Horne. "He can't accept doing things the legal way. If he'd paid attention to the law in the first place, he would have kept up his taxes and never fallen so far behind it was hopeless for him to claw back out."

Still wearing a cold, lopsided smile, Bradley said, "That's the first truthful thing I ever heard come out of you, Van Horne. You're right—as far as you and this so-called posse of yours, it is useless. For you, the jig is up.

"Me and my crew slipped back here this morning looking to get the drop on what we thought were some rustlers dogging our herd. In a way, I guess that's what you are. But I'd have more respect if you were the kind we expected—the kind of skunks who at least have the honesty to call themselves outlaws and do their stealing from behind a gun instead of from behind crooked, paid-off officials and slippery paperwork."

"What difference does it make?" Van Horne sneered. "Either way, you're going to fill us full of lead and leave our carcasses out here for the coyotes. Isn't that your intent?"

"Don't put any ideas in his head," growled an anxious-looking Chance Barlow.

"You gun down a Texas Ranger," Malloy intoned, "you won't be able to run far enough or long enough to ever get away. Sooner or later, you'll be hunted down."

Bradley wagged his head slowly back and forth. "That threat might mean something if we were the kind of hombres Van Horne would have you believe. I want you to think about that, Ranger. You're going to have plenty of time to ponder the things you've heard here this morning while you're embarked on the little hike that lies ahead of you."

Van Horne scowled. "What hike? What are you talking about?"

Ignoring him, Bradley jerked his chin in the direction of his men. "Roman, Shad . . . you two keep the Ranger and the rest of those ferocious posse members under your guns. The rest of you men spread out and gather up all their gear—guns, saddles, horses. That stuff will all be leaving with us. Check to make sure none of the men have any weapons hidden on them. Somebody better make a search of Van Horne's tent, too. I doubt he's got the guts to carry a weapon of his own, not when he can pay for somebody to do his gun work just like he pays for everything else . . . but you never know."

As Bradley was reeling off all of this, Van Horne's eyes were steadily bulging larger. Finally, he blurted, "You can't be serious! You're not going to deprive us of all those things and then just . . . just *leave* us here. That's savage, that would be inhuman."

Bradley eyed him coldly. "Nobody's saying you have to stay here. You have the right to strike out in any direction you choose—as long as it's not the way we're going. You ought to be able to find a town or a ranch of some kind in three or four days. That's the little hike I mentioned a minute ago.

"After the recent rain, you shouldn't have any trouble finding water. We'll leave you your pack animal. You better hope whoever picked the supplies it's carrying did a good job so you'll have what you need to sustain yourselves."

Van Horne couldn't control himself. Obscenities spewed out of his mouth.

Bradley's gaze grew even icier as he put a stop to Van Horne's tirade with a jerk of his rifle barrel. "Say another word, I'll strip you and your men of your boots, too. Now get over there with the rest and keep your trap shut!"

CHAPTER 35

It was daylight by the time the Rafter B crew got back to their own camp. Shad lagged behind for a while to make sure Van Horne's outfit got headed off in an opposite direction.

Once in camp, Mac wasted no time starting to work up breakfast. The sequence of preparations he went through came more or less automatically, which was a good thing because a large portion of his mind was occupied with thoughts far removed from putting together a meal.

He'd fallen in with a gang of rustlers.

Down deep, Mac felt he had come to know the folks he'd been traveling with all this time—especially Colleen, Shad, and Norris Bradley—pretty well. Well enough to believe they must see their actions as justifiable, for all the reasons Bradley had laid out to Ranger Malloy.

But right there was the kicker—the presence of Malloy and the explanation he'd given about how his assignment was sanctioned by a high-ranking Texas judge. That effectively trumped Bradley's version of the matter. No matter what shenanigans may have been pulled behind the scenes—and Mac knew all too well how such things could take place when a wealthy, influential man like Van Horne was involved—the current legal standing put Bradley in the wrong and branded him a lawbreaker; a "rustler" of this herd that, by his account, still rightfully belonged to him.

For Mac, none of it boiled down to a moral issue. In that regard, his choice was clear. He knew and liked Bradley, so he believed him and would be willing to side with him. But from a purely practical standpoint, there were other considerations he had to take into account.

If the Rafter B outfit ran seriously afoul of the law before Bradley got the herd sold and Mac headed for California, he'd be hauled in with the others to face rustling charges. In his case, that could turn into something a lot bigger. If some alert law dog somewhere along the line happened to make the connection between him and the widely circulated Wanted posters linking back to those New Orleans murder charges, he could be well on the way to ending up with a hangman's noose around his neck.

The bitter irony of the whole thing wasn't lost on Mac. So many people with so many secrets, all tangled together and spilling every which way like a hill of beans. The Forrests—or Fausts, to be accurate, and now just Belinda/Brenda on her own—anxiously fleeing past deeds and deceptions. Mac himself, haunted and relentlessly pursued by a dark cloud of betrayal and death. And at the heart of the entanglement was a bold act of theft, fueled by self-righteous anger and retaliation.

Mac shook his head in wonderment as he twisted and gouged his fingers into the blob of biscuit dough he was kneading. For the first time since accepting the offer to join the Rafter B outfit, he found himself wishing that instead he had let them chase their own blasted stampede that first night and just kept to himself.

So lost was he in this whirl of thoughts that Mac didn't notice the approach of Norris Bradley until the ranch owner spoke from the other side of the drop-down table.

"Imagine there must be a passel of questions running through your head right about now, Mac."

Mac lifted his face. The man standing across from him had come away from the recent encounter looking distressed and haggard, as if he'd suddenly aged five years. Mac suspected his own expression might carry some similar traits.

"Gotta admit that, yeah, there is," he replied.

Bradley heaved a weary sigh. "It's a devil of a thing we're embarked on here, me and my Rafter B bunch. But to a one, we all entered into it willingly and with full understanding of how things stood . . . only that was never a courtesy extended to you. Or to the Forrests, either, as far as that goes—even if it turned out they had their own secrets they were running from."

Yeah, and they're not the only ones, Mac thought sourly.

"I feel mighty low about holding back on the facts. Especially where you're concerned, Mac." Bradley's gaze was sad and earnest and penetrating. "You pitched in wholeheartedly and became a key member of our crew, right from the get-go . . . and I showed my gratitude by never giving you a hint that joining us put you at risk for being branded an outlaw."

"If the only law to worry about is represented by that bunch we left back yonder," Mac said, "then that part of it don't seem like much of a risk. Likelihood of them regrouping and catching up again before you make Miles City seems mighty slim. I'm guessing your plan, once you sell the herd, is to find some far-off corner of nowhere and start all over again."

"We've made ourselves outlaws, Mac. What makes you think our plan ain't to scatter far and wide and just keep riding the wild side?"

Mac's mouth pulled into a humorless smile, and his head gave two slow shakes, one in each direction. "You ain't no outlaw, Mr. Bradley. No matter the brand that's been slapped on you. Same is true of the men riding for your brand—men who've been with you for years, either by blood or otherwise. What's more, there's Colleen to consider. You'd never steer her toward the wild side, not all the way, not in a million years."

Bradley huffed. "You think you've got me all figured out, eh?"

"Yeah, mostly I do. Now. That don't mean I ain't still sore about getting the brand of a rustler running-ironed onto my hide in the process. The only question that leaves is whether or not it might be burned shallow enough for me to find some way to rub it off."

"You'd be a fool not to set off pronto for finding that out. Nobody—not that dumb sap of a Texas Ranger, not Van Horne or any of the rest of his crew—knows you by name and they only got a murky look at you. You make the break from us now, you'd leave no association to the Rafter B that anybody could ever make stick. No matter what else happens."

Mac took his eyes off Bradley and let his gaze drift over the camp, lingering on the idle activities of the familiar shapes and faces of the men he'd gotten to know and had grown comfortable being around. And over on the edge of the area, somewhere out of sight inside the medicine wagon where she was still comforting Belinda, there was sweet, tender Colleen.

As if from a distance, a rush of recent thoughts and spoken words echoed inside his head: *He'd fallen in with a gang of rustlers* . . .

His eyes returned to Bradley. "Those things you told that Ranger, about how your ranch got sold out from under you through corrupt double-dealings . . . That all true?"

Bradley's eyes were as bright as fresh-forged steel. "Every word."

"Nothing else you could have done? No way to save it?"

"I put thirty years of blood and sweat into that place. My wife and one of my sons are buried on the land. You think I would have pulled up stakes and abandoned all of that if there was any way to avoid it?"

The two men held each other's eyes for several seconds.

Until Mac abruptly shifted his attention back down to his biscuit dough and returned to kneading it. "I'd best get back to working up this breakfast. Might be a good idea for you to step out of the way, Mr. Bradley," he suggested. "If those hungry hounds out there get too impatient for their morning grub, they might trample you."

CHAPTER 36

From where he sat on his canvas folding chair—which that piece of trash Norris Bradley and his gang of thieves thankfully had not deprived him of—Caleb Van Horne squinted sourly up at the eight men standing before him.

At the end of an agonizingly long day spent plodding across expanses of open country under a hot sun boiling in a cloudless sky, Van Horne's entire disposition was sour, to put it mildly, and his appearance did nothing to hide it. His eyes were bloodshot from sun glare, his shoulders slumped, his belly sagged even more than usual. The dust caked on his face was streaked by half-dried sweat tracks running down over his heavy jowls and collected to form blackened deposits in the folds of fat under his chin. Even the hat he normally kept so pristine, his high-crowned, cream-colored Stetson, appeared wilted and dust-smudged where it hung on a corner of the chair's backrest.

Addressing this worn-down apparition, Chance Barlow managed to look equal parts relieved and smug. He stood in the midst of the other five men, new arrivals to the sparse evening camp in the process of being set up to close out this punishing day. The newcomers all bore the unmistakable mark of gunmen. Narrow, suspicious eyes, grim expressions, a poised, never-quite-relaxed way of carrying themselves.

And, of course, the tools of their trade—guns and heavily loaded cartridge belts.

"Here they are, Boss," Barlow crowed proudly. "I told you we could count on 'em showin' up. And, boy, they couldn't have picked a better time, eh?"

"The hell they couldn't," Van Horne growled. "They could have been on hand this morning when that blasted Rafter B bunch jumped us! That not only would have trimmed Norris Bradley's wick once and for all, but it would have saved me the mortifying day I've been forced to endure."

The man standing to Barlow's left, a tall, broad-shouldered hombre with washed-out blue eyes set in a long, strong-featured face, said, "Chance told us about the hard luck you had at the start of the day, Mr. Van Horne. Sorry we wasn't able to catch up with you sooner. But we're here now, and we're ready and able to make up for lost time. You'll find us to be just the ticket for setting things square with those who did you so wrong."

"I want their heads on stakes!" Van Horne said. "I want their guts sliced out and strung from here all the way back to the Panhandle!"

"You call the tune, we'll make 'em dance to it," the tall man replied without emotion.

Smiling broadly, Barlow said, "Let me introduce you to these fellas who are gonna help make whatever you want happen, Boss."

Barlow started with the tall man on his left, whom

he identified as one Zeb Mahoney. Gesturing to each subsequent hombre as he named them off, he presented: Garcia, a moderate-sized Mexican with a scraggly mustache, a set of bandoliers crisscrossed over his chest, and a brace of black-handled Colts riding in holsters tied low on his narrow hips; Selkirk, a transplanted Australian with a precisely cocked gambler hat on his head, intense dark eyes, a cruel slash of a mouth that ruined what otherwise might have been a handsome face, and a matching brace of ivory-handled .38s, one in a holster on his right hip and one in a shoulder holster on his left side; Clay Coburn, a whip-thin individual with lifeless slits for eyes, a fist-sized Adam's apple bobbing in an elongated throat under a weak chin, and a pair of thin-bladed throwing knives worn in an underarm rig on his left side, just above a long-barreled revolver holstered butt-forward for the cross draw; and, finally, Walt Purdy, a massive black man wearing a Union Cavalry kepi and armed with a mare's-leg Winchester in a breakaway holster strapped to his right thigh.

When he was finished, Barlow added, "Take it from me—you ain't gonna find a better bunch for the job you want done."

Before Van Horne could respond, a new voice spoke as Garfield Malloy came striding up and stepped into sight from behind Purdy's considerable bulk. His Texas Ranger star was prominently displayed on his shirtfront.

His gaze traveled down the line of newcomers and then swept over to include Van Horne. Malloy announced, "The job to be done, the one that's always been before us, is to retrieve the stolen herd of cattle and apprehend the rustlers responsible so they can be brought to justice in a court of law. That's the way it still stands—even in spite of this morning's unfortunate incident."

There was a moment of silence. Mahoney's eyes touched on Malloy's face and then his badge and then cut sharply to Barlow. "What is this all about?" he wanted to know.

"Nothing to be concerned over," Barlow was quick to say.

"You think not, eh?" Mahoney focused hard on the Ranger's star again, then asked, "Is that real?"

Barlow's forehead puckered. "Well, uh . . . Yes. Yes, it is."

"But you still think it's nothing for us to be concerned over. Is that what you just said?" Mahoney's eyes were suddenly boring into Barlow as intently as they had regarded Malloy's badge. "In fact, you figure it's something of such little concern that you even failed to mention it in the wire you sent. Speakin' for the boys and myself, I find that to be pretty careless of you, Chance, old pard."

"Here now," Van Horne huffed, injecting himself back into the conversation. "The wording of the wire you received came from me. Mentioning Ranger Malloy's presence seemed of no consequence to the matter at hand. Not from your perspective. Men like you sell your guns for money, isn't that the long and short of it? I'm of the belief that my name is familiar enough to you so that you know you'll be generously paid for the job I want you to do. That being the case, contingencies such as who else may or may not be involved hardly require your sanction."

Mahoney canted his head to one side and regarded

the plump speaker as if he didn't quite know what to make of him.

Off to Mahoney's right, on the other side of Garcia, Clay Coburn leaned out and said, "Did you understand all that he just rattled off, Zeb? He was flingin' so many big words I sorta lost track. I think one or two things in there might've rubbed me the wrong way, but I ain't sure."

Selkirk, the Australian, smirked. "Anyone using words of more than one syllable is likely to cause you to lose track, Coburn."

"Yeah, and that kind of lingo is right up your alley, ain't it, you foreign fancypants." Coburn gave a rude snort. "How about you kiss my hind end? Them ain't fancy words, but I reckon you get my message plain enough. And in case you don't—"

"Knock it off, you two!" Mahoney barked, ending the exchange before it went any further.

"What is this?" Van Horne demanded, rising ponderously from his chair. "Is this what I paid good money for? Based on this behavior, how can I trust you to succeed at what I want done when the men in your ranks seem primed first and foremost for going at each other's throats?"

Mahoney was ready with a sharp response. "You let me worry about the behavior of my men. When the time comes, they'll know whose throats to go after. And as far as money paid, good or otherwise"—here the tall man again canted his head and eyed Van Horne appraisingly—"you bring to mind what I think, under the circumstances, is a fair question for me to ask."

"And what might that be?"

"Considerin' the sorry shape you got left in by the

Rafter B's little surprise raid—no horses, no saddles, no shootin' irons, nothing but whatever rations you got on one pack animal—I can't help but wonder what else they might've picked you clean of?"

Van Horne's reply came only after a long pause. "If you're worried as to whether or not I still have funds to pay you and your companions, you can rest at ease." His tone clearly signaled that his imperious manner remained intact despite his current disheveled appearance. "My wallet and its contents are intact."

Mahoney displayed a pleased smile at that news.

"Furthermore," Van Horne added, "even if he had emptied my wallet, I can assure you that it merely would have required a visit to the nearest town with a bank and a telegraph office before sufficient replacement funds would have been available to me. Sufficient enough to more than satisfy the requirements of you and your men."

"Now this conversation has righted itself and we are definitely on the right track," Mahoney declared, his smile even wider.

"Good. Then I assume the compensation offered in Chance's wire is agreeable?"

"It got us here, didn't it?"

"So now we come down to what you're going to do to earn it."

"I thought you made that clear enough a few minutes back. Heads on stakes, guts strung from here to the Panhandle."

"Now hold on a minute," protested Ranger Malloy. "You certainly didn't take that as a *literal* description of the task to be done here, did you? I already explained what the mission of our posse is. There will be no arbitrary gunning down of Bradley's bunch unless it's a matter of self-defense—and there surely will be no heads on stakes!"

"A minute ago," Mahoney said, directing his words to Van Horne, "you questioned some conflict among my men. With all due respect, I find myself needin' to turn that back on you. Who's layin' out the plans for how we're supposed to go about things now that we're here?"

"Make no mistake. There ain't but one boss in this camp, and that's Mr. Van Horne," stated Barlow.

"Then why do I have to listen to this law dog stick his two cents in every handful of minutes?" Mahoney wanted to know.

"Because I *am* a law dog," Malloy told him. "It may be true that this overall undertaking is under the leadership of Mr. Van Horne. But I still have a responsibility for seeing to it that things are conducted within legal limitations."

"Everybody calm down," Van Horne ordered. "Yes, Ranger Malloy has a role to play in this. But like Chance said, the final decision on anything falls to me." He paused a beat and focused his gaze meaningfully on Malloy. "In the event of a difference in opinion for how we will proceed, our resident lawman and I will settle the matter separately . . . and discreetly."

The two men locked eyes and held while everyone else waited to see how Malloy was going to reply.

Before he could say anything, however, Curly Pierce—unaware he was interrupting a somewhat tense moment—came walking over from where he and the other posse members had the campsite completed and a good-sized fire crackling in its midst. The bottom edge of the sun had by now slipped behind the western horizon. The air was starting to cool, and long shadows stretched out from the copse of trees beside which the camp was laid out.

"We got your tent set up and a pan of hot water ready inside so's you can get washed up, Boss," Pierce announced. "They's a pot of fresh coffee ready, too, and the boys are startin' to fix supper. I reckon these here fellas"—he tipped his head to indicate Mahoney and his men—"will be joinin' us for grub as well?"

"You reckon correctly, Curly," Van Horne answered. "Why don't you show them where they can spread out their gear. Chance, go along and make the necessary introductions. After supper, you, me, and Mr. Mahoney will get together again and firm up plans for how we'll proceed come morning. In the meantime, I'll have some words in private with Ranger Malloy. Then I'll be along to make use of what Curly has prepared in my tent."

Once the others had drifted away, Van Horne wasted no time pinning Malloy with another hard glare. "You are threatening to undermine my authority, mister," he said in a strained voice. "And that I will not stand for. Do I need to remind you—yet again—that your purpose here, your assignment, is to *aid* me? Not fight against me!"

"The only thing I'm fighting against," Malloy said, holding his ground, "is seeing this whole thing turn into a revenge bloodbath with any thought of justice through legal means thrown out the window. And that's the way I see it headed more and more. If I had any doubts before, they've been pretty thoroughly removed by the arrival of Mahoney and the rest of that bunch he rode in with. Every stinking one of them fit descriptions on Wanted posters I've seen scattered all through Texas. If I was within my regular jurisdiction, I'd take the whole lot into custody. Asking me to ride along with them instead goes mighty hard against my grain—no matter your special 'arrangement' with Judge Ballantine or anybody else!"

Van Horne bared his teeth in a thin, humorless smile. "Sounds to me like you're treading on some awfully dangerous ground, Ranger. Not only are you bucking me, but now you're threatening action against Mahoney and his whole crew. Need I remind you that not only do they outnumber you five to one, but in your present condition, you haven't even a single weapon with which to face them? If they got wind of some of the things you just said, I fear it might be extremely difficult to stop *them* from taking some very unpleasant action against *you*."

Malloy's eyes narrowed. "Are you threatening me?"

"I'm merely making some observations, you ideological fool." Van Horne snorted disdainfully. "I don't know what you thought you were getting into when you rode out with me, but it's time—now that your eyes are finally opened—to open your brain, too, and face the facts. Don't you realize how beneficial it can be for you to ingratiate yourself to me? Even Judge Ballantine, with his own power base already established, not to mention that simpering tax assessor, recognized how they could gain by bending matters to align with my best interests.

"When this is over, I can put in a good word to your higher-ups and practically guarantee you accelerated advancement through the ranks. What's more, I have intended all along—and I assumed this was understood, but perhaps I need to make it clear—that you will also be rewarded in a more direct and more personal way. Everyone knows that the earnings of a Ranger are not nearly adequate for the job they perform. In your case, I have in mind a generous bonus to help offset that abysmal miscarriage. You certainly wouldn't consider that a threat, would you?"

"No," Malloy said in a chill tone. "But I might consider it a bribe. And I see one nearly as distasteful as the other."

Van Horne's face reddened. "See here, you. I've about had it with your high-and-mighty tone. You may have forgotten your place, but I haven't. Nor have I forgotten what this is all about and has *always* been about . . . I aim to see Norris Bradley severely punished for trying to turn the tables on me and leave me looking the fool. Nobody does that to me and gets away with it! And I don't need no law or court or any of that nonsense to set the matter straight. All I ever needed from you was cover for the actions I deem necessary when we catch up with Bradley. If you know what's good for you, then you had better get your head right with that and do it quick!"

CHAPTER 37

Malloy watched Zeb Mahoney and his men ride out at first light the next morning. His thoughts were as bitter as the scalding coffee in the tin cup he held, waiting for it to cool before he took a drink.

Although he hadn't been invited to participate in the meeting that took place after supper last night, he'd managed to position himself where he was able to overhear most of the discussion that resulted in the plan Van Horne, Barlow, and Mahoney had settled on. The initial step they came up with, aimed at correcting the plucked-clean condition in which the Rafter B riders had left the original posse members, sounded reasonable enough. One of Mahoney's men—Purdy, the powerful black giant—claimed to have some familiarity with this general area and knew of a couple fair-sized ranches off to the east where replacement horses and saddles could likely be attained, especially with Van Horne's money available to cover asking prices.

There'd been some debate about paying a visit to the Rafter B remuda and getting the needed horses there instead—either reclaiming the ones that had been taken or grabbing suitable substitutes. That notion had been abandoned out of concern for prematurely alerting the Rafter B crew that Van Horne had acquired reinforcements. They'd find out about that development in due time, once all of Van Horne's posse was re-outfitted and ready to ride down on them.

As Barlow pointed out, the longer they let the Rafter B bunch push the cattle, the shorter the distance and easier it would be to complete the drive once the herd was reclaimed. "Those Rafter B fools are welcome to all the hard work," he had said, "then we'll take over with only the effort it takes to pull a few triggers."

"And I know just the spot for the takeover," Mahoney had interjected. "I did some work up Miles City way a couple years back. I recall that about a day's ride south of town, the land turns pretty rugged for a considerable stretch. Lots of rocky hills and ridges. Not the kind of terrain you want to be driving cattle over. But there's a pass through it—a gap, the locals call it. Buffalo Kill Gap. Name comes from the old Indian tribes of the area, Sioux probably, and the way they used it for their big buffalo hunts. Some of the hunters would whoop it up behind a buff herd, get it runnin' into the opening, while other bucks waited up on the cliffs to either side. When the buffs came crowdin' through, they'd cut loose on 'em with arrows and spears—rifles, too, if they had any—and slaughter 'em by the dozens, maybe a hundred or more. Then they'd go to work harvestin' the carcasses so their tribe could stock up months' worth of all the things a buff provided 'em."

"Pretty efficient, it sounds like," Van Horne commented. "But I'm not sure I see the relevance to my stolen cattle herd."

"I do," said Barlow. "Bradley will have to use that same gap to push the herd through that rugged country in order to reach Miles City, right? That means if we got there ahead of 'em, it could be our boys waitin' up on those cliffs. Only when the herd is down in the gap, it won't be cattle they open up on—it'll be the Rafter B wranglers. When they're out of the way, we'll gather up the herd after it passes through the gap and finish off the drive to Miles City."

"With our men positioned right and only six or seven of Bradley's crew to deal with, one or two volleys ought to take care of the whole job," Mahoney summed up bluntly.

There was a moment of silence before Van Horne responded in an excited tone, "I like it. I like it a lot!"

After hearing that, if Malloy had harbored even a sliver of doubt about this whole thing having become nothing but a vigilante mission, a slaughter—which apparently had been in Van Horne's mind right from the start—it was long gone. Just like his lofty notion about being on hand to make sure the rustlers got brought to justice legally.

What was more, the resistance he'd shown and the things he'd said—especially last evening to Van Horne—had very possibly signed his own death warrant. Van Horne likely now considered him not only of no use but maybe even a liability. And if Barlow or Mahoney got wind of him making noise about noticing how several of the new men fit descriptions on Wanted posters, that would seal the deal. They wouldn't hesitate to pump him full of lead and throw his carcass in the nearest gully.

The departure of Mahoney and his men—and their guns—made Malloy believe he'd gotten at least a temporary reprieve from that fate. Otherwise, he reasoned, they would have come for him in the night. It was possible, he supposed, that Van Horne hadn't yet mentioned what had transpired between the two of them. Or it could be a decision had been reached that they'd wait for the return of Mahoney before any action was taken against him.

As he sipped his bitter coffee and pondered on his fix some more, Malloy hit upon another possibility. The more he pondered on it, the more he grew to believe he had a good hunch what could be in store for him. Since those scattered ranches Purdy claimed to know about were quite a ways off and it might require visiting both of them to acquire enough horses, the men who'd ridden out weren't expected back until sometime tomorrow. Meaning those left here in camp would have nothing to do except bide their time until then . . . bide their time and perhaps look for the right opening to make their move on the uncooperative ranger.

That could mean they'd wait for night to fall again— though it wasn't out of the question they might try some trickery sooner. Barlow and Pierce were the ones to watch, of course. Van Horne didn't have the guts, and the five wranglers would most likely be kept out of it. In fact, having them around might be the reason Malloy was still alive. Killing a Texas Ranger, even one a long ways off his range, wasn't something of minor consequence. And having witnesses made it all the more problematic.

But if Barlow or Pierce could lure Malloy away from camp on some pretext . . .

* * *

In the Rafter B camp several miles farther north, restlessness had started to set in. What had, in the beginning, been a welcome reprieve from spending hour after hour, day after day in the saddle, pushing lazy, stubborn longhorns when they didn't want to go toward where they didn't want to get to, was beginning to become borderline boring. Sitting around doing nothing *sounded* good, but in practice, to men used to a steady diet of activity and hard work, it soon had an unnerving quality.

It would have been different if it was the weekend after payday and they were in a town chewing through free time drinking in a saloon or cavorting with soiled doves, maybe blowing their hard-earned wages in an all-night poker game. That would be normal. But out here there were no saloons or soiled doves, and playing poker on a camp blanket for matchstick stakes was hardly high excitement.

And a kind of gnawing anxiety that came from knowing Van Horne's "posse" was somewhere behind them—even though they'd been stripped of their weapons and set on foot miles from anywhere—didn't help, either. Not when you considered they were at least on the move, making a kind of progress no matter if it was backwards, while the Rafter B outfit was stuck just waiting. Waiting for a stupid river to tame itself down . . .

"Well, at least the ice has washed out of it," Shad reported, trying to inject a hopeful tone after returning from his most recent check of the river. "I take that as a good sign. Means all or most of the higher-up water has broken loose and flowed on down."

Bradley, on the receiving end of the report, sighed.

"But you still feel the current is too strong for us to take the herd across?"

"Be an awful big risk, Boss," Shad said with a regretful nod. "If we had twice as many men and without the two wagons, it might be worth considerin'. But the way it is, if we're strung out too thin to contain the cattle and some of 'em start flounderin' and gettin' sucked off by that current . . . well, it could turn ugly mighty fast. And that's still without knowin' how solid the bottom is or havin' crossing boundaries yet marked."

Roman, who had ventured over, along with Mac, to hear the latest on how things stood, said, "How about taking two or three of us fellas back with you and getting at least that much done this afternoon? Way you're saying, it sounds like the river is manageable for a couple good horsemen. We could test the bottom and, if it feels good, go ahead and mark crossing points."

"Be some worth in that, sure," Shad agreed. "I was plannin' on goin' back out again anyway and scopin' things farther downstream. If I could find a spot where the land flattened out some and the river ran a little wider and shallower, and still had a solid bottom, that would be a big help."

"I'd like to tag along for a look-see, if nobody objects," Mac said. "I could get noon grub out of the way a little early and then we could head out right after."

Nobody objected, so it was settled.

"Speaking of grub," said Bradley, "how are our food supplies holding up, Mac? Laying over like this is obviously lengthening the time we figured we needed to be stocked for."

"We're still in pretty good shape," Mac told him.

"Got plenty of flour, beans, and coffee. And I went out yesterday afternoon and picked a mess of greens that I know how to fix with spices and such to make 'em right tasty, so they'll help stretch out a few meals. Meat's the thing we might get a little sparse on—without butchering another of our own cows, that is. But Henry and George are out hunting again now, as a matter of fact. If they have any luck bagging a deer or antelope, even a handful of jackrabbits, that would help and also add some variety."

"Let's hope they have better luck than anybody's had so far," said Roman.

Bradley said somberly, "I'm determined to head out tomorrow and get across that blasted river. So get it set in your minds, and I'll spread the word to the others."

A short while later, with some time to kill before getting started on the noon meal, Mac was by himself over beside the chuckwagon, trimming and washing some of the greens he had picked. The sun was climbing toward its midday peak in the sky, beating down hot on the back of his neck as he bent over the task.

He felt the momentary disruption of a shadow and looked up to see Colleen standing there. She looked fresh and pretty, and the sunlight glistened extra bright on her hair.

"What are you doing with those weeds?" she wanted to know.

"They're not weeds. They're greens that I'm cleaning so I can fix them for supper later on," he explained.

"Are they good to eat?"

"They will be the way I fix 'em."

"What are they anyway? If not weeds, I mean."

Mac grinned. "What are they called, you mean? I have no idea. I just know that if I boil 'em and mix 'em with some bacon grease and the right spices I can make 'em taste decent and they'll help fill folks' bellies. I'm trying to stretch things, you see, to make sure our food supplies last."

"How did you learn to do that? Aren't there some plants that are poisonous to people? If you don't know what these are, how do you know they're safe?"

"Haven't poisoned anybody yet." Mac's grin widened. "Leastways, not all the way to death."

Colleen arched a brow. "Now you're teasing me."

"A little bit maybe. But look at it this way—the Rafter B is a pretty good bunch to do some experimenting on. You all survived Brandenburger's cooking before I came along. I'd call that proof that your constitutions must be mighty strong. So chances of me serving something that would harm anybody after what he put you through I'd say are pretty slim."

"I guess that's one way of looking at it," Colleen said, though not without a trace of skepticism. "But I guess instead of asking so many frivolous questions at this stage, I should have been paying closer attention all along to the way you whip up such good food. Let's face it, if I'm ever going to land me a husband, I ought to know how to cook the poor devil at least one or two dishes he won't want to throw back in my face."

Mac scowled. "Any fella who'd do that wouldn't be worth your time to begin with."

"Still and all, that might be a good place to start."

"There you go again, selling yourself short," Mac responded with a sigh. "You know darn well that, as pretty as you are, there are plenty of hombres who'd consider themselves lucky—and rightfully so—to claim you for a wife, no matter if you couldn't cook a lick."

"Or," Colleen said, turning a bit coy now, "I could solve the whole problem by latching onto a fella who was already good at cooking himself."

"Could happen, I reckon," Mac allowed, dropping his eyes and going back to work on the greens.

"Doggone it, Mac, you know I'm talking about you. Look at me," Colleen insisted.

Mac lifted his face and met her gaze.

"The two of us haven't had the chance to speak of it before now, but I know you learned the truth about our outfit—the real story behind our drive—when you went with the others to confront Caleb Van Horne yesterday. Father told me." Colleen's eyes were peering deeply into his eyes and beyond. "Father also told me that he encouraged you to ride away from being branded an outlaw and a rustler along with the rest of us, but you didn't leave. Why didn't you, Mac?"

He couldn't find the words. He just gave a faint shake of his head.

"I know that we're heading out again tomorrow, across the river and on to Miles City. Father expects to be there in about a week." Colleen's eyes continued to penetrate, to search. "What will you do then, Mac? Is *that* when you'll ride away, set off for California like you've been saying all along? Or can I hang on to the belief that maybe, just maybe, the reason you didn't ride away even after you heard the ugly truth from Van Horne and that Texas Ranger . . . was at least partly because you weren't ready to ride away from me?"

In a husky voice, Mac admitted, "Yes . . . that was part of it."

Some of the intensity left Colleen's eyes, and the caress of a pleased smile touched her lips. "That's all I needed to hear. I won't press for more. That's enough for now."

CHAPTER 38

"Hey, Malloy, you still got those field glasses you've been carryin' slung around your neck? Or did Bradley's bunch make off with 'em?"

From where he sat soaking up some sunshine, Malloy thumbed back the brim of his hat and looked up to find Chance Barlow standing over him.

"Yes, I've still got my binoculars," he replied. "Bradley's men didn't seem to take any interest in them when they searched through my stuff. Why?"

"Because I've got an interest in 'em—and you," said Barlow. "I don't know about anybody else, but I'm getting pretty sick of sowbelly, beans, and hardtack. So, since we're gonna be stuck here for the rest of today and tonight and a chunk of tomorrow, I was thinkin' maybe somebody oughta use the time to go out and try to bag some fresh meat for a change."

"That's a real enterprising idea," Malloy said. "But how do you intend to bag the game for that fresh meat—throw rocks at some critter if you're lucky enough to run across one? And what do my field glasses have to do with it?"

From where he'd been carrying it muzzle down at

his side—in a manner that kept it initially unseen from Malloy's vantage point—Barlow raised a Henry repeating rifle and held it up.

"Reckon this oughta take care of the baggin' part," he declared. "And I figured if you came along with those field glasses, you could help spot something for me to shoot."

Malloy's gut tightened at the sight of the Henry being brandished in his face. He fought to keep his expression from showing anything, but his thoughts instantly flashed to the hunch he had formed earlier about how his resistance to backing Van Horne's increasingly obvious plan for vigilante justice had very likely put him at risk. If he wasn't willing to trade off his badge and provide cover testimony, then he couldn't be trusted not to offer incriminating testimony instead. It was as simple as that. And if that was the conclusion Van Horne had reached, then there was no better way to make sure Malloy didn't say the wrong thing than to eliminate him.

And what better way to do that—and be left with a reasonable explanation for it—than by means of an unfortunate hunting accident?

"And if you're wonderin' where this came from," Barlow added, holding the Henry up even higher, "Mahoney was generous enough to loan it to me before him and his boys took off this mornin'. One of the other fellas left one for Pierce, too—you know, to give us some protection until they return. If they can, Mahoney promised to try and fetch back some permanent replacement guns for all of us. 'Spect it must be especially hard on you goin' unheeled, eh? I mean, you bein' a law dog and all, you must feel practically nekkid without a shootin' iron, right?"

Barlow's eyebrows raised, and at the same time, one corner of his mouth lifted into a crooked grin. *Is he taunting me?* Malloy wondered. *Is he getting some kind of sick pleasure knowing he plans to lead me off somewhere and back-shoot me?*

Maintaining an outward indifference, Malloy said, "Is Pierce coming hunting with us?"

"Naw. He's gonna stay here and look after the camp. Besides, he's got some kind of bunion after all that walkin' yesterday. He's moanin' and carryin' on almost as bad as the boss after our trip on shank's mare."

Nice try, Malloy immediately thought. More likely, Pierce would be following along, keeping close but unseen, to increase the odds that one of them would get him in their sights all the quicker.

"Speaking of the boss," Malloy said, glancing over toward the tent where Van Horne was holed up, "I take it he won't be joining us, either?"

"You kiddin'?" Barlow scoffed. "I ain't sure he even knows which end of a gun the bullet comes out of. If we succeed in bringin' back something, though, you can bet he'll participate then, when it comes time to chow down on it."

"Yeah," Malloy grunted. "I've noticed he crowds pretty close when there are vittles to be had."

"Speakin' of which . . . If we're gonna try to improve what any of us have got to crowd up to in the way of vittles, we oughta get after it." Barlow eyed him impatiently. "You gonna grab those field glasses and join me or not?"

Malloy paused a minute, as if he really had any choice, then said, "Sure. Wouldn't miss it."

* * *

Yesterday's trek, reversing over the earlier route taken by both the cattle herd and themselves, was now on the flatter, less hilly stretches of short-grass prairie. To either side, especially to the west, however, there also lay clusters of higher hills cut by deep, sharp gullies often choked with evergreen growth.

It was toward one such cluster that Malloy and Barlow set out, reasoning they'd have a better chance to find deer or antelope in such terrain at this time of day. With the sun an hour or so from its noon zenith, the animals would more likely be holding to shade and cover, waiting for dusk to go in search of water.

Yes, it was reasonable hunter's logic, Malloy told himself. It was also good logic for getting him off to an even more remote spot, well away from the wranglers back at camp, where he could "accidentally" catch a bullet between the shoulder blades and have it blamed on mistaking him for a deer or some such moving through the trees and underbrush.

As he and Barlow strode along, the Ranger made sure he stayed close to his companion's side and paced himself not to move ahead. In the event Barlow tried to turn the Henry on him, he not only didn't want to make himself an easy target but also meant to stay within reach of grabbing the rifle for himself if he got the chance. The only thing that prevented him from making such an attempt as soon as they were out of sight of the camp was not knowing where Pierce was. Malloy didn't believe for a minute that Van Horne's other private gunman had stayed back in the camp.

But before that could be determined, he and Barlow reached the edge of the broken land they'd been walking toward. The ground straight ahead fell away in a series of deep, crooked gorges and gullies with jagged limestone walls and thick evergreen growth packing the narrow floors like green fog. Up high, to the right, there was more limestone, rising to sharp-peaked ridges lined with rows of stunted, stubborn pine trees.

Pausing to catch his breath, the Henry cradled in the crook of his left arm, Barlow pointed with his right and said, "If there are any deer in there, they'll be down in those gullies amidst the brush."

"Uh-huh," Malloy agreed. Then he added, "You know, I spotted two or three nice plump jackrabbits in some of that higher grass we just passed through. They make good eating, too."

"I know. I saw 'em. Rabbit's okay, but not as good as venison. Not to my taste," Barlow explained. "If I'd've popped at those rabbits, I would have scared away any deer that might be around close. This way, even if we come up empty on the deer, those stupid rabbits will still be hoppin' around back there, and I can always bag some then, as second choice."

"If you say so."

"I do. Now here's the thing. I'm figurin' on makin' my way down into this middle gorge right ahead here. I'll be movin' real slow-like, hopin' to flush something. So if you take those glasses of yours up on that ridge"—Barlow pointed again—"you oughta be able to see anything slinkin' out ahead of me. You'll need to move along slow and easy, too, just like me, but keep out of those scrubby trees so you stay visible. If you spot anything, don't holler out. Just point, I'll be watchin' for you to do that. When I get your signal, me and this Henry will take over from there."

Yeah, I bet you will. You and your Henry will take over all

*right—or maybe it will be Pierce and his rifle, if he happens
to be the one in the best position once I'm exposed up there on
that ridge like a tin can on a fence post.*

But no, he couldn't let it come to that, Malloy told
himself. He made one last desperate sweep with his
eyes, trying to catch some sign of Pierce, whom he remained convinced had to be somewhere not too far
behind them. He saw nothing.

It wasn't enough to stop him from going ahead with
what he had in mind, though. If he waited, Barlow
would quickly grow suspicious and the element of surprise, the only slim chance he had at all, would be
gone. He could only hope that Pierce—wherever he
was—would also be caught by surprise and unable to
react in time to stop his attempt dead in its tracks.

"Well, go ahead. Get started," Barlow urged. "I'll let
you get partway up before I—"

Malloy didn't let him finish. With Barlow standing
to the right of him, the Henry still crooked in his left
elbow, Malloy suddenly swung his right arm in an
upward sweep, knocking the barrel of the Henry high
and then driving it back against the side of Barlow's
head. At the same time, the Ranger twisted his whole
body and reached with his left hand to grasp the rifle
just behind its hammer. Leaning in with all his weight,
he pushed the weapon ahead and barreled as hard
as he could into Barlow.

The gunman was knocked backward and staggered
by the attack. The rifle barrel slammed to the side of
his head didn't hit as squarely as Malloy meant for it
to, instead skidding off and delivering more of a
glancing blow. It was still enough to momentarily stun
Barlow, though, and the follow-up of Malloy throwing
his full body weight into him knocked the gunman off

his feet. Trouble was, he never lost his grip on the Henry, and Malloy, fighting to yank it away from him, was dragged to the ground also.

The two men rolled over a couple of times, thrashing and cursing, their struggles taking them closer to the rocky lip where the ground broke away and spilled down into the brushy gorge. Barlow was bigger and stronger than Malloy. Having failed to gain a better initial advantage, the Ranger knew a prolonged physical battle wasn't likely to end in his favor. Because neither man could risk using his fists for fear of losing their grip on the rifle, both were wildly kicking and pumping their knees in efforts to land a telling strike to stomach or groin.

Desperately, in the midst of this, Malloy found an opening to ram his forehead hard against Barlow's face, aiming to mash his nose in order to clog his breathing and blur his vision with the sting of involuntary tears. The maneuver worked even better than hoped for. The blow landed solidly, causing Barlow to throw his head back with a howl of pain, and at the same time he paused in his kicking—giving Malloy a second opening, this time to drive his knee up into his opponent's crotch.

The double dose of punishment was enough to make Barlow lose his grip on the Henry, and abruptly Malloy was able to roll free of the entanglement with the rifle held in his hands alone. He scrambled to one knee and immediately aimed his newly attained prize at Barlow.

But it was quickly evident that Barlow no longer posed a threat, at least not anytime soon. He lay curled up on the ground, agonized moans coming through the streams of blood pouring out of his nostrils and down over his mouth.

Malloy knew he had little time to savor his accomplishment, however. Not if he was right about Pierce following somewhere close behind.

The thought had barely crossed his mind before the proof of his suspicion reared its ugly head. The crack of a rifle shot reached Malloy's ears and in the same instant the punch of the bullet hit him in the shoulder, just under the outer tip of his left collar bone. The impact spun him a hundred and eighty degrees around, dropping him to both knees. Fiery pain coursed down through his entire body but he fought through it to keep hold of the Henry rifle and to stay upright. *Spin the rest of the way around, shoot back!* his mind screamed. But a second bullet screamed in, preventing even the slightest such attempt. This round tore through the meaty part of his right trapezius muscle, jolting him forward.

Malloy hit the ground facedown. The Henry fell from his hands and went clattering off to one side. A third shot gouged into the ground mere inches from where he'd fallen.

Issuing a roar of pain and rage, knowing he had one slim chance remaining to get out of this alive, Malloy mustered all his strength to push up onto his hands and knees and then shove desperately forward, hurling himself ahead and over the lip of the gorge. Sizable chunks of dirt and gravel, loosened by the recent rains, broke away from the edge under the weight of his lunging body. He went skidding down the slope in a minor landslide of rocks and clumps of dirt and rattling pebbles. Through the clamor, he heard two more shots cutting the air higher above him.

He picked up speed, rolling and flopping, and then began to crash through brush and evergreen growth. Small branches snapped and broke away, their points scraping and gouging into him. He felt the breath being pounded out of him as he continued to tumble uncontrollably and then, suddenly, he reached the narrow, boulder-strewn bottom. All at once the Ranger saw a large, moss-speckled rock rushing toward his face then an instant later something exploded inside his head and the world turned black and silent.

Chapter 39

"Chance, are you okay?"

Groaning, Barlow rolled onto one side. His knees were still drawn up, and he was hugging his stomach down low. Above the mangled nose and mouth, his eyes glared up at Curly Pierce leaning over him. "What do you think? Do I look okay?" he growled. Blood bubbled from his lips when he spoke.

Pierce took a wadded, grimy bandanna from his pants pocket and held it out. "No, I can see he clipped you good. Here, use this to try and stop the bleeding."

Barlow took the bandanna and pressed it gingerly to the lower part of his face. Through the blood and the wad of cloth he said, "That sneaky varmint! I heard shootin'. Did you get him?"

"Yeah, I hit him twice. Knocked him over the edge and down into this deep gorge. Then I came over and poured another half dozen rounds down into the brush he went crashin' through."

"Did you kill him?"

"Well, yeah, I think so. I'm pretty sure I did."

"Van Horne ain't gonna want to hear 'pretty sure'! Did you or didn't you?" Barlow demanded.

Pierce scowled. "I can't say for certain. But I hit him twice, like I said. And look at all the blood spilled here. Even if he was still alive when he went over the edge, he ain't gonna stay that way for very long. Not after that fall and especially not out here in the middle of nowhere with nobody to tend his wounds."

Barlow rolled onto one hip and then, slowly, got his feet under him. Pierce came over and helped him stand up. Barlow took a wobbly step closer to the lip of the gorge and looked down.

"Careful, that edge might not be done crumblin' away," Pierce cautioned.

Barlow glared for a long minute down into the ragged cut in the earth. "If I thought for a minute there was any life left in that star-packer, I'd go down there and throttle it out of him."

."Don't be stupid. In your condition you can hardly stand," Pierce said. "He's dead, I tell you . . . or as good as. Worm food. Not even the crows or buzzards can get at him through all that brush. The grubs and the insects will have his remains all to themselves for a good long spell."

Barlow wiped away some blood and then folded the bandanna, trying to find a part not already soaked. "We really ought to go down and make certain," he mumbled partly to himself.

"You go ahead if you want," Pierce said, frowning. "But it's a waste of time. You're in no shape to try, and I'm already hobbled on account of all that walking we did yesterday. I say it ain't worth riskin' worse injury for an hombre with two slugs in him. He's dead, I tell you, or soon gonna be. More important to get you back to camp and have your nose and mouth tended to proper."

Barlow wiped his mouth again and looked at the thick smear of fresh blood when he pulled the bandanna away. "All right. It's hard to argue when you put it that way." He put a hand low to his abdomen and winced slightly as he turned and stepped back from the gorge. "But when we tell it to Van Horne, we say we saw his dead carcass for certain—you got that?"

"Got it."

"See that you don't forget. Now hand me my rifle and let's get out of here."

Malloy came to in pieces. At least that's how it seemed.

His first awareness was of pain. Throbbing, burning pain.

Memory drifted in. He recalled getting shot, falling. He recalled his face rushing toward a rock.

When he tried to open his eyes, the right one resisted. There was a gummy wetness holding the lid shut. Malloy lifted his eyebrows, worked his jaw. With a series of blinks he got the eye open. Vision through it was blurred until he reached up with one hand and wiped away some of the gumminess. His hand came away smeared with half-congealed blood. When his vision started to clear, he realized the eye itself wasn't damaged. The damage was higher up, above it. Reaching again, Malloy felt the gash on his forehead. The blood there was gummy too, starting to congeal, meaning it didn't seem to still be bleeding.

All this exploration had been done with Malloy's

right hand. When he shifted his body and attempted to push to a sitting position, which meant also using his left hand and arm, the pain in his shoulder on that side knifed through him and caused him to immediately drop back. He lay there, his breath suddenly coming in rapid gasps, the waves of pain continuing to radiate down through his arm and chest.

When his breathing had leveled off and the pain had subsided back to a dull throb, he craned his neck to peer as best he could at the shoulder. He saw the bullet hole, saw the still-oozing blood and the stain spreading down over his shirt. If he meant to make it the rest of the way through this, he thought, he'd have to find a way to get that bleeding stopped or the blood loss would finish him off.

Make it the rest of the way through this . . .

Malloy's mind raced, and for the first time since regaining consciousness, he thought about Barlow and Pierce. He lay very still and listened intently. He'd never seen him for sure, but of course it had to have been Pierce who shot him. Where was he now? And what of Barlow?

The congealed blood indicated he had been lying here for a while. But how long? Gazing up through a narrow opening in the evergreen growth crowded in around him, he could see a slice of the sky and a corner of the sun. The latter hung slightly off-center, so it was roughly an hour past noon. He and Barlow had started out about an hour before noon and had traveled for maybe forty-five minutes before reaching the broken country. It hadn't taken long after that for the shooting to start, which meant he must have been lying down here, unconscious, for close to an hour.

And it also meant that Barlow and Pierce evidently hadn't bothered coming down to make sure of their handiwork, so the cold-blooded snakes had left him either for dead—or for dying. But no, Malloy mentally amended with an icy smile, he shouldn't call them names for that. They'd done him a favor.

Because he *wasn't* going to die in this lonely gorge. He didn't know exactly how, but he was going to endure, find a way to survive and make them—and Van Horne—pay for their greed and corruption and for trying to make him part of it until they decided to kill him off instead!

Fueled by this resolve, the Ranger again attempted to sit up, using only his right arm. With slow, careful, determined movement, he rose to the point where he was able to lift himself and take a seat on the very boulder he had slammed his head against. He sat like that for several minutes, catching his breath, running things through his mind, reaching across with his right hand to hold his left arm snug and steady against his body. It was obvious that any success at surviving would hinge on addressing the shoulder wound. That meant getting the bleeding stopped and then stabilizing the arm to minimize further aggravation to the damage.

Toward that end, Malloy scooped up a handful of dirt and moistened it with spit and blood into a mud pack. He pressed this tightly over the wound. Pulling the bandanna from around his neck, he looped it under his left armpit then up and over the shoulder. With one end of the bandanna clenched between his teeth and the other gripped in the fingers of his right hand, he pulled it tight and formed a knot to keep pressure on the mud pack and hold it in place.

Next, Malloy removed his belt from its trouser loops and then rewrapped it around himself at midrib level with his left arm inside. Cinching the belt tight once more held the arm securely in place to prevent any movement—inadvertent or otherwise—that would aggravate the shoulder wound.

With these steps taken, the Ranger felt ready for the rest of his challenge to stay alive and survive . . .

And deliver justice to the men who had done this.

CHAPTER 40

"If there was any question about taking the herd across this morning, that right there settles it."

The "right there" Norris Bradley referred to with a tilt of his head was a bank of dense black storm clouds rising above the horizon off to the northwest. "Another hard rain—which those clouds sure look like they have in 'em," he added, "could churn up that river all over again and possibly keep us here who knows how long."

"I don't need convincin'," said Shad Hopper, standing next to him.

"Nor me," agreed Roman, standing on the other side of his father.

The three were grouped, each with a cup of coffee in hand, near the chuckwagon where Mac was busy fixing breakfast. The other men scattered around the camp were still in the process of crawling out of bedrolls.

After taking a sip of his coffee, Shad said, "The river oughta be tamed down even more this mornin', and that shallower crossing we found a ways downstream yesterday will also help. I don't think we'll have much trouble at all gettin' to the other side."

"As long as we make it before that storm hits," pointed out Roman. "Don't look like it's movin' in too fast, but you never can tell. If the wind starts whippin' up, it could be on us in no time."

Bradley scowled in the direction of the storm clouds for a handful of seconds. Then, abruptly, he called over his shoulder back toward the chuckwagon, "Whatever you got going there, put a shortcut to it, Mac! Go ahead and finish a batch of biscuits if you're far enough along, but that and some coffee will have to do until we're across the river." Turning back to the middle of the camp, he raised his voice and hollered out to the others, "Shake the dew off your lilies and hop to it, you rascals! Stow the bedrolls and stomp into your boots. We got a herd to move!"

For the next hour there was a flurry of activity that, to the untrained eye, might have at times looked somewhat chaotic. But in fact, it was seven veteran cowhands each knowing and performing—with a hastily gulped cup of coffee and a biscuit—their individual roles when it came to stowing gear, breaking camp, rounding up and saddling a mount, then fanning out to encircle the herd and prepare them for getting on the move again. Colleen put the medicine wagon and her attention to Belinda behind, and once again returned to her remuda duties. Belinda herself, who had for days hardly ventured outside her wagon, also had to pitch in and see to hitching up her own team.

"We'll take the wagons across last," Bradley ordered. "I need you on horseback, Mac, to help contain the herd during the crossing. Afterwards, you and Shad can come back and fetch the wagons—you on yours, him driving the medicine wagon."

"What about Belinda?" Mac asked.

Bradley frowned. "She'll have to stay and wait with her wagon. She can bring it to the crossing point if she wants, then wait there, alone, until somebody comes back for her. I'll explain to her how it has to be."

No sooner was Mac once again mounted on his big paint than they were ready to move out. The sun was climbing brightly in a clear sky to the east, but to the northwest, the bank of mean-looking storm clouds edged steadily closer.

After days of lazy grazing, the cattle weren't exactly eager to get moving again. But some prodding and pistol shots fired over their heads along with a few well-placed cracks of Shad's whip got them in the mood quick enough. Toward the river they headed in a strung-out mass, bawling and complaining but moving along at the pace set by the drovers pushing them. The remuda and Belinda Forrest in her wagon brought up the rear.

Upon reaching the river, they veered to the right and followed the muddy, recently overflowed bank another mile to the wider, shallower spot that Shad, Roman, and Mac had marked yesterday. The current was slower here and the bottom under the muddy water good and solid.

The lead cattle balked briefly when first faced with entering the flow. But they were loosened up and settled into their pace by then, and the mass of other cows crowding up from behind—not to mention the yipping, cussing cowboys urging them on—didn't allow any time for contemplation. They plunged in, and the rest followed with only minor displays of resistance.

When all was said and done, the crossing went well enough to almost be called anticlimactic. Eight hundred head taken over in only about forty minutes, with a loss of just four—weaker specimens who got caught in quirky swirls of current and couldn't fight their way free. A half dozen more would have met the same fate if not for some timely and expert lasso-throwing by Roman and Shad, who pulled them to safety.

Once the last cow and rider had scaled the opposite bank, Bradley called for the men to find somewhere close by where all could hold in place while the remaining parts of the outfit, the wagons, were brought across. A wind out of the northwest was picking up and hastening the approach of the storm clouds. It seemed pretty certain they were in for another drenching by early afternoon.

Sitting his horse just back from the river's edge with Shad, Roman, and Mac again gathered about him, Bradley said, "Sorry to prod you fellas right back into the drink, Shad and Mac, but you'd best not tarry about getting those wagons on over. That doggone storm looks like it's in more and more of a hurry to get to us. And you're going to want to be on this side when it does."

"No need to worry about sending us into the river again," said Mac. "Like you said, that storm is going to be on us in no time, so we're going to stay soaked one way or the other."

Shad made a sour face. "Brrr. Don't remind me. That cold river water bit deep into these old bones, and I was lookin' forward to warmin' 'em in some sunshine for a spell. Fat chance of that now, by the look of things."

"If you want, Shad, I can go over and fetch that medicine wagon," Roman offered. "Give you a chance to soak in at least a little bit of sunshine before—"

Bradley cut him off, stiffening in his saddle and saying, "Hold it a minute. Is that crazy woman starting across on her own?"

The eyes of the other three whipped around, following his gaze, and sure enough, they all saw that Belinda Forrest was whipping her wagon team into motion and urging them into the river. As they watched, the horses plunged in, pulling straight and strong. But the wagon, once fully out on the water, immediately began drifting off course with the current. What was more, the light, top-heavy conveyance began to bob and sway erratically.

"We've got to get some ropes on that rig to keep it upright or she's gonna lose it," Shad barked.

He was already loosening his lasso from the side of his saddle and gigging his horse out into the water. Roman took the exact same action. Mac followed suit, except for pulling free a lasso. He had one on his saddle as well, but was honest enough with himself to admit that his roping skills were too lacking to be of much use. He'd do more good if he was able to reach the wagon team and try to steady them.

By the time the three riders approached the rig, it was starting to founder. The wagon was fast taking on water, twisting in the current and tipping wildly. The added weight and countermovement made it impossible for the horses to continue on a straight course across the river, threatening to drag them sideways.

They were fighting frantically, eyes bugged with terror as they sensed the futility of their efforts.

Shad and Roman rode to the upstream side of the wagon and roped it at the front and rear, then turned their horses to swim hard against the current, trying to both hold the wagon upright and check its drifting-away momentum. While they were doing that, Mac reached the team and grabbed the halter of the up-stream leader, talking to the animal, trying to calm it and coax it to keep pulling, keep fighting even as he swung his paint to also swim against the current and aid in the struggle.

But they weren't even halfway across the channel yet, and the rig had drifted so far downstream from the intended crossing that the river was narrowing and the current was picking up speed and strength. Up on the driver's seat of the wagon, Belinda appeared to have given up all hope. She'd let go of the reins and was just holding on to whatever she could grip in order to try and keep from getting thrown overboard by the swaying and pitching.

Up on the bank, more Rafter B riders had appeared. Henry and George Bradley heeled their mounts out into the water and came swimming hard to be of assistance.

Above the increasing volume of the current, the slap and creak of the wagon, and the anxious shrieks of the pulling team, Shad hollered, "We can't hold it! Start cuttin' those horses loose to try and save 'em! Somebody grab the girl!"

A fraction of a second later, one of the wagon's sub-merged wheels struck an unyielding object thrusting up from the riverbed. There was a loud *craack!* of splintering wood, and the wagon gave a fierce lurch.

Belinda was upended from her seat and thrown into the water on the downstream side of the wagon. She managed a short, terrified squeal before going under.

Mac didn't hesitate. With Henry and George arriving to start cutting loose the horse team, he launched from the saddle of his paint, clambered across the backs of the pullers, then dove off on the other side to go after the girl.

He spotted her as soon as he broke the surface. Ten feet away, flailing, twisting in the rush of water. Mac reached ahead and began pulling himself toward her in long, steady strokes. He was a good swimmer and moving fast with the current. Belinda appeared to have some swimming skills of her own, but she was panicking, fighting the current, trying to swim *against* it rather than going partially with it and putting her efforts into angling toward one of the banks. The only good thing about that was that her struggles held her somewhat in place and allowed Mac to reach her more quickly.

"I've got you! Quit struggling, I've got you," he said, spitting water as he grabbed a handful of clothing and pulled her to him. The current spun them in a tight circle as he got hold of one arm and pulled her closer still.

But panic still had hold of her, too. She flailed and grasped wildly at him, scraping his face, clawing at his shirt. Her eyes were as wide and frightened as those of the team. She babbled something, but it was unintelligible. The way she struggled and grabbed at him threatened to pull them both under.

"Stop it! Stop it!" Mac said sharply. "Try to relax and swim with me toward the bank. If you keep fighting, you'll drown us both."

But the wildness in her eyes didn't subside. Neither did her thrashing about. Mac inadvertently swallowed some muddy water and went into a brief coughing fit.

"Blast it, hold still!"

A sudden loud noise, the magnified creaking and splintering of iron and wood being violently twisted out of shape caused Mac's head to snap around and look frantically upstream. He saw the medicine wagon, having been temporarily hung up on the sunken object that had caught its wheel, suddenly break apart and pull free in huge, shattered pieces—all of them now hurtling straight for him and Belinda!

Their chances of getting out of the way in time, especially with her fighting against him, seemed all but impossible. But Mac wasn't ready to give up that easy. The first thing he did, without hesitation, was to throw a slashing right cross straight to the girl's jaw. It knocked her cold.

The instant her body sagged in his arms, he twisted away, hooking his left arm under her chin, and began stroking with his right arm and kicking furiously with his feet. At first he went straight with the current, letting it and his added effort propel him along, trying to increase the distance between him and the oncoming wreckage. Then, gradually, he began angling toward the bank.

As his breath started burning like fire in his throat and lungs, he heard shouts coming from over on the bank, just a short way ahead. Then he saw them—Sparky Whitlock and Laird Nolan. They were mounted, riding their horses along the edge of the water, whirling their lassos. Mac kept swimming as hard as he could, never letting up until he saw the loop of Nolan's lasso spinning just above his head and then dropping down over him. He thrust up his arm to make sure it was inside the loop and then grabbed it, for added assurance, as the rope settled across the back of his neck and over his shoulder and started to cinch tight. The scratch of that coarse braid felt sweeter and more wonderful than the caress of the most beautiful woman imaginable. And not even the sudden jolt as Nolan braced his horse and then commenced tugging with all his might to pull Mac and his burden from the river was enough to diminish the illusion.

Out they came, geysering water, dragged skidding and slipping up over the muddy bank and then rolling to a stop on the grass. In the final seconds before being yanked from the current, Mac felt the unmistakable tap of something solid bump the very tip of his boot heel and through the water splashing across his vision he saw a massive, twisted section of the medicine wagon go swirling past. That's how close it came to slamming into and almost certainly drowning him and Belinda . . .

CHAPTER 41

Much as he hated to admit it, the ordeal in the river had left Mac battered and spent. As a result, against his not very strenuous protests, he hung back to recuperate a bit while George and Henry went to fetch the chuckwagon.

As for the medicine wagon, it was a complete loss. But at least its team had been saved and no one else was injured in the disastrous attempt to try and get the rig across.

No one except for Belinda. In addition to a sour stomach from all the river water she'd swallowed, there was also the matter of a chipped tooth and swollen jaw she suffered as a result of the punch Mac had landed to make her stop struggling.

Upon regaining consciousness, Belinda immediately and sincerely began apologizing for her actions. "I—I thought I could get the wagon across by myself. I didn't want to bother someone else with having to do it. Instead, I ended up bothering so many of you in an even worse manner." She paused to cough up more river water. "Not only that, I subjected you to far more danger than you would have had to deal with if I'd just waited. And yet, after all my lies and everything Herbert and I put this outfit through, you still risked your own lives to save mine. Even you."

The last part was directed squarely at Mac. The words and the penetrating gaze that accompanied them were somewhat unsettling.

Nevertheless, Mac met her eyes and held them. "Even me," he echoed softly. "As in . . . even the man who shot your husband?"

Belinda blinked and then averted her gaze. "I didn't mean it that way," she said, almost a whisper. "I—I just meant I'm grateful. As for the other, I understand that you didn't have any choice. I know Herbert was being dangerous and irrational. But still . . . even though things had become very strained between us, he was an important part of my life for so long . . . It's just not easy to . . . to . . ."

Her voice trailed off and she went quiet. She leaned her face into her palms and began rocking slowly back and forth.

Colleen stepped up and adjusted the blanket that had been draped over Belinda's shoulders, pulling it more tightly around her. She looked up and swept her gaze over the men who stood gathered around. "This isn't a good time to be trying to drag a lot of talk out of her," she said to no one in particular.

It was her father who responded. "Wasn't nobody looking to badger the gal," he stated. "We'll step away. You go ahead, stick with her a bit. When we get a fire going, bring her over to get dried out some more, leastways until that doggone storm hits."

With that, he led Mac, Shad, and Roman off toward

a grove of cottonwood trees where Nolan and Sparky were stirring up a campfire. "When Henry and George get here with the chuckwagon, we'll boil up a pot of coffee," Bradley said. "That and some beef jerky—maybe some leftover biscuits if there are any—will do for grub until supper time. Storm or no storm, I mean to cover some ground today with the herd. We've lost too much time and I want to get to Miles City before anything else goes wrong."

"If Miles City holds some kind of guarantee to the end of our troubles, I'm all for that," Roman said, but not without a trace of skepticism.

When they reached where Nolan and Sparky were feeding more branches into the fire, Mac went up to Nolan. Loud enough to make sure everyone could hear, he said, "Laird, I got something to say to you. Miss Belinda a minute ago expressed her gratitude to me for saving her life. Truth is, and everybody here knows it, if it hadn't been for you and your lasso, neither me nor her would have made it out of that river alive." He extended his right hand. "Words don't cover it, but I want you to know how grateful *I* am for you saving our hides."

The leathery-faced old wrangler took the offered hand and the men shook. Then, pulling his hand away, Nolan abruptly arched one shaggy brow and said in a dubious tone, "If I was to think on this very long, it might be that I don't want no credit for savin' the life of a rascal like you. You're still plenty young, hard to tell what kind of scrapes you might still have ahead of you. Might not be healthy for me to be sharin' in the credit for something you haul off and do in the future."

The others looking on chuckled at this bit of ribbing.

But Nolan wasn't done. "On the other hand," he said, "I don't want to pass up the part about you providin' me a page for the record book."

Grinning, knowing he was in for some more ribbing, Mac said, "What record book? What are you talking about?"

Frowning with mock seriousness, Nolan said, "Just think for a minute. You got to be about the ugliest critter anybody ever flung a loop at, right? And Miss Belinda, even with you all wrapped all around her, is dead certain the prettiest. So there you have it—I roped me the prettiest and the ugliest all in one toss. Wouldn't you say that's one for the record books?"

Everybody laughed, none louder than Nolan's own whoop as he scooted back to avoid the toe of Mac's boot aimed in a kick at his rear end.

The laughter was still dying down when they all heard a different kind of whoop coming from the direction of the river. "That'll be the boys returning with the chuckwagon," Bradley said. "Come on, let's go see if they need a hand."

By the time the men quit the trees and reached the riverbank, the chuckwagon was already on its way across. Henry Bradley was on the driver's seat, working the reins of the steady-pulling mule team. Young George was riding alongside, leading a second horse, the one Henry had ridden off on. The squat, sturdy chuckwagon was built watertight and heavy, intended for periodic river crossings, so everyone was relieved to see it moving along smoothly in line with the mules.

Having first confirmed that much, what all eyes next shifted to and locked on was the figure of a third man—a stranger, hunched forward, clinging desperately, unsteadily to the saddle horn—mounted on the horse George was leading.

"It's that Texas Ranger we saw with Van Horne's bunch the other day. Name's Malloy," Henry Bradley was explaining. "He claims he had a falling-out with Van Horne after he got to thinking about some of the things he overheard during and after we paid our little visit. When he spoke out too much, they shot him and left him for dead. He's got a couple bullet holes in him, no doubt about that. He's in a pretty bad way."

"How'd you happen on him?" Roman asked.

"When we got back to the chuckwagon, he was there waiting," answered George. "After he survived being left for buzzard bait, he patched himself up as best he could and started walking to try and reach our camp before we lit out. He retraced the way Van Horne's bunch had gone after we put them afoot. Dragged himself through part of the day yesterday and all through the night. Says he came for help and also to warn us."

"Warn us about what?" Bradley growled suspiciously. "We already know all we need to about that lowdown skunk Van Horne."

Malloy wagged his head weakly. "No, you don't.

There've been some new developments since you thought you'd settled with him."

Once the chuckwagon and its accompanying riders were across the river, Malloy had been lifted down from his saddle, carried over to the grove of trees and laid out on a bedroll near the crackling fire. Now everyone, even the two women, were gathered around to hear his story.

The Ranger was in a battered, exhausted condition from his ordeal yet was determined to say his piece. Some gulps of fresh water and a couple of belts from one of the chuckwagon's whiskey bottles seemed to have revitalized him enough to keep him talking, even as Shad Hopper carefully pulled open his shirt and began examining the shoulder wound.

With a handful of ragged pauses and a few grimaces of pain whenever Shad probed a little too hard, he related everything—the false premise that had put him in Van Horne's company to begin with, his gradual discomfort and suspicions as time had passed, and then finally the bringing in of Zeb Mahoney and his pack of gunnies.

Judging by their expressions, most of those looking on and listening seemed to be guardedly accepting Malloy's tale. All except the elder Bradley.

"If this pack of reinforcements—these almighty dangerous hombres—showed up two days ago," he said, his suspicious tone intact, "how is it that you, staggering and half crawling, managed to make it to the river ahead of them?"

"He told you, Pa," said George, obviously a little annoyed by his father's stubborn resistance. "Mahoney and his men went off to fetch horses and guns for the others—Van Horne and his original crew. On account of how far they had to go, they weren't expected back until sometime this morning. Could be they haven't even started out after us yet."

"But no matter when they do," Shad pointed out solemnly, "it ain't gonna take 'em long to gain ground on us. Sounds likely for tomorrow, maybe even yet tonight."

Mac said, "If this oncoming storm hits hard enough, the way it looks like it could—that just might work in our favor. If it re-floods the river, like we were worried about for our own sake, let's hope it makes a problem for Van Horne's bunch instead. Keeps 'em from crossing right away and sticks 'em on the other side for a while, no matter how fast they make it this far."

"Be nice to think it could work that way," allowed Shad. "But keep in mind that a pack of hardcases with blood in their eyes and no wagons or cows in the mix might be apt to brave a fast-runnin' river where others wouldn't try."

"You make a good point," Roman admitted grudgingly. "Except I'd hate to apply the word 'brave' to any action taken by Van Horne or the pack of mongrels he's got runnin' with him."

"That's just it," said Bradley through gritted teeth. "There isn't one admirable quality you can apply to Caleb Van Horne. Sure as blazes not brave. But tricky, cunning, devious . . . That's what makes me so leery about this Ranger showing up with all these claims he's making."

For the first time, Colleen spoke up. "For crying out loud, Father. Do you think he shot himself—or allowed someone else to do it—just to try and play some kind of clever trick on us? The fact he's been shot at all, since you took all the weapons away from Van Horne's men, should be enough to confirm his story about those other desperadoes arriving and providing the guns that were used on him."

"She makes a good point, Boss," said Shad. "This shoulder wound looks too serious to me to be some kind of trick for putting us off our guard. And I'll tell you something else. It's too serious to let it go untended much longer, or it's gonna get a whole lot worse."

Bradley scowled. "What are you saying?"

"I'm sayin' it's dang near a miracle he's made it this far and kept the bleedin' from drainin' him out. If we put him on a horse or jostle him around on the chuckwagon without treatin' that wound more, the bleedin' will most likely start in again and finish the job on him." Shad's mouth pulled down in a long frown. "What's more, the bullet is still in there. Probably in fragments, what with the way it busted up the bones in his shoulder. If somebody don't go in and get all or most of it dug out, and pronto, then he's going to die."

All eyes came to rest on Bradley, watching and waiting for his response.

"And in case you need any more bad news," said Roman, raising his voice to be heard over a sudden gust of wind, "that storm is rolling up on us mighty fast."

"No matter whether we stay or start driving the herd through the storm, we're never going to outrun men riding hard after us," Colleen declared. "But if we wait here and try to treat this man's wounds, at least we might have a chance to save his life. And if Van Horne's bunch is planning to go on ahead and set up an ambush for us closer to Miles City, like the

Ranger says, then it won't matter. We're still going to have to deal with them when the time comes."

Bradley withstood her unwavering glare for several seconds. Then, in exasperation, he puffed out his cheeks and expelled his own gust of air. "Get that chuckwagon pulled around to make a windbreak, then start putting up some tarps for added shelter. Shad, you're the closest thing we've got to a doctor, so you'll have to be the one to go in after that bullet. Mac, dig out those coal oil lanterns you've got in your wagon and, while you're at it, better grab another bottle of whiskey. Somebody start pouring it into Malloy to get him ready."

"Good idea," grunted Shad. "Grab enough to be able to pour some in me, too."

CHAPTER 42

For the better part of an hour, Shad worked on the Ranger's shoulder wound. Cutting, probing, extracting pieces of lead from the pocket of mangled meat and bone; then closing it, stitching and packing and bandaging to halt the bleeding. Through it all, the storm raged, having arrived mere minutes after the procedure began. Lightning flashed, thunder rolled and shook the ground, the rain came down in wind-whipped sheets.

In the dimness introduced by the darkened sky and the tarp enclosure within which the procedure was forced to take place, the main illumination coming from a pair of coal oil lanterns, Shad went about his business silently and intently. Sweat poured from his rugged features almost as profusely as if he were standing out in the downpour. But Colleen was by his side every minute, repeatedly wiping his face and occasionally pinching a blood vessel with her fingers to help control the bleeding. Mac and Roman stood close by also, holding the lanterns.

When the shoulder had been tended to as best as

possible, Malloy's other wound—the bullet hole through the muscle to the right of his neck—was a relatively simple matter of cleaning and plugging the two ends, entrance and exit.

After that, there wasn't much left to do but wait. Wait for the storm to subside. Wait to find out if Malloy had the strength to recuperate. Wait to see if Van Horne and his pack of curly wolves had any surprises in store between here and the now-anticipated ambush at Buffalo Kill Gap.

Wait for a new day to once again get the cattle drive underway . . .

By evening, the storm had passed.

To everyone's appreciation, Mac took the opportunity to prepare the day's first full meal. He kept it simple—fresh biscuits, leftover rabbit stew from the success he, Shad, and Roman had had bagging some fat hoppers the day before, and another mess of greens, which had proved popular when he served them previously. He heaped the helpings high and with Boss Bradley's permission added a generous slosh of whiskey to the cups of fresh-brewed coffee for all who wanted some—which proved to be most everybody, strictly as a preventative measure against the damp and cold, it was understood.

As he'd given fair warning of intending to do as soon as his medic role was fulfilled, Shad had hit the whiskey ahead of everyone else. But no one took issue with his having earned the right. And of course the patient, Malloy, had earned his right to imbibe copiously even earlier, for the purpose of numbing himself against the pain of what he had to endure.

It was some time later, after the meal was over, after the herd had been checked and bedded down for the night, that Roman summoned his father and Mac for a confab removed from the rest.

"I been thinkin'," he announced. "Came up with a notion I feel is worth following up on."

"You got our attention," said Bradley. "What's on your mind?"

Roman jabbed a thumb over his shoulder. "That river back there. I went and took a look. It's runnin' high after the storm, but nothing like we faced when we first came on it. I don't figure it's going to slow Van Horne and his gunnies too much when they get to it."

"Uh-huh. We sorta figured that already."

"The thing is, knowing when and where they might cross," Roman went on. "If we believe what the Ranger told us—and that appears to be what we're doing— then they ain't coming in no hurry to overtake us, even after they've been joined back up by those new hombres with replacement horses and guns. Reasoning that way, they likely holed up somewhere and waited out that storm. Meanin' they won't likely try the river until tomorrow in daylight."

Bradley nodded. "I agree with all that so far. But if they mean to loop around us and set up their ambush in Buffalo Kill Gap, then there's no telling where they'll cross."

"Not for sure, no," Roman said. "But if they stay on line according to how we've traveled up to now, I say there's at least a fifty-fifty chance they'll reach the river about where we first did. They don't know nothing about Malloy makin' it to us and us being slowed by patching him up. They'll figure we went on some distance after making our own crossing, so there'd be no reason for them to cross anywhere else other than where we already tested the bottom. *Then* they could start their swing around us."

Bradley frowned, showing some impatience. "Again, I don't necessarily fault anything you've said. But what's your point?"

Some added excitement edging into his tone, Roman said, "My point is this: What if a couple of our boys—me and Mac, I'm suggesting, since we're the best shots in our crew—hang back and baptize Van Horne's heathens with a blessing of lead? We could hold to cover on the bank, wait for 'em to get out in the middle where they couldn't make no sudden moves, and then cut 'em to pieces."

Neither Bradley nor Mac gave an immediate response. Both looked caught off guard, maybe a little stunned, by the suggestion.

Until Mac said, "I like it!"

Bradley wasn't quite so quick to buy in. "Now hold on a minute," he said. "That's a mighty tempting notion, I've got to admit. But stop and think, it would also be a very harsh act. Staging your own ambush, cutting down men in cold blood . . ."

"They're not men, they're vermin," Roman was quick to say. "It'd be turning their own kind of tactics back on 'em. And every one we cut down would be one less left to try and do as bad or worse to each and every one of ours, including Colleen, Pa. It was bad enough before, but with the kind of filth riding with that Mahoney hombre now in the mix . . . if they got the better of us and didn't kill her outright, then there'd be even worse—"

"I don't want to hear that!"

"Of course, you don't," Roman snapped back. "You think I do? I never want such a thought to cross my mind. But we have to face facts, Pa. This thing has turned meaner and nastier than we ever bargained for. And the only way I see for us to get through it is to turn meaner and nastier ourselves . . ."

CHAPTER 43

A full hour ahead of daybreak, they once again set the herd in motion. Their route was plain enough that the sunless yet clear early morning sky provided sufficient light to see by.

Shad took the lead. Belinda drove the chuckwagon with the wounded Malloy laid out as comfortably as possible on a pile of blankets behind the seat. Bradley, Colleen, and the rest of the crew—save for Mac and Roman—worked the cattle and the remuda.

After seeing the others off, Mac and Roman returned to the riverbank to take up concealed positions. They chose a low mound about halfway between where they'd first considered crossing and where they actually did. The mound provided a good view of the river for a long stretch in either direction. A line of brushy growth augmented by some large, twisted pieces of driftwood that they dragged up from the water's edge gave them cover from behind which they could shift and move several yards back and forth parallel to the river.

Each man was armed with a pair of repeating rifles—Winchesters being Mac's choice, Henrys selected by Roman—in addition to their sidearms. This gave them thirty-plus rounds of individual firepower before ever having to reload.

"If that ain't enough to put a serious dent in 'em," muttered Roman, "then we'd better trade in our guns for knitting needles."

The plan was for them to wait at the river, behind their cover, until noon. If Van Horne and his gunnies didn't show up by then, it would be assumed they had found a crossing somewhere else, and Mac and Roman would drop back then ride to catch up with the herd. If their targets *did* show up here, however, they would find a baptism by lead in store for them.

Time dragged as they waited for the sun to rise. The pre-dawn gloom seemed to add to the somberness of the situation.

They talked little, except for one exchange prompted by Roman, when he said, "Seems like things have worked out for me and you to keep getting involved in gun work together. What do you make of that?"

Mac didn't answer right away. When he did reply, he said, "I'm not sure. Each time, it seemed like the right—or at least the necessary—thing to do. Looking back, though, I guess a part of me will always wonder if there might have been a different or better way."

Both men were somber and quiet for a spell. Then Roman said, "And now, here again thanks to me, you're poised to shoot and kill some more. Seems like hanging around with the Rafter B in general and me in particular is turning you more and more into something you don't want to be. And this, what with me volunteering you like I done, will likely turn out to be the bloodiest piece of work yet."

"I could have said no," Mac reminded him. "But

you put it best when you laid it out for your father. These ain't men we're fixing to deal with—they're vermin. For the greater good, they deserve to be gotten rid of just like any right-thinking person would put down a pack of rabid dogs. I can live with being part of that."

They appeared not long after the sun was fully risen above the eastern horizon. The last tendrils of morning mist had lifted off the river and the churning, boiling water, still a muddy brown from storm run-off, was managing to pick up a few glints of sunlight. The air was motionless, the only sound that of the hissing, rushing current.

They rode up on the opposite bank, thirteen strong, surveying the challenge before them.

"Don't seem likely that high water is going to be enough to hold 'em off," whispered Mac. "I think the show's about to begin. You ready?"

"I didn't pick this front-row seat just to watch the sun come up. Yeah, I'm ready," Roman answered.

Across the river, the thick torso and bulging gut of Caleb Van Horne made him easily identifiable. Mounted to his right was Chance Barlow, known previously to Roman from back in Bellow County and encountered before by Mac during the raid on Van Horne's camp. To the fat man's left was an hombre neither of the waiting ambushers had ever seen before—a tall, rugged specimen with an elongated face wearing a grim expression. It seemed reasonable to figure him as being Zeb Mahoney, the leader of the new recruits Ranger Malloy had spoke of.

As if prompted by this thought, Roman said, "If there was ever any doubt about that Ranger fella bein' on the level with the things he told us, I'd say all those ugly new faces and the fact Van Horne's original outfit is armed and on horseback again pretty much settles it."

On the opposite bank, the thirteen riders began to shift in the downstream direction, continuing to study the two banks and the river in between. Any conversation within the group was blotted out by the sound of the rushing water, but it appeared that some in their ranks were recognizing—as Shad had done for the Rafter B outfit—that the spot where the river widened and ran shallower presented their best bet for crossing over.

Anticipating this, Mac and Roman shifted with them.

Although the intervening storm had obliterated all signs of the Rafter B's crossing, Van Horne's bunch reined up at almost the exact location on the bank where the cattle had been driven in. They palavered there for a minute or so, exchanged some general gesturing and jawing, and then the man Mac and Roman had judged to be Mahoney abruptly wheeled his horse and gigged the animal into the water. After a few seconds' hesitation, the rest came plunging after him.

Dropping to one knee at about eight feet from where Roman was doing the same, Mac brought his Winchester smoothly to his shoulder and, out the side of his mouth, said, "Remember the way you explained it to your pa. Let 'em get nearly to the middle so they can't quickly turn and make a run for it. Then we start making it so they don't exist no more."

CHAPTER 44

All the riders were in the water when Mahoney spotted the single eyeblink-quick flash of sunlight reflecting off of something in the line of brush on the low mound across the river. He had no way of knowing what caused it, but his instincts told him that, whatever it was, it didn't belong there. And his years of staying alive amidst danger and violence furthermore told him it *just might* be the sun winking off a gun barrel—which made it enough to propel him into action.

First, he threw up his right hand, signaling a halt to those splashing behind and on either side of him. An instant later he dropped that hand in a blur of motion and raked the long-barreled Colt from the holster on his hip. Without hesitation, he extended his arm and triggered three rapid-fire rounds into the brush where he'd seen the suspicious flash.

This intent to flush out whatever might be there came close to working. While not completely flushing the source of the flash, Mahoney's shots did reveal the movement of a human shape, though barely discernible, that was forced to scramble back from the unexpected volley. That, in turn, was enough for Mahoney to wheel his horse sharply as he began hollering, "Ambush! Ambush! Everybody back. Scatter!"

There was immediate chaos in the river. All of Van Horne's riders were only too willing to obey Mahoney's command and turn back toward the bank. But two of Mahoney's own men—Garcia and Selkirk, each packing a brace of pistols—couldn't resist delaying flight until they'd first thrown some lead, even though they had just the slimmest idea of what and where their target was. They merely began pouring rounds into the same clump of brush Mahoney had fired at.

Garcia and Selkirk trying to hold their horses in place while they burned powder caused some of the other riders attempting to make it back to the bank to jam up against them. The result was a good deal of wild shooting, cussing men, and shrieking, confused horses.

For their part, Mac and Roman—whose rifle had been the one that gave off the telltale glint of sunlight resulting in him nearly getting his head blown off by Mahoney—were quick to try and take advantage of this bit of bedlam. With their intended targets not as far out into the river as they'd hoped for, the partial jam-up of horses and men still provided a chance for them to do some of the damage they meant to accomplish.

Having repositioned about ten yards down from where Roman had drawn fire, the ambushers once again slammed their rifles to their shoulders and opened up on the gun-wolves hired to come after them. Their rifles roared and bullets sizzled across the churning brown water.

One of Van Horne's wranglers threw up his arms and toppled from his saddle, the first man to go down. Only a few feet away, a horse panicked by the combination of swirling water and the shooting and shrieking of the other horses, thrashed wildly and threw itself inadvertently into the path of a bullet.

Van Horne and Curly Pierce were among the first to regain the bank they had left just minutes earlier. The bulbous, flailing form of Van Horne was naturally a prime target for the ambushers. Both of them began pouring lead in his direction. He screamed in terror, realizing this, and dug his heels and whipped his reins in a frenzy, urging his horse to run from the scene.

Before the bewildered beast could respond satisfactorily, an even shriller scream escaped from the fat man as a bullet tore a long gash in his thigh. He reacted so violently, pitching back in his saddle with the reins clenched tight in his fists, that he caused the horse to twist half around and rear up on its hind legs. As a result, two slugs meant for Van Horne smashed into the horse, killing it instantly. The unfortunate creature collapsed as Van Horne toppled off the back side and landed on the ground in a heap, where he was promptly protected by the carcass of his fallen mount.

Seeing all this take place right before his eyes, Curly Pierce did his best to come to the aid of his boss. He yanked the Winchester from his saddle scabbard and began returning fire on Mac and Roman, their positions identified now by the powder smoke from their own rifles. All Pierce succeeded in doing was drawing their attention to himself instead. He paid for it by having a pair of heavy-caliber slugs blow his chest apart. He flew from the saddle in a mist of blood and gore, dead before he ever hit the ground.

Mac and Roman shifted their positions again and quickly redirected their fire.

The turmoil of colliding horses and men in the water had begun to untangle itself somewhat. Garcia and Selkirk were still bent on throwing lead instead of turning away, but the others who'd initially had their way blocked by this display of stubbornness had mostly found their way past it by now and were scrambling to make it to shore. Roman concentrated on the two shooters whose rounds were relentlessly slashing through brush and whacking against the stacked driftwood. None of these shots were coming particularly close, but Roman saw no sense in allowing their aim to improve.

Mac, in the meantime, began seeking riders who had made it up onto the bank, trying to stop as many as he could before they got away. Another of Van Horne's wranglers fell as a result of this. Adjusting his aim a few feet to the left of where that man toppled, Mac suddenly found Chance Barlow looming in his sights. Without the slightest hesitation—with *eagerness*, in fact—Mac squeezed his trigger. Unfortunately, he turned out to be a little too eager and his shot sailed wide of the gunman, the miscalculation helped by an unexpected side step by Barlow's mount.

As Mac was jacking home a fresh cartridge and fixing to tighten his aim, Barlow—evidently having felt the heat from the near miss—locked his eyes on where the shot had come from and swung up his revolver in response. Both men fired at the same time. Instantly, Mac knew his shot was again off the mark. With this realization came the simultaneous crash of Barlow's bullet tearing through the brush only inches from his head, causing him to reflexively duck down lower.

When Mac rose up again, half a yard from where

he'd fired before, Barlow was on the move. He wasn't spurring his horse *away* from the river, however, but rather was urging it parallel to the bank. It took a second for Mac to understand that he was headed toward Van Horne, apparently intending to go to his aid. Mac smiled a wolf's smile, anticipating the prospect of having the two men clustered together. He began tracking Barlow with the front sight of his rifle, holding fire until the gunman reached his boss.

Meanwhile, Roman's focus on Garcia and Selkirk paid off when he scored a direct hit on the Mexican. He planted a bullet just above the point where the bandoliers crisscrossed over Garcia's chest. The impact sent the hired gun somersaulting backward out of his saddle and into the swirling river. Seeing this was enough for Selkirk to finally decide it was time he retreated. After a last discharge from both of his pistols, he holstered them with a flourish and then wheeled his horse toward the bank. Roman didn't let him get away completely unscathed, though. As the Aussie was spurring his mount up out of the water, Roman got off another shot that caught a piece of Selkirk's left shoulder, causing him to twist violently in the saddle, almost falling off. But he managed to hang on, at least long enough to gallop away without Roman being able to plant another bullet in him.

Everyone was up out of the water now. Most were fleeing straight back across the landscape of low, rolling hills, trying to get out of range from Mac's and Roman's rifles.

One exception was Chance Barlow, attempting to come to the aid of the fallen Van Horne. Helping them was none other than Zeb Mahoney, who sat his horse boldly facing in the ambushers' direction as he began laying down covering fire with a Winchester Yellowboy. Backing him up was Clay Coburn, repeatedly levering and firing a rifle of his own. Between the two of them, they were chewing up the brush and driftwood close enough to where Mac and Roman were positioned to make it more than a little hot for the pair.

Leaning down from his saddle as he reached the fallen Van Horne, Barlow got hold of his plump target and dragged him upright. One of Mac's bullet's skimmed Barlow's hat off his head and sent it spinning away. Undeterred, the gunman, in an adrenaline-fueled surge of desperation and determination, managed to drag his boss the rest of the way up so that he lay belly down in front of him. Reining his horse around sharply, Barlow then bolted away.

The fire from Mahoney and Coburn was effective enough to keep Mac and Roman from scoring any more kills. The closest either one came was a shot from Mac that wounded Barlow low in the back. Mac saw him jerk in the saddle, but the durable so-and-so stayed upright and kept riding away.

And then, abruptly, with the withdrawal of Mahoney and Coburn—throwing lead even as they spun around and rode off—it was over.

Except for the bodies lying on the opposite shore—Curly Pierce, the nameless Van Horne wrangler, and Van Horne's dead horse—the scene Mac and Roman gazed out on looked once again exactly as it had only minutes before. The rapid flow of the river had swept away the blood and the bodies of the men and the horse that had met their ends in its water. The sounds of gunfire and of shouted curses and screaming horses were all ended, too, and there was only the steady rushing hiss of the current.

Silently, moving as if weighed down by sudden melancholy, Mac and Roman got to their feet and walked toward where they'd left their horses tied.

CHAPTER 45

"It had to be those Rafter B devils! It's the only thing that makes sense," insisted Chance Barlow, his teeth bared in a grimace as one of the Horned-V wranglers finished tying the bandage wrapped around his middle, patching the fist-sized chunk of meat torn from his flank by a bullet.

"How does it make sense?" countered Mahoney, scowling. "Why would any of the Rafter B bunch hang back to stage an ambush after they'd just got done puttin' your whole outfit on foot, weaponless, and havin' every reason to expect it would be a week or more before you ever got to that river?"

"Precaution, that's why," Barlow stated stubbornly. "Norris Bradley is the crafty and careful sort. That flooded river must have kept him and the herd from crossin' for another day or two after they hit our camp. He *thought* we were miles and days from any ranch or town where we could get re-outfitted, but he couldn't be certain. He don't know this territory all that well. So, *just in case* we found a way to get healed back up quicker than seemed likely, he left a couple of his boys behind for a while to sting us again if we showed up—this time more permanent-like."

Bitterly, Mahoney said, "Well, whoever it was got that much done for at least four of ours. I lost a top man in Garcia."

"And I lost a friend in Curly Pierce," Barlow responded, the bitterness in his own tone matching Mahoney's. Then, his voice easing back some, he added, "Reckon it would have been even worse, Mahoney, if you hadn't caught wind of something being wrong as quick as you did. For that, I guess we're all—all who are left, anyway—plenty obliged."

Mahoney waved him off. "I don't want nobody's gratitude. It was a piece of luck that I spotted a wink of sunlight off a gun barrel, that's all. But it wasn't enough to stop the damage they were still able to do. What I really want is another chance at those bushwhackers. I'm havin' trouble believin' that it could have been anybody from the Rafter B crew, but I got no better explanation. And in the end, who it was don't really matter for what we got left ahead of us. We still need to get Mr. Van Horne's cattle back, and now we need to deliver payback to those who bloodied us, no matter who they were."

"Heads on stakes, that's the answer! Guts strung out for coyote pickings!" declared Van Horne, speaking for the first time in a number of minutes. The words came out slurred and thick sounding due to the fact that the fat man, after gulping down copious amounts of whiskey to dull his pain from the bullet wound in his thigh, was quite drunk. He was perched once again on his canvas folding chair, right leg extended out straight before him. His pant leg had been split up one side from cuff nearly to waist in order for wrangler Smith to be able to access and treat the wound. The latter amounted to a deep bullet burn, laying open several inches of meat but not deep enough to strike bone. The pain was nevertheless considerable, and Van Horne was hardly one to suffer discomfort well.

The ambush victims, now whittled down to nine in number, were gathered in a shallow draw among some jagged rock outcrops just over a mile from the river crossing they'd attempted to make. The spot was selected for the cover the rocks would provide in the unlikely event their ambushers came in pursuit. A small fire had been built for the purpose of heating water to treat the wounded men and for cooking a pot of strong coffee.

As Barlow, Mahoney, and Van Horne continued to discuss their situation, the other men stood gathered close around, sipping from steaming cups of the bitter brew and from time to time joining in.

"I'm all for that heads-on-stakes idea," Mahoney said in response to Van Horne. "I liked it the first time I heard it, still do. But it seems to me we're in a position where we need to take a step back and sort of rethink exactly how it is we're gonna go about that."

"What's the matter with goin' ahead and stagin' our own ambush like we been plannin'? In Buffalo Kill Gap?" Coburn wanted to know. "Ain't that still a workable notion? I'd like more than ever for the chance to lay some fire down on those Rafter B cow pushers."

"Same here," agreed Selkirk, his left arm in a sling due to the shoulder hit he'd taken. "I not only owe those blokes for this shoulder, but they also cost me those bandoliers of Garcia's that I took such a fancy to. Reckless as he was, I always figured it was just a matter of time before he got himself killed. Then I planned on sort of inheriting them. Never counted on the greedy jake getting swept down a bloody river and taking them with him."

"Nobody's sayin' we won't ambush them at Buffalo Kill Gap," said Barlow. "But we've got to face the fact that pullin' it off now, what with our number havin' been cut down from thirteen to nine and three of the nine bein' wounded . . . well, that makes a difference."

"Speak for yourself," protested Selkirk. "I can shoot with either hand, and those fools made the mistake of leaving me my *best* one. How about you, Barlow? You saying that chunk of meat tore out above your hip has taken the fight out of you? And nobody ever figured Mr. Van Horne for gun work to begin with, right?"

"I've got plenty of fight left in me, bub. You don't need to worry about that," Barlow was quick to reply. "But we still lost a quarter of our force. That needs takin' into consideration. Even Mahoney said as much."

"That's right, I did." Mahoney backed Selkirk down with a hard look.

"But if there's still eight of us willin' and able to fight, then why wait?" said Walt Purdy, his dark face glowering. "We're fightin' men by trade, they're nothing but cowpuncher rabble. I never understood all this pussyfootin' around, waitin' for a place days down the road to ambush 'em. 'Specially not now. Why not just ride after those rascals, shoot 'em outta their saddles when we catch up, take back Mr. Van Horne's cattle, and be done with it?"

Mahoney chuckled. "You make that sound awful easy, Walt. And maybe we could pull it off just like you say. Keep in mind, though, that at least one or two within that rabble have showed themselves to have their share of bark, meanin' that takin' 'em your way would likely come at more cost to us. And then, even after we skinned the bark off the men, we'd still have eight hundred head of cattle on our hands needin' four or five days of drivin' to get 'em to Miles City. You in the mood for that much cowboyin', Walt?"

Purdy's expression turned sour. "You know I was raised on an Iowa dairy farm. Onliest cows I know about are the kind who stand still to get milked twice a day. I got no truck with the kind you gotta chase all over creation on a horse."

"Well, there you go. I got no taste for chasin' around stubborn cattle, either, especially not for a whole week. Yet that's what we'd have on our hands— what finishin' our job would require—if we got in a hurry to take out those Rafter B men the way you're suggesting." Mahoney paused, gave that much a chance to sink in. Then he added, "That's why I still think hittin' the Rafter B at Buffalo Kill Gap is our best bet. And, yeah, maybe we could go ahead and pull it off with the crew we got left. But I also think there may be a way to do it smarter and improve our chances in the long run."

"How so? What have you got in mind?"

"What I'm thinkin'," Mahoney explained, "is that, if we hurry, we'd be able to reach Miles City, arrange a couple of things to help our cause, then make it back to the gap still in time to be waitin' for our Rafter B friends."

"That's a lot of extra riding. What would we gain by goin' through all that?" Barlow asked.

"Two things," Mahoney told him. "First of all, we could get some proper doctorin' for the three of you who've been wounded. Yeah, you're lucky that none of you seem to have any lead in you and maybe you all can tough it out—but maybe infection or some such could still set in, and that could seriously hamper us from dealin' with the Rafter B."

"I'm all for that," proclaimed Van Horne, his excitement for the idea seeming to sober him somewhat. "This leg is killing me, and I sure would welcome some attention to it from a proper doctor!"

Barlow eyed Mahoney. "You said two things. What else?"

"More men. Replacements for the ones we lost," Mahoney said with an air of smugness. "Montana's big and wild. Bound to have plenty more of the kind of men we need, and bound to be some of 'em in Miles City. They'll be easy to spot if you know what to look for. All of this, of course, dependin' on if Mr. Van Horne is willin' to shell out what it'd take to hire 'em. How about it, Boss? You agreeable to reinvestin' what you ain't gonna have to pay Garcia, Pierce, or those two wranglers no more?"

Van Horne waved his whiskey bottle, took another swig, and declared, "Whatever it takes to get heads on stakes!"

CHAPTER 46

For the next three days, the cattle drive pushed steadily north, covering close to twenty miles a day. The weather stayed clear, the terrain presented no serious hardship, and best of all, there was no further sign of Van Horne or his gun wolves.

At first, after Mac and Roman rejoined the drive following their river ambush, Shad Hopper rode tirelessly in wide circles around the moving herd, wearing out two or three remuda horses each day, always on the lookout to make sure there were no signs of an unwanted presence anywhere near. The chuckwagon, continuing to be driven by Belinda, kept pace with the cattle rather than rolling on ahead. Mac still did most of the cooking, but between meals, he worked from the saddle as an added wrangler to help keep the cattle in line and on the move for the sake of pushing every inch of daily distance out of the critters. In recognition of this double duty, he was excused from taking any nighthawk turns.

By the third day, Shad had eased up some on his scouting. No one in the outfit was ready to relax, not by any means, but there came a point where it seemed reasonable to pull one's horns back a little. Especially given the information supplied by Ranger Malloy about Van Horne's plans to hold off on making his big move until they reached Buffalo Kill Gap. The question mark now hanging over that, however, was whether or not having their force whittled down by the ambush might change Van Horne's plans.

"I don't see why it would," Roman said as he sat with the others around the central campfire on the third night after supper. "If anything, it seems to me it oughta give 'em all the more reason to stick with that plan. There's fewer of 'em now, remember, so they'll need the advantage of hitting us by surprise all the more."

"I'm inclined to agree," said Shad, exhaling a puff of pipe smoke. "By my reckonin', I figure we're only a couple of days out of Miles City. Means sometime tomorrow, late in the day I expect, we ought to come in sight of that stretch of broken land and the gap leadin' through it. If Van Horne's varmints had took a mind to come after us in some different way on account of the boys' ambush—out of anger or retaliation or whatever—you gotta believe they would've done it by now. That's what I been on such careful lookout for. But havin' not seen hide nor hair of 'em, I'd say that makes it pretty clear they must still be figurin' to try pickin' us off when we go through that gap."

"What about waitin' for us in town and maybe bringin' the law into it?" asked Sparky Whitlock. "Those skunks have had plenty of time by now to ride on to Miles City ahead of us. And knowin' how tight Van Horne is with that crooked judge back in Bellow

County, they could have traded wires back and forth
and filled the law in Miles City with all sorts of convincin' lies against us. Enough so that a posse—a *real*
one, not like the pack of curly wolves Van Horne
dragged along with him—might be primed and ready
to jump all over us as soon as we show up."

Norris Bradley's mouth stretched in a tolerant
smile. "That's smart thinking, Sparky. Smarter, I feel,
than what we can expect from Van Horne." The ranch
owner paused, his smile fading. "No, I take that back.
Much as I hate to admit it, Van Horne doesn't lack
smarts. But in our case, I don't think playing it smart
is what's driving him. At least not any longer. I think
it's too personal now. From Van Horne's perspective,
I don't think there's room for the law anymore. I don't
think he'll be satisfied with anything short of us going
down under the muzzles of his hired guns."

"I go along with that," spoke up Malloy from where
he was seated among the others. In the pulsing fire-
light, his boyishly handsome features took on some
shifting shadows that at times made him look harder,
grimmer than his countenance usually conveyed. He
held himself erect and steady—though this was at
least partly due to the supporting nearness of Colleen,
who had become very attentive to the wounded man.
When she wasn't in the saddle pushing along the
remuda, she was seldom very far from his side.

Mac had noticed that, and even though he'd been
fighting against developing feelings for Colleen practically since meeting her, now he experienced a pang
of jealousy every time he saw these displays of attention by her.

"During the time I had the displeasure of being in

Van Horne's company," Malloy went on, "I saw him change from mostly just wanting his herd back and seeing all of you severely punished . . . to something deeper and more personal. Nothing short of bloody and permanent revenge. I think the longer the chase lasted, the more discomfort he went through from being on the trail, and the more reluctance I started to show for the part I was supposed to be playing all started to add up. And then, when you waylaid us and took all the guns and horses, I think that's when Van Horne truly went mad. By the time Mahoney and his hardcases showed up, he was ranting about wanting your heads on stakes—and I think he meant it literally!"

Nobody responded to that until Roman said, "All right, with that pleasant thought in mind, I guess it comes right back around to whether or not we can expect an ambush to still be waitin' for us at Buffalo Kill Gap. I'm sayin' that's the way all the signs point. Anybody else?"

"I see it the same," said Mac. "Unfortunately, our ambush left enough of the varmints alive for them to maybe figure they can still get the job done. They got no way of knowing the Ranger gave us warning, re- member. So seven or eight men, most of them skilled gunhands, shooting down on a narrow passage from high rocks . . . What's to discourage 'em from going ahead with it?"

"I thought you said you wounded a couple more in addition to those you killed," said Henry Bradley. "You counting on some fight still being left in them, too?"

"Let's say I'm not betting against it," Mac replied. "We clipped about three of them as best I could make out. You got to remember, the lead was flying pretty intense there for a couple minutes, so taking time for an exact tally wasn't part of it. One of the ones I know we *did* hit, though, was Van Horne himself. Trouble was, it was only in the leg. We were both firing at him so we don't know for sure who can take credit for the hit."

"Worse than that," muttered Roman, "neither do we know who missed nailing him more seriously."

"For what it's worth, from what I saw and heard," said Malloy, "I don't think Van Horne ever figured to play a big part in the shooting, anyway. So losing him in that regard isn't going to make much difference in how the rest proceed."

"Just like that cowardly, conniving dog to set a bloodbath in motion yet keep his pampered hands clean of it," Bradley snarled in disgust.

Mac shrugged. "Whether he is or not, don't really change the overall picture. Getting back to Henry's question, all I can say, again, is that I think there's enough left of Van Horne's force to go ahead and try to ambush us in Buffalo Kill Gap."

Again there was a stretch of quiet. All the faces around the fire looked deep in somber thought.

This time it was Shad who broke the silence, saying, "All right. Nobody seems to have a good argument against expectin' the ambush. So, if that's the case and if I'm right about us comin' in sight of the gap sometime late tomorrow, that means we're pretty soon gonna be facin' whatever's there waitin' for us. So now the question becomes: How are we gonna deal with it?"

This time somebody had a response right away. "I been thinking on that. A lot," said Bradley.

All eyes immediately swung to him. He paused, perhaps for a touch of dramatic effect, and then continued, "Not too long ago, there was a couple young fellas we all know who set out to fetch back a handful of cows that had been run off by some lowdown rustlers. Thinking back on their telling of how they dealt with those no-good hombres, I recall a gap between some rock walls being involved and a purposely whipped-up stampede of the stolen cattle being brought into play and getting rammed right down the throats of the rustlers who'd placed themselves in that gap. That struck me at the time as a pretty clever way for those young fellas to take care of the business they had before 'em. Reflecting on it again, it strikes me now that not too much of a variation on that same trick just might be what could help us take care of this new piece of business we've got ahead of us . . ."

CHAPTER 47

"A saddle and gear, one of the horses from the remuda—all missing," reported George Bradley, his jaw set firmly.

Hearing this, Mac gritted his teeth and said, "She took off sure enough. No two ways about it."

"I don't understand. Why would she do something like that? Where would she go?" asked Colleen in an anxious tone.

"Where she'd go, seems plain enough, would be to head for Miles City," responded Shad. "She knows it's due north, the way we been aimin' for days now, and she must have heard me say how I reckon it's only a couple days off. A couple days pushin' our herd means less than a day for a lone rider on horseback. As to *why* she took a notion to light out, that I can't say."

"With that gal, there's no tellin' what runs through her head to make her do what she might haul off and do," said Roman sourly.

Everyone was standing near the chuckwagon, where Mac had first noted the absence of Belinda Forrest when he came over to start making breakfast. The way things had been arranged for the past few days, ever since Belinda began driving the chuckwagon by day with the injured Malloy riding in the back, was that at night Mac would spread his bedroll off with the other wranglers, apart from the wagon. The two women would remain with the wagon, their own bedrolls laid out underneath, while the healing Malloy remained in his nest up behind the seat. When Mac came around before daybreak to start fixing the morning meal, he worked as quietly as possible so as not to roust the others any sooner than necessary.

This morning, after he'd been going about his preparations for a while, he noticed that Belinda's bedroll under the wagon was empty. At first, he figured she had gone off to answer nature's call or perhaps some other personal business. But after an unreasonable amount of time passed without Belinda returning, Mac had seen fit to wake Colleen to see if she might have an explanation. When she didn't, things had escalated to the point of waking the others and eventually reaching the conclusion that the woman had fled.

As they stood now, pondering this development in the just-breaking dawn, Norris Bradley's gaze settled on his daughter. "You're the one who's been closest to her of late—about the only one to actually speak with her, given how she's kept apart from the rest of us, all sort of aloof, ever since the shooting of her husband and that shenanigan she pulled at the river. She give any indication of having anything like this in mind?"

Colleen shook her head, long hair sweeping back and forth across her shoulders. "No. Nothing. Like I said, I don't understand it at all."

Bradley's eyes cut to the Ranger. "How about you, Malloy? You been riding in the chuckwagon with her every day for the past three days. You were kinda out of it for the first day or so, but here lately you're spryer and more alert. You and Belinda must have talked some. She give any hint that she was forming a notion to take off?"

"Not a thing," Malloy answered firmly. "That's not surprising, though, considering how, in all the time we spent together, I doubt she said more than twenty or thirty words to me. I tried, believe me—you know, out of boredom, to help pass the time. But no matter what subject I tried to bring up, she had no interest in it."

"I saw that, too. How Belinda was particularly cold and aloof toward Gar," commented Colleen.

Mac winced a little at hearing her use Malloy's name—"Gar," even, instead of Garfield—with such easy familiarity.

"Even right at the beginning," Colleen continued, "when he was in great pain and half delirious, she was almost completely indifferent. Just . . . just *cold*, that's the word I keep coming back to. I guess maybe that was a sign right off that something was going on inside her, but I didn't know what to make of it."

"I know what to make of it. Your word 'cold' is right. She's a cold, calculating witch, that's all there is to it," Roman said bitterly. "Oh, she could turn on the sweetness and the heat when she was angling for something. Me and Mac and who knows how many other suckers got a taste of that. But under it all was always the conniving witch."

"That may be," allowed Bradley. "But what's so cold and conniving about her lighting out on her own like this?"

"Don't like to think it," said Shad, the corners of his

mouth pulling down, "but a hunch occurs to me. Maybe she's anglin' for a way to put herself on what she sees as the winnin' side of things."

Bradley displayed his own frown. "I don't follow you."

"I think I do," said Mac. "While it's a fact that Belinda ain't been joining in on many conversations lately, that's not to say she hasn't been listening and paying attention to the rest of us. Meaning she not only heard about us being close to Miles City, like Shad said a minute ago, but she also would've heard how we figure Van Horne's gang of hardcases is laying in ambush for us between here and there. And given her calculating, self-serving ways, it ain't hard to believe that her taking off like she's done is a sign that she thinks she can serve herself better by throwing in with Van Horne. In other words, who she sees as coming out on top once the gunsmoke clears. That about what you're thinking, Shad?"

"You summed it up real purty."

Bradley's scowl turned into an angry scowl. "If that's her game, if she set out to stack her chips with Van Horne, then she'll blab everything she knows to get on the good side of him. How the ranger survived to warn us, how we're expecting the ambush, what we've got in mind to deal with it."

"That's about the size of it. The whole works," Mac conceded.

"But why would she do that?" Colleen said. "After all we did to help her! Mac risked his life going into that river to save her, even once we knew the truth about her lies and scheming ways and after her husband shot Roman! After all that, she'd betray us to a devil she knows is out for nothing short of our destruction?"

Gently, Bradley said, "You can never understand

that kind of behavior, dear, because your mind doesn't have the capacity to imagine ever acting in such a way."

"I understand plain enough," said Roman, his face flushed with anger. "That witch has gone beyond just being ungrateful. If she makes it to Van Horne ready to tell everything she knows, she's a serious threat to all of us. We don't know for sure when she took off, but we know which way she's headed. I say we quit wasting time standing around talking when one of us oughta be takin' out after her. Get me a horse, George, I'll do it!"

Bradley held up a restraining hand. "I appreciate how you feel, son, but it's no good. Your chances of catching her are slim, and there's the risk Van Horne might have some men posted on the edge of that broken land, watching for our approach. The sight of you, a lone rider, getting close might be too tempting for them not to try and pick you off. We don't have any men to spare, and I'm not ready to lose a son."

"He's right, boy," said Shad. "That gal ain't worth the risk. She's likely made it too far, anyway."

Roman's mouth pulled tight and he looked ready to argue. Then, slowly, the tension visibly lifted off him and he expelled a long, ragged breath.

"All right," he said. "So what now? If we're in agreement that she's gone ahead to alert Van Horne about everything we know and had planned, how do we play it from here? What changes do we need to make?"

Bradley gazed off to the north for a long moment, as if thinking he might see an answer there. Then, exhaling his own heavy sigh, he said, "I don't know. Not yet. But I do know we're not turning back and we're not going around. Whatever happens is going to play out at Buffalo Kill Gap. So the sooner we get there, the sooner we can bring this to an end. We can chew on some new ideas during the course of the day. For right now, let's remember we're conducting a cattle drive and get these blasted critters moving!"

It was that blasted Ranger showing up that forced her hand, Belinda thought bitterly. If not for him, she would have been willing to stick with the Rafter B outfit all the way to Miles City and trust they wouldn't turn her in for her part in the New Mexico murder she'd confessed to Mac about.

But the presence of the Ranger changed everything. New Mexico bordered on Texas, and it was well known how alert and far-reaching those determined law dogs who wore the famous star-in-a-circle badge tended to be. They made it their business to know not only the outlaws who operated strictly in their jurisdiction but also anywhere close. And from all reports, they had memories like steel traps. Malloy had proven as much when he told about recognizing Van Horne's recent hires as all being wanted men for misdeeds scattered over a wide swath.

Having Malloy in the wagon with her, always trying to make conversation, always looking at her, had worn her nerves raw. Belinda was used to having men look at her, but not in the way he did. She could *feel* him either recognizing her completely or at least recognizing features that ought to mean something to him. Something to the lawman part of him.

There was no way Belinda was willing to face charges for her part in that New Mexico business. Not after everything she'd already been through since then.

And especially not alone, not after Herbert and his insane jealousy had gotten himself killed.

As a result of the Ranger having joined them, the notion to flee the Rafter B outfit had formed in Belinda's mind. She'd forced herself to hold off until she was sure they were close enough to Miles City for her to make it the rest of the way there on her own. But then, upon hearing how Van Horne was expected to have a small army of gun toughs waiting in between to ambush the Rafter B, her plan had changed drastically.

She'd been vaguely familiar with the name of Caleb Van Horne before hearing it in connection to this cattle drive. Or more accurately, this cattle *theft* she had fallen in with . . .

Van Horne. Claimant to vast land and cattle holdings, as well as a wide range of other businesses throughout the Texas Panhandle. Powerful. Ruthless. Wealthy.

Suddenly, Belinda had seen the potential in adjusting to a different plan. A far better one. If she could ingratiate herself to the powerful Van Horne—and she felt confident she had information for doing exactly that—then she not only would ensure her break with the Rafter B and that meddlesome Ranger but possibly, with her considerable wiles, she might manage to place herself in very comfortable position for the future.

These thoughts raced through Belinda's mind as she spurred on the sturdy mount she'd taken from the Rafter B remuda. She'd been riding for hours now, the sun ascended almost to its noon peak above her. She had stopped once, briefly, to water and rest both the horse and herself. But she hadn't been able to contain for very long her sense of urgency to keep pushing hard.

As they galloped on over roughening terrain, Belinda could feel the horse tiring under her, and her own exhaustion was starting to weigh heavy, as well. She knew she would have to stop again before long or risk pushing the horse beyond its limit.

And then, as she was looking around for a stand of trees or some rock outcrop that offered a patch of shade, she saw it up ahead. Up where the land grew even more broken and rocky and then heaved up into a high, jagged ridge extending as far as she could see off to the east and west. But right in the center, almost directly in front of where she was headed, there was a V-shaped opening that looked like it had been sliced by the swing of a giant ax.

"Buffalo Kill Gap, it has to be," Belinda said under her breath.

And then, a swell of excitement pushing away her exhaustion, she said in a louder voice, "Keep it up just a little longer, horse—we're almost there!"

CHAPTER 48

"It can't be, I tell ya. She's lyin'. It's some kind of trick that Rafter B bunch is tryin' to pull to confuse us, maybe get us feudin' amongst ourselves!"

Chance Barlow was frantically spouting these words as he was being backed into a shallow vertical crevice worn into the rock wall above a high ledge on the west shoulder of Buffalo Kill Gap. Crowding him on either side, forcing the backup, were Zeb Mahoney and Clay Coburn. Both men wore looks of narrow-eyed menace on their faces, and each had one hand resting on the butt of a gun holstered on his hip.

Standing a few feet off to one side, Caleb Van Horne and Belinda Forrest looked on. Van Horne's eyes shone, and the expression on his face was a mix of anger and excitement. Pressing herself against the fat man, as if seeking support and protection, Belinda appeared highly apprehensive.

"There's lies involved in the gal's tale, all right," snarled Mahoney. "But they're lies that trace straight back to you. You said that Ranger was dead! You said you and Curly made sure."

"N-no! I never said that," Barlow protested. "It was

Curly. I was just goin' by what he claimed. The Ranger jumped me and knocked me loopy for a few minutes, remember? That's when Curly showed up and plugged him. Poured a half dozen or more rounds into him and knocked him over the edge of that gully. There was blood all over. He *had* to be dead!"

"You said you made sure," Mahoney repeated.

"He was dead, I tell you! Nobody could have lived through that."

Mahoney edged a half step closer. "But somebody did—and it was that Ranger! He lived and he dragged hisself to the Rafter B camp and told them all about us. How me and my boys had showed up to reinforce your sorry bunch and then the plan we put together for ambushin' their outfit right here in this gap. That explains how they knew to wait for us at the river with their own ambush and killed four of ours—including one of my top men!"

"I know, I know," wailed Barlow. "I lost a good friend that day, too. It still didn't seem possible that Malloy could have had anything to do with it."

"Well, it *should* have! You should have thought of it as a possible explanation," Mahoney insisted. "That gave you a second chance to tell the truth, to own up to what you didn't have the guts to own up to in the first place. But you didn't. You still kept it all to yourself and left the rest of us not knowin' to expect they'd be showin' up prepared for us."

"So what? We've still got them outnumbered and outgunned. The advantages are still all ours. If they're stupid enough to come on ahead anyway, like the girl claims, what difference does it make if they know we're here waiting for 'em?"

"What difference?" echoed Mahoney, baring his

teeth in a humorless smile. He turned his head and looked at Van Horne. "The difference, to me, is a mighty big one. I don't favor ridin' with a lyin' yellow weasel who sees members of his own crew mowed down because he held out on 'em and then thinks it don't matter. Way I see it, what really don't matter no more is him. You got a problem with my way of lookin' at it, Boss?"

Van Horne's head moved slowly back and forth. "Consider yourself in charge now, Mr. Mahoney. Handle the matter as you see fit."

Barlow's eyes bugged. "No! Boss, I always did whatever you wanted. One mistake shouldn't—"

Barlow was so focused on making his plea to Van Horne that he completely missed the very faint hand gesture Mahoney made to Coburn. In a smooth, fluid motion that appeared totally unhurried yet took place with remarkable speed, Coburn's hand left the butt of his gun and swept up alongside his chest, passing over the underarm rig that held his brace of throwing knives. As it moved away from the rig, the hand was gripping one of the knives. Thrusting his arm forward in a quick, piston-like movement, Coburn plunged the knife to its hilt into Barlow's chest, directly over his heart.

Barlow stopped talking. His eyes bugged even bigger and his mouth hung open, releasing a string of drool. Coburn's arm worked piston-like again, this time sinking the knife at a slightly upward angle but once more directly into the heart.

Barlow's eyes stayed open but turned dull and unseeing. Lifeless. A bubbling sound issued from his mouth, pushing more drool out with it. Unable to fall because of the rock crevice he had backed into,

Barlow could only sink slowly downward as his knees buckled and folded under him until he ended up sitting Indian-style, as motionless as the rock into which he was wedged. Coburn reached out, casually wiped his blade on the dead man's shoulder, then slipped the knife back into its sheath.

Continuing to look on, staring raptly all during the stabbing, Van Horne now wore a pleased smile. He had two reasons for feeling pleased. One was seeing the incompetent Barlow dispatched. The other was because of the way curvaceous Belinda was pressed so tightly against him, her face turned away in shock by what she had just witnessed and buried against Van Horne's shoulder.

"If you want," Mahoney drawled indifferently, "he can be the first head for one of your stakes."

Van Horne's smile faded. "That won't be necessary. We'll save that special treatment for the Bradleys and the mongrels closest to them."

Mahoney nodded. "However you want it. Speaking of those mongrels . . . What have you got in mind for them now, based on this new information we've got? They've got to figure we'd end up with their runaway and that one way or another, she'd spill to us everything she knows."

"Yes," said Van Horne, gently touching Belinda's hair where it was splayed across his chest. "How fortunate for us she's been willing to share with no need for coercion."

Belinda lifted her face from Van Horne's shoulder. Scowling as she swept back her hair, she said, "I have no reason to protect the interests of anyone in that pack of rustlers! They gunned down my husband,

and before his body was even cold, practically every man in the outfit took a turn at trying to maul me—or worse!"

"Yeah, I'm sure that was real rough on you," said Mahoney, his tone lacking genuine sympathy and in fact bordering close to sarcasm. "But my job—the one I just inherited—is to focus on the here and now. And that means what to expect different from the Rafter B boys now that you've skipped ahead and filled us in on things they were countin' on us not knowin' before."

"You think that will cause them to change their plans?" asked Van Horne.

Mahoney shook his head. "Can't say. Way I see it, though, the best thing we got goin' for us is that they've come this far and have got to be mighty anxious to plow on through the rest of the way. What's more, considerin' the lay of the land and all, they ain't got a lot of options for gettin' where they want to go."

Van Horne looked at Belinda. "Their plan, from what you gathered, was to stampede their herd through the gap and try to use that as a distraction to make it clear of our shooters up on the rocks. Is that right?"

"I didn't hear anything real detailed," said Belinda. "But that was the gist of it, yes."

Turning his attention back to Mahoney, Van Horne said, "Would something like that have any luck to work against us?"

Mahoney pooched his lips thoughtfully for several seconds before replying, "Won't lie to you. Yeah, it might give us some trouble. Eight hundred longhorns poundin' through this gap, dust rollin' thick enough to choke and sting eyes. Boilin' up as high or higher than where we're standin' now and their men ridin'

through in the midst of it . . . Be mighty hard, shootin'
down through that, even for crack marksmen to pick
'em all off. No tellin' how many might make it through."

"Damn!"

"That ain't to say we couldn't ride out after the
ones who *did* make it, and finish 'em off that way," Mahoney was quick to add.

"If we're going to end up fighting them like
mounted cavalry," Van Horne snapped, "then we
might as well go out and ride into them that way to
begin with."

Mahoney shrugged. "Makes no difference to me.
Doin' it like that, though, goes back to leavin' the
cattle scattered—and on the wrong side of the gap to
boot—when the shootin' is over."

Van Horne's face reddened. "The cattle are mine,
I'll reclaim them one way or another. Even if I have to
hire more men from town to bring them the rest of
the way in. First and foremost, I want that blasted
Bradley and all of his seed dead and done for!"

"Then I say we ride back and have it out with 'em,
nose to nose, once and for all," stated Mahoney.
"Without the element of surprise, tryin' to take 'em in
this gap while they're stampedin' through—a tactic
I don't see 'em changin', no matter what they figure
the girl told us—will only drag things out and maybe
work more to their favor than ours."

"Are you confident we have sufficient force to
take them in a charge of that sort?" asked Van Horne,
frowning.

"Look around." Mahoney swept his arm, indicating
the heavily armed men scattered at various high
points in the rocks on either side of the gap, already
positioned and primed for the arrival of Bradley's

outfit. "With the added guns you hired in Miles City, we're back to a full dozen—well, make that eleven, what with the resignation of Barlow. Eight of us seasoned gun hands, plus your three wranglers. According to the girl, Bradley's got only a total of ten, and that's countin' his daughter and the crippled Ranger. Among the rest, there ain't but about two who have more than passin' experience at gun work. With those kind of odds, Mr. Van Horne, I'd feel confident chargin' straight into the Devil's parlor."

In an icy tone, Van Horne said, "What I expect is for your goal to be quite the reverse, Mr. Mahoney. I want you to ride out and *deliver* fire and brimstone!"

CHAPTER 49

Garfield Malloy sat rigidly perched on the driver's seat of the Rafter B chuckwagon, gazing intently ahead as he deftly worked the mule team's reins with only his right hand. His left arm was wrapped tight against his body, immobilizing it to prevent any movement that would aggravate his shoulder wound.

Turning his head slightly to one side, the Ranger said over his shoulder, "We're getting mighty close. Somebody's going to have to make a decision before much longer."

Two feet behind him, squatting in the emptied-out bed of the conveyance, Mac replied, "It's Boss Bradley's call to make. Don't worry, he's seeing the same things you are. He'll know when to signal which way we're going to play this out."

It was late in the afternoon. The sun was descended close above the western horizon. For some time now the landscape had been growing steadily more broken. The cattle herd plodding behind the chuckwagon was stirring up a perpetual cloud of brownish dust—gold-tinted at times when the slanting rays of sunlight hit it just right—that partially enveloped the animals and then trailed off in their wake until it dissipated far behind in a gentle breeze.

Under the canopy of the wagon, in the space created by stripping away all the food supplies and cooking paraphernalia and leaving them stacked beside the trail some miles back, crouched four other men besides Mac—Shad, Roman, Sparky, and Nolan. Back with the herd, riding point, was Norris Bradley. His sons Henry and George were a ways behind him, one on each flank, and bringing up the remuda at the rear was Colleen.

These adjustments had been made in accordance with the plan Bradley and Shad came up with to counter possible changes expected from Van Horne once he received information from Belinda. Learning from her that the Rafter B outfit knew of the pending ambush awaiting them in Buffalo Kill Gap and how they'd intended to stampede straight on through, it was reasoned Van Horne and the lieutenants leading his hardcase army would likely consider some different tactic, though one still aimed at wiping out Bradley and his crew, then seizing the herd.

The terrain and the nearness of Miles City, however, actually left Van Horne only very few options as far as a change in tactics. Assuming he was still bent on making this personal and keeping the Miles City authorities out of it, that meant a confrontation had to go ahead and take place out here in this harsh, remote locale. That pretty much boiled down to Van Horne's gun-wolves either going ahead with the ambush in the gap, banking they were skilled enough to pick off all or most of their targets plowing through amid a stampede . . . or riding out and settling things in a face-to-face exchange from horseback.

If it was the latter, the heavily armed men now concealed in the wagon were in place to spring a mighty big surprise on any incoming riders. From the perspective of those on the approach, it was hoped that the appearance of the chuckwagon rolling ahead of the herd would be taken as merely standard procedure. And the visible figures of Bradley and his two sons would be seen as front wranglers, with the assumption that the rest would be strung out behind, obscured by the churning dust cloud. If those coming on the attack bought all of this, when they drew near enough to the chuckwagon the canopy would be peeled back and an outpouring of blazing lead from the previously concealed men would greet the would-be attackers with devastating effect.

That was Bradley's altered plan—revised on the expectation that Van Horne's force might try something different. But if the gun-wolves stayed in the high rocks and stuck with their ambush attempt, then the men hidden in the wagon would revert to horseback and proceed with stampeding the herd through the gap.

Given that the high, ragged ridge and the gap splitting it at the middle—an opening already with a blood-drenched history—now loomed less than a mile away, one faction or the other was soon going to have to commit.

In the back of the wagon, cramped, jarred and jostled by the continued onward movement, tension was building in some of the men. But the wagon rolled on, creaking and jostling its silent cargo.

Until, at length, Malloy once more spoke over his

shoulder. "Looks like the ball is about ready to pop, fellas. I see riders coming out of the gap, headed our way. A whole mess of 'em."

"They look friendly?" Mac said wryly.

"Don't see no smiles. I'm pretty sure they're not a welcoming committee coming to greet us with open arms."

"More like open gun muzzles," Mac muttered.

At the rear of the wagon, Roman said, "I just signaled my pa. He sees 'em, too."

Mac hitched forward and peered over Malloy's shoulder. The approaching riders were coming at a steady canter, and as he watched, they fanned out wide over the intervening expanse of barren, mostly flat ground.

Emitting a low whistle, Mac said, "Don't know where they got 'em, but that pack has added some new wolves to it since what we last saw back at the river."

"How many are there?" Roman wanted to know.

"Looks like about ten . . . eleven . . . a dozen, give or take. Plenty to go around."

"Van Horne with 'em?"

"Don't see no sign of him."

Roman grunted. "Figures that pampered skunk would do everything he could to avoid the shooting."

"I don't see Chance Barlow, either," said Malloy. "I can make out Zeb Mahoney and some of his men. Selkirk . . . Purdy. Also see some faces I don't recognize. New recruits from somewhere."

"They had time to ride ahead and pay a visit to Miles City. Must have hired some more guns there," Mac said.

"Whoever they are," replied Malloy, "they don't show no signs of slowing down. Appears like they're not interested in trying for a parley."

"Good," said Shad, his jaw set hard. "We got no words for 'em anyhow . . . just lead."

CHAPTER 50

When the Van Horne riders had approached to within a hundred yards, Mac put his hand on Malloy's shoulder and said, "Get ready to swing that mule team, Ranger. Once you do, set the brake and then drop down low before the lead starts flying. Boss Bradley needs you alive to be a witness back in Bellow County if we come out on top of this scrape."

"Don't worry, I know what I have to do," Malloy responded curtly.

Glancing around behind him, Mac said to the others, "You ready, fellas?"

"I was born ready," growled Shad.

Roman nodded. "Pa's signalin'—go ahead and let 'er buck!"

Mac touched Malloy's shoulder again, this time just a quick slap. "You heard the man, Ranger. Turn 'em."

As the approaching riders, now at fifty yards, broke from a canter into a full gallop, Malloy braced his heels against the footboard of the driver's box, leaned back on the seat and hollered to the team, "Gee! Gee, you hammerheads!"

Upon hearing the right-turn command and also noting the urgency in Malloy's tone, the mules swung sharply in accordance. The wagon swept around, too, causing the men inside to momentarily grab the walls to keep from getting tossed off balance. Once the team and wagon were positioned perpendicular to the path of the oncoming horsemen, Malloy instantly brought everything to a jolting halt by hauling back on the reins and setting the brake with a hard kick of his foot. A moment after that, he swiveled on the seat and dropped back into the bed next to Mac, saying, "Your turn—take 'em!"

Mac and the others were tugging at the previously loosened canopy, yanking it from its frame and flinging it away. Before the canvas ever hit the ground, some of the men were leveling their rifles and cutting loose with the first rounds of the conflict.

The maneuver worked perfectly as far as catching Mahoney and those riding with him by surprise. That initial volley made the air sizzle with lead, and three of the horsemen were immediately knocked from their mounts.

None of them, unfortunately, was Mahoney. Unscathed, he spurred his horse onward, shouting frantically, "Don't break! Don't break! Ride them down!"

The line of men to either side of him faltered and slowed slightly, but held together and kept coming. Handguns drawn, all were extending their arms out ahead and triggering return fire at the wagon and its occupants. The air filled with the roar of rifles and the crack of pistols. Dust and powder smoke swirled thick, cut by bullets slicing back and forth.

Mac stayed in the wagon bed, crouched behind its

wall, levering and firing his Yellowboy in a steady rhythm even as incoming rounds hammered and rattled the boards shielding him. To his left, Shad was working similarly with his Colt revolving rifle.

Roman had dropped off the back side of the wagon and was now on his belly underneath, his Henry pouring lead from there. Sparky and Nolan were on the ground at the rear of the wagon, firing from behind the drop-down table as Bradley, Henry, and George came galloping hard from back by the herd, adding to the leadstorm with their drawn pistols.

Mahoney and his hardcases kept coming.

A slug sent another one somersaulting backward off his horse and then, a moment later, the horse caught its own round and went down screaming.

Nolan took a hit and keeled over. Sparky immediately knelt and began pulling him to better cover behind the wagon wheel. Bullets chewed the ground all around them until one found Sparky, too, pitching him backward in the dirt.

Bradley and his two youngest sons closed in, cursing and throwing lead wildly in retaliation. Behind them, the cattle began to scatter and turn away from the gunfire. The mule team hitched to the chuckwagon, due to a combination of training and the sturdy wagon brake, pawed some with their front hooves but otherwise held amazingly steady in the midst of all the fury around them.

Big Walt Purdy, one of the initial attackers to be knocked out of the saddle, staggered back to his feet and began advancing determinedly toward the Rafter B men, even without a horse under him. His black face was shiny with sweat and his massive chest was streaked with blood, but still he plodded forward, extending a long-barreled .45 ahead of him and shooting as he came. Mac drew a bead on him, and with a caress of his trigger finger planted a slug in the center of his broad forehead. When the big man went down this time, he didn't get back up.

Continuing to lead the charge, Mahoney seemed also to be leading a charmed existence. More than a dozen bullets had sliced the air within inches of him without ever managing a strike. At one point, Roman had him square in his sights, but an instant before he fired, a random incoming round kicked a geyser of dust into his eyes and his slug went wide by a yard.

For his part, Mahoney got off a shot of his own a moment later that plowed off-center into Shad's chest and sent the trail boss toppling heavily back onto the floor of the wagon.

Extending his arm and leaning forward in his saddle to make that shot, however, finally exposed the hardcase leader to a bullet that broke the charm. It caught him in the throat, angling up into the brain, blowing the top of his head away in a spray of gore and bits of skull.

Mac snapped his head to the right, looking in the direction from which the kill shot on Mahoney had come—and there was Malloy, with a smoking revolver in his good hand and a satisfied glint in his eye.

"I thought you were supposed to stay down," Mac barked.

"And miss out on all the fun? I don't think so!"

Any further exchange of words between the two, for the time being, was forced aside by a sudden volley of shots banging into the side of the wagon behind which they were hunkered. Both men promptly raised their weapons and concentrated on triggering a heated response.

With Mahoney down, the remainder of the attack quickly faltered and fell apart.

Selkirk and Coburn were the next ones to bite the dust, and the remaining man recently hired in Miles City—a rat-faced little runt in cowhide chaps—quickly followed. Van Horne's three wranglers, who had been hanging reluctantly in the rear the whole time, wheeled and rode away as fast as they could spur their horses. No one pursued.

All of a sudden it was over.

Van Horne's pack of curly wolves were wiped out. The Rafter B crew fared better, but didn't make it through without paying some tolls. Laird Nolan was dead. Sparky and Shad were wounded, both injuries serious but neither appearing life-threatening. The same was true for Norris Bradley who, in an ironic touch of misfortune, had ridden up just in time to get in the way of the final shot thrown wildly by the runt in the cowhide chaps as he fell from his saddle after being struck in the temple by a bullet from Roman.

Colleen, thankfully, didn't make it up from the remuda until after the shooting was done. Also thankfully, she was on hand to start tending to the wounded men.

All three were laid out on the canopy canvas from the chuckwagon. As his daughter began cutting away his pant leg to get at the bullet in his thigh, Norris Bradley propped himself on his elbows and scowled up at Roman and Mac.

"You know this ain't finished, don't you?" he rasped.

"The big, fat head rattler is still waiting somewhere, safe back in the nest."

"More like he only *thinks* he's safe," Roman replied.

His father nodded. "That's what I hoped to hear. You know I wanted in the worst way to be the one to corner that poisonous critter myself. But now, with this"—he jerked his chin toward his leg wound—"that don't seem to be in the cards for me. So I'm looking to you two again."

"Done," Roman and Mac said in unison.

CHAPTER 51

"Don't come any closer or I'll put a bullet in her brain!"

Those were Van Horne's words as he jammed a silver-plated, over-under derringer against Belinda's temple while he held her body in front of his, her head wrenched back at a painful angle by the thick handful of hair he clutched in his free hand. His face was flushed and covered by rivulets of sweat, he was breathing hard from exertion, and his eyes were wild, desperate. Belinda's eyes were wide with pain and fear.

That was how Mac and Roman—also accompanied by an insistent Garfield Malloy—found the pair when they reached the back side of Buffalo Kill Gap. The way they would reason it out later was that Van Horne and the woman had remained up in the higher rocks on one shoulder of the gap, where they also later found the body of Chance Barlow, in order to have a good view of the attack by Mahoney and his men. What they ended up seeing, of course, was the hard-cases faltering and failing.

When the three surviving wranglers turned tail and

fled out through the gap directly below their position, making no attempt to stop and help what they now obviously considered their former employer, there was nothing left for Van Horne except to attempt flight himself. But the climb back down to the floor of the gap where their horses waited took too long due to Van Horne's ponderous weight compounded by the wound in his thigh. As a result, they'd only just made it to the animals when they were suddenly confronted by the arrival of the Rafter B men and the Ranger.

Survival instinct and raw desperation led Van Horne to attempt turning his tenuous new ally, Belinda, into a bargaining chip. Pulling from a hideaway vest pocket the one personal weapon he ever allowed himself, he jammed the derringer against her head, challenging the men who'd come after him to call his bluff.

"What makes you think," Roman replied in a casual drawl as he leaned forward to rest a forearm on his saddle horn, "we give a hoot whether or not you put a bullet in the head, no matter how pretty it is, of somebody who's done nothing but lie and scheme and double-cross us?"

Van Horne's eyes darted nervously, uncertainly across the faces of all three men as Mac and Malloy edged their horses up on either side of Roman. Licking his lips, he said, "You can't be serious. You'd disregard the life of this woman so easily, rather than consider a deal with me?"

"You seem to have a mighty short memory," Mac responded. "We just got done disregarding the lives of a whole handful of men. They weren't much, but at least they took what they had coming straight ahead, not trying to find somebody else to hide behind."

"And one of the men who lost his life back there," added Roman, "was one of ours—worth all the rest of yours and about ten of you, you cowardly bag of guts. That makes it real hard to stomach the thought of makin' any kind of deal with you, no matter what."

"Please. Don't let him kill me," said Belinda in a small, strained voice as Van Horne continued to crank her head back. "I . . . I know I done you wrong. I'm so sorry . . . But I don't want to die."

Roman looked at her coldly. "Like Mac said, a whole bunch of folks just died. Some of them was likely sorry, too. But neither did it do them any good."

Van Horne's eyes locked on Malloy. "You. You're a sworn officer of the law. A proud Texas Ranger . . . All the while we rode together you spouted about justice. You can't let them just . . . just *execute* me. Stand by and let the girl be killed . . . You can't *allow* that!"

Malloy just looked at him.

Van Horne licked his lips again, his mouth dry in spite of the sweat pouring down over his face. His heavy body appeared to waver somewhat, but his grip on Belinda's hair never lessened and the derringer's muzzle remained pressed tight to the side of her head. "I'll put myself in your custody," he said, still addressing Malloy. "Take me in, I'll throw myself on the mercy of the court. I'll sign a paper, I'll confess to bribing the judge and the tax assessor. I'll sign the ranch and the cattle back over to Bradley right up front. Please, show some mercy."

"Like the mercy you showed me," Malloy grated in a low voice, "when you sent Barlow and Curly out to kill me and leave my body for the buzzards?"

"That was a mistake, a bad one." Van Horne's breath was coming in ragged gasps. "It was Barlow and Mahoney . . . they talked me into it. I . . . I never should have listened. But look at me. Haven't I already been punished, made to pay for so much wrongheadedness? Coming after this herd, seeking personal vengeance . . . it's all been one of the biggest mistakes of my life. I've been shot, I'm wore out, exhausted. I know that's still not sufficient, so take me back to Texas where I can finish paying my debt. I'm ready to face whatever it is."

Roman made a half-gagging sound in his throat. "Oh, that's rich. Back to Bellow County, eh? Where you can start right in again greasing palms and calling in favors to slick the skids for you. Yeah, that sounds like your idea of justice, all right. But it ain't the kind you're gonna get, fat man."

Van Horne started to reply, to plead some more, but held his tongue and instead canted his head slightly in a listening pose. Then the others heard it, too. The rataplan of a horse's hooves, a single rider coming rapidly through the gap.

Roman didn't take his eyes off Van Horne. Mac and Malloy turned for a quick glance to see who was coming.

"It's young George, riding lickety-split," said Mac.

Half a minute later, George reached them and reined his horse sharply. His face was crumpled into an anguished expression.

"What is it, George? Is there something wrong?" asked Mac.

"Afraid so," said George in a strained voice. "It's Shad Hopper . . . he died."

Shad. Dead. The words fell like a hammer on Mack and Roman and both sucked audible intakes of breath.

"His wound was worse than we first thought," George went on. "Pa figured the bullet must've sorta rattled around inside him and got too near his heart. There was nothing nobody could have done." George swallowed hard. "He talked a little bit. Told Colleen he was okay, to take care of Pa and Sparky first. Then he took a sudden, real deep breath and . . . and wouldn't breathe no more." George's voice cracked on the final words.

Mac stood stock still for a long moment. Then he turned slowly back to face Van Horne. "Evil . . . can't . . . win," he stated loudly, clearly. Then, smooth and fast, he pulled the Smith & Wesson from his waistband, extended it to arm's length, and fired one shot.

The bullet entered half an inch above Van Horne's right eye. His head snapped back like it had been jerked by an invisible wire, the cream-colored Stetson spinning off in a splatter of bright crimson. The fat man's body twisted away from Belinda and started to fall, his dead fingers loosening their grip on her hair but the hand holding the derringer spasming as that arm dropped limply to his side and a round was triggered from the little gun. Van Horne collapsed heavily to the ground.

For several heartbeats, everyone remained very still. Mac continued to hold his arm extended and a slow curl of smoke drifted up from the muzzle of the Model 3.

And then Belinda doubled forward and fell.

The four men quickly knelt around her. Only then

did they see the wet red stain spreading across the front of her blouse under rapidly rising and falling breasts.

Looking around, it was Malloy who recognized what had happened. "Ricochet," he said. "When that derringer went off, the bullet struck the rocky ground and bounced up into her."

"Damn!" Mac bit out between clenched teeth.

Belinda's eyes fluttered open and swept across the faces leaning over her. They came to rest on Mac. Her mouth twitched but no words came out.

"I . . . I'm sorry," Mac said hesitantly and in a husky voice. "I didn't mean for you to get hurt that way."

Belinda's mouth curved in a faint smile. Barely above a whisper, she said, "You saved my life once . . . I guess I wasn't meant to keep it . . ."

Then her eyes closed once more and never opened again.

CHAPTER 52

In the morning, they gathered together the bodies of Mahoney and his men and laid them out in a row near where the battle had taken place. Off to one side of Buffalo Kill Gap, they similarly laid the bodies of Van Horne and Belinda. Authorities in Miles City would be notified and the task of returning to do with the remains whatever they deemed proper would be left up to them.

On a grassy rise a mile or so beyond the gap, where the landscape had again given way to a stretch of rolling prairie, they took the cleansed and wrapped bodies of Shad and Nolan from the bed of the chuckwagon and buried them there. As both were men of the grasslands and wide-open spaces, it seemed as appropriate a place as any. Bradley said some words and young George sang the "lay the sod o'er me" refrain from "The Cowboy's Lament" in a soft, lilting voice with a tear running down his cheek.

After the burial, the procession—Malloy and Colleen on the wagon seat; Bradley and Sparky, the two wounded men, as cargo; and the three Bradley brothers mounted alongside—prepared to go on into

Miles City to give notification, set follow-up actions in motion, and seek proper medical attention for their wounded. The cattle herd, for the time being, was left back where they had scattered. It was reckoned that the buyer Bradley had lined up, probably after dickering for a price shave, would provide some men to help round up the longhorns and drive them the rest of the way on in.

That left one critter out of the outfit, however, who was ready to scatter and not join any trip into Miles City.

Mac.

"This seems like a good spot for me to call the end of the trail," he explained from the saddle of his trusty paint horse. "The trail being taken by the Rafter B, that is. Ain't a decision I make lightly, nor one I make without some regret. Even though I was a latecomer, I grew to feel part of the Rafter B. It was something I was proud to be, and I hope it showed. But everything's different now. It ain't over for the rest of you, but it is for me." He tipped his head toward the west. "California's still waiting for me. I figure it's time I got back on course."

"There's other doggone places besides California, Texas being one of 'em," Bradley said. "You can stay part of the Rafter B. We'd be proud to have you. With Malloy here ready to testify against Judge Ballantine and that crooked tax claim, I'm going back to fight for what I got swindled out of, and I think we got a strong chance to win."

"You're in the right. That'll make the difference," Mac said, the words a weak echo inside his head. "So going back is the right thing for you . . . but it ain't necessarily the same for me."

Malloy regarded him. "You distancing yourself from some kind of trouble back there, Mac?"

"Gar!" Colleen said admonishingly.

Gar again, Mac thought. He also noted how closely together they were sitting on the wagon seat.

Meeting Malloy's gaze, Mac said, "Could be. Then again, maybe there's trouble I want to avoid running *toward.*"

"I don't follow you," Malloy responded.

Mac smiled thinly. "I shot Van Horne in cold blood, right in front of you. Even though he was a piece of scum, it's not something that sits especially easy with me. I don't expect it does with you, either. And you've made it well known you're all about justice and due process. If we was to both land back in Texas, who's to say the star you wear wouldn't start causing what you saw to eat more and more inside you until you felt obliged to try and do something about it?"

Twin streaks of color ran up the sides of Malloy's face. Mac couldn't tell for sure if it was anger or embarrassment. His gaze continuing to bore into Mac, he said, "Here's a curious thing about Van Horne getting shot. Just at the moment it occurred, an odd little breeze came through that gap and blew a speck of dust into my eye. For all I could tell, Van Horne started to swing his stupid little derringer toward you and you had to fire in self-defense."

"You know, it's the craziest thing," spoke up Roman from where he sat his horse off to one side of Mac. "The same thing happened to me. By the time I blinked my vision clear, it was all over."

"I didn't have no trouble with dust, but you were smack in my way, big brother," joined in George. "I didn't see exactly how it went, either."

Mac swept his gaze over all three of them. Grinning faintly, he said, "Always suspected Texas had more bull artists than longhorns . . ."

"It's a big state. We got room for both," replied Bradley.

Mac sighed. "Maybe someday I'll come around for a closer check on that. And I appreciate hearing about that curious dust devil back there in Buffalo Kill Gap, I truly do . . . But for right now, I'll admit there's still other memories and other reasons pushing me toward California. And that's all the explaining I care to do. Hope you understand."

"We don't," said Roman with a wry smile. "But we respect your right to your own business. For the record, let me say I'm mighty glad I didn't shoot you that night we first ran into each other. Be careful some other hotheaded fool don't have better luck."

"I'll try to do that," Mac assured him.

"What about the pay I owe you?" said Bradley. "Wire me when you land somewhere, I'll send it to you."

Mac waved a hand. "Don't worry about it. Put it toward some nice markers for Shad and Nolan."

Finally, Mac did what he'd been avoiding. He settled his gaze on Colleen. She was looking back at him with moist eyes. "Sorry we never found time for me to give you that cooking lesson," he said, smiling sadly. "But like I been telling you right along, I got a hunch when you get back to Bellow County, you're going to find a fella who don't give a hang whether you can cook or not."

She mouthed his name, but barely any sound came out.

Mac cut his attention to Malloy. "And you, Ranger, I'd advise you be extra careful not to let any more dust get in your eye that could cause you to miss something else important that might be right in front of "—here an another glance at Colleen and then back—"or maybe even beside you."

Malloy blushed again. "I'll be sure to remember."

With that, Mac swung his arm in a broad wave, then wheeled the paint and rode off at a gallop. A man could make all the plans he wanted to, Mac thought, but in the end they didn't amount to much more than . . . a hill of beans. But that didn't mean he ought to stop trying.

With the climbing sun at his back, he headed toward the horizon where that sun would be setting out ahead of him later today and for many more days to come.

Chuckwagon Trail Recipes

DEWEY "MAC" MACKENZIE'S HILL OF BAKED BEANS

What you're gonna need:

A hill of beans *(okay, that's about a half a pound of the dried ones)*
¼ cup chopped onion
¼ pound bacon
¾ cup maple syrup
1 teasoon salt
½ teaspoon dry mustard
Dash of cayenne pepper, if there's any handy

Put them beans in about 5–6 cups cold water and allow to soak overnight. Beans should be just slightly covered by the water when they's nice and juicy.

Build yourself a cracklin' fire when the beans are ready to cook. Have a good pile of wood or coals to keep the fire going. Nobody likes a fire that ain't hot enough.

Drain off them beans and place in your kettle, and add enough fresh water to cover beans. Put your kettle over the coals and bring to a boil. Don't put the lid on until the whole thing starts to boil. Keep it at a slow boil for a half hour or so.

Remove from heat. Drain your water and keep it handy. Add in onion, and cut your bacon into 3 or 4 chunks and toss into beans, and mix 'em all up real nice.

In separate bowl, take the water you drained off and mix with the syrup, salt, and mustard. Stir and pour back over the beans. Keep stirring—you ain't done just yet.

Put the lid on the kettle, put it back on the hot coals and keep a medium heat for about 4 hours. Now and then, give them boys a stir—and do keep your good eye on the water level! Turn up the heat and cook for a couple more hours so it thickens right up.

And for gosh sakes, don't burn 'em.

Your Mac Mackenzie beans are ready and'll feed half a dozen or so hungry cowboys. Also, sleep upwind of your buddies—these are beans we're talking about, and they've been known to give folks the wind.

CHUCKWAGON STEW

What you're gonna need:

  2½ pounds beef cubes (5 cups)
  2 tablespoons flour
  1 tablespoon paprika
  1 teaspoon chili powder *(there's more of it later)*

2 teaspoon salt
3 tablespoons lard (or vegetable shortenin')
2 onions, sliced
1 clove garlic, mince and mash it
1 28-ounce can of tomatoes
3 tablespoons chili powder
1 teaspoon ground cloves
½ teaspoon dried red peppers, crushed
2 cups chopped potatoes
2 cups chopped carrots

Coat beef in a mixture of flour, paprika, that
1 teaspoon of chili powder, and salt. Brown the beef
in hot lard or shortening in a large pan or a Dutch
oven, if there's one to be found.

Add onions and garlic, and cook those until soft.
Throw in your tomatoes, the rest of that chili
powder, and your cloves and peppers.

Cover it up and let it simmer for two hours. Throw
in the potatoes and carrots, and cook until the
vegetables are done (usually about 45 minutes).

Should feed about four or five hombres—unless Fat
Tommy Bullfinch is on the drive. Then it'll feed just
two, and both of those are Fat Tommy.

Keep reading for a special excerpt of the new
Duff MacCallister western
by William W. and J. A. Johnstone

KILLER TAKE ALL
A DUFF MACCALLISTER WESTERN

Scotsman turned cowboy Duff MacCallister traveled
far and worked hard to start a new life in America.
And anyone who tries to mess with his dream
is in for some serious Highland justice . . .

The cattle town of Chugwater may not look like
much to outsiders. But for Duff MacCallister and
the determined settlers who've staked their futures
there, it's a land of opportunity. That's why the
whole town is fired up by the latest news. Young
railroad developer Jacob Poindexter wants to run
a rail line through Chugwater, making it easier to
transport cattle. Everyone is on board with the
plan—at first. Duff begins to suspect that Poindexter
is only after the most valuable land and he's using
strongarm tactics to force reluctant ranchers to sell.
Things only get worse when Poindexter's hired
guns show up—and the violence really begins . . .

But Duff's got a plan of his own. With a little help
from some well-armed friends, he's going to flush
this phony out of Chugwater—and run his hired
killers out of town on a rail . . .

Look for **KILLER TAKE ALL,** *on sale now.*

Chugwater, Wyoming

Thad Gorman counted out twenty-six dollars for Bob Guthrie, owner of Guthrie Lumber and Supply. "Here's what I owe you, Mr. Guthrie." Gorman smiled. "I got a good price for my wheat, and I thank you for carrying me on your books."

"Ahh, it's all part of doin' business, Thad. Why, most of the ranchers and farmers run a tab with me." Guthrie chuckled. "And I run a tab with my suppliers. Did Sue come to town with you?"

"Oh yes, Sue and the two young'uns. They're over at the mercantile now. She's payin' off Fred Matthews and stockin' up with things we been puttin' off till we had the money."

"What about Slocum? Did he come into town also?"

"I expect he'll be in tonight. I just got paid myself, so I haven't paid him yet."

"How's Slocum workin' out for you?"

Gorman chuckled. "Well, he's not the friendliest feller I've ever known, but his work has been all right."

"You were a good man to hire him," Guthrie said. "Not everyone would be willing to hire someone like Drury Slocum, a man who had spent five years in prison."

"I guess so. But it seems to me like ever'one deserves a second chance. Anyway I guess I'd better go pick up Sue 'n the kids before they spend all my money."

When Gorman stepped into the Matthews Mercantile a couple of minutes later he was greeted by a little girl who held out a doll. "Papa, look what I have! Isn't she beautiful?"

"I suppose so, but she isn't as beautiful as you are." Gorman smiled at Ethel, his six-year-old daughter.

"Huh, there's nothin' beautiful about a doll," Jimmy said. He was Gorman's nine-year-old son. "I got me a pocketknife," he added proudly.

It took half an hour for the farm wagon loaded with purchases to reach the family farm. When they drove into the yard they were met by Drury Slocum, Thad's farmhand and only employee.

"Did you get the money for the crop?" Slocum asked.

Gorman smiled. "Drury, you see all things we bought while we were in town. Do you really have to ask that question?"

"I'll take care of the team," he said as he began to disconnect the two gray mules from the wagon.

"Mr. Slocum, would you like to take supper with us tonight?" Sue asked.

"Nah, soon as I'm paid I'll be goin' into town."

"Look at it this way, Drury. You have to eat. If you eat with us, you won't have to spend money for food in town," Gorman said.

"Yeah," Slocum said. "Yeah, that's right, ain't it?"

* * *

An hour later Slocum came into a house that was redolent with the aroma of fried chicken, biscuits, mashed potatoes, and gravy.

"Drury, are you ready to be paid?" Gorman asked.

"Yeah."

Gorman reached over to the sideboard where lay the three hundred seventy-five dollars he had been paid for his wheat crop.

"I'll be giving you thirty-five dollars," Gorman said. "The extra five dollars is a bonus."

"I'll take it all," Slocum said.

Gorman smiled. "Yes, I didn't think you would turn down the extra five dollars."

"No, I mean I'll take all the money." Slocum pulled his pistol and pointed it at Gorman.

"Mr. Slocum, what are you doing?" Sue called out, her voice high-pitched with fright.

Slocum didn't answer. He pulled the trigger, shooting Thad Gorman in the chest from point-blank range. The bullet lodged in Gorman's heart, killing him instantly. Slocum then turned his gun on Gorman's screaming wife and crying children, firing three more times.

With the four members of the Gorman family lying on the floor, Slocum grabbed two pieces of chicken and two biscuits and left the house.

Slocum was in the Wild Hog Saloon later that same evening. His plan was to be very visible in town, then when word came that the Gorman family had been murdered, he would have the alibi of having been in town. That way, he wouldn't have to go on the run. But something he overheard from a nearby table caused him to change his mind.

"It was the hired hand that did it. Mrs. Gorman was still alive when Duff MacCallister 'n Elmer Gleason stopped by to buy some hay from 'em. She told 'em it was their hired hand that done the killin'. They tried to bring her into town, but she died before they could get her to the doctor."

Not everyone in the saloon knew that Slocum worked for Gorman, and those who did hadn't noticed that he was there. Slocum got up and went through the back door as if going to the privy.

He had no horse of his own, nor did Thad Gorman. Slocum had come into town riding one of the two mules Gorman owned. He had considered stealing a horse, but he didn't want to take a chance. He needed to get out of town as quickly as possible.

But the mule wouldn't cooperate.

"Get up, you worthless, long-eared galoot!" Slocum said, trying to urge the mule into a gallop.

He headed south, and no matter what he did to force the mule into a gallop, it wouldn't respond. Then quite unexpectedly, the mule balked, bucked, and threw Slocum off its back. The mule decided to run then, leaving Slocum stranded on the road.

Sky Meadow Ranch

"There is someone in the mine," Wang Chow said to Duff and Elmer Gleason the next day. Wang was speaking of a gold mine, played out now, that sat at the extreme north end of Sky Meadow.

"How do you know?" Elmer asked.

"Tracks go into mine but do not come out," Wang said.

"Well, let 'im snoop around," Elmer said. "He won't find anything, and if he does, we can give him a commission for finding it."

Before Duff had built Sky Meadow, before even he and Elmer Gleason were friends, Elmer had discovered and was working an old mine that had been abandoned by the Spanish more than a hundred years earlier. Legally the mine and all proceeds belonged to Duff, but he shared the money with Elmer, and Elmer invested back into the ranch so that he was not only the ranch foreman, but a junior partner.

"Elmer, have you considered that it is nae someone looking for gold?" Duff asked in the heavy Scottish brogue that he had not lost in all the time he had been in America.

"Well who else could it be?"

"Perhaps it is the one who murdered *Xiānshēng* Gorman," Wang suggested.

"I'll be damned. That's what you was thinkin' too, ain't it, Duff?"

"Aye."

"Well then, maybe we should go have us a look," Elmer suggested.

"I'll go in first," Elmer said when they reached the mouth of the mine. "There don't nobody in the whole world know this mine better 'n I do." He was justified in making such a comment, since he had actually lived in the mine for almost six months.

Elmer went in first, surrounded by a bubble of

golden light cast from the torch he had lit. Duff and Wang followed, but were just outside the light.

"All right, mister, you can just stop right there!" a voice called from the darkness before Elmer.

"Who the hell are you?" Elmer asked.

"It don't matter who I am. You're in light 'n I ain't." Elmer started to reach for his gun.

"Uh-uh," the voice said from the darkness. "I already got my gun out, 'n if you pull that 'n of your'n, I'll shoot you." Slocum appeared then, holding a pistol in his hand and pointing it at Elmer. "You know who I am, Gleason?"

"Yeah, Slocum, I know who you are. What I don't know is why the hell you are here. After what you done I figured you'd be long gone by now. Hell, ever'body figured that."

"Yeah, I would be if that damn mule I stole from Gorman hadn't throwed me 'n run off. You got a horse here?"

"What if I do? I ain't goin' to let you have it."

Slocum's laugh was short and without any real glee. "You think I'm askin' you for it? I ain't a-askin'. I'm goin' to kill you 'n take it." He extended his hand and Spulled the hammer back.

A bright muzzle flash lit up the mine even beyond that of the flickering torch, and the sound of the gunshot was almost deafening in the closed in area. The gun flew from Slocum's hand as Duff and Wang suddenly appeared. A narrow wisp of smoke curled up from the end of the Enfield Mark 1 pistol Duff was holding.

"We'll be for taking you in now, Slocum," Duff said.

"How you plannin' on gettin' me there? Like I said, I ain't got no horse to ride."

"You can walk, can't you?" Elmer asked.

"What do you mean, *walk*? It's five miles to town," Slocum complained.

"You don't have to walk if you don't want to," Elmer said. "We can drag you into town."

Connect with

Visit us online at
KensingtonBooks.com
to read more from your favorite authors, see books
by series, view reading group guides, and more.

for sneak peeks, chances to win books and prize packs,
and to share your thoughts with other readers.

facebook.com/kensingtonpublishing
twitter.com/kensingtonbooks

Tell us what you think!

To share your thoughts, submit a review,
or sign up for our eNewsletters, please visit:
KensingtonBooks.com/TellUs.